A slow shake of her ... but, determined to have the last word, Jane commented, "Then it would appear, taking account of your recommendations, proposals and strategy, that I have no case to uphold – except you've forgotten how easily we rub each other up the wrong way."

David smiled broadly, "I'm out of the office a lot. Look, I expect you're ready for something to eat. Why don't we adjourn to a quiet restaurant around the corner from the station? You can get to know me and judge if it could work, and I can discover just what I might be letting myself in for."

Worried, she murmured into her lap, "I'm not sure that's a good idea."

"What? That I should discover what I might be letting myself in for?"

Jane clicked her tongue and snapped, "No, of course not! I mean mixing business with pleasure."

It was clear that David was suppressing his mirth, but he still said with great seriousness, "Well, Jane, I am heartened to think that dining with me could be considered a pleasure."

Lips pursed, she took a deep breath and released it with the words, "You know what I mean! After all it was you who reminded me earlier of what happened last time I attempted to spread my wings."

"And I would remind you, Jane, that you felt God had appointed me to be your guardian angel."

RUTH JOHNSON

JANE
The Heart's Desire Series

BOOK 1

EMANUEL PUBLISHING

First published in Great Britain in 2007

This novel is entirely a work of fiction.
The names, characters and incidents portrayed in it are the work of the
author's imagination. Any resemblance to actual persons living or dead,
events or localities is entirely coincidental.

ISBN: 978-0-9554898-0-8

A catalogue for this book is available in the British Library

The words and music of 'Healing Stream' are copyright
© Lou Lewis, Zimrah Music,
39 Union Road, Exeter, Devon, EX4 6HU
and used with kind permission

'Joy to the World' written by Isaac Watts
'It is well with my Soul' written by H G Spafford and P P Bliss

Printed and bound in Great Britain by:
Cox & Wyman Ltd, Reading, Berks

Published by Emanuel Publishing
36 Kenmore Crescent
Bristol BS7 0TL

www.emanuel-publishing.com

Look out for further details on
www.emanuel-publishing.com
for other proposed books in the
Heart's Desire Series:

Jill
David
Rosemary
Janice
Matt

ACKNOWLEDGEMENTS:
Thank you to all those dear friends who read and inspired
me to continue writing and publish this book.
My special thanks go to:
Janet Beaty my first reader and encourager;
Carolyn and Wendy Bond who spurred me on;
Tasha Tombs who said, "You must publish this";
Richard Herkes of Kingsway who wanted to publish this!
and Brian Minney who spent hours proofreading and
preparing for printing.

Trust in the Lord and do good; dwell in the land and enjoy safe pasture; Delight yourself in the Lord and he will give you the desires of your heart. Commit your way to the Lord and trust in him and he will do it..
Psalm 37: 3-5

DEDICATION
This book is dedicated to the 'Jane'
who 35 years ago influenced and changed my life.

And to my beloved husband and children who,
over the years, put up with me shutting
myself away to write.

LONDON, 1966

CHAPTER 1

The large Georgian mansion was ablaze with light and alive with people. On the first floor, the conference room with its magnificent chandeliers, large French windows and light oak panelling resounded with laughter, voices, and the strains of a small orchestra imported for the company's Midsummer Ball.

On the third floor, Jane changed her evening dress for a navy office suit. A quick brush restored her matted reddish brown hair neatly around her heart shaped face. With overnight case and bag she headed for the back stairs.

Her plan was to leave without being seen. To achieve this she needed to get to the basement, cross the courtyard and go out the back gate. Her stiletto heels clattered on the stone staircase. She slowed to dampen their sound. The nearer she got to the first floor the sound of the band playing 'March of the Mods' became louder. No-one would hear her on the back stairs, she just had to hope no-one would decide to use them until she'd reached the bottom of the stairwell. She moved quickly down, then remembered - the back gates were locked at six o'clock! In an effort to relax she took a deep breath and exhaled slowly and began the last flight down to the ground floor. Could she make it through the front door without being stopped? Even if she did there was still the semi-circular drive to…. Jane gasped as the light clicked off leaving her in darkness. Fright caused her to halt and tighten her grip on the stair rail. What now? Nothing but relative silence and the realization that the light was on a timer, it wasn't someone playing a joke or anyone with ill intent. Relieved, she carefully negotiated the last few steps, pushed open the huge oak door to the ground floor and was pleased to find the dimly lit passage empty. Despite her inner trembling she didn't pause. She tiptoed along the stone floor to the entrance hall and backed in a clandestine manner against the wall to first peer right to the double door entrance and then left to the main staircase.

Voices! People were descending. Soon they'd turn and come down the wide sweep of stairs. Jane's mind raced. Could she make it along the central carpeted section and out the door before they saw her? If she slipped between the columns lining the hall she would be hidden, but the stone floor and her heels would make it impossible to be quick and quiet! There wasn't enough time. She slipped back into the shelter of the stairwell. With the door slightly open, she listened as the group approached.

Chris County's well bred voice reached Jane's ears. "...witty and amusing, as well as being interesting and informative."

Envy filled a younger man's words. "I don't know how he did it. He may have forgotten his notes, but he held everyone spellbound."

"Experience Julian, experience! I've heard many speeches in my life, but I'd agree with Chris that David Reinhardt's was exceptional."

"Well, Marcus, I'd say that David Reinhardt is definitely exceptional!" purred a female voice. "Mmm, that body, that smile!"

The men chuckled as a second female voice whined, "Honestly Donna, you're awful! You told me he was middle-aged and boring!"

"So, I've changed my mind! But he'd still eat little girls like you for breakfast!"

Chris laughed, "Women! Trust them to be more impressed by a body and smile than an ad-libbed speech."

Julian chipped in, "I bet that he's got a photographic memory."

Donna mimicked Marilyn Munroe's deep sexy lilt. "I bet a night with him would be more than a photographic memory!"

Jane moved deeper into the darkened stairwell as Marcus came into view a few yards from her hiding place. His retort, "Well, my dear, you'll have to make do with having ogled him during his speech. The man's got a fiancée."

Chris joined Marcus. "And you should see her, she's a peach! Now I wouldn't mind a night with her."

Donna tottered past in a snake-like pink sequin dress. Undeterred, she preened as she said, "Well, David Reinhardt certainly gives the impression of the cat that could manage both the peach and the cream!"

Over the laughter, Chris commented, "I like that, Donna — a good editorial quote in the next company magazine."

"You wouldn't dare!"

Ribald remarks wafted on the air until the main doors closed behind them.

Jane breathed a sigh of relief. Members of the Press Department were well known for their inquisitiveness. If they had seen her.... There was no explanation as to her need to rush home, or why, earlier, she'd behaved so out of character.

Sounds at the top of the stairs jolted her back to the present. If she was going to leave without being seen it was now or never. She smoothed down her pencil-slim skirt, adjusted her handbag and picked up her case. With straight back, her small nose tilted upward, she strode out across the hall as if on important business.

Intent on her goal and listening for those behind, she jumped as Jill Hart, emerged from the room behind the reception desk. "Ah, there you are Jane. At last! I've been searching for you. I'm not on duty now, you know."

Conscious of those approaching, Jane scarcely slowed.

Jill frowned and folded her arms across her buxom chest. "I like to enjoy myself as much as anyone else, so if you will order a taxi you might at least be here waiting for it."

Bewildered, Jane stopped. With her hand on the door she asked, "A taxi?"

"The driver said it was ordered for eleven. He's been waiting for you." Jill pushed back straying strands of long black hair towards her French pleat and stated, "You've changed! I thought you were staying at Pam's flat tonight."

Anxious to be gone, Jane opened the door. "Sorry, Jill, can't stop!" With a rueful smile she added, "I've got a taxi waiting." At Jill's hurt expression, she added, "Talk to you Monday."

She could feel Jill's fixed gaze as the cabby called, "You Jane Mackenzie?" At her nod, he continued, "I don't mind waiting, Missy, but you might – money's fast ticking away, and you ain't gone nowhere yet!"

The taxi was paid for!

"Where to then, luv?"

People were about to spill from the building, she thought fast and jumped inside. "South Kensington station, please." Once the cab was out of the drive she slid back the glass partition. "I'm told this has been paid for, is there enough…."

The cabbie interrupted, "To South Ken? Yes luv! Yer can go anywhere up to five quid."

Surprised she exclaimed, "Five pounds!" That was half a week's salary! Who could afford that? The cabby looking in his mirror chuckled at her amazed expression. "Someone, me duck, it seems likes you – and us taxi drivers. I've been told to put any change in our fund."

"Did you see the m... err, person?"

"No, I was at the back of the rank." He removed his cap and scratched the top of his balding head. "Me mate at the front, 'e come over saying 'e was off in a tick, but a fare was wanted in twenty minutes. 'E put the money in me 'and, give me yer name and pick up address, then 'e was gone!"

"Would you still have money for your fund if you took me to Osterley?"

"Oh, yeah!"

"Right, then, Osterley, it is." She sat back to enjoy the ride.

Had he ordered this taxi? He'd either plenty of money, or suffered a rush of conscience. Was there a mundane but honest statement to describe this evening's bizarre experience? She shivered involuntarily, but comforted herself that she was safe, and on her way home. Her face reddened when she considered that perhaps the stranger wasn't entirely to blame for his behaviour.

The transformation of the conference room and the sumptuous dinner by candlelight had made her feel she'd been transported to a bygone era. People swirled around the room in evening dress while the general hum of voices vied against the classical medleys. Nikki Clarke broke the spell by drawing the attention of those at the table to a couple smooching across the room. With a shake of her head she commented, "I sometimes wonder at the wisdom of these parties. There'll be embarrassment for some on Monday."

Pam laughingly rebuked her. "Oh, don't be such a spoilsport. It's only a bit of fun. You're beginning to sound like Rosemary."

"Heaven forbid! Did you hear how she was going on about the company dropping its standards by using the local colleges to provide the food and music?" The answer was lost on Jane as her mind wandered, remembering she should have rung Bruce about their music practice tomorrow. As Nikki purported to know everything about everything she waited for an opportunity to ask her where she could find a telephone with an outside line.

"Mr Reinhardt's office, but don't even think about it."

The reputation of Mr Reinhardt, one of the six directors, went before him. Men spoke of his business acumen, women of his love life. During her three months employment at ITP (International Trade Promotions), Jane had often heard in hushed and awed tones, "Mr Reinhardt's arriving", or "Mr Reinhardt's leaving", but she'd never seen this imposing character. Her mistake had been to say to Rosemary her office companion, "I'm dying to meet this elusive Mr Reinhardt."

Rosemary's nose had lifted and, with a toss of her long dark hair, the usual prelude to one of her plummy sneers, she'd answered, "Oh good heavens, Jane! Mr Reinhardt makes an after dinner speech, an opportunity to reward employees with a few chosen words. He certainly doesn't fraternise with junior secretaries!"

The musicians moving from the podium signalled it would soon be time for this magnanimous Mr. Reinhardt to make his appearance. A sudden thought made her grin. Supposing, just supposing, that while Mr Reinhardt was addressing his staff she popped out and made use of his office telephone! He would never know, and she could pay the switchboard for the call.

No-one noticed her leave the table or slip across the corridor and through the door to the backstairs. At the sound of polite applause, which she guessed heralded the arrival of the man of the moment, she ran up the stairs to the floor above.

Five minutes was all she needed so she sauntered, as though lost, down the empty corridor. Mr Reinhardt's secretary's office door was slightly open. With one finger she widened the gap, until in the shadowy light, she could see Mr Reinhardt's office door. A hysterical giggle rose in her as she quickly crossed the room, but as her hand twisted his office doorknob, sudden guilt choked it.

The darkness of the room was like a black abyss. With

caution, and the assumption that Mr Reinhardt's desk would be across the room, she pressed forward with outstretched hands. Her hand, felt the back of a leather-buttoned settee which she used to guide her in deeper. When the settee ended she carefully moved forward, but almost immediately collided into someone. Startled, she recoiled! Her heart thudded, expecting to be confronted. Nothing happened. With a tentative hand she reached forward, her someone it seemed the shade of a large table lamp. As she breathed again, she wondered if perhaps this hadn't been such a good idea. Although it might be a good one to switch the lamp on, it was unlikely anyone would see its glow from the corridor, and she wouldn't bump into the unknown again.

The light revealed a room larger than expected. Shelves filled with large academic books lined the wall between the offices. Set at right angles were two maroon chesterfield settees with lamps at each end. Opposite the settees, and in front of a heavily curtained window, stood a large antique desk containing three telephones. Her eyes took in the perfectly centred large green blotter, the neat pile of foolscap typed sheets on one side and the black leather bound diary on the other. Above the blotter a combined stainless steel desk lamp and pencil holder were joined by a serrated paper knife with a carved handle, and a heavy, matching wooden ruler. Her lip curled – overall it would seem Mr Reinhardt was as fastidious as magnanimous.

To sit in the deep leather chair behind the desk did seem rather cheeky so she'd stretched across the width of the desk, dialled the number and rested on her elbows. Bruce's immediate answer gave her time for a brief chat and the blowing of a goodnight kiss.

It was in the split second of replacing the receiver in the cradle that the light went out. This time there was someone in the room because legs – warm, large and definitely male – pressed against hers. Sprawled across the desk she took stock of her situation. Disconcerted now, rather than fearful, she reasoned that, in the pitch darkness, he was as blind as she. What were his intentions? And what could she do to defend herself? Slowly she stretched her left hand across the desk towards the blotting pad – her fingers touched the cold steel of the knife. She may want to hurt, but not maim or kill! Her hand found the ruler, she drew it toward her. Now armed, she pushed herself up from the desk, but instantly felt diminutive against his size and height. In the small space he afforded they were welded together, their rhythmic breathing the only movement and sound. Why didn't he move, or speak? Her limited knowledge of self–defence told her to keep her arms down in front of her. If his arms encircled her, she could bring them up suddenly and, hopefully, break free.

Large hands rested on her shoulders. Being guilty of trespass she expected arrest. Instead light and sensitive fingers flexed against her skin, moving upward, caressing the area around her neck and ears. A shiver vibrated down her spine. Nonplussed, she tried to squirm away, but movement was impossible pinned between him and the desk. Was this someone's idea of a joke? If it was it was about to backfire. And if he wasn't going to speak, then neither was she! If she appeared compliant, he would be surprised by a sudden attack. The hands that had been on her shoulders now slid downwards to explore her curves with a tantalising light, fluid motion of a swimmer doing a slow, miniature breaststroke. She attempted to wriggle free, but this caused even more disturbing sensations. When she bent forward he took it as an opportunity to kiss and caress the back of her neck and ears. Waves of debilitating pleasure washed over her. In weakness she leant back against him. He was wreaking havoc on her escape strategy.

Bruce's touch had never made her feel breathless and

writhe with pleasure. Surely this only happened in romantic novels? Enveloped in erotic sensation, she wondered what it would be like if she were naked. The abnormality of that thought brought her to her senses. This man was having fun at her expense. A series of sharp, pleasurable tremors reverberated through her making her treacherous body shimmy wantonly against him. His hands tightened under her breasts, his fingers stretching over them. It was the moment he tweaked her nipples through the thin fabric of her dress that the red alert finally sounded in her brain.

Anger provided the fuel she needed to act. This stranger had captured, touched and caressed her in an intimate way. Fury erupted within her at his effrontery. At speed she bent forward, pushed back and twisted in the small space. With all the force as she could muster she jabbed him with her elbow in the stomach. He gasped and stepped back giving her enough room to turn, aim the ruler at what she deemed the correct height and thrust it into him. Her accuracy, rather than the hardness of the blow, caused him to grunt. His hands left her to tend his pain.

Free to run she careered blindly across the room. An upright chair in her path nearly sent her flying. She righted herself, took two steps and bumped again into the wretched lamp. Hand out, she found the settee to guide her to the door. A hand brushed her arm. To counter it she moved sideways. Drawn by a chink of light from the corridor she headed toward it. He caught her arm. She twisted it round in a manoeuvre to force him to let go. But he'd closed the distance between them and pulled her towards him. Her cry of "Let go!" with other exclamations, were stifled as her face met with the lapel of his jacket. Furious, she pulled back her head to demand, "Who are you?" Her words muffled as his large hand drew her head against the hard muscle of his chest.

How she wanted to pummel him. But with her arms

pinned between their bodies she could do nothing. Secured within his arms, her struggles were met with silence. If he expected her to stop fighting he could think again! She drew back her foot and managed an ineffectual kick. A further attempt was thwarted as he tucked her flailing body under his arm. At that she yelled, "You beast! Put me down!" He ignored her and prised the ruler out of her grasp. "No!" she howled. She shrieked, "How dare you! You won't get away with this. Let me go! Who do you think you are? You can't do this!" The futility of that remark brought a frustrated squeal. "What sort of man are you anyway? Have you nothing better to do than wait around and prey on innocent girls?"

An exasperated sigh broke from him. So she'd finally got through! Her triumph was short-lived. A moment later he sat heavily on the settee taking her with him. Her body jerked across his lap and her face rested on the cold leather of the seat. She struggled to get up. The first slap of the ruler connected with her bottom. In the hope of avoiding further blows she frantically wriggled and cried out, "Stop! Stop!" He said nothing. The repeated hard smacks of the ruler turned her cries into silent, repentant tears, the reaction to her instinctive belief that she was being punished because she deserved it. Her thoughts had flown back ten years....

She had been a strong–willed child and caning, although infrequent, had always been well deserved. Her father, a strong disciplinarian, had believed in the Bible's words, "spare the rod, spoil the child", but no one would have called him cruel. Once he saw tears of real repentance, he would stop. And after she had sobbed "I'm sorry, Daddy," he would draw her into his arms, to cuddle her and assure her of his love.

The blows from the ruler ceased. Stunned, more with humiliation than pain, she found herself being lifted and placed on the settee. Now he'd had his revenge Jane expected him to leave. But he didn't. The leather creaked beside her. Fingers touched her tear–stained cheeks. She jerked her head away. But as they skimmed her face a quiet relieved sigh filled the silence. Before she could think of escape, an arm slipped around her. This action, so reminiscent of her father's care, was enough to allow herself to be nestled and cuddled.

It was probably less than a minute before he drew away, took hold of her face in his hands and let his thumbs gently trace her cheekbones. She strained to see through the blackness. There was a dim, blurred movement and then soft, cool lips met hers. The gentle, nuzzling kiss was tender, yet so erotic it brought a fresh onslaught of newly awakened desire. Her natural reticence and his mistreatment of her were forgotten as her traitorous body responded. This time his groan wasn't in pain, but birthed from the same longings running rampant through her.

"Missy, we're just coming into Osterley. What's the address?"

Jane dragged away from fevered memories, opened her eyes and concentrated on directing the cabby to the end of her road. Travel by taxi was not something that she, her family, or her neighbours did so if anybody spotted her, the news would soon reach her mother's ears.

After a rummage in her bag, she found a mirror, and examined her face. When animated, it could be considered attractive, but now it looked drawn, her hazel eyes too large in her face. Her hand touched her mouth where with his finger he'd sketched her lips before leaving as silently and suddenly as he arrived. Bemused, she'd sat for several minutes staring into the blackness, her body continuing to yearn for the unknown.

"'Ere you are, Missy. 'Ome at last! And if, luv, you ever find the identity of our benefactor, thank 'im for me."

'Benefactor' was not the word she'd have chosen! If

caught trespassing you would expect to be confronted, not fondled. But then, if she had protested in the beginning, he might have acted the gentleman and stopped.

Jane alighted from the taxi and turned into the cul-de-sac. It was a relief to see her house lights were out. No need then to make any explanations for not staying at Pam's tonight. A blush suffused her face. Even reliving the experience, her body produced a fierce sexual ache. Was it unusual to reach 22 before discovering your body's sensuality? In the two years she'd been dating Bruce, she had never been aroused and, on the rare times when Bruce got what she called 'overheated', she'd been more put off than turned on!

Her mother always said, "a husband should be someone who is a good and trustworthy friend, whose company you enjoy." And there was nothing wrong with that as far as it went, but now she wanted more. So was Bruce the right man for her?

The garden gate's creak refocused her thoughts to the stranger. He had only made noises: murmurs of delight; a painful grunt; a passionate groan; sighs of exasperation and relief. Had he been afraid she might identify his voice? Well, he'd certainly heard hers! Did he know who she was? What was it that Nikki had said? "There'll be some embarrassment on Monday." She groaned and hoped there wouldn't be any for her.

CHAPTER 2

"Wake up, Jane! Come on, you're going to be late." Her mother's voice tore Jane from a vivid dream of the comic strip character Batman rescuing her from a speeding, driverless taxi. "I thought you were at Pam's until I saw your handbag in the hall."

Late? Pam? Oh – it was Saturday! Jane pulled herself up and accepted the proffered cup of tea. Her mumbled thanks were met with her mother's brisk words, "Well, I'd better get a move on. Bruce called yesterday and said the practice was at ten, so you'll have to hurry."

Relieved her Mother wasn't expecting to hear why she'd come home Jane drank her tea and reflected that Pam and Jill might not be so accommodating.

Distracted by thoughts of the stranger, she didn't arrive until the rehearsal had started. As she headed for the stage her eyes rested on Bruce. His head jerked in time with his violin bow, causing his mousy hair to slip over his brow. He certainly couldn't be described as tall, dark or handsome – more short, swarthy and weedy. She felt no onslaught of love, or any great feeling of affection at the sight of him. He was gentle, kind and reliable, and once he had an instrument in his hands, both he and it, came alive. Were they only drawn together by their musical abilities? The beat of the Irish jig got faster and sweat broke out on Bruce's forehead. Those not playing began clapping. It was music to make your spirit rise, your voice sing and your feet dance. As she responded, Bruce noticed her. His brown eyes lit up. His brief, but warm smile made her feel mean at her sudden negativity toward him. The tune accelerated to a climax, the clapping got faster, then it was over and Bruce stepped down toward her.

"There you are. I expect you left Pam still sleeping."

He patted her arm as his lips brushed her cheek. "I suppose your 'do' went on a bit."

John Myrrh, the trumpet player, intervened before she could answer. "Now you are here Jane, we really would like to get started. We've a lot to practice before tomorrow night."

To Bruce she threw a quick grimace, grinned at John, snapped to attention and saluted. The group's laughter echoed in her ears as she barked out a smart "Yes, Sir!" and goose-stepped to the piano.

For two years, the music group had been struggling to gain acceptance in their church. At first they'd been known as the 'Young People's Group' and given an occasional 'spot'. The older people had called it a cacophony of sound and likened it to the Beatles' rock stuff. But after the Queen had bestowed the Beatles with the MBE last year, they too had found favour and approval. Now, with their willingness to combine traditional hymns and new music, they were leading the worship every Sunday evening.

John, laughing with the others, asked no-one in particular, "What are we going to do with her? You certainly liven up the place, Jane, but from those shadows under your eyes I guess this isn't the only thing you liven up!"

Bruce frowned. Jane quickly ran her fingers over the keys and began playing. The diversion was enough for Bruce to dutifully return to the stage to pick up his violin. He never lost his temper, never openly criticised her, but he did get morose - particularly about her life outside of church activities - and remarks like John's didn't help. The denomination Bruce had come from had strict religious roots which he found difficult to let go.

The telephone call to Pam was easier than expected. Pam barely listened to her feeble excuse of not having felt well before she launched into the tale of her activities the previous night. "I was nearly the last to leave so when I couldn't find you I guessed you'd gone off somewhere!" She finished with a suggestive laugh, "Hopefully with someone! What about that tall chap, Ian, from the Print Department? It's obvious he likes you. Mind you, I bet he wouldn't be the only one if you'd only show a bit more of those shapely legs of yours!"

Jane winced. Pam had volunteered to take up her skirt claiming calf length was 'out'. Instead of the couple of inches Jane had expected, Pam had nearly made two skirts out of one. Jane could still hear her Mum's scathing reaction and see Bruce's blush of embarrassment. It had been enough to make her vow never to wear the skirt again!

"What's that fat old foreman's name....?"

"Do you mean Sam?"

"Oh yes, Sam, that's right. Don't know why you're so friendly with him."

Annoyed, she'd replied more sharply than intended. "Because, Pam, in my first week I was nearly in tears from Rosemary's constant sniping. Sam not only noticed, but he sat me down in his little cubby hole of a room, gave me a cup of tea, and told me to ignore her, believe in myself, and give the job a chance."

There was an awkward pause, before Pam said hurriedly, "Right! Okay! Well glad you're feeling better — I'll see you Monday. Bye!"

Despite her determination to enjoy Bruce's company that evening, he suddenly seemed very dull. So, when her mother invited Bruce and his father, Ted, to Sunday lunch she groaned inwardly. Her father had died of a heart attack three years earlier, and although she appreciated her Mum liked Ted's company, it made her feel claustrophobic.

That night she tossed and turned worrying about the identity of the stranger. Now she understood the phrase, 'we got carried away', she wondered if it were possible for friendship, chemistry and love to come together.

Sunday she felt tired, snappy and unappreciative of Bruce's predictable, dependable and helpful self. Later, getting ready for bed, she reflected that Bruce and the word 'boring' were synonymous. There were no surprises, or romantic interludes, and although they didn't live together their life was similar to a married couple – and those who knew them assumed that one day they would be. Was that what she wanted? She slipped into bed, closed her eyes and let her thoughts drift. If, as she believed, God had a plan for her life, then meeting the stranger must have been part of it. But she couldn't see to what purpose? A picture formed in her mind of a tadpole swimming contentedly with others and the world around it. Was God warning her not to step past her comfortable boundaries? Tadpoles however didn't remain swimming; they grew and changed into frogs. Was the stranger to be part of her metamorphosis? Was it time to grow up and move out beyond the snug confines of her life into the real world? She meditated on the picture and fell into a deep sleep.

The next morning Jane entered the back gates and crossed the courtyard of the mansion that served as offices for ITP. In what had been the servants' wing of the house, the first floor was now offices where Rosemary worked for Mike, the Public Relations Officer, and she, his assistant Paul. It was hard to believe that this beautiful house was buried amongst office blocks and the large Georgian terraced houses in the west end of London. This secretarial position was lower than her previous employment, but a few months ago she'd been swayed by the financial rewards and exceptional benefits to join ITP. And, if Rosemary hadn't disliked her and determined to make her life a misery, she would have enjoyed her job. This morning was no exception. After she'd taken a brief break and chat with the telephonists, the usual hectoring began. "And where have you been? You're here to work, not socialise. I'm still waiting for you to finish Paul's report so I...."

Pam entering the office seemed oblivious to Rosemary's flow for she cut across it. "Hi, you two! So, Jane, have you recovered from Friday night?" Pam disappeared behind the partition to use the photocopier.

When she reappeared Jane was ready to answer. "I still felt a bit sick yesterday." She added silently – of Bruce, not food. "But I'm fine now, and that delicious smell coming up from the kitchen is making me feel really hungry."

Rosemary's head lifted to sneer, "It was probably the rich food on Friday that upset you." She stood, tossed her shiny curtain of hair, and gathered up her typing, "But, Jane, I don't suppose you're used to drinking wine either."

Jane made a face at Rosemary's back as she headed out of the door. Pam caught it and grinned.

"It was disappointing though to miss Mr Reinhardt and his speech." Rosemary stopped, and pointedly blocked her view as she took up the conversation. Pam retrieved her photocopying and headed towards the door while Rosemary's plummy voice continued on full throttle. "If, as he says, ITP's success is down to every member of staff and he wishes to mellow the lines of hierarchical working by having an open door policy, he must mean he wants to get away from the 'them and us' mentality. I'm not sure...."

Unable to resist, Jane spoke to Rosemary's back. "So it would seem that Mr Reinhardt is happy to fraternise with junior secretaries like me."

The toss of dark mane and contemptuous look in her direction was accompanied by Pam's guffaw, which she stifled into a cough as Rosemary continued to address her. "I'm not sure that's a good thing, it could bring a lack of respect from more menial staff. This was the first Ball I've heard about when the directors mingled after the speeches, and if I'd known that Mr Reinhardt would dance with all the Department Head secretaries I would have stayed longer."

Jane was never sure if Rosemary's posh accent was genuine, but was sure that on this occasion it had a wistful edge.

Pam's abrupt "Really! Got to rush" indicated to Jane her feelings towards Rosemary's snobbery. Rosemary took Pam's place at the photocopier.

Moments later Jill poked her head around the door. With a conspiratorial grin she proclaimed, "Oh good, Jane, you're alone. I've been dying to know why you were in such a rush on Friday. Don't you live somewhere near Heathrow?" She clicked her tongue and with raised her eyebrows said, "You must earn a good salary to afford a taxi."

"Jane ordered a taxi?"

Jill threw Jane a horrified look mouthed "sorry" and swiftly announced, "Must go. Thought Pam was here. See you at lunch."

Rosemary flounced back to her desk with a look of disdainful incredulity. "You went home in a taxi? How much was that?"

Jane bit back a rude reply. "Expensive, but not feeling well it was worth it." To avoid further questions she added, "Well mustn't chat, you know – Paul's report to do." She ignored Rosemary's hard stare and resumed her typing.

The sound of voices and steps heading downward to the canteen heralded the relief of lunch time. The queue had already reached the top of the stairs, and joining it she began scanning for those who had the potential to be her mystery man. There were plenty of candidates: too old; too young; too thin; too short! As the line moved down it gave her the opportunity to view those joining above. Could the man have been someone's boyfriend or husband? How dreadful, but it was the likeliest explanation for his actions and silence!

Once in the canteen her eyes roved over those already seated. Julian was in discussion with the older man, Marcus and sharing their table with two men from the Films Department. They fitted the build of the stranger, they had the boldness and certainly wouldn't want to be identified because they both were married.

"'Ere you! Do yer want dinner, or are you making a meal of them fellahs?" Jane turned around. Doreen, the cook, spoon in hand, was hanging out of the hatch to see what, or who, was holding up the queue.

Sam's old, croaky voice rose above the chatter, "I might have guessed! It's young Jane. Hurry up and get your dinner, I'm starving."

Embarrassed but not wanting to show it, she hurried forward with a big smile and loud voice, "Oh sorry, Doreen, I got carried away with wondering which was the best dish!"

Doreen grunted as she looked out over the canteen, "Well, I guess in this day and age, you can try out as many as you like."

Jane's smile turned weak. That wasn't her philosophy, but now wasn't the time to say so. In fact, if she were honest, conversation with an unattached, attractive man out of the context of work often made her feel awkward and naïve. That was probably why she tended to gravitate to Sam, his fatherly eye and friendly department always felt like an extended family into which she was welcome.

To get to a free table in the far corner she passed Sam. "Methinks, Sam, it would take some while before you starved!" She gave a meaningful look at his stomach. Sam, running his hand over his bulging paunch, pulled himself to his full 5ft 8ins height. "I'm not fat, I'm just not tall enough." Ian sniggered. Sam muttered, "I don't know! You young people! You take them under your wing, you teach them all you know, but they have no respect."

Jane seeing Ian miming along to Sam's words, grinned and moved on. She liked ITP's canteen. It was the pivot of the friendly social atmosphere of the whole company. The salary of her two previous jobs had included luncheon vouchers which gave plenty of options of places to eat, but not the people to eat with. Here you could be eating with a department head one day, and the next with Sam and Ian, who ran and maintained the huge lithograph machines in the basement printing department.

Today Sam and Ian joined her. Sam, having enjoyed his food, burped, grinned and stated, "You know this is much better than me Missus' grub, but don't go telling her that."

As neither he nor Mrs Bennett came to company events because, he said "they were full of tofts", Jane wondered how she'd have the chance to tell her.

Behind Sam the canteen doors swung to admit a group of middle-aged, expensively suited men heading towards a reserved table by the kitchen door. These were probably the kind of 'tofts' Sam had in mind. Her eyes followed them and, to her surprise, Doreen left the hatch and emerged from the kitchen with an obsequious smile. As one of the 'tofts' spoke to her, she began to nervously screw the corner of her apron. Intrigued, Jane bent and whispered across the table, "Don't either of you turn round now, but who are the men sitting in the opposite corner?"

Sam gave a wicked chortle. "Why? Do you fancy them?"

"Sam! You're awful! They're way out of my league, in both age and class!"

"Don't sell yourself short, our Jane! You're one of the best."

Jane gave a derisive laugh and returned her gaze to the six men. The one who had spoken to Doreen was now seated facing her. He looked younger than the others, probably mid-thirties. However, his harsh, square features and the grim line of his mouth were enough for her to understand why Doreen seemed intimidated. He glanced unexpectedly in her direction and caught her contemplative gaze. She diverted her eyes to her plate, but not before seeing his black eyebrows rise and his eyes widen.

What arrogance! She should have stared back. Her gaze drifted back towards him. His eyes met hers. The grim lips twitched with amusement. This time she gave him one of Rosemary's haughty stares. Who was he? A cold shudder ran down her back. Perhaps he knew something she didn't? She determined not to look over there again. But she could sense his continued interest.

It was a relief when Sam sat back with a grunt of satisfaction and Ian suggested, "Time for a game of table tennis?"

Sam groaned, "Only if I want indigestion."

Unnerved by being watched, Jane was quick to rise. That condescending man certainly wasn't going to think she had any interest in him! Sam grinned knowingly and took his time. With her eyes fixed on Ian, she chatted as they moved through the tables and out the doors. A man's laughter boomed out from the canteen. Ian, being tall, peered through the door's round window, but jumped back as Sam rushed out. "Hey Sam! You nearly knocked me over."

Sam ignored him, grabbed Jane's elbow, shot her along the corridor and out through the back door into the courtyard. Taken by surprise, she allowed herself to be steered across the cobbles and through the pots of riotously coloured flowers towards the ivy covered walls of the main house. Breathless, Sam stopped to open the basement door and managed to say, "Not... much... time..." before bulldozing her into the cavernous corridor towards the games room. Puzzled, Jane tried to shake free. Sam held on. Once inside the room he let go, flopped on the chair nearest the door, and used his forearm to wipe the sweat from his brow.

Ian arrived as Jane asked, "Sam! What was that all about?"

"You didn't see, did you? I daren't say anything until I got you here in case you tried to go back."

Irritation combined with perplexity made her snap, "Didn't see what? Go back where?"

Sam's face broke into a huge grin. "You know those men you were interested in?"

Jane frowned and nodded.

He chuckled, "No wonder you thought they were out of your league!" From his back pocket Sam pulled a handkerchief and blew his nose noisily. His eyes twinkled with merriment. "I'm surprised you haven't seen them before." In a habitual gesture he smoothed the long thin strands of white hair across his bald patch and said thoughtfully, "But then they don't often eat in the canteen, and if they do it's usually at second sitting and ...."

"Sam!"

He grinned, ".... and it is unusual to see Mr Reinhardt."

A vision of the harsh face with the slicked back, black hair and equally dark penetrating eyes rose before her, "Oh, no! Don't tell me he was the one facing me?"

Sam nodded. "Let me finish...." He paused to smooth his belly. "Okay – don't look at me like that. I'm getting to it. Mr Reinhardt looked over at you, then said something to his fellow directors which made them turn in your direction."

Jane visibly bristled.

"There, there! I knew you wouldn't like it." Sam shrugged. "I don't know what made him laugh, but I guessed if you thought it was something to do with you, you'd rush back in there."

Jane headed for the door. Ian blocked her way. "Come on, Jane. Let it go." He grinned. "After all you were eyeing them up earlier."

Sam took a deep breath and looked upwards. "If you went marching in there, heaven knows what would happen."

He was right, but Jane wasn't going to admit it. A verbal attack on a Company Director in front of his staff wouldn't enhance her job prospects!

"I haven't forgotten what happened when our Ian here made a pass at you. He knows better than that now, don't you Ian?"

Ian grinned ruefully. A smile flickered across Jane's face at the memory. Ian had taken her praise for his table tennis playing too literally and responded by giving her a snogging kiss! The retaliation of her hand had been of equal passion! Fortunately, Ian hadn't taken offence, but Sam thought it a huge joke and thoroughly enjoyed the opportunity to circulate the story about the fiery 'Miss' from the Public Relations Department.

Ian handed her a table tennis bat. Automatically, she returned his service. So that was Mr Reinhardt! How could anyone think his grim austereness was attractive? But it would account for why people held him in such esteem. However, his reaction to her glances proved he was as supercilious as he was supposedly benevolent! And certainly she wouldn't agree with Donna's description of sexy! Why had he been watching her? What had he said that was so amusing? Had it been about her? Maybe the stranger told Mr Reinhardt about the incident in his office?

Unseen, the ball hurtled past her outstretched arm. It had been Mr Reinhardt's office – He was of the right build.... No! Oh, please… no!

Sam's voice penetrated her thoughts, "Concentrate Jane. Come on, you'll beat him."

It couldn't have been, could it? The thought of him.... No, he wouldn't have dared, she might have recognised him. But not in the dark! And he hadn't spoken! Oh surely not! That would be awful! Dismay began to trickle in, but sudden realization came as a flood of relief. Of course it wasn't him - he'd been giving his speech. Minutes later she whacked the ball for a final time across the table and heard Sam declare, "Game to Jane. Well done!"

The afternoon dragged on endlessly. At the unusual sound of someone knocking at their office door she leapt to answer it. About to say, "there's no need to knock", she stopped, her mouth open, at the sight of a pageboy dressed in Regency costume, his arms filled with red roses.

The size of the bouquet impeded his aristocratic bow as he announced, "I have a bouquet here for Miss Jane Mackenzie."

Her voice came out as a shriek, "For me!"

The officious smile turned to a cheeky grin, "If your name's Jane Mackenzie, then they're yours. See!" He tapped at her name on the envelope stapled to the corner.

Rosemary joined her, gave an incredulous gasp and scowled at the boy. "There must be some mistake?" She tossed her head toward Jane, "No-one would send her such a marvellous bouquet."

The boy stepped back nervously, "Look 'ere, I don't want no trouble. That's what the card says, don't it? So 'ere you are, take 'em." With that he thrust the flowers at Jane and scuttled away down the corridor. As the door to the hall swung to let him out, Jill, hair pins and hair coming adrift, rushed in.

Jill almost knocked Rosemary down in her excitement to peer at the bouquet. "How marvellous, Jane. There must be at least three dozen roses in there."

Rosemary tossed her hair, her voice sour, "I wouldn't have thought anyone Jane knew could afford to spend that kind of money!"

Although it was the truth, Jane asked herself why did Rosemary always have to be so nasty?

Jill gave Rosemary a hard look. Then turned to ask, "Come on Jane, tell me, tell me. Who's the man? He must be really something to buy flowers like that."

Baffled, Jane shook her head. Once or twice Bruce had bought her flowers, but nothing like these. Could it be her stranger? He really was a bit special if he could pay for taxis and flowers. As elated as a detective finding a clue, Jill pointed. "Look, Jane, look, there's a card."

Jane's throat went dry. To delay she moved back into the room and placed the flowers on the photocopier. But at Jill's insistence she removed the silver-edged card from the envelope. 'The roses are red, the words unsaid, but my heart is true, it's saying "sorry" to you'. The squiggle after the rhyme could have been anything. As the simple message gave nothing away she passed the card to Jill.

"So, who is he?"

"I don't know."

"Oh, come on, Jane, you must do. He's apologizing for something. It's so romantic to receive flowers. And these are so gorgeous. Is this man really such a mystery?"

In attempt to make light of the truth, Jane chuckled, "He certainly is."

"Oh! A secret admirer!"

"I doubt it. Anyway the 'he' could be a 'she'!"

"Oh, don't be silly. Of course it's a man. Only a man would send flowers like that. Look, I'm sure if you tried you could work out this signature. This could be either D or B, maybe K or even R." Jill frowned, "Do you know anyone with those initials? What do you think, Rosemary?"

Rosemary having returned to her desk looked up. "Oh, don't ask me. I neither know, nor want to know, any friends of Jane's. As for an admirer – huh!"

Jill pursed her lips, and with hand on hip retorted, "Oh really! Well, with your attitude I'd be surprised if you had anyone you could even call a friend, let alone an admirer!"

Rosemary's olive skin flushed.

Keen to avert a row, and with sudden inspiration, Jane said in a bright voice, "Of course, it could be Bruce. And there are others. In fact Don, Keith and Roger all have the right initials!"

Fortunately Jill didn't ask if any of them had offended her, or could afford such an extravagant gift. Instead Jill gave Rosemary a hostile look, then suggested, "Come to Reception. I'll find you some vases. You can't possibly take them all home on the tube." With that Jill headed back down the corridor replacing hair pins as she went. At the swing door she turned with a grin, and called, "Of course I could always order you a taxi!"

Jane chortled. Rosemary said tersely, "You'd better get those flowers off the photocopier." With the coldness of Rosemary's stare Jane wondered if her Mum was right and that Rosemary was jealous of her. Why, though, she couldn't fathom. Rosemary had a better secretarial position and if she weren't always so sullen, she'd be beautiful with those large, dark, expressive eyes and a perfectly shaped mouth. Compared to Rosemary's hourglass figure and long shapely legs, she was plain, short and thin. Jane could only think that when God had made her she had come from a second-class mould. But in fairness to her creator, he had given her a bubbly personality and a happy disposition. She picked up the flowers and smiled. All things considered, she had the better deal – looks died, but personality remained!

Jill, with several vases and clutter on the Reception Desk, was rummaging through the hall cupboard and spoke without turning. "I think, Jane, there are taller ones somewhere in the back here, but are any of those any good?"

Jane deliberated, leant forward, and then jumped as a deep voice boomed from behind her. "Hello, what are you two up to?"

Several of the vases on the desk wobbled ominously –
Jane grabbed one as Jill exclaimed, "Gosh, you startled
us!"

Jane spun round to look up into the mocking, square-
jawed face of the man she now knew to be Mr Reinhardt.
Earlier he'd neither seemed so tall, nor so broad. The sharp
nose, the piercing black eyes under the slicked back, raven
hair seemed to intensify his imposing presence. She felt
like prey to a vulture. A cold shudder ran through her. Jill,
though seemed neither perturbed nor intimidated, and her
happy chatter served to keep his attention.

Jill paused for breath. Mr Reinhardt turned his focus to
Jane. "So, who sent you, as Jill calls it, this magnificent
bouquet?"

"Oh, it's so romantic!" Jill chirped.

Mr Reinhardt's eyes lifted heavenward.

"It's not just that. It's mysterious too, isn't it, Jane?"

With a faint smile, Jane prayed that Mr Reinhardt
would find something more important to do. His lips
twitched with the same aggravating amusement she'd seen
earlier. She groaned inwardly, wondering what Jill was
going to say next. Undeterred at Mr Reinhardt's lack of
response, Jill rattled on, as Jane became unnerved at his
steady gaze. Embarrassed, she looked around the large
imposing hall, up at the two enormous glass chandeliers,
then down to the patterned carpet. How she wished the
floor would suddenly open and, like in a Rupert the Bear
story, she could slip down a hidden chute into a faraway
land. All the while she knew he was observing her and,
by his wry expression, was finding the whole thing very
diverting! How on earth could she stop Jill?

In the hope that she could quell Jill with a look, she
concentrated her gaze on Jill's face, noting that her rather
square features were softened by the long, curly strands of
black unruly hair which frequently escaped. These seemed
to reflect her scatty, chatty nature, but, endearing as it was,

Jane wished she didn't feel the need to repeat to this man the snappy verse on her card. If she couldn't distract Jill, perhaps she could make an excuse and leave.

"So, Miss, err...."

Jill supplied her name. "Jane Mackenzie."

Jane, now forced to look at Mr Reinhardt, was taken aback at the sensual, slanted way in which he was regarding her.

"So, Miss Jane Mackenzie, do you think you can forgive the gentleman in question?" The mocking smile broadened as his eyes went to her feet, then travelled upward in a slow, deliberate appraisal of her body. Amused, he met her stony look to taunt, "Were his misdeeds such that they deserved such an apology?"

Disconcerted by the sexual insinuation being conveyed, she took a deep breath, stretched herself to her full height and said coldly, "The answer, Mr...." She paused, as though as unaware of his identity as he had been of hers.

His eyes widened.

Jill's carefully enunciated, "Mr Reinhardt," she knew was a warning, but indignation had replaced her embarrassment and she was not going to back down.

Her expression hardened, she stared into his seductive expression and stated firmly, "The answer, Mr Reinhardt," she paused, then decided to go for it and be damned, "is as impertinent as your question. Mind your own business."

Jill's gasp was audible. A quick glance revealed her friend's mouth dropping in horror. She stood her ground, her gaze didn't flicker, although her stomach did as she watched the provocative amusement fade from his eyes.

Mr Reinhardt's sudden uproarious laugh and slap of gusto against his thigh took Jane by surprise, and obviously astonished Jill. People crossing the hall turned their heads. Jane blinked – he was amused! His voice reflected his mirth. "Well! Well! Well! Jane Mackenzie, you are indeed one fiery little lady." His face came in line with hers. His nearness made her want to step back, but she determined not to. In a quieter voice he mocked, "In which case, Jane Mackenzie, may I be forgiven for my interest in your affairs?" He gave a gentle laugh.

Had he deliberately used the word 'affairs' to annoy her? She clenched her hands to restrain the urge to slap the seductive smile off his face. The speed with which his head returned to its normal elevation, a good foot above her upturned face, left her in no doubt he'd heard Sam's tale. Her churning stomach belied her outer calm and confidence as she stood tall to reply, "Mr Reinhardt, if I thought your interest in my..." her green–flecked hazel eyes flashed in bold hostility, "...life was sincere, then I wouldn't need to forgive you but, as it is, I just think you're amusing yourself at my expense. However, if you must know, the gentleman in question was forgiven even before he sent the flowers." Despite her shaking knees, she turned to the desk, picked up two vases, thanked the stunned Jill, and with a brusque, "Good afternoon, Mr Reinhardt," she marched across the hall back to the relative sanctuary of her office.

Once the swing door closed behind her, her outward confidence collapsed. The magnitude of what she had said, and to whom she had said it, caught up with her. She stumbled along the corridor into her office, put the vases on her desk, her bottom on her chair, her head in her hands and thanked God that Rosemary was missing.

What would happen now? Would she lose her job? There were plenty of others, but she liked it here. Paul was a thoughtful boss and the work interesting. Should she send Mr Reinhardt an apologetic note? No, why should she? A small grin flittered across her lips. On this occasion he'd certainly got more than he bargained for. Then rationality took hold. Perhaps he hadn't meant it like that and was just being polite. But, either way, she felt sure she hadn't heard the last of it.

With unsteady hands she unwrapped the flowers. Hopefully news of her bouquet would spread no further. With a grimace she concluded that the altercation in the hall proved one thing beyond a shadow of doubt, if Mr Reinhardt had caught her in his office he would have confronted, not fondled, her!

She was on her way back from the tap in the courtyard when Jill at the top of the stairs called her. Startled she jumped. Water slopped out of the two vases over her and on to the floor. Jill giggled. "Sorry! I didn't mean to frighten you. I just wondered where you were. Whatever got into you? There aren't many people who would dare to speak like that to Mr Reinhardt. I couldn't believe it."

That information wasn't a surprise! Jane pulled a face. Her last glimpse of Mr Reinhardt had shown his features tightening into a forbidding mask. Oh dear! This wasn't the first time her temerity had been her undoing. Her voice trembled, but she had to ask, "Did he, did he say anything after I left?"

Jill shrugged, "Not a lot. He watched you disappear, ignored me, turned on his heel and, with head bowed, walked off muttering, 'Well, well, well.'"

"Oh, Jill, I was positively shaking inside!" She held out her hand, "Look, I still am, but he's not to know that is he? Do you think I should apologize?"

"No! I think he was astonished by your reaction, but I shouldn't worry — he'll realise he deserved it. Now tell me about that gentleman who was forgiven before he sent the roses and what he did that needed such an extravagant apology. Then you'd better decide what to do with them before they cause you more trouble."

40

CHAPTER 3

The news of her bouquet had circulated the offices. But light-hearted banter about the mystery sender only lasted a few days. And there were no repercussions from her run-in with Mr Reinhardt. She'd taken half the bouquet home and was surprised her explanation of it being a colleague's apology for upsetting her was accepted. Her Mum thought the words on the card were lovely but, if she'd known the full truth, both she and Bruce would have been shocked by the stranger's actions, and her response.

In the hope of finding out something more, she had plucked up courage and visited the florist shop in Knightsbridge. The young assistant had giggled, the manageress had been haughty and unhelpful, and then snubbed her by hailing another customer while Jane was still talking to her. So the card was the only clue to the stranger's identity.

It had been two months since that night. The incident would seem unreal if she didn't awaken sometimes in the night in a breathless sweat, dreaming she was with him. Also she was recognising her growing discontent with her comfortable, secure and cocooned existence.

Several weeks after her run-in with Mr Reinhardt, she and Rosemary had met at the front door as he was coming out. In politeness, he stood to one side to let them in. Fascinated, she watched as Rosemary, with a toss of her long silken hair had stepped in front of her, bestowed Mr Reinhardt with a little smile, and in her soft, posh voice had said, "Oh, thank you."

Mr Reinhardt had acknowledged that with a punctilious nod, then looked at Jane. She pasted on a bright smile, swallowed nervously and hoped her voice sounded steady as she acknowledged him by saying, "Good afternoon, Mr

41

Reinhardt."

Mr Reinhardt revealed an immaculate row of straight white teeth as a wide smile lit up his austere features. On a slight bow he acknowledged her, "And a good afternoon to you, Miss Jane Mackenzie." To her astonishment, he added a slow, deliberate wink, before striding out through the door.

That, with the astonishment on Rosemary's face, made it hard not to turn her smile into a smirk. Back in the office, Rosemary hit her with a barrage of questions. "You didn't tell me you'd met Mr Reinhardt. How does he know your name? Why did he wink at you? Don't tell me that you've been sucking up to him too?"

Jane took a deep breath. She determined to ignore the jibe, but couldn't resist a facetious reply. "No, Rosemary, I won't." Before Rosemary could respond she headed for door to escape to the Ladies'. But she left with a parting shot, "I expect its all part of Mr Reinhardt's fraternising strategy – the one that includes junior secretaries like me!"

That day, the atmosphere in the office changed. Even the constant asides about her Christian faith ceased. If this was due to Rosemary mistakenly thinking that she and Mr Reinhardt were fraternising, well – let her think it. If Mr Reinhardt's simple wink could accomplished that, then she decided her cynical thoughts and opinions of him should be forgotten.

What couldn't be forgotten was the stranger. She joined ITP's social club in the hope of meeting him. The club's disco in a marquee by the Thames had been fun. She'd enjoyed the Proms at the Royal Albert Hall, followed by drinks in the pub afterwards, where a lively debate had started about whether the pop music of today would become the classical music of tomorrow. At both events she observed people's behaviour and found their attitudes to life were often very different to hers. And Bruce's continuing reluctance to join her at office activities seemed to exacerbate his lack of adventure which alienated her further.

As the weeks passed, she was losing hope of ever discovering the stranger's identity. Still dreaming, she finished typing one metallic sheet and was just putting another in the typewriter as the office door was flung open and slammed against the wall.

Rosemary, eyes ablaze, stormed in towards her, gave her hair its customary toss and threw the papers in her hand down on her desk. In a voice that was a tight scream she declared, "It seems, you – and I just can't imagine why – have been asked to stand in as Andrew Carlton's secretary! Nikki Clark won't listen to reason! I'm far better qualified than you, and I have far more experience than you. But they want you." Her lip curled in disdain, she shook her head in disbelief.

Jane's brow furrowed, "They do?"

Rosemary looked down her nose at her and repeated, "They do! And what they say goes. I can't understand it! The policy is, if help is needed, a secretary whose boss is away fills in. Mike's away so that should be me. Instead, I'm told I have to stay and run the department with Paul."

In the hope of placating her Jane ventured, "Well, that shows what a vital part you play – I can be dispensed with, you can't. Anyway, what's so special about Andrew Carlton?"

Rosemary's pretty face took on a scowl, "Good heavens! Don't you know anything?"

"I know he's the Head of Finance and has a suite of offices on the top floor."

"Exactly!"

Further questions were halted by Paul's arrival. "You've heard, Jane?" he asked.

Hoping Rosemary might appreciate her support, Jane put forth reasons why Rosemary would be better working for Andrew Carlton. Rosemary nodded in agreement.

Distracted, Paul ran his fingers through his hair. "Believe me, Jane, I've already tried those arguments. But Nikki said she had been told by Mr Plaidon that you must go, so I can only conclude he doesn't trust me, in Mike's absence, to run the department without Rosemary's backup."

Rosemary preened, then scowled as Jane blurted out, "That can't be true."

"Well, that's the way it looks to me."

"If I were you, I'd ask Mr Plaidon himself. And if he's not available, talk to one of the other Directors."

Paul looked thoughtful and agreed, "You're right," then turned on his heel and left.

Rosemary drummed her fingers on the desk, while Jane, having been given no instructions to the contrary, continued typing Paul's long and urgent report. A quarter of an hour later, Paul returned, appearing much lighter of heart.

"Jane, could you show Rosemary what needs doing and then make your way to Andrew Carlton's office."

Fury filled Rosemary's face. She bit out, "Can I speak to you outside?" Paul stepped back as she stormed out the door before him. Even though Paul closed the door she could still hear enough to know Rosemary was haranguing him as they moved toward his office. When she eventually returned she was sullen and silent, so whatever Paul had said had obviously upset her. Jane could only guess that she was still to work for Andrew Carlton, so made ready and popped her head around Paul's office door. "I assume I'm still to go. Rosemary said nothing. I did tell her what I had to do, but I doubt she was listening so I've typed out some instructions and left them for her!"

"Making sure she can't blame you when, in temper, she gets it all wrong, eh!" Paul gave an unperturbed laugh. "Oh by the way you were right, the decision was nothing to do with my abilities, more yours!"

"Mine?"

Paul gave a ironic smile, "Apparently, certain of your actions have come to Mr Plaidon's attention and he believes you are more capable of dealing with Andrew Carlton's... let's say, 'caprices', than Rosemary would be."

Jane blushed. Just what tales had reached Mr Plaidon's ears, and what were Mr Carlton's 'caprices'? As she pondered, Paul continued, "You'll be fine and a lot happier than I'm going to be." He waved his hand in dismissal. "Go on, enjoy yourself."

Andrew Carlton's secretary had a carpeted office, a huge L-shaped desk and the very latest IBM electric typewriter with a golf ball of characters which moved instead of the carriage! It was going to be a bit difficult to get used to, but if she was to enjoy herself this was a good place to start! A note propped up in the typewriter keys gave a list of tasks, all of which were easy to accomplish. She gulped as she turned the note over. On the bottom was a single initial, 'A', which wasn't unlike that scribbled on the apology card. Could Andrew Carlton be her stranger? Tonight she'd compare the two initials. She stowed the note in her handbag.

At lunch, she was eager to tell Sam and Ian of the day's developments. Although they confessed to never seeing the man their garnered description made him out to be an unmarried, blonde Tarzan. When Jill arrived, Jane's news was received with a frown and comment, "That's odd! That's not what Company policy dictates."

"Rosemary said the same – so why insist on me?"

Jill grinned. "Maybe Andrew Carlton knows about Rosemary's reputation as a sullen, snobbish prig and asked if he could have her cheeky, impulsive office mate instead."

"Huh! The question is, does the cheeky, impulsive office mate want him?"

"Maybe, if she likes Greek God features – you know, bright blue eyes, wavy blond hair and a tall, athletic, bronzed body."

With a smile, Jane asked pointedly, "A suitable candidate?"

Jill's reply was cut off by Sam's irritated outburst. "You've been asked to work for the man, not marry him! Now he's definitely out of your league...." At Jane's look of surprise, he went on less dramatically, "Let's just say, he's a man of the world – if you get my meaning."

"Oh, dear. Now you're making me feel nervous."

"Take no notice of him," Jill chuckled. "Your fun–filled charm will break down any barriers, and let's face it, if he gets out of line you'll soon put him right."

Ian touched his cheek, "Um, I can vouch for that. Woe betide him if he looks too long at those shapely legs and sexy bottom!"

Jane gave him a hard look, and then said airily, "Words, Ian, words. I can tell you they can be just as stunning!"

Jill sniggered into her hand, while Ian and Sam gave each other a look that said, 'women'! Then, trying to be more serious, Jill remarked, "I've heard Andrew called a sheep in wolf's clothing."

Ian butted in, "You mean wolf in sheep's clothing!"

Jane and Jill spluttered with laughter, and Sam hissed "Sssh! Everyone's looking in this direction."

But Sam's embarrassment didn't douse their amusement. Their conversation got sillier, their laughter got louder, until even Ian was groaning. Sam kept shushing them until, with urgency in his eyes, he leant forward and spoke in an unaccustomed snarl. "For goodness sake, the pair of you – shut up!" Then he sat back to give someone behind them an apologetic smile.

Nonplussed, they stared at Sam, then turned together to see a pair of trouser legs standing between them. They grinned at each other and together their eyes travelled upward. Even before they reached Mr Reinhardt's smiling face, the laughter had died in their throats.

"Well, well, girls! You are enjoying yourselves! Do share the joke."

Jane took a deep breath and exhaled slowly, hoping Jill would answer. But her face was as white as Jane's was red. She mumbled something that Jane guessed, rather than heard, to be "Oh God!"

Well Jill might not believe in God, but she certainly had the right idea! It wouldn't be wise to again tell a Company Director to mind his own business, especially in a canteen full of people. With Jill mesmerised by the pattern of the tablecloth, Jane felt she had no alternative but to stand and face their challenger, and reasoned that honesty was the best policy.

Even as she tilted her head back to address Mr Reinhardt, she determined not to be put off by either his wry expression, or the unexpectedness of making what was quickly turning into her first public speech. On what she hoped was a sweet smile, she began, "Mr Reinhardt, I am sorry if Jill and I disturbed your lunch. Please accept our apologies." Her eyes studied his tie as she continued mournfully, "Unfortunately it isn't a joke to share…" She took a deep breath, then fixing her eyes back on Mr Reinhardt's face, "…because I was comparing a part of my anatomy with that of someone else." Her eyes challenged him. "And, as a gentleman, I'm sure you'll ask no further." Under Mr Reinhardt's steady gaze, she felt rather than saw that the room had stilled to await his response.

As she watched, those dark brooding eyes filled with warm amusement, and his mouth broke into a wide smile. Then he declared loudly, "Jane Mackenzie, in my entire life I've never met anyone quite like you!" His response to her sceptical expression was to slap his thigh and roar with laughter.

The whole canteen, seconds earlier charged with tension, now seemed to share the mirth that gripped him. Stunned, Jane tried to take it in. To her it was anything but funny, but she managed a watery smile as she glanced round at the laughing faces. Self-conscious, she sat down and glanced at Jill. Poor Jill. Her face was tight and white. Concerned Jane leant sideways to comfort her. With closed eyes she pulled back. Oh, no! No! It couldn't have happened. Had she really just placed her lips on Mr Reinhardt's cheek? She opened her eyes. His, wide with astonishment, were staring into hers. Surely he didn't think she'd deliberately kissed him in full view of his employees? The ridicule and laughter this was going to bring in the days ahead was bad enough, but what of his reaction? She watched as incredulity crinkled into amused lines around his eyes, which were now filling with mirth. His lips twisted into a wry smile. He moved toward her ear and murmured, "If you feel the need to kiss me, Jane, perhaps in future you could do it in a more private place."

Mortification turned her face crimson and her limbs weak. Not knowing what to say or do she stared down at her plate while Mr Reinhardt, having straightened, towered over her to ask Sam for a glass of water before bending again to speak to Jill. The rest of the diners, decided the floorshow had ended and reverted to talking and eating, which she mimicked, but the food seemed to stick in her throat. Sam pushed a glass of water under her nose. In thanking him, she caught Jill's churlish expression and Mr Reinhardt patting her shoulder. Then, in passing, he did the same to her as he returned to his table across the room. Embarrassed, Jane could only stare at her plate. Would she ever be able to look him, or anyone else, in the face again?

The scraping of Jill's chair on the floor caused her to look up. The expression on Jill's face was murderous. Tentatively she asked, "Are you alright?"

Jill shook her head and stalked out of the canteen. Sam

patted Jane's arm. "She'll be alright, luv. I don't think it's you she's cross with. But you've certainly been and gone and done it – got yourself really noticed, young Jane."

Ian grinned. "What a stunning performance. So what did Mr Reinhardt say to you after you kissed him so prettily?" The surly look she gave him made him chortle. "That bad, eh?"

Not wanting to be the subject of more banter, and anxious to regain her equilibrium before meeting Mr Carlton, she got up. "I think I need some air."

Sam nodded sympathetically.

However, instead of getting some air, she went back to her new office where, half an hour later, Andrew Carlton appeared. As described, he was the epitome of a Greek God. She stood to take his outstretched hand as he introduced himself. "Hello there. I'm Andrew Carlton. Please call me Andrew." Already unnerved by previous events, it didn't help when he added in a feigned Scottish accent, "And ye must be Jane Mackenzie, the wee lass who kissed Mr Reinhardt in the canteen this lunch time?" She swayed weakly again the desk. Amused Andrew dropped the accent. "I think Jane you'd better she sit down. I just know we're going to get on famously. Don't worry – gossip spreads like wild fire but, believe me, it's quickly forgotten."

Andrew's wink probably meant he hadn't forgotten the other tales about the "fiery Miss" in the Public Relations Department and the floral apology she had received. One way or another, Jane felt she was getting a reputation she didn't deserve.

However, during the next few hours, her working world changed. Andrew was fun and the work was challenging and interesting. His relaxed style was reflected through the Accounts and Payroll Department, giving her the opportunity to talk and laugh with the twenty or so people who worked for him. As his Secretary, she fielded his calls, organised his appointments, and dealt with the constant stream of visitors who passed through her office en route to his.

The only person who ignored her, but hounded Andrew between chain-smoking and coughing was Maud. She'd the habit of suddenly emerging from her office in a billowing grey cloud of cigarette smoke, to erupt with caustic remarks – sometimes to no-one in particular. So, along with the prematurely lined face, raspy voice, red hair and fingernails she'd earned the title of 'The Dragon Lady'.

It was four days before she came face to face with Maud in the Ladies'. She gave a her a cautious smile. On a gust of stale cigarette breath, and with a sight of crooked brown teeth, Maud grated out, "So that blue-eyed snake's got you, eh? " She peered into the mirror as if to see Jane better. "Interesting choice!" Before Jane could comment she went on, "How's Evie doing?"

Puzzled, Jane repeated, "Doing?"

"Yes – doing! How is she?"

Jane shrugged. "Enjoying herself on holiday, I expect."

In the mirror, Maud stopped adding black mascara to her false eyelashes to snap, "Umph! I bet she wishes she was."

Jane frowned. "Why? Has something happened to her?"

Maud weighed her up and down, then answered abruptly, "Woman problems."

"Oh, I see. I'm sorry. Maybe that's why Andrew didn't mention it. Perhaps we could take up a collection?" Black, eye-lined eyes stared at Jane in the mirror. "You know, buy her some chocolates, flowers or something to cheer her up."

Maud gave her a hard look, threw her make-up back in her bag and barked out, "She needs more than that, poor cow, but you do that and I'll take it to her." Before Jane could ask or say anything else, she'd gone.

Never slow to act, Jane was already collecting when

Andrew returned from lunch. He seemed a little taken aback, but delved into his wallet and produced a ten-shilling note. Seeing her surprise, he gave her an engaging smile. "I like to be generous. But if Evie doesn't come back, will you stay?"

"Is there any reason why she shouldn't?" Andrew gave a non-committal shrug, so she chirped, "I've certainly no objection, if no-one else has. You're a pleasure to work for, Mr Carlton."

With a small, shy smile at her enthusiasm, he walked out.

Her heart fluttered. If he was her 'stranger', as she suspected from the initialled note, then the longer she worked for him the more likely he'd be to confess.

CHAPTER 4

The weekend dragged as thoughts of Andrew kept pervading her mind. Obviously Maud wasn't one of his fans – when she'd told her of his generosity she'd practically breathed fire, snarling, "Oh, he's generous alright – but don't you be fooled by it!" At that, she'd practically grabbed the goodies for Evie out of her hand and stalked off.

Mr Reinhardt's words also plagued her. What had he meant by "In my entire life I've never met any one quite like you"? Was that a compliment, or an insult? And his suggestion that, "If you must kiss me, could you do it in a more private place" – the very thought made her cringe! Now had Andrew invited her to kiss him....

On Saturday afternoon Bruce, sensing her frustration, suggested they went for a boat trip down the Thames. She agreed, but her thoughts were far from agreeable. Ten miles up the road was about as far as he was willing to go. Last year, she'd launched a major campaign to persuade him to go to Majorca and then, when he had finally said 'yes', she found his Dad and her Mum were joining them. Once there, everything had been the subject of complaint. It was doubtful that would be repeated. Now Andrew was well travelled!

Bruce and she didn't have dates: they met at church meetings and then he brought her home; he would pop in and suggest somewhere, then they went out. At church, because everyone considered her and Bruce a couple, they were invited everywhere together. It was making her feel stifled, she wanted a change from this cosy but boring existence – what she needed was some excitement.

So, on Monday, it was that longing which stopped her from pointing out to Andrew that allowing her bottom to be patted wasn't in her job description!

On Tuesday, when he delicately kissed her fingertips, and whispered, "You type so beautifully," she'd giggled delightedly.

Wednesday brought an unexpected lingering kiss on the back of her neck, which sent a tingling sensation down her spine. This time, she gave a smiling but haughty rebuttal. However, it obviously wasn't strong enough to deter him, for he continued to touch her whenever he passed.

The following afternoon, he suggested they went for a drink after work. Her refusal was met with "Oh, playing hard to get are we?" Her explanation that she always went to a Bible Study on Thursday evenings merely drew a cynical laugh.

Friday morning, Andrew appeared preoccupied. She was disappointed. He hadn't confessed to being the stranger, and there'd been no talk of her staying on another week. That meant on Monday she'd be back with her small desk, manual typewriter and Rosemary!

In between his meetings, she blurted out as he passed, "I'm going to miss you if Evie's back on Monday."

His eyes took on a big sad look and his hand pulled boyishly at his ear. "That seems the way of it. She's not like you. She takes everything so seriously – no sense of fun." He pulled a face. "Evie thinks anyone who enjoys life is fickle. To think I nearly had that misery Rosemary here. Thank goodness they saw sense and sent you instead. Working with her must be much the same."

So it was Andrew who had persuade Mr Plaidon she should work for him – why? Did he know something she didn't? Was he the stranger? Jane smiled up at Andrew. She had only seen Evie once or twice. She wasn't a particularly attractive girl, but she didn't appear to have Rosemary's sullen nature. Nevertheless, she could sympathise with Andrew. "If she's unhappy why doesn't she leave?"

"I was rather hoping she might, but I am told it is I who should change." Unable to think of a suitable comment she said nothing as Andrew opened a file and pointed to a complicated table, "Evie hates typing these – she'll probably think I've saved this to spite her!"

"Let me do it then. It'll take a while, but I can stay late because I've nothing planned this evening."

Andrew brightened. "Oh, Jane, would you? Would you really?"

She laughed and basked in his delight. "If it'll help, then I'd be happy to."

"In that case, as soon as you've finished, I'll take you out to dinner." Andrew it seemed noticed her hesitation because he went on, "A 'thank you'. And after – we'll hit the town."

Those playful, pleading eyes looking at her were so endearing. His enthusiasm brought her to a giggled reply. "Oh, I think dinner would suffice."

"Right then." He headed across her office, "I'm out for the rest of the day, but I'll pop back for you later."

The door closed and she frowned. Her spontaneous reply had taken her by surprise and, for no reason she could fathom, she wondered if it were wise.

In the lunch queue, she decided it would be better to tell Sam and Ian about her unexpected date rather than they find out elsewhere. Sam's face clouded with apprehension. "Not sure that's a good idea, young Jane – it would seem that man's got a bit of a reputation."

Ian grinned, "Sam! This girl's got a reputation!" He straightened his face, "That incident with Mr...."

Jane interrupted. "Oh, stop it! Anyway, any gossip you've heard about Andrew probably stemmed from Evie. Apparently she's just like Rosemary! I've explained why Andrew is buying me a meal, and there is nothing more to it than that!" At Sam's cynical expression she continued,

"Andrew's unassuming, a pleasure to work for, and I'm sure he'll be fun to be with."

Sam's eyebrows lifted, "If you say so, girlie, but rumour has it he's no gentleman."

"Rumours! Honestly Sam, this place is always full of rumours. Look how stories about me have got out of hand!" Ian sniggered. Jane gave him a stony look then, to illustrate her point, went on, "Okay then, take Mr Reinhardt. There is always talk and rumour about him. He looks stern, seems unapproachable, his manner can be intimidating, but the other day I think he was trying to be friendly."

Ian spluttered, "Just like you were in giving him that kiss?"

Her eyes narrowed and she snapped out, "I didn't kiss him!"

"Okay then, what did he whisper in your ear?"

Sam patted her hand, his eyes twinkling affectionately, "Don't worry, luv, I think Mr Reinhardt liked the fact you were honest. and ...."

Doreen's piercing voice came from the hatchway. "Who's holding up the queue?" Jane saw the smirks on the faces of those around and leapt forward as Doreen continued, "Aha! It's Jane again. Might have guessed it was you, ducks." She shook her head, "What yer bin up to this time?"

Jane sighed, "I wish I knew. Cottage pie, chips and peas, please."

Before Doreen could fill her plate, Pam arrived at the counter with Jill, who asked, "What's all this about dinner with Andrew Carlton?"

Jane sighed. Oh no, surely it wasn't on the grapevine already? Apprehensive, she glanced at those around. Thanks to Jill's shrill tone it soon would be!

"'Ere you are, luv," Doreen gave Jill and Pam a cross look. "Now, if you two will get to the back of the queue,

I'll give everyone else their dinners!"

Jill, not to be distracted, walked beside Jane saying more quietly, "You may think that Andrew Carlton could be your stranger, that he's some sort of nice, cuddly teddy bear but, believe me, he isn't!"

"Oh, come on, Jill you're exaggerating."

"No, I mean it."

Seeing her friend's concern, Jane conceded, "Look, get your lunch and we'll talk about it".

Jane, determined to get in the first word began by praising Andrew Carlton's virtues and in triumph concluded, "And, I don't see how he can turn into a wolf during a meal in a restaurant, do you?"

Jill wavered. "I suppose not, but please be careful, for sometimes it's not what you say, but the way you say it."

Pam, who was normally not bothered about who did what to whom, unexpectedly spoke up. "Andrew Carlton may not venture out much from the third floor, but I doubt he's a stranger to the tales about you. He probably sees you as a challenge to his male ego."

"Oh now, Pam! That's ridiculous!"

Pam's smile faded, "Look, all I am saying is, 'beware'. Now can we drop the subject?"

Jane looked at her watch for the tenth time that evening. It was now 7.00pm. Had Andrew changed his mind about dinner tonight? Should she change hers? To be wined and dined by such a handsome man a few years older than herself would be any girl's dream. And he didn't make her feel like an unsophisticated nincompoop.

On the other hand, if he did turn out to be the stranger, would he expect to continue where they'd left off? That could be awkward, for to be taken by surprise and fondled was one thing, but encouraging a man who didn't share her faith and principles was quite another. She pulled a piece of paper from the rack and started to write.

As if on cue, Andrew arrived. Did he guess she was writing her excuses? It seemed so, because he kept up a steady stream of conversation as he steered her out of the office, along the corridor and into the lift. "I'm so pleased you said 'yes'. I am so looking forward to your company out of the office. I thought you'd not want to go too far so I thought we'd go to this pleasant little restaurant just round the corner from my flat in Kensington. After our meal, we can go on to a night club, dance for a while to get us in the mood, and then back to my place."

A quick glance at him revealed his playful, provocative smile. He already knew she wouldn't go along with that, but she gave him a haughty reply just in case. "Now don't get any ideas, my man. Dinner is just fine at the restaurant, but after that it will be nearly time for bed."

Andrew gleefully rubbed his hands together. "Oh, jolly good!"

"Oh! You know what I mean!"

They left the lift laughing, but as they started across the hall, Andrew fell silent. Jane followed his gaze. Mr Reinhardt was sitting with his feet up on the Reception desk. Presumably he was waiting for someone. She had not seen him since the incident in the canteen nearly two week ago, and rather wished she hadn't now. Was there any hope of leaving without him asking at least one question? As she heard his voice boom across the hall her heart sank – obviously not!

"What are you two still doing here?"

Why did the man always made her feel guilty? She pinned a smile on her face.

Andrew's stilted, nervous tone surprised her. "Jane's been working late. Helping me out. Very kind. Don't you think?"

Mr Reinhardt gave Andrew a long hard stare, lowered his legs from the desk and bent forward to say coldly, "Um. Is that so?" He eyed her up and down, and said more cheerily, "That's good of you, Jane. You're off to your home now."

She swallowed hard and strove to be pleasant. "Well, not yet. Andrew – I mean Mr Carlton – he's taking me out for a meal. A 'thank you' for my work. Isn't that kind of him?"

Mr Reinhardt rose. His build was similar to Andrew's, yet, perhaps due to his dark grimness, he seemed more intimidating. "So, Andrew, where are you taking Jane?"

Andrew's hand, which had slipped reassuringly under her elbow, tightened, but his reply sounded nonchalant. "Oh, a little place off Kensington High Street." Mr Reinhardt's questioning gaze didn't waver from Andrew's face and, under that penetrating stare, she could understand Andrew's struggle. "Err, you may know it. Um, it's a pleasant place, *La Bohème*."

Mr Reinhardt frowned and gave a speculative hum. They turned to leave, but jumped as he barked out, "Off with the old and on with the new then, Andrew?"

Andrew's jaw clenched, his face reddened. Incensed at Mr Reinhardt's interference, Jane moved forward to face him. Any reply Andrew may have been forming she cut across to burst out, "Look Mr Reinhardt, I don't know why you feel the need to ask so many questions, or be so rude. Andrew and I are going out for a meal. We don't need your approval, or disapproval. This isn't company time, it's in our time." Both men gaped at her. "Come on Andrew." Drawing on his arm, and with a quick toss of her head, she threw an emphatic, "Goodnight, Mr Reinhardt!" and passed through the door.

The heat of Mr Reinhardt's glower at their backs was almost tangible. Inwardly she sighed, if only she would think before she spoke. That man could make her life very uncomfortable. But then, it seemed he already had the knack of doing just that!

Jane instinctively drew closer to Andrew, as they

walked away. About to speak she was taken by surprised when Andrew's mouth came down to cover hers. If she hadn't guessed the kiss was for Mr Reinhardt's benefit she would have pushed Andrew away, especially as it wasn't the cool, sensual massage she was expecting, but more a warm slimy rub! To avoid it continuing too long, she caught hold of Andrew's hand and drew him laughingly towards the car park. The moment they rounded the corner of the building he strode ahead toward his car while she quickly turned and wiped her mouth against the back of her hand.

With panache, Andrew whisked open the door of his bright red E-type Jaguar and bowed as she moved to slide in to the low bucket seat. Before she could lower herself in, Andrew wedged her between himself and the car, muffling her protest by his kiss. Memories of the stranger stopped her pushing him off, but there was no adrenaline rush and certainly no sense of being wooed. The moment he came up for breath, she put her hands on his chest to ward him off and demanded, "Get off me, Andrew!" His response was a boyish chuckle. "I don't like being grabbed. I'm not that sort of girl."

"Really?"

"Yes! Really!"

Her vehemence caused an amused smile and a raised palm of surrender. "Okay, Jane, okay!" He moved away to let her into the car, "I know, just playing hard to get."

Annoyed, she said fiercely, "No I'm not."

"In that case, please accept my deepest apologies." he bowed deeply. "Your carriage awaits."

Still cross, she gave him a haughty look, then slid into the low slung, sleek car, with its long bonnet and black leather upholstery which it seemed reflected the lifestyle he enjoyed. Jane's thoughts were not on the car as the engine alternated between a roar and a purr along the road, but on her wisdom in going out with this man.

She could still picture Mr Reinhardt's grim face, and remember his words, "off with the old, on with the new." Andrew didn't like Evie, so he would hardly have taken her out for meals. Did he mean a previous girlfriend? A love affair? It didn't feel right to ask. But Mr Reinhardt's attitude clearly showed he didn't like Andrew. Why not?

As if reading her thoughts, Andrew chuckled, "My goodness, Jane! You certainly put the old man in his place. Did you see his face? You've certainly got a way with words." He gave a derisive laugh. "Since it was out of office hours he can't sack you for insubordination. Watch your back, though. He doesn't like being crossed and he'll be looking for a way to get you out."

So, it was mutual dislike! Andrew had a point though. Interfering or not, Mr Reinhardt was in a position to demand respect. But intuitively she knew that however annoyed he might be, he'd never do anything unscrupulous.

Andrew stopped and parked outside a five-storey Victorian apartment block. Jane stated the obvious. "This isn't the restaurant."

He chuckled, "10 out of 10! It is, however, the best place to park. And now we're here, we might as well pop up to my flat and have a couple of drinks."

Alarmed, she replied quickly, "I'd rather not, if you don't mind. I'm rather hungry and I hate eating late. I get indigestion when I go to bed on a full stomach."

Andrew's eyebrows raised in a suggestive manner.

Disconcerted, she opened the car door asking, "Which way to the restaurant?"

Andrew, obviously put out, came around to her side of the car and after saying briskly, "This way," headed off and remained silent during the two-minute walk.

At *La Bohème*, Andrew was welcomed by name. The table he requested was instantly prepared and this, with the arrival of the pre-dinner drinks, restored his smile and charm. His chosen table was at the far end of the room and, when seated, she found they were almost surrounded by oak panelling. One glance at the leather-bound menu caused her to stifle a gasp. The cost of a starter was twice the price Bruce had paid for her three course meal when he'd taken her out in April to celebrate her birthday. Did everyone spend this kind of money regularly? Andrew apparently did. No wonder the waiters treated him with such deference!

The meal was an experience she thoroughly enjoyed. Each course came exquisitely decorated with vegetables or fruits – a grape and peach flower, an exotic celery design, a tomato rose. The recommended sweet was an island of pastry with fruits, surrounded by a blue sauce in which sat a profiterole swan filled with cream. Each bite was an adventure of texture and taste. If nothing else, tonight had given her ideas for her own cuisine.

The only thing that spoiled the evening was that, the slower she savoured the food, the faster the wine slipped down Andrew's throat. She had only managed one glass before a second bottle appeared, followed rapidly by a third that he said would enhance the sweet course. Having insisted that she empty her glass to try it, he consumed the remainder. Next, he ordered a brandy with his coffee. His usually bronzed tan was beginning to look florid, while his thick, curly blond hair fell in damp tendrils across his brow, and a heavy-eyed, sexy look had crept into his Greek-god-like face.

"It's been a wonderful meal, Andrew." Jane glanced at her watch. "But I think it's time I went home."

His brow creased. "No, no, you can't go yet. Next stop, a few drinks at my club."

"Thank you, Andrew, but I did say I'd only come for a meal."

"Now come, Jane. Neither you, nor I, took those words seriously." His eyes roved over her suggestively. "You know how irresistible I find you."

Jane was not used to being mentally undressed, and the revulsion in her eyes made him curl his lip. "Oh, come on, stop the play acting."

Her heart sank. He may not be slurring his words, but the drink was making him act as though he were a god she should obey. Then, as if to reassure her, he reverted back to his friendly deep huskiness to say, "Relax, we're going to have a good time – a memorable night."

Nervous, she babbled, "Look I'm sure we would, but I have to get home. We can't be far from an underground station so don't worry about me, I'll find my own way there."

"No!" His reply was so harsh that she jumped. For a moment, she thought he was going to hit the table. But it seemed he suddenly noticed that the restaurant had filled up, for his voice took on a quieter, more persuasive note and, while downing yet another brandy, he assured her a taxi would take her anywhere she wanted to go.

"I'm sorry, Andrew, you had other plans for this evening, but I must go, thank ...." She bent to pick up her bag and gasped as pain shot up her arm. Andrew, having grabbed her wrist, was now twisting and squeezing it. Hissing, "Let go, Andrew," she tried to free herself. He allowed her to sit up, but slid his hand down to hold hers. Not wanting to cause a scene, she demanded with icy quietness, "Andrew! Please let go of my hand!"

His reply was a lewd laugh. She tried to pull away, but he wouldn't let her.

"I'll call the waiter."

"Hmm, now comes the 'ice maiden' act I've heard about." His fingers squeezed her small hand with a vice-like grip. "If I let go, I suppose you'll slap my face?" Jane's eyes flashed with anger, while he purred with silky menace, "I assure you, my dear, if you do, you will receive back twice what you give." His mouth curved in a mocking smile and his eyes narrowed. "But then, some girls like it that way." In shock she stared at him. He peered at her over his raised glass, then laughed knowingly, "And maybe you're one of them." Her friends had been right. He'd changed from sheep to wolf, and this was far more scary than her encounters with Mr Reinhardt! Nausea was beginning to replace the pleasant after-dinner satisfaction. Andrew was the right height and build. He could afford expensive taxis and flowers. And only the stranger knew how pliant and responsive she could become. How her imagination had run wild! This bronzed, drunken hulk was not the portrait she'd painted in her mind. She suppressed a sense of loss.

Andrew's voice, thick with drink, dark with menace, broke into her thoughts, "Now Jane, let's leave without fuss. I can, and will, handle with ease any scene you might make, but rest assured that once outside I will deal with you."

His derisive laugh, and the febrile glitter of his eyes as they raked over her, told her this was no idle threat. She had every reason to believe he'd enjoy 'dealing with her'. Her stomach churned in fear. Could she escape once they were outside in the darkness of the street? How far was it to the main road? Perhaps while he was paying the bill she could tell the waiter she wanted to leave alone in a taxi.

His drunken drawl grated out, "Well Jane? I'm waiting."

Determined to outwit him and trying to buy a little time, she laughed lightly as though it was a joke, "Oh, come on, Andrew. Don't be so melodramatic. I said I would come out with you for a meal – I have, and I enjoyed it. Surely you're not threatening me? That would be silly!"

He moved closer. The smell of alcohol wafted from his breath as he whispered, "Perhaps it is you who is silly?" His hand tightened again over her wrist and, pulling it under the table, he twisted it so hard that she gasped with the pain. Tears pricked her eyes as his lips curved to snarl, "Girls like you don't get expensive meals for nothing."

It was difficult to control her mounting panic, but she must if she was to escape. The people sitting at the table opposite probably believed he was holding her hand, her eyes wet because he was being romantic and tender. There was no doubt in her mind he'd have an equally good ploy should she burst into tears, beg someone to help her, or refuse to leave.

Like a chameleon, he suddenly changed to smile and coax her, "Oh Jane, let's not row. We're going to be so good together. I'll play your game, but let's leave first."

The thought of being alone with Andrew, and 'good together' was frightening. She prayed for deliverance, her silence taken for agreement as he tipped back the remainder of his brandy.

In the hope of reasoning with him, she spoke into those glittering, jumping eyes, "Andrew, I'm sorry, I'm really sorry if my actions led you to believe I was – I am – playing games with you. I'm not, honestly. I really thought this was a meal to thank me for my work...."

A snarl contorted his features and under the table he twisted her wrist and arm so fiercely that she thought it might break. She cried out, "Andrew — you're hurting me!"

But his response was to look around the restaurant with a congenial smile before growling near her ear as if whispering sweet nothings, "Keep quiet, or you'll find this is only a sample of the payment you're going to get."

In the hope of drawing on his better nature she beseeched, "Please, Andrew, let me go.... I really don't know anything about men and their ways."

He gave her an invidious grin. "Oh, come on Jane! This is the swinging sixties – the era of sexual freedom – you really don't expect me to believe that! You know what you want – I know what I want." He shrugged. "But, as I said before, save the play-acting until later."

If he thought she had been play-acting, then now was the time to really start! She opened her eyes wide, put on a sad look and, moving nearer to his florid face, said penitently, "Andrew, I'm sorry. Can we start again?" By smiling and giving a sideways flutter of her eyes she hoped her expression would be considered provocative. "Now, if you'll just let me go...."

To her surprise he believed it. Her wrist was released. Slowly she moved her hand, while her mind raced with ideas of escape. With a forced smile, she asked, "I must go to the Ladies' before we leave. Do you know where it is?"

Andrew pointed towards it as he chortled, "That's more like it! I'll meet you by the front door."

Jane put on a bright smile, picked up her bag and cardigan but froze as she turned to leave. In the aisle, Andrew was blocking her way. "One for the road, eh!" he murmured drunkenly, and thwarted her attempt to twist away by clamping his hands over her ears and tilting her head upwards. His mouth ground into hers. His tongue forced itself down her throat. If the gesture was meant as a promise of the 'fun' they were going to have, she was thankful they were still in the restaurant.

Sickened, shaking and red faced, she managed a smile, turned and, with eyes fixed on her goal, walked between the diners to the front door. Glancing back, she could see him watching her over the oak partitioning. To reassure him she painfully waved her fingers at him before pushing the door into the Ladies' toilet. Inside, she leant back against the door and fought the urge to slide to the floor and weep. But she knew her ordeal wasn't over yet. There was no time to waste. Giving a brief rub to her arm and wrist, she peered out. Andrew, his back towards her was putting on his jacket. It was now or never.

As she passed the man at the desk, she put a finger to her lips and gave him a playful smile. With a puzzled look he glanced toward their table, no doubt checking someone was going to pay the bill, and then smiled back. Seconds later she was out in the street.

Not wanting to go by the restaurant window, she turned left and ran as quickly as she could in her tight skirt and three-inch heels. A car drove by, but otherwise the street was quiet and empty, making her easy to spot. It would be better to disappear into the dark warren of side streets. She judged the main road past Kensington Gardens must be in that direction.

Jane crossed the road and took the first turning right. In the hope of confusing him if he followed her, she took the second turning left. The next two right turns were dead ends, but the third, a narrow one-way street, revealed a main road with bright lights at its end. Now out of immediate danger, she gave in to the burning sensation in her chest, slowed to a steady walk and adjusted her shoulder bag to use it as a sling for her throbbing arm. The road ahead was obviously Kensington High Street. She sighed with relief and thanksgiving.

Several cars drove past her. At the sound of each engine she glanced round worriedly, but when brakes squealed and a car halted beside her, her fears were realized. Immediately she broke into a run, and headed for the High Street – she'd be safe there. The sound of a car door slamming told her Andrew was following her on foot.

She reached the High Street and quickly looked left and right. Her heart sank. The shoppers had long since gone. The pavements were empty. Cars purred steadily by. A man in the distance was walking away from her – could she catch him up?

She glanced behind and saw Andrew was gaining on her. Despite the pain growing in her chest, she tried to run faster. If only someone would appear from one of the darkened shop fronts or closed doors. The sound of thudding footsteps warned her Andrew was almost upon her. His hand curled round her bruised arm and swung her round. In pain and fright, she cried out and tried to jerk free. But Andrew's arm encircled her waist. Pulling her against him, he half dragged, half carried her back down the road.

Once back in the narrow street, his hand shot up and grabbed her hair, pulling her head back to cut off her shouts. Slightly breathless, he purred over her upturned face, "So, another of your little games, eh? Escape and capture!"

His lips ground hers painfully against her teeth, and his tongue forced her mouth open. Furiously, Jane kicked and twisted against his hateful invasion of her mouth. She pushed hard and tried to run, but his arm locked round her again, dragging her backwards into his chest. Desperate as his hand clamped over her mouth to stop her shouts, she tried elbowing him, but delightedly he murmured, "Now for the taming of the shrew!"

Her hands strove to pull away his hand from across her mouth. She tried to bite him. An attempt to plant her stiletto heel through his foot caused a brief loosening of his arm, but only to painfully hoist her up, so her feet didn't touch the ground. His warm, alcoholic breath fanned her cheek. "Not only a devious little vixen, but spirited with it!"

She swung her leg backward in the hope of kicking him.

Andrew sniggered, "I guessed you'd be a bit of a challenge, but then we know that makes everything so much more exciting, doesn't it?"

A cold frisson ran through her. If there had been remaining doubts, they were gone! He was her 'stranger'. It seemed that drunk, Andrew's sadistic side — which she'd chosen to forget from that night — was now uppermost. Obviously he'd enjoyed beating her then, and would do so again. She aimed her shoe at his leg again and had the satisfaction of stabbing into flesh.

He groaned, but his grip tightened. "Struggle all you like, but I warned you – if you hurt me, I'll hurt you." With that, his knee violently jarred into her spine. Pain rocketed through her. Her eyes filled with tears. Her stomach sickened. Andrew continued as though making cheery conversation, "I do congratulate you, Jane, on the way you left the restaurant. You've certainly spiced up the evening."

The street seemed to be getting darker. The bonnet of his car came in sight. Panic mounted within her. Her inability to pull his hand from her was making it hard to breath. Still struggling, she prayed silently to God for his divine intervention. Her heart was banging like a drum. Every part of her body thrummed with the beat. It became a growing pressure in her head – her eyes closed against it. She tried to summon her thoughts, but they seemed to swirl in a maelstrom of discomfort and pain which twisted downwards, drawing her into the centre of a suffocating black hole.

The purr of a car engine seeped into her brain. Slowly her mind refocused. She felt sick. Her head was slumped forward, but her body was held by the safety belt. Revelation brought a flash of terror – she must be in Andrew's car! Jane breathed slowly and willed herself to think and not be sick. This could be her last opportunity to get away. Would falling out of a speeding car be preferable to what Andrew had in store for her? Would that stop him? He seemed so determined that he'd probably pick her body off the road and punish her further. His flat couldn't be far. When he stopped, maybe she could make a run for it? Tears filled her eyes. It was hopeless – there was no escape. She sniffed to relieve her running nose.

Her head shot up as a voice boomed, "So, young lady, I think this time you bit off more than you could chew."

Astonished, she took in Mr Reinhardt's chiselled profile silhouetted against the orange glow of the street lamps, and then uttered thoughtlessly. "Oh no, not you!"

Amusement tinged his retort. "Preferable though, I hope, to Andrew Carlton?"

Relief flooded over her. She managed, "I'm...I'm sorry," then burst into tears. A box of tissues appeared under her nose. Once she'd stemmed the flow she asked in a rush, "What are you doing here? How did I get here?" And then, with a hint of panic, "Where are you taking me?"

Mr Reinhardt slowly moved his head from side to side in disbelief, "It seems, Jane Mackenzie that you are irrepressible."

Another bout of nausea stopped any response.

With a glance in her direction, he fumbled in his pocket and flipped a packet of mints into her lap. "Suck on these. They'll help."

Surprised at his understanding, she stared at him as he concentrated on the road.

After a minute, he glanced at her with amusement and again instructed, "Suck a mint, Jane." Once satisfied she had obeyed, he spoke again, his cultured voice quieter than usual. "Now, to those questions. I'll take the last first, and ask you where do you imagine I'm taking you?" They were heading west out of London, but her mind was blank. She shook her head. "I'm taking you to your home, of course." He gave her a questioning glance, "I assume that's where you want to go?"

This man was rising rapidly in her estimation, but he still made her nervous. "Yes, yes, home," she echoed, then tentatively asked, "But how do you know where I live?"

"Oh, I know a lot of things and, if I don't, I make it my business to find out!"

Her retort was immediate and without thought. "Yes, I noticed. I've been the victim of your enquiring mind on more than one occasion!"

Mr Reinhardt's hearty laughter exploded within the car.

Jane stared at him. He threw her a wry smile and continued speaking with his eyes focused on the road. "Now to the 'what are you doing here?' question. I was eating at the same restaurant as you and Carlton. I saw, and was puzzled by, your odd signal to the *Maître d'* and you leaving alone. It wasn't long before I realized why. Carlton, obviously drunk and very belligerent, muttered no end of foul language on hearing that 'the young lady has slipped out'. I watched as he stormed out of the door, fortunately in the opposite direction to you. It then occurred to me that perhaps he hadn't given up on you, but was getting his car to chase after you. Worried about what he might do if he caught up with you I decided to find you myself."

Grateful for his concern, she rubbed her wrist and arm and whispered, "Thank you."

"I spotted you walking towards the High Street. I did consider offering you a lift," he glanced across at her, "but decided you probably wouldn't welcome my intrusion — especially if I'd misunderstood the situation."

With a rueful grimace, she bent her head. This was one occasion that she could thank God for Mr Reinhardt's interfering nature!

"At the top of the road I stopped and watched you walk to the end and, assuming you were safe, I was about to go when Carlton swung round the corner and screeched to a stop beside you."

The reminder brought back her nausea. Her fingers shook as she undid the paper to get another peppermint.

"I decided then my suspicions were valid when I saw you run into the High Street, I thought he might follow you by car, but I didn't expect him to grab and drag you off the street. But, when I saw you come round the corner, and kiss him so passionately, I thought perhaps this was some sort of game you were playing."

Tears filled Jane's eyes. So he, too, thought she was playing games. Why?

Mr Reinhardt's voice became grim. "However, it soon became obvious that you were being forced against your will."

Jane looked across at him. A passing street light revealed his jaw clenched in abhorrence. In remembrance of how near she'd been to disaster, she sobbed, "How... how can I, ever thank you? I... I was so scared. At work he was so nice. But he changed. He thought... he wanted ... he hurt me...." She trailed off into deep wrenching sobs that were impossible to subdue. To try and stop she took large gulps of air and tried blowing her nose. The soggy pile of tissues grew in her lap. Eventually with a spasm of shivering she managed, "I'm sorry I've caused you so much trouble."

Aware that the car was pulling into the kerb, her eyes widened with fright as she envisioned another assault. Why was he stopping?

"It's alright, Jane. There's nothing to fear. I'm not going to hurt you. I just think you need this more than I do." Baffled, she watched as he stepped out of the car, shrugged out of his jacket and walked round to open her door. "Now put this round your shoulders." Obediently, she popped the seat belt and sat forward as he placed his jacket, heavy with personal items, around her. "You're in shock. This will warm you."

His kindness made her eyes brim with more tears. On a hoarse whisper, she managed, "Thank you." Carefully he tucked the jacket inside the car, helped her refasten the belt and closed the door. Jane drew it around her. It felt deliciously warm, smelt pleasantly of him, and was so large she could snuggle into it. She watched him walk around the car. In his shirtsleeves, he seemed far less imposing and formidable. The engine started, they rejoined the traffic, and she helped herself to another peppermint while waiting for him to continue.

"Now for the answer to your question as to how did

you get here?" He flashed her another wry smile. "Carlton was walking backwards towards his car and didn't see me. I wasn't sure of the best way to deal with him until you conveniently passed out. Carlton realized it and took his hand from your mouth and your head slumped forward." Mr Reinhardt's voice took on a cheery quality. "I tapped him on the shoulder, and, as he turned, I thumped him hard on the jaw." Mr Reinhardt's obvious satisfaction brought a small shaky smile to Jane's lips. "I don't think he even saw who'd hit him. He just went down like a sack of potatoes with you on top. Before he could come round, I picked you up, put you in my car and drove off." He turned to give Jane a wide smile. "And now, if you'll forgive my enquiring mind, may I ask why did you go out to dinner with Andrew Carlton?"

"He asked me, and said it was a 'thank you' for working late."

"But you'd been warned about him."

"People often say things about others, but I like to judge for myself. I didn't believe them because he seemed very charming and nice. I suppose I thought I knew better."

"You're honest, I'll give you that – but not very worldly wise."

Jane shrugged. "Probably not. But when I say 'no' to Bruce he takes it as that. Obviously, 'men of the world' think differently."

They stopped at traffic lights, which gave Mr Reinhardt the opportunity to look at her while he questioned, "Excuse me for asking another of my impertinent questions, but is Bruce the only man you've ever been out with?"

Jane nodded. "Yes. You see, I became a Christian when I was fourteen. Bruce came to the church when I was eighteen. We became friends and in the last two years seem to have become a couple. But a few months ago, something happened which made me wonder if Bruce is the man for me. So I told myself I needed to spread my wings and meet new people. When I was asked to work for Andrew I thought... well, never mind what I thought. But I did try to refuse his invitations, resist his advances."

She glanced across at Mr Reinhardt and noticed that although his eyes were now intent on the road ahead, his faced had hardened and he had the steering wheel in a tight grip. He must be really annoyed hearing about Andrew's behaviour and she could now understand why he disliked him. "I nearly wrote a note refusing, but he came in, and I couldn't see how a meal in a restaurant could be dangerous, so ...." With a hard gulp she pressed on, "But God seems to have had mercy on me, in the form of you, Mr Reinhardt."

He gave a cynical laugh. "I have to say, Jane, that I'm not sure if I believe in God. Therefore, I very much doubt that He'd appoint me as your guardian angel. But I can assure you that 'men of the world' as you call them are not all like Andrew Carlton. However, I'm sure the lessons learnt this evening will make you more circumspect in the future."

An immediate retort arose at his superior attitude, but in the light of his kindness she remained silent.

For the next few miles they were engrossed in their own thoughts until Jane remembered their earlier meeting and blurted out, "Oh, by the way, I'm sorry about the way I spoke to you earlier." Mr Reinhardt said nothing as the car filtered into traffic at a roundabout. Nervously she hurried on, "I know you're a hard-headed business man, but when people talk about you in future I'm going to tell them that underneath the stern face, the loud bark and the awkward questions, you are really a very kind and thoughtful man."

A roar of laughter burst from him. Now what had she said that was so amusing?

"My God, Jane! Ooh, sorry! My goodness, Jane, you

really are like a breath of fresh air. These days, there aren't many people who'd be quite so frank with me!" The car slowed. "Look, I'll turn right here and drop you at the end of your road. It will seem then as if you came home on the train as usual."

She felt awkward but, out of politeness, she felt she must ask, "Would you like to come in for a coffee before driving back?"

"Thank you Jane, I think not. Maybe another time." He put on the interior light, "Your bag's down there. It might be wise to do something with those red eyes before your mother sees you."

Beneath his jacket, her clothes were a tangled mess, but a quick inspection showed that nothing had been torn in the struggle. With only a powder compact and lipstick, she did her best while he watched in silence. He smiled appraisingly, "Right. Yes. That's better. Off you go then – get a good night's sleep. Don't worry about Andrew Carlton." His voice took on a grim tone, "I'll deal with him." He switched off the light and resettled himself.

"Mr Reinhardt?" She wriggled out of his jacket.

He turned, "Yes, Jane?"

"You'd better have this back."

He smiled. Putting out two fingers as a hanger, he twisted to place his jacket carefully on the back seat.

"Mr Reinhardt?"

"Yes, Jane!"

In noticing his slightly exasperated tone, she spoke quickly before her courage ran out. "The other week you said if I wanted to kiss you could I do so in a more private place, so I hope this is private enough...." She leaned across the gap and planted a kiss on his cheek. He stared at her as though her lips had burnt him. Quickly backing out of the car she stammered, "It's a thank you. Thank you for rescuing me and being so kind. See you at the office."

Without waiting for a response she closed the car door,

waved and walked briskly away in an attempt to cover her embarrassment. Why had she done that? Why had he looked so startled? Now he'd probably think she deserved all she got, yet it was only the kind of kiss she'd give a relative or friend. As she turned the corner, she glanced back. Mr Reinhardt was watching her. He gave her a brief salute, but she was at her front gate before she heard the engine start and the car drive away.

CHAPTER 5

Sam and Ian had left the canteen to play table tennis, and Jane was just finishing her coffee when Miss Pawson, Mr Reinhardt's secretary, joined Nikki Clarke at an adjacent table. Grace Pawson was in her fifties, probably the oldest woman employee of ITP. Despite a little middle-age spread, she retained a youthful face and, although her brown hair had a thick drizzle of white, it was always beautifully curled and styled. She was unmarried, but far from being frumpy or grumpy.

When Jane overheard Miss Pawson quietly say to Nikki, "Poor David. He's having a really awful day," she just had to listen! "First there was that fracas in his office," Miss Pawson shook her head and frowned. "I can't remember when I've seen him so angry. Hardly surprising that he needed headache pills later. And then – if that wasn't enough – a registered parcel arrived just before I came down for lunch and, when he opened it," Jane strained to hear as Miss Pawson lowered her voice, "it was Felicity's engagement ring!"

"Oh no! I bet he was upset!"

Miss Pawson shrugged. "Hard to tell. He just grunted, snapped the box shut and returned to his office."

"But they've known each other for years. What could have happened to upset her that much?"

Jane, staring over the top of her coffee cup, was asking herself the same question. Had Felicity been in the restaurant with him on Friday night? If so, she probably would be unhappy at being abandoned for some silly secretary who'd got out of her depth on a date. But surely that wouldn't be enough to break off an engagement?

The arrival of Jill and Pam stopped Jane brooding further. However, back in the office, she was unable to concentrate. Rosemary's churlish voice was just querying, "Haven't you finished those letters yet?" when Jill came bursting in, her face glowing with excitement.

"Hi, Rosemary. Hey, Jane! Guess what happened to Andrew Carlton on Friday night? Apparently he stopped just off Kensington High Street and as he got out of his car someone jumped out of the shadows and knocked him out."

Without thinking, Jane sniggered.

Surprised, Jill retorted, "That's not very nice after he took you out for such a lovely, expensive meal."

Rosemary, incredulous, snapped, "You! You went out to dinner with Andrew Carlton?"

Jane ignored her, and spoke to Jill. "Well, he did have rather a lot to drink. It can make you unsteady on your feet."

"Umm!" Jill deliberated. "I've heard Andrew likes his drink. Do you think he fell over and knocked himself out? Anyway, when he came round, his pockets had been emptied and his car stolen!" Rosemary and Jane gasped in unison. "He spent the night at the Police Station trying to identify his attacker."

Jane's wide-eyed concern wasn't for Andrew. It was for his 'attacker' who, if identified, would also be accused of robbery.

Jill continued eagerly, "And if that wasn't bad enough – this morning, Mr Reinhardt called Andrew into his office and gave him a real rollicking. Several people heard snippets, mostly Mr Reinhardt's words. You know what his voice is like!" Jill grinned and, enjoying the telling such a juicy piece of gossip, she didn't notice the colour draining from Jane's face. "Well, it turns out that Andrew said to John Forsythe, 'Reinhardt's summoned me! If he's about to question what I do, and who I spend my time with, outside office hours, I'll be telling him it's none of his business'. George Earnshaw was delivering post to Miss Pawson's office when he heard Mr Reinhardt arguing with Andrew. He assumed it was Mr Reinhardt who thumped the desk before shouting, 'Ask for it! Ask for it! Are you also saying Evangeline asked for it?' George didn't hear Andrew's reply, but he did hear Mr Reinhardt roar, 'Don't give me that! You'll be telling me next it was all Jackie's fault too! I don't think so! Mr Reinhardt's tone lowered so George got as near as he dared to the door between the offices, and caught Andrew's disparaging laugh and tone as he said, 'So you made a mistake! She's just like all the others'.

Rosemary and Jane stared, spellbound, as Jill went on gleefully. "Apparently Mr Reinhardt bellowed, 'Enough'! It was so loud George said he jumped and, believing Mr Reinhardt was going to open the connecting door into Miss Pawson's office, he hared out into the corridor. But moments later Mr Reinhardt's private office door opened and the people in the offices opposite heard him boom, 'Just get out of my sight. I want you out of the building in thirty minutes'. No-one caught Andrew's words as he left, but whatever it was Mr Reinhardt barked at him. 'Don't you threaten me! You just get that desk emptied and be out of here in half an hour, or it will be me calling the police, not you!' I don't know what Andrew Carlton thinks he has on our Mr Reinhardt? Nikki said from what she's heard – but isn't at liberty to repeat – Andrew Carlton got what he deserves!" Jill raised her eyebrows. "Heaven only knows what he's done! I suppose we could hazard a guess! Mr Reinhardt's a fair man; he wouldn't sack someone for nothing. Andrew's antagonism, though, won't have helped him if he needs a reference, and Nikki suspects he'll find it hard to get a job at all. Now the police are…."

The telephone rang as Jane struggled to come to terms with what she was hearing. Her faith demanded that she forgive as she'd been forgiven. Even though she had forgiven Andrew for his treatment of her, and asked God to forgive her if she'd unwittingly led Andrew on, she couldn't help feeling responsible for all this happening to him. Rosemary's thrusting the telephone under her nose now, reminded her this all started because she'd gone to Mr Reinhardt's office to use the telephone. And the scowl on Rosemary's face was enough to make Jane believe that even receiving a telephone call was a crime, so when she heard Miss Pawson asking her to come up to Mr Reinhardt's office, she felt she had committed one!

Fortunately, Jill was so busy chewing over events with Rosemary that they barely noticed her leave. The moment Jane entered the hall, she saw the police car parked on the drive. Had Andrew Carlton identified his attacker? If so, she could be speaking up for Mr Reinhardt sooner than anticipated!

Breathless, having run up the two flights of stairs, she bowled into Grace Pawson's office to state, "You want to see me."

Miss Pawson looked drawn and seemed to have grown older since lunch! She frowned at Jane. Her voice was clipped and ,efficient. "No, Jane. The police. Mr Reinhardt asked me to get you."

Mr Reinhardt's connecting door opened. They both turned as a burly, middle-aged man emerged to enquire, "Did you manage to get hold of Jane Mackenzie, Miss Pawson?"

Jane stepped forward, "That's me!" She caught the flash of surprise that crossed his face – perhaps she wasn't quite what he'd expected?

He walked slowly towards her as though studying her before saying. "Detective Inspector Jordan, CID." She shook his outstretched hand and bit nervously at her lips. The Inspector's speculative gaze was distracted as Grace made to leave. "Ah, Miss Pawson, don't go. We would like to get this matter cleared up as soon as possible and, as we're very short of WPCs, would you mind staying? This isn't an official statement, more fact finding, but I'd prefer it if you were here – if Miss Mackenzie has no objections."

"But you might need me as a character witness?"

A smile flickered across the Inspector's face. "I think, Miss Pawson, that Mr Reinhardt's standing could provide him with a great many of those, and you'd serve him better as a silent witness to my questioning."

Perplexity wreathed Grace Pawson's face, but she returned to sit at her desk while the Inspector perched on the corner. "Right Miss Mackenzie, do sit down. Now, do you have any idea why we want to talk to you?" At her nod, he continued. "I believe you were involved in an incident off Kensington High Street on Friday evening?"

"If you mean what happened between myself, Andrew Carlton and Mr Reinhardt, yes!"

"I do indeed, Miss Mackenzie. Perhaps you'd like to give me your version of events?"

"Not a version, Inspector. The truth."

The Inspector's face hardened. "I should hope so, Miss Mackenzie!"

It was difficult to judge what effect her detailed description of the evening was having on the Inspector as he wrote in his notepad, but she was grateful he didn't interrupt. When she'd finished, she shrugged. "Well, that's it."

His noncommittal "Hmm" made her heart sink. Surely he couldn't believe that Mr Reinhardt would rob Andrew Carlton. It was ludicrous, and she said so in no uncertain terms.

Unmoved by her outburst, the Inspector folded his arms. "And, tell me, Miss Mackenzie – if you weren't involved in the robbery, how do you know about it?"

Jane could feel the blush spread up her neck and face, but she wasn't about to be intimidated. "I know, Inspector, because the news is already being gossiped all over the building. Mr Reinhardt hit Andrew to rescue me. I know I was unconscious at the time, but I don't believe Mr

Reinhardt would rob Andrew of anything."

The Inspector smiled faintly, "That, Miss Mackenzie, is where we do agree. But the problem is Mr Carlton wants to charge Mr Reinhardt with assault, and from your own admission, Mr Carlton does have a right to do that."

Those words hit her like a blow! Instead of helping Mr Reinhardt, she'd given them an open and shut case. So much for telling the truth! It just wasn't fair. Vexed she spat back, "Surely it can't be a chargeable offence if you hit out to defend someone? If it is, you can tell Andrew Carlton that if he presses charges on Mr Reinhardt, then I'll press them on him."

Annoyance registered on the Inspector's face. "Now look here, young lady, we're not playing games. You can't go pressing charges on people for the fun of it!"

The patronising words, 'playing games', ignited her desire for justice. "Now that's where you and I agree, Inspector Jordan. Andrew Carlton is doing just that in an attempt to get back at Mr Reinhardt for giving him the sack! Oh yes, that's on the grapevine too. Believe me," she swallowed hard, "if Mr Reinhardt hadn't intervened on Friday night, Andrew Carlton would have raped me!" Grace Pawson gave a horrified gasp. Jane fiddling with the buttons on the sleeve of her blouse, snapped, "Look at this!" The Inspector's eyes widened as she pulled her cuff further up her arm revealing the black and blue bruising to her wrist and lower arm. "I think with these and other bruises I would not be seen to be playing games in pressing a charge of assault on Andrew. And not just so he drops the charge against Mr Reinhardt, but to stop this happening to someone else in the future."

The Inspector's face darkened. "That's your story, Miss Mackenzie! I must tell you that Mr Carlton's is rather different. He claims he was attacked because Mr Reinhardt wanted you, and couldn't bear the thought of anyone else having you."

"What? Surely you can't believe that! Mr Reinhardt only left the restaurant because he saw I was trying to escape from Andrew. After he rescued me he drove me straight home. So how can that be true?"

"The truth, Miss Mackenzie, is what we are trying to establish. What we'll need to know is the approximate time you spent in the restaurant, in the street and in Mr Reinhardt's car. Is there anyone who can verify the time you arrived home? Now we'll need you to accompany us to the police station. We need to get photographs of those bruises and a written statement."

Those words, 'verify the time you got home', repeated themselves inside her head. Would the Inspector think it odd that she hadn't awakened her mother to tell her of the attack? How could she prove she hadn't gone off with Mr Reinhardt afterwards? In the need to defend herself, she replied vehemently. "Good heavens, Inspector! I feel as I've been found guilty of a crime, not the victim of one. I would have expected the police to be on the victim's side, not on the assailant's. No doubt if Andrew Carlton had raped me you'd have said I'd led him on, or he didn't do anything without my consent!" Thoroughly stirred up, she made a stab in the dark. "Why don't you question some of his former girlfriends, or his secretary who has just spent two weeks in hospital? Perhaps if they knew I was willing to stand against him, they might have something they'd like to testify about."

She stared defiantly at the policeman. When he spoke, his voice gave nothing away. "Miss Mackenzie, there is one more question I would like to ask?"

"Yes?"

His cool eyes bored into her, "Are you and Mr Reinhardt having an affair?"

Totally incensed, she leapt up. "What!" In her fury, words poured out. "I hardly know Mr Reinhardt. We've never been out together. We certainly are NOT having an affair; and in fact until Friday night I've never even seen Mr Reinhardt outside these four walls."

She stopped for breath and the Inspector asked, in an infuriatingly calm voice, "But you knew him well enough to believe you were safe his car?"

"No – yes."

"Well, which is it?"

"Both! He's a well respected man at work, he'd rescued me from Andrew's clutches, and he reassured me I'd nothing to fear from him and was driving me home."

"And you believed him?"

"Why shouldn't I?"

The Inspector's cynical expression made her realise just how ridiculously trusting she was. "Didn't you think it was a bit of a coincidence that he was dining in the same restaurant after you'd told him where you were going?"

She shrugged, "I didn't think about it."

"Come on, don't give me that. You and Reinhardt agreed to meet?"

Jane frowned, "Why would I want to do that?"

"Have you forgotten that you've been seen kissing Mr Reinhardt?"

That was the final straw. Her hands balled into fists at her side, and she only just stopped herself stamping her foot in frustration. "I don't believe this!" Her face flushed in anger and embarrassment. "If you're talking about that the time in the canteen, I DID NOT kiss him! My lips met his cheek because the wretched man stuck his head between Jill and I as I leant across to speak to her."

A glimmer of amusement flickered across the Inspector's face, "Are there any other times I should be asking about?"

"No, there are not!" But even as she emphatically denied it, she remembered differently and added, "I am not in the habit of kissing men I don't know. Even you can't take a kiss on the cheek as some kind of 'grand passion'!"

The Inspector's lips twitched as though to smile, but his was reply was short and abrupt. "Thank you Miss Mackenzie, you've been most helpful." Jane didn't like the sound of that − helpful to whom? "Now I'd better make arrangements for you to be seen by a doctor and get that photographic evidence. Miss Pawson, is there an empty office with a telephone I can use?"

As the Inspector left the room, Jane sat down again with a thump. If only she'd kept her temper and not said all the wrong things. Oh Lord, what is happening! If God dished out punishment, surely Friday night's incident would be enough for seeking excitement in the world? What would people think seeing her leaving with the police? Tears trickled down her face. People were sure to talk. Her mother always said 'there's no smoke without fire'. Well, there was plenty of smoke here but, in all honesty, no fire. After this she would have to leave. She told herself there were other jobs, but would her reference, like Andrew's reflect that there had been a problem? The more she thought about it, the worse it became.

A hand on her back made her jump. She thought it was the Inspector ready to cart her off to the police station. Instead it was Miss Pawson. "Poor Jane. What an ordeal you've been through. Here, drink this. It'll make you feel better."

She gave a weak smile. It wasn't over yet − she still had to face going to the police station. But she took the glass and sipped the liquid. "Ugh".

"Look, you're shaking. Have a drop more." Obediently, and to the surprise of Grace, Jane threw the remainder of the liquid down her throat, then coughed and spluttered at the burning in her throat.

Warmth gradually began to spread through her. Perhaps things weren't quite so bad after all.

"Miss Mackenzie." The Inspector looking friendlier than before came in, "Are you okay? You're looking rather

pale. Perhaps you'd like to freshen up before we leave —
Miss Pawson could you go with her, please?"

Wasn't she safe to go on her own? Were they afraid
she'd run away? In the safety of the Ladies' the emotions
bubbling up inside her burst out. "Oh, Miss Pawson, this is
awful, just awful! Mr Reinhardt's in trouble because of me.
I thought Andrew was a nice man. I—I didn't know."

Grace Pawson put a motherly arm round her shoulders.
"All you did was accept a dinner invitation — you did
nothing wrong and I'd say you had a lucky escape. There's
nothing for you to worry about. And don't worry about
David either, he'll sort it out. Tell me, would you have
gone to the police if this hadn't happened?" Jane shook her
head. "Just as I thought. Then it's for the best. Andrew
thought he was making trouble for David, but I rather think
he'll find it's.... Oh dear, what's the matter? You don't look
well. Here, sit on this chair."

"I feel… odd. The room's tipping at a funny angle."

"Put your head between your knees. I'll get Jack, he's
the first-aider."

Jane wanted to say, "Don't leave", but Miss Pawson
had already gone. Nausea rose from her stomach. She
didn't want to be sick on the floor. The room swayed as she
stood. The toilet door seemed at a peculiar angle and too
far away. She lurched and stumbled toward the washbasin.

The pain in Jane's head caused her to moan. Something
cold and hard was underneath her. She was lying on her
side. For a second she opened her eyes, saw a man's shoes
and closed them against the brightness of the light. The
shoes must belong to the male voice repeating her name. It
must be he who was placing something cold on her aching
head. A draft of cold air hit her, along with the sound of
Mr Reinhardt's boom. "Good God, man, how did this
happen?" His voice triggered her memory – she was in the
Ladies' toilet. The man beside her, who she presumed was

Jack, rose to his feet to answer. "She must have fallen and knocked herself out on that washbasin, but she's coming round."

Jane squeezed her eyes against Mr Reinhardt's loud angry voice as he asked, "What did you say to the girl to get her in this state?"

The Inspector's voice replied from further away. "Nothing that Miss Mackenzie didn't seem able to handle."

Mr Reinhardt gave a disbelieving grunt.

Jane tried to lift her head, but it caused such a sharp pain that she only managed a moan.

Jack knelt beside her again and adjusted the cold compress. "We'll get you somewhere more comfortable soon." Then addressing whoever else was in the room he suggested, "I think we should call an ambulance. She could have concussion."

Oh no, not an ambulance! First Andrew Carlton, then the police, now this! At the sound of movement near her head she managed to murmur, "No ambulance," and, unsure she'd been heard, opened her eyes to repeat it and saw a different pair of shoes.

To her surprise, it was Mr Reinhardt crouching beside her. In an unusually quiet voice, he explained, "Jane, you've had a nasty bump and gashed your forehead."

She struggled to move her head to look up at him, and winced with pain as she pleaded, "Please, no ambulance."

He patted her shoulder reassuringly, and then arose. "This is ridiculous! When that's doctor of yours coming? Surely we can move her from the cold floor." Several pairs of shoes clicked across the lino and then the stone floor of the corridor as everyone seemed to leave. Voices answered Mr Reinhardt, but she couldn't hear their words. Less dazed she moved slightly, contemplated getting up, and was about to attempt it when Jack returned to crouch before her to announce, "We've decided to move you. Try to relax."

Jane felt an arm slide under her knees, and another under her back. Efficiently and effortlessly, she was lifted and carried against a broad warm chest. Her head hurt too much to move, but she was aware of a soft, silky material against her cheek.

Jack rushed by. "I'll open the doors."

Worried that she'd be sick going down in the jerky lift to the emergency room on the first floor, she opened her mouth to issue a warning when, to her surprise, she felt herself being lowered and realized she was in Mr Reinhardt's office, on one of his settees. Even more astonishing was the discovery it had been Mr Reinhardt's strong arms which had carried her here.

"Another cushion here, Grace. Yes, put that towel over it. Good. Right, Jane, now lean back." Slowly he withdrew his arm. "There. Comfortable?"

She managed to whisper her thanks before her eyes widened in horror at the large bloodstain on Mr Reinhardt's shirt. At her horror-stricken look, he glanced at the ugly red patch and said reassuringly, "Head wounds always bleed a lot. You'll be fine."

"But – your shirt?"

With a wry smile he squatted beside her. The knuckle of his forefinger rubbed her cheek. "A minor detail under the circumstances."

The minor detail instantly became major as she threw up in his lap. He flinched, but said nothing. In deep distress, she opened her mouth to say 'sorry' and added more to the mess.

Grace exclaimed, "Oh goodness" and jumped forward with a box of tissues.

Mr Reinhardt pulled several out of the box. "Here, Jane take these. Do you think you're going to be sick again?" A nightmare of misery and vulnerability rendered her speechless. "Umm. Grace, bring over that waste paper bin." He chuckled, "I think I'm going to have to call you

'Calamity Jane'! First you mess up my life, then my shirt, and now my suit. What am I going to do with you?" Mortified, she closed her eyes and lay back against the cushions as Mr Reinhardt cleaned himself up while issuing further commands. "Ah, Jack. Put those blankets from the first-aid room on the other settee. Could you find some towels? Grace, I think Jane could do with a glass of water. This carpet will need disinfectant. I'll chase up the doctor. Oh, and when you get a chance, ask Jill to get me some fresh clothes."

Tears of remorse edged out from under Jane's eyelids and mingled with the blood trickling down her face. A tissue gently dabbed her cheek. She opened her eyes and found herself gazing into Mr Reinhardt's warm, dark ones.

"Jane, don't get upset. The doctor will make you feel better, and by then everything will have sorted itself out. You'll see. Now lie back and rest."

Obediently, she closed her eyes. The irony of the situation struck her, for it was here in this very room, on this very settee, that she had met the stranger. It seemed it had finished where it had started. Part of a Bible verse came to mind, 'ask and it shall be given unto you ....' Did God have a man who would be kind and solicitous like Bruce, interesting and fun like Andrew, and have the ability to turn her on? Jumbled thoughts swirled in her mind. She longed to sleep. Voices drifted in and out of her hearing, but nothing made much sense. A door opened. Jill's voice said something about a doctor. Had Jill seen her? Hopefully not, or it would soon be all round the building. Jane opened her eyes to see a pleasant, bearded man of similar age to Mr Reinhardt walking towards her. If this was the doctor, he wasn't the middle-aged, gruff police surgeon she'd expected.

"Hello, I'm Dr Stemmings. I believe you're Jane and you've been in the wars!" With a sympathetic smile he drew over a chair so he could sit beside her. After a quick preliminary examination he proclaimed, "Well, you don't appear to have done anything that a few stitches and a bit of rest won't repair but, to make sure, you ought to have an x-ray."

Mr Reinhardt, who'd been prowling nearby, gave a heartfelt sigh. A memory stirred in Jane's mind, but was forgotten as the doctor rose and nearly head-butted Mr Reinhardt. Amused, she watched as the doctor skilfully manoeuvred Mr Reinhardt out through his office door while saying, "Now if you don't mind, I think I'd better get started. This may take a while, if I need anything I'll ask your secretary. I understand you are a busy man and have much to attend to, so I won't keep you." With a final glance in Jane's direction Mr Reinhardt shut himself out, while Dr Stemmings returned to her side and grinned as he saw the laughter in her eyes. "Right then, I gather your head injury is from today, but you also have some rather nasty bruises – a lucky escape I hear. Though the way you're feeling now I don't suppose it feels like it. Would you like a friend or colleague to join us, or are you happy for me to go it alone?"

Thinking the fewer people involved the better, she mumbled, "Carry on."

"First, let's get you more comfortable with a painkiller. Then I'll get some stitches in that gash in your head. After that, I'll take a look at those bruises. To save you any more distress, I've been asked to take the photos in case they are needed for evidence."

Eventually, the doctor left and the ordeal was over. Four stitches and more photos than she'd anticipated. His examination had been thorough, finding plenty of bruising to confirm her testimony, but for now she was just too weak and exhausted to consider the outcome. Fortunately, he'd given her something for both the sickness and pain. Drowsy and warm from the blankets Grace had arranged over her, she drifted into a deep sleep.

When she awoke, awareness returned gradually. She opened her eyes to find it was dark, but for a small glow of a light behind her. She moved her head – it hurt. In the dimness she could see shelves full of academic books. She pulled herself to sit up.

Almost immediately, the voice she was beginning to associate with every ill wind of fate that came her way, spoke from across the room, "Don't try and get up." Almost instantly, Mr Reinhardt was beside her with a cushion. "Here, this will help." His hand helped her sit forward as he slid it in behind her. "There, that should be more comfortable."

In a voice not much more than a whisper she asked, "What time is it?"

"About nine-fifteen, but don't worry – everything is under control." Mr Reinhardt switched on the lamp at the end of the settee and sat on the chair vacated by the doctor. In a voice filled with an emotion she didn't understand, he said, "This was my fault. This wouldn't have happened if it hadn't been for me. I just can't tell you how sorry I am."

Surprised at his words she moved her head and winced in pain as she asked, "What for?"

"Careful. Does your head still hurt? Just close your eyes and lie back." A cool hand rested gently on her brow to ensure her capitulation. "Right, just relax and listen. It's this business with Andrew Carlton. I should have had more sense."

Without lifting her head off the pillow she opened her eyes and, seeing he was now sitting in front of her, managed to say with spirit, "I don't see how you work that out. You're a hero. You rescued me."

But even as she was speaking he was shaking his head. "No, Jane, I'm not! Now, don't say anything. It's important that you just listen to what I have to tell you. I think you're going to be very angry with me, but please don't react violently – remember your head. You see...."

The connecting door with Grace's office opened. "Is she still sleeping?" The appearance of Grace not only halted Mr Reinhardt's words, but caused a combination of annoyance and frustration to cross his features. "I've finally managed to speak to Jane's mother. Apparently she's been cleaning the church. Obviously she was very anxious when I told her of Jane's fall, but she doesn't drive and wanted to come on the train to be with her. I assured her there was no need and we wouldn't send her home alone." Grace's eyes moved from Mr Reinhardt's face to look down on Jane's. "Oh, Jane you're awake. How do you feel?"

"Terrible," she answered truthfully. "And when my mother sees me I'll probably feel worse, because she's never going to understand or believe me. I shall be cross-questioned and lectured about my stupidity. Then I'll probably have to go through it again with Bruce. He won't go on and on, but I doubt he'll understand." After that long speech, she sighed and shut her eyes. Everything seemed too much to bear.

Mr Reinhardt's voice boomed cheerily, "Oh, come on Jane! What's happened to that fighting spirit? I'm sure falling and banging you head hasn't knocked that out of you. It won't be that bad, you'll see." A gentle rub of a knuckle of a forefinger down her cheek caused her eyes to flash open. He meant it as a comfort , but the déja vu sensation was such that she turned to stare at him and caught his dark brooding gaze. In an almost embarrassed hesitancy he asked quietly, "Are you – are you all right?"

Grace, now perched at the end of the settee, gave him a questioning look, then filled the slightly awkward silence by saying, "Don't worry about your mother. David... er, Mr Reinhardt and I agreed that it was better that she only knew that you'd had a fall in the Ladies' and knocked yourself out."

"But what about the police?" She glanced at them

apprehensively. "Once they start questioning and probing, she'll find out."

Mr Reinhardt smiled triumphantly. "The police won't be doing anything. Andrew Carlton dropped all thoughts of an assault charge when he heard that if he charged me, you would charge him. On hearing that photographs had been taken of your heavy bruising, and that you'd suggested there may be others who might want to testify against him, he apparently left the Police Station in a great hurry and before the police could question him further. They are now following certain leads they have been given, and Andrew Carlton may indeed find justice at his door."

Jane rather suspected, looking at Mr Reinhardt's grim face, that he'd been the one to furnish the police with some of his suspicions. There was a brief silence as they considered his words then Mr Reinhardt, in jubilation, his voice swelling in delight, boomed out, "So you see, Jane, you did it again! Stood up and fought and won. Grace said you were quite magnificent! So how can I thank you? You not only spoke up for me, but for others also. Well done!"

Mr Reinhardt was pleased with her. He appreciated her frankness. And her Mum need only know she had fallen. The disappointment that her stranger hadn't lived up to her expectations was tempered by the hope she'd been used to bring Andrew to justice. Her heart lifted in thanksgiving and she smiled — it really was over. Mr Reinhardt balanced himself on the edge of the settee between her and Grace, and smiled down on her.

She looked up at him and, despite the age difference, she was suddenly aware of why women found him attractive. It was only as he bent towards her that she realized his intent. An inbuilt belief that you didn't allow a man to kiss you on the lips unless you were 'going out' with him made her turn her head. Immediately she remembered the time on this very settee when she hadn't been quite so reticent! His lips planted the kiss on her cheek. His breath fanned the words, "Why the need to be so shy?"

Jane blushed and, in bewilderment, looked at Grace. Grace patted her leg reassuringly and stood. "It seems all things have worked together, and I'm sure good will come from it. Now we'd better do something about getting you home." She looked at David Reinhardt as he stood in contemplation, jangling the loose change in his pocket, and added, "I'll give your Mum a ring and tell her that you'll soon be on your way."

Now she was left alone with Mr Reinhardt, to get past the awkwardness, she reminded him, "What were you about to tell me before Grace came in?" He stared thoughtfully ahead as though having difficulty in remembering. "It was something about Andrew Carlton and I was going to be angry with you."

"Oh yes! Right! Yes! Grace and I did discuss whether you'd feel uncomfortable about not quite telling your mother the truth, but it was I who persuaded Grace it was for the best."

Jane gingerly nodded her head. "I think the less Mum knows, the less she'll worry. But, really I'm surprised, Mr Reinhardt, that as I got you into this mess you're not angry with me."

"Well, I think we've both learnt a lesson here." She wondered what lesson he could have possibly learnt as he moved forward, patted her shoulder and once more sat on the chair beside her. "I also think that, after what we've been through, you could in future address me as David."

Taken aback, she replied tartly, "That's very kind of you, but I'm not sure I should, or could."

The warm gaze with which he was regarding her, flickered with emotion. Had her words caused him pain, or anger? His voice when he spoke was quiet and surprisingly humble. "Jane, I should like it if you would. You see, it's my wish that not just you, but many more employees will treat me less formally. I feel that respect should come from what you know of a man, not from his title, status or position. I believe people are more motivated if they feel they are working together rather than serving anonymously in some hierarchical structure. In view of that and recent events, my hope is that you might feel you could treat me less formally and begin by calling me David." He tilted his head questioningly.

The majority of his words she guessed came from his Midsummer speech, but the sincerity with which he uttered them made her anxious to reassure him. "In that case, well, yes. I see. It'll feel odd at first, but I expect I could get used to it!"

"Good – that's a start then." He stood and stretched, "Now, we'd better follow the doctor's orders, organise an x-ray and get you home to bed."

CHAPTER 6

"Well, that was a nice family evening."

Jane closed the front door on Bruce and Ted, and privately sighed at her mother's enthusiasm. Ted wasn't her dad, and he and Bruce weren't family! After three years, and knowing that death was only a temporary separation, didn't lessen the daily pain of the absence of her dad's love and wisdom. Grief welled up. Not wanting to talk she headed upstairs. The bedroom was cold – she shivered. Should she put on the electric fire or just undress quickly and jump into bed? She chose the latter and quickly flung off her clothes before diving into the tunnel of bedclothes made warm by the electric blanket. In the warmth, she snuggled down and murmured a prayer. "Lord, what shall I do? I feel in a rut. I don't want to hurt anyone, please show me the way forward."

How could she break up with Bruce? Her Mum would be very upset, but she shouldn't feel trapped because of that. Bruce wasn't very sociable – at church he only spoke when he was spoken to. He loved classical music, yet he'd refused to join her on ITP's visit to the Proms.

She closed her eyes. Her mind drifted over the last few months. It had been hard not to let slip what had happened with Andrew Carlton, especially when the day after her head injury Mr Reinhardt — David — had visited her at home.

That afternoon she'd been snoozing in bed while her mother was weeding in the front garden. David's voice had heralded his presence! While she was wondering if she ought to get dressed, her mum arrived to whisper, "That boss of yours is downstairs. He insists you shouldn't get out of bed, but wants to see you. What shall I say?"

Her response was to smile and say, "I suppose you'd

95

better show him up." To her surprise, her mum had clicked her tongue in disapproval, but had complied. Although when she showed David in, she had made it clear he was to sit on the stool in front of the dressing table, while she perched on the bed. The funniest thing had been when the doorbell rang. David, obviously catching her mother's dilemma of leaving him alone in Jane's bedroom, had stood and offered, "Shall I go downstairs, Mrs MacKenzie, while you answer that?"

Flustered, her mum had jumped up saying, "No, no, that's alright. I won't be a moment." But, as she turned at the door her face had been a picture, because David had sat on the bed in the place she'd just vacated!

Jane had no idea what her mum said to Bruce, but she and David had only exchanged a few words before Bruce uncharacteristically burst in. It hadn't helped that the bunch of flowers in Bruce's hand had been upstaged by David's bouquet and box of chocolates. Bruce's face had reddened in a mixture of anger and embarrassment. To David's credit, he'd immediately risen and, having introduced himself, had suggested that Bruce take the prime spot on the bed. Poor Bruce didn't know what to do. He'd never been in her bedroom, and for him to sit on her bed when she was in it would be unthinkable! His insignificant stature and unease were highlighted by David's size and manner. In an attempt to help, she offered Bruce the dressing table stool and a chocolate, but David's cheery, "She's as light as a feather. I think she could do with a bit of fattening up, don't you?" seemed to fuel Bruce's anger and animosity. After five minutes of making polite conversation and receiving only monosyllabic replies from Bruce, David excused himself, calling jovially as he went down the stairs, "Goodbye, Mrs Mackenzie! Thanks for letting me see Jane."

Jane frowned at the memory. Bruce had found plenty to say about David's bombastic approach and loud voice when her mother had brought up the tea and biscuits. At least her mum had the grace to admit how thoughtful David had been for, realizing they hadn't a car, he had not only driven Jane home, but en route had taken her to the hospital for an x-ray. And, surprisingly, her mum had even laughed while telling Bruce how, despite her and Jane's protests, David had carried Jane from the car to her bed. Her mum's dismissive glance at David's flowers and her scornful dismissal of, "Mind you, he must have more money than sense," were obviously for Bruce's benefit, so Jane had stifled the retort that David was not only a qualified barrister but also one of ITP's directors.

That had been six weeks ago, and the gossip about her date with Andrew Carlton had long since been forgotten. The police had merely requested her to sign a written statement. Her injuries and time off work had been attributed to slipping on a wet patch in the Ladies'. And for once, Jill had neither mentioned to anyone that Jane had recovered in Mr Reinhardt's office from her fall, nor spoken of it since, making Jane wonder if Jill had been told to forget what she'd seen.

A week after Andrew's dismissal, to the astonishment of the Finance Department, Maud the dragon-lady was appointed new Finance Director. Evie returned to work and sought Jane out to quietly whisper her thanks, although she seemed reluctant to comment further. And, according to David, Jane's threat to charge Andrew had encouraged others to come forward but, as Andrew had left the country before he could be arrested, it was probably wise to wait before worrying her mother over her involvement.

News of David's broken engagement had leaked out, followed almost weekly by rumours that he'd been spotted here and there with different women. It seemed his words to Andrew, "off with the old, on with the new," could now be applied to him One evening, meeting David on the drive, she had managed to say, "I'm sorry to hear about your broken engagement," but hadn't had the courage to ask if her unfortunate date had been the cause.

He had looked down at her, his look rueful, but said manfully, "Probably for the best, Jane. Marriage is built on trust and understanding. It's better to find out that the foundations are inadequate before, rather than after − less hurt and damage all round."

Pleased that he seemed so positive, she'd commented, "Friendship is a good foundation, but can be mistaken for love." She went on dreamily, "When I marry I want that extra spark, that excitement, that chemistry between two people." Caught up in the thought, it was a few seconds before she refocused on David and had been disconcerted at the strange way he was looking at her.

But whatever he had been thinking, the unexpected burst of his characteristic laugh made her jump. And with the slap of his thigh, he boomed the words, "Is that so!" and marched off leaving her to stare after him.

She doubted she'd ever understand men! Still trying to get to sleep, her mind raced comparing Bruce, David and Andrew. In church, the morning sermon had been Psalm 37: 'Trust in the Lord and do good: dwell in the land and enjoy safe pasture.' The incident with the stranger had certainly taken her from 'safe pasture'. But surely you could be 'safe' and still enjoy life?

Jane sighed and pulled the pillows round her against the draught from the window. Rosemary's attitude towards her certainly stopped her enjoyment of being at work. Since the day she heard her call Mr Reinhardt, 'David', it was as if she had committed a terrible sin. For someone to be quite so nasty there had to have been something in Rosemary's life that had caused her to be the way she was. Only God knew and maybe it was He, not she, Rosemary was rejecting? Jane began to pray for her, but fell asleep..

She awoke to a dark and miserable Monday, typical for the end of October, which did nothing to lighten her mood. Rain was falling, turning the brown and golden leaves into piles of rotting rubbish. On her walk to the station cold gusts of wind blew them up around her legs, leaving the occasional leaf sticking to her stockings. Winter and its associations enveloped her as she trudged to the station.

The platform was crowded as usual. The usual people were waiting for the usual train to take them to the usual destination, from where they would go to the usual office to sit at the usual desk to do the usual tasks. A couple of people wished her good morning, but she doubted anyone felt it was good. The papers were still full of harrowing pictures and recriminations from Friday's tragedy, when a coal tip had slipped, burying the village school in Aberfan and killing over 100 children. The mood didn't lighten as the train arrived full. An umbrella stabbed her in the back, a heavy man stood on her toe, it was six stops before she got a seat and the thought of having to endure Rosemary all day made Jane wonder if it was time to look for a new job.

At the realization she was scowling at people, she told herself that a nice Christian girl who went to church regularly, read her Bible frequently and prayed almost as naturally as she breathed, should not be bad tempered, frustrated, or thinking uncharitable thoughts. So much for 'doing good'!

David and Jill were walking from the car park as she turned in at the gate. She slowed, not wanting to chat, but they had seen her and were waiting for her to join them. Jane pulled her coat around her and grimaced. Jill called, "Yes, winter is on its way." But as David held open the door for her he chuckled, "Cheer up Jane. You'll soon be nice and warm inside. Where's that sunny personality?"

Her response was a wintry smile before scurrying

across the hall. David wasn't be far behind, but she was unprepared for him to overtake her and block her path. He asked sympathetically, "Am I allowed to enquire the reason for this morning's long face?"

"Oh, you're allowed to ask — but it's not something I wish to answer."

"No doubt that's a polite way of telling me to mind my own business?"

On a grumpy expression she shrugged, skirted round him and backed against the heavy swing door. To her surprise, as she looked up she intercepted a knowing smile from Jill to David. Was something going on there — maybe a romance budding? Jill was a receptionist by choice. From the little Jane knew of her background, it was obvious she was in David's league.

Several weeks earlier, when Jane had talked of wanting to live a little, Jill had suggested, "Come out with me. There's always some fellahs to chat up and I'm never in a rush to get back to my horrid bed sit."

That evening, they'd got to know each other a little better, but she'd felt intimidated by the men in the bar and left Jill to chat up a chap she'd fancied. That evening she'd discovered Jill's father was a high flying businessman, and unlike Jane's, who'd been the hugging sort, had the belief that endeavour and education made a man/woman. Jill's brother had taken up his opportunities, extended his education, and had a good job which often meant long hours and pressing responsibilities — something Jill certainly didn't want. So, despite a higher education, she was content to be a receptionist until Mr Right appeared, bringing marriage, home and family.

Her words, "Why work yourself into the ground for money? I have enough to live on, enjoy my freedom and I manage a holiday abroad once a year," had given Jane the idea of holidaying with Jill, and they'd decided to visit the travel agent to see if there were any cheap last minute deals. But the following week, Jill had seemed reluctant. Was this because she had begun dating David?

For an hour or so she felt uplifted by thinking about Jill and David, but gradually the laborious retype of documents for the Brussels Exhibition onto metal plates for printing, and Rosemary's constantly dour face and snide comments, dragged her back into depression. Unable to be civil any longer, she went to find refuge, but in the corridor bumped into Paul, her boss, who insisted she talk to him in his office. "So then, Jane, tell what's wrong? You're usually such a ray of sunshine."

"I think I just need a break. Is there any possibilities I could have the rest of the week off?"

Paul frowned. "Is there any particular reason for you feeling like this?"

"Oh, you know what they say – a change is as good as a rest."

"And what change have you got in mind? I hope you're not thinking of looking for a new job?"

Her face must have given thoughts away, for Paul sighed, "I see. Well, take a couple of days off, have a rest. You've still got holiday due to you, you'll feel better in a few days time."

"I won't! Have you any idea what it is like working seven hours a day in an office with someone who criticises and hates you? It's really getting me down and, much as I like it here, I've had enough."

Paul gave a long sigh and asked, "Can you leave it with me for a few days?"

"To do what? Speak to Rosemary? That'll make it worse."

"Look I don't want to lose you. Don't make any snap decisions. Make sure it's what you really want. I think I'd better do what you usually do." Paul gave a sideways smile.

Jane's forehead puckered. "What do I usually do?"

"Pray!" Paul grinned, lifted his eyes heavenward and asked, "God, could you please change Rosemary into a pleasant human being, so Jane can be happy working here?"

"I'd be shocked if you got an answer to the first half, but I suppose she could always leave for the second half to be answered."

Paul chuckled, "You're always saying miracles can happen. So let's see what God can do!"

Even awaiting miracles didn't speed the day's end. When the afternoon drew to a close she didn't rush off, but instead waited for the majority of people to leave so she could chat to Jill. On her entry into the hall, Jill was busy tidying the reception area.

"Oh, Jane, you're still here. I thought I'd missed seeing you on your way home. Have you cheered up since this morning?"

Jane countered the question with another. "I missed you at lunch time. I've been dying to talk to you. What's going on between you and David? Don't deny it — I saw that smile you gave him this morning." Jill glanced around the hall, straightened and unsuccessfully attempted to push her ever-straying hair back into its knot. "Oh come on, I've told you about the stranger, my date with Andrew, my romantic thoughts — now it's your turn. Come on, tell. How long have you and David Reinhardt been going out?"

The hum of embarrassed agreement made by Jill as she moved back behind the Reception Desk was enough for Jane to say, "Well, Jill, I'm glad for you. He could be your Mr Right. From what I have seen he is kind, caring and thoughtful! Still, I expect you already know that." On a saucy smile, Jane added, "And some would say he's very sexy — can't see it myself, but there, he's too old for me." Jill tidying the desk, nodded in a preoccupied way. "We must keep in touch because if there are wedding bells I want an invite." Immediately she realized her slip, so hurried on in the hope Jill wouldn't notice. "You know, I think you'd make a striking pair. You're both tall with black hair and eyes." A giggle escaped from her. "Imagine your babies."

Jill turned to the cupboard to add to a pile of magazines which threatened to slide over and out. Jane continued, "Mind, he would seem meticulously tidy, and let's face it, you're not!" With the cupboard door safely shut, Jill turned, a worried frown creasing her brow. "What's the matter?" asked Jane, "Don't take it all so seriously. If you enjoy each other's company I am sure he won't care if you're a bit untidy."

"You said, keep in touch? Where are you going?"

Jane shrugged, "Nowhere at present, but who knows what might happen. Depends how quickly your wedding bells ring."

"But why leave? You like the company, the job, the people, and they like you."

"You forget the one exception – my office mate! I've got Rosemary all day, and Bruce is almost living at my house. I can't see how to break free from Bruce, but I can from Rosemary. Paul has given me the rest of the week off, so I'll just look around and see what's available. Maybe nothing as good as here."

"What about a transfer here?"

"I hadn't thought of that! Is that possible? Do you know of a vacancy?"

"I can't think of one. Nikki would be the…" The lift door banging distracted Jill's attention. The look on her face told Jane that the person who had just emerged was the one person, with his questions, she'd rather not meet just now. Sure enough, the familiar voice boomed, "Hello, girls!" Did they look guilty? For almost instantly he queried, "And what are you two cooking up?"

To Jane's surprise Jill was unexpectedly bold. "David we are in the middle of a private conversation. If Jane wants to tell you then that's up to her — if she doesn't then let her be."

David frowned as Jill held his eyes in silent challenge. Jane tried not to smirk, for Jill was not only calling him David, but was confidently standing up to him!

Undeterred, David asked, "So, Jane, what have you been up to?"

It might have been said pleasantly, but the man really did have an intimidating air, and she wasn't going to be intimidated. She deflected his question and smiled sweetly, "Nothing much, how about you?"

David looked at Jill. His eyes sharpened, his gaze speculative, as she nervously twisted a column of curly hair in her fingers. Like a vulture determined to get his prey, David swooped to delve. "You know, Jill, how much I hate office gossip. And remember, the definition of gossip is to talk about another person's problem with someone who can't resolve it. So I hope you two haven't been indulging in that?"

Jane's mouth opened in astonishment. He was the one who was always interfering and being nosey! "I don't know how you could say that, when it is you who has the knack of appearing and asking the wrong questions at the wrong time."

His mouth twisted with a suggestion of a smile. "Is that so, Jane? I would have said I have impeccable timing."

Jane, suspecting she'd had a hand in wrecking David's engagement, had no intention of damaging this budding relationship by letting David think Jill had been gossiping.

"Well, we haven't been gossiping and I have a problem which I am quite capable of resolving. So you've got it all wrong, because I was telling Jill I'm looking for a job."

"What!" The loud exclamation made them both jump. David stepped nearer and towered over her. Jet black eyes bored into her. She could only suppose that by wanting to leave ITP she was, in his eyes, committing a heinous crime.

"Ah! So my timing is still impeccable. And what is wrong with the job you have?"

Her mother's voice saying 'least said, soonest mended' echoed in her mind, so she replied with a shrug, "Just circumstances."

David's brow creased, then he questioned, "Your mother? Bruce? You need more pay? Is this something to do with the way you were feeling this morning?" At each suggestion she shook her head. Exasperated he asked, "Then what are these 'circumstances'?"

She bit back 'mind your own business', but there was no denying the haughtiness in her voice as she replied, "In the light of it being judged as gossip, I'd rather not say." David's jaw clenched. His mouth moved into a grim line. "And I haven't started looking for another job yet. I didn't intend saying anything until I'd found something else. I might not even go, but I really don't know why either you or Jill should be so upset – especially in the light of recent events."

David's response at her shy smile was to glance at Jill as he echoed, "Recent events?"

Jill, who had been fiddling with her hair throughout his interrogation, suddenly burst out, "I suggested there might be another secretarial job available here."

David's eyes riveted on Jill as if to read her mind, then said slowly, "I'm sure when a secretarial position becomes available, Jane could have first option."

Anxious to finish the conversation, Jane's words rushed out. "That's very kind, thank you, but in the meanwhile I'll look around. I've got the rest of this week off., but I won't make any hasty decisions." She stopped, for it seemed neither Jill nor David seemed to be listening. Jill was gazing worriedly at David, while he seemed deep in thought. A door banged in the nearby corridor, a current of air caught the chandeliers, which tinkled gently. What were they waiting for? God to speak? An urge to giggle rose up – perhaps that was the angels heralding His presence?

Jane flinched as David clapped his hands and said with great jollity, "Of course! That's it! The very thing." By the satisfied smile across his face she wondered if God had given him a revelation. Those black eyes refocused on her. "Tell me Jane, what do you think of Grace?"

Her brow puckered at the strange question. "Umm... grace? Well, as a Christian I believe that we are saved by God's unmerited favour — in other words, grace."

"No, no, not that grace! Grace, my assistant."

"Oh sorry. Umm... yes she's very nice. She was very kind to me when...."

"Good. Good. Grace has always said that help from someone who knows nothing about our exhibitions would be more trouble than it was worth. But as you work in the Public Relations Department, that argument won't apply."

The realization of where his mind was going brought an emphatic, "I don't think so."

"What do you mean, you don't think so? It's perfect! I don't know why I didn't think of it before."

Irritated, thinking he really could be a difficult man, Jane replied with asperity, "Look, it may seem perfect to you, but not to me. So let's forget about it, shall we? I'm going home!"

In the time it took to adjust her bag and step towards the door, David had blocked her path.

Jill instructed, "Leave it, David!"

He ignored her to challenge Jane, "At least let's discuss it. I'm sure we can thrash out any problems. Let's adjourn to my office." His stern gaze seemed to defy her to decline. The last thing she wanted to do was 'thrash out' anything with him.

He obviously expected her to capitulate for he turned to Jill, "No need for you worry. I'll sort this out." Jill, however, did look worried, and glanced uncertainly between them before casting a sympathetic glance in Jane's direction. "After all we don't want Jane going off on one of her harebrained, 'must spread my wings', schemes again, do we?"

That did it.The frustration and tension of the day exploded into hot molten fury.The only way to control the words she longed to spit out was to keep her mouth tightly shut while she seethed inside. The condescending....! Who did Mr High and Mighty Reinhardt think he was? Oh, yes! The esteemed and revered Director of the Company. Well, that didn't give him licence to make facetious comments about her or demand an explanation for her decisions. Without further ado, she pushed past him and strode off across the hall to the stairs.

David's voice boomed out after her, "And where do you think you are going?"

She turned to drawl sarcastically, "Why Mr Reinhardt to your office. It will be less embarrassing for you when I tell you exactly why your idea isn't a good one. And be quick about it, for my Mum's expecting me home for tea." The astonishment on his face filled her with a heady triumph she called goodbye to Jill and headed to the stairs. However, she wondered if she would be allowed to return after tonight!

About to enter the stairwell, she glimpsed back and saw Jill's finger stabbing into David's chest. So she knew him well enough to give him a telling off! Serve him right! She gave a grin of satisfaction, then felt a pang of remorse. Oh dear, the whole point was to not cause trouble between them.

A glance at her watch told her it was nearly six o'clock! In a determined gesture, she pushed her hair behind her ears, climbed the stairs and considered how the man who was known to hate gossip was himself an interfering, insufferable busybody.

The connecting door to David's office door was ajar, should she go in? No. Better to stay and wait in Grace's office. It was obvious from the neatly stacked files and well filled 'in tray' that Grace did have a heavy workload, her responsibilities far beyond shorthand typing. So it was quite possible she needed an assistant, but equally it would be quite impossible to work for David – he'd probably wind her up far more than Rosemary's antagonism and insults did. She may have glimpsed behind his stern exterior but, even so, 'kind, caring and thoughtful', didn't describe his business persona.

He had slipped up, though, to speak of her 'spreading her wings' in front of Jill. It meant he'd told her about the Andrew Carlton incident, and so they must be closer than she thought! So if he shared that with Jill, what had Jill shared with him? She began to pace up and down. Would Jill have repeated the impression that Bruce and her mother had of David?

Where was he, anyway? And why was she waiting? Probably because David's authoritative air was like her father. He used to say when angry, "Go to your room." Her arguing didn't stop his tongue-lashing and, when younger, being given the stick, but she'd respected his stance and been aware of her boundaries. When she grew into her teens, provided she wasn't rude, he would laugh at her temerity and question, "How did such a mild mannered man as me get such a strong-willed child?" Even now, a smile broke out as she remembered her mother's derisive laugh at that remark, and her dad's response of a playful pat on her mum's bottom. Their love for each other had always been evident. Tears sprang to Jane's eyes — oh, she missed her dad.

She rubbed her eyes with a finger, then glanced at her watch. Half an hour had passed. Where was that wretched man? Was he doing this on purpose to rile her? She'd said her Mum was expecting her. She usually rang if she was going to be late. That thought triggered memories of using David's telephone and of the stranger. Once again, this office was to be a place of confrontation — however this was one she could handle! The lift gate clanked open and shut. Jane stiffened, took a deep breath and braced herself.

Without glancing in her direction, David strode through the room, saying briskly, "Right! Come on through, Jane. I had several things to do before I could see you." He flicked on two table lamps and indicated to the hard-backed chair in front of desk. "Do sit down."

Seated in the large, comfortable seat behind the desk, David switched on the light over his blotter, glanced over his meticulously tidy desk, picked up the ruler and tipped back the chair. From the shadow he gazed at her while twiddling the ruler between his fingers. Jane seethed at his high-handedness, lack of apology for keeping her waiting, and now being disadvantaged because she couldn't see his face clearly, when he could see hers.

Amusement tinged his voice. "Do sit down Jane. Why didn't you come in and make yourself comfortable? After all, it's not the first time you've been in here, is it?"

Wary, she perched on the edge of the chair. What was he getting at? Had he found out about the night of the stranger? She parried the question, "Isn't it?"

"Surely you've not forgotten lying on that settee with your head injured?"

Relieved, she answered quickly, "No. No, of course I haven't. That was different."

"It was different…?"

Was he taunting her? The way he kept twisting that ruler round and round was beginning to unnerve her. She stammered, "Yes. No! Yes."

He leaned forward into the light. "Which is it, Jane?"

This had nothing to do with their business tonight. He

was baiting her, but she'd nothing to fear from him. "Look, David, you wanted an explanation as to why I can't work with you and Grace – I'm here, I've waited for you. I don't know why, but I did, so could we get on with it."

David continued examining the ruler and asked, "Did you want to use my telephone to ring home?"

Jane stared at him. He gave her a wry smile. Annoyed she pursed her lips and snapped, "No thank you. Now, the matter of this job?" Keeping eye contact, she defied him to sidetrack the conversation again.

"You don't have to pay for the call. This one has an outside line." With a flourish of his hand he indicated the red telephone, then went back to gently tapping the ruler against the palm of his hand. If he was trying to disconcert her, he was succeeding. "Do help yourself, Jane."

Despite David's straight face it was apparent he was finding this very funny. Head bent, she squeezed her hands together. Of course — Andrew Carlton had probably told him he'd caught her in here using the telephone. Heaven only knew what else Andrew had told him during their row, probably using her responses to justify his actions. Her face was began to heat — how much did David know?

"Well, Jane? David, with his elbow on the desk and his head resting on his hand, was scrutinising her face.

This was becoming an uphill struggle. She took a deep breath. As she exhaled, her words burst forth, "Just stop harping on about me ringing home. If you'd let me tell you why I can't accept your job offer, I would be on my way home by now." His lips twitched in amusement while he continued to tap the ruler against the palm of his hand. "Look, if you're wanting to know if I've been in here before I had my accident, you could have asked me straight out." David leant forward, replaced the ruler and gave her a questioning look. "Yes, the answer is 'yes', which I'm sure you already know. And yes, I came in and used your telephone. It's not a crime is it? And I paid for it. But if you think I'm dishonest, then you wouldn't want to employ me and that solves my problem." She picked up her bag.

"That's not my conclusion. I didn't for one minute think you weren't honest."

"I guess Andrew Carlton told you he caught me in here and…." She paused and David's eyebrows drew together. Her face reddened and she ended lamely, "…well, it was very embarrassing."

"Oh, I see."

He didn't see and she wasn't going to enlighten him! Jane's exasperation was rising. Now, having passed the moment of anguish thinking he might know all that had passed between her and Andrew Carlton, she stood up. "I'm going. There's no point in continuing. You wanted a reason." She waved her hand nebulously into the air, "This is it! You seem to enjoy hounding me, baiting me, then pouncing on me like a vulture catching its prey…."

That roar of laughter, for which he was famous, hit the air. The room reverberated with it. Not finding anything funny, she folded her arms and stared crossly at him. In between chuckles of laughter, he queried, "So Jane, what happened to — I quote — 'underneath the stern face, the loud bark and awkward questions, you are really a very kind and thoughtful man'?"

Jane glared at him. "Nothing happened! But within these four walls you are still the hard-headed businessman with the stern face, loud bark and awkward questions. And you still continue to amuse yourself at my expense. Oh, yes! You can laugh. Go on, why don't you? You boom into my life with your questions, you rock my boat until you've finally taken the wind out of my sails and then watch as I bob about at sea." She stalked toward the door. "It's such good sport isn't it?"

David's laughter died in his throat. "Jane! Wait!" He leapt up to urge, "Jane, please! Hear me out! Please, please, don't go."

It was the change in tone that halted her footsteps.

"I really don't deliberately set out to antagonise you. Please come back and sit down. You see I felt from my very first encounter with you, that it was I who'd been hurtled round by a hurricane. I tell you, when the wind is in your sails, my boat gets rocked far more than yours! And, when calm is restored, the very direction of my life seems to have changed!"

At his unexpected confession she slid on to the edge of the chair, and leant forward to explain. "I, I never mean to. It's just you always seem, well...to put it bluntly, you are nosey, interfering and insistent. It annoys me, so I retaliate." His face tightened. Perhaps she'd been a bit harsh, so she added, "But I haven't forgotten that it was those things...well... that time − I was grateful for your interfering nature."

The wry smile brought her to consider how it lit up his heavy, square features − even the skin around his eyes crinkled and softened those penetrating dark eyes. Oh dear, she'd been staring. She dropped her gaze and aimed her words at the desk.. "I know we've been through quite a bit together, but really there is no need to feel some sort of responsibility for me." Jane looked up in hope of a response, but David seemed deep in thought. "It's not that I don't appreciate your offer of a job, but I'm sure, having had time to think about it, you will realize it wouldn't work. Working with Rosemary has been difficult, but working for you! Well that would be a recipe for disaster. I wouldn't just rock your neat, efficient boat − we'd clash with such force we'd probably both be capsized and one of us, I suspect me, would probably drown!"

Laughter ricocheted around the room. Now what had she said that was so amusing? She scowled. David sat forward and bantered, "I'll risk it, if you will. I'm a good swimmer and have my life saving certificates − so, no need for you to fear drowning!"

Jane glared at him. "You may be willing to risk it, but I'm not, and for several reasons." David's eyebrows lifted questioningly. She plunged on. "First, is there really a job? Second, if there is, then surely Grace should have a say in who gets it. And third, even if Grace is happy for me to work in your office, it would mean several steps up the secretarial ladder. To give me the job would look like favouritism, or ..." Her eyes focused on the wood carving around the outer rim of the desk. She gulped, and said quickly, "... or something else. Which I am sure neither of us would appreciate. And then there is Jill. There's always gossip and that could hurt her, and your relationship."

David was silent. She felt triumphant. That had floored him! Time to leave! She stood as David asked, "If I found a way to overcome all your reservations — would you consider working with Grace?"

The chance of that was so unlikely she said stiffly, "Maybe."

It seemed he'd taken that as a yes, because he leaned back in his chair, steepled his fingers against his mouth and went into a state of meditation.

Now what? Should she stay, or go? David Reinhardt had a reputation for being an expert at problem solving, his decisions known to be well considered and sensible. Tentatively, she looked around her and when he said nothing more decided to sit again. How many futures had been mapped out at the oval boardroom table at the far end of the room? This place certainly had been life changing for her. Her gaze drifted to David, his steepled hands reminding her of the nursery rhyme: 'Here's the church, here's the steeple, open the doors and see all the people'. An idea came into her head. She chuckled.

David bent forward, the heavy gold signet ring on his little finger reflecting light. He asked, "Now what's going on in that overactive brain of yours?"

With a grin, she leant back in the chair and said

confidently, "I've just thought of a solution that would solve all the problems."

"Is that so?"

Ignoring what she perceived as sarcasm, she went on, "I don't know why, but it seems you want me to stay working for ITP?"

"Of course. When we find good employees we want to keep them, and, if they have a problem we like, if possible, to seek a resolution."

"Right! Well this, I think, could be a very suitable resolution to my problem and yours. Grace needs someone to help her, preferably someone who's been involved in public relations because she doesn't want to waste time training them?"

He sighed wearily, "Yes, Jane, but I fail...."

"Let me finish."

David glowered and fell silent.

To string it out, Jane controlled her laughter and said in as serious a voice as she could muster and using David's vocabulary, "Therefore, logically, the easy, effective and efficient solution for both of us, and one which I'm surprised you haven't thought of, would be to promote Rosemary to work with you."

David, with a loud groan, slumped his head into his hands.

"It's brilliant, isn't it?" Her choking laugher belied her innocence.

He looked up. "Good God, girl! Any more ideas like that and I'll cheerfully throttle you."

"Precisely. That's why Rosemary would be a better choice."

David groaned. "What have I done to deserve this?"

Amused, she watched as he sat back and linked his hands behind his head. Well, he'd have difficulty getting out of that.

Elated at her victory she was taken aback when he

asked, "If you could give me a few quiet minutes to think, I really do feel I can come up with a better solution than yours."

Jubilant, she said perkily, "I doubt it!"

David raised his eyebrows then tipped back his chair, leaving her with a view of the cleft in his upturned chin. Jane smiled to herself. Those harsh features were a façade he used to his advantage, and he was certainly a man for whom she was gaining respect and perhaps even, admiration. The fact he was so much older than her was probably why, unlike Donna, she didn't think he oozed sex appeal, but she could see his attraction and he would make Jill a good husband. Perhaps she should add some of David's better traits to her prayer for her dream man!

"Right Jane, first and foremost...."

She dragged herself back from her musings to comment, "It sounds as if you're addressing the court."

David ignored her and continued in a magisterial tone, "It seems to me that you believe you have conclusively and effectively summed up your case. So now, I will do my utmost to convince you otherwise." She doubted it, but widened her eyes in expectation — she was enjoying this. "Now, if you will just listen, I'll detail my solution."

At that moment, her inner voice told her this man held her future in his hands.

CHAPTER 7

David had given her no chance to interrupt his proposals. And they certainly made her conclusions seem very feeble. Now, with elbows on the desk, chin between his hands, he asked, "So Jane, in removing the obstacles have I solved your arguments?"

Her nod was reluctant. "But your tactics will have to work."

"They will. The question is, will you accept the position as Grace's personal assistant?"

"Are you sure you didn't bludgeon poor Grace into saying she'd be delighted to have me?"

Amusement twitched at his mouth. "Now would I do a thing like that?" Jane's eyes widened questioningly. "Jane, I am only ever gently persuasive. Bludgeoning is not my style." He ignored her cynical expression. "When I rang Grace with my suggestion, she agreed you would be suitable, and pointed out several obstacles, which I assured her I could overcome." He flourished his hand towards the telephones, "Feel free to ring her yourself."

A slow shake of her head was a sign of her defeat but, determined to have the last word, Jane commented, "Then it would appear, taking account of your recommendations, proposals and strategy, that I have no case to uphold — except you've forgotten how easily we rub each other up the wrong way."

David smiled broadly, "I'm out of the office a lot. Look, I expect you're ready for something to eat. Why don't we adjourn to a quiet restaurant around the corner from the station? You can get to know me and judge if it could work, and I can find just what I'd be letting myself in for."

Worried, she murmured into her lap, "I'm not sure that's a good idea."

116

"What? That I should discover what I might be letting myself in for?"

Jane clicked her tongue and snapped, "No, of course not! I mean mixing business with pleasure."

It was clear that David was suppressing his mirth, but he still said with great seriousness, "Well, Jane, I am heartened to think that dining with me could be considered a pleasure."

Lips pursed, she took a deep breath and released it with the words, "You know what I mean! After all it was you who reminded me earlier of what happened last time I attempted to spread my wings."

"And I would remind you, Jane, that you felt God had appointed me to be your guardian angel."

Did the wretched man have an answer for everything? She tried another tack. "What about Jill? Won't she be expecting you?"

"No. I told her I was going to persuade you by fair means or foul to take up my offer. Jill will draw her own conclusions as to which method I used, and be only too happy that I achieved my goal."

She stiffened at his confident assumptions but said, more mildly than she felt, "You're very sure of yourself, aren't you?"

"No, not always Jane. With you, never!" David stood and stretched his long body. "But, no doubt if you work with Grace you'll see more of me and my failings. In the meanwhile, however, can you be persuaded to eat with me, and ring your mother to tell her you should be home around eleven?"

The thought of dining with the boss had been rather daunting, but the reality was far from it. The restaurant proved to be moderately priced, pleasant but not intimate, and when David ordered a half bottle of wine, stating, "I don't like more than one glass when I'm driving," another fear was allayed.

As David entertained her with tales of his early years living with his parents and two sisters on a farm near Bristol, Jane began to mellow under the wine and his charm. So much so that when he demanded that she tell him about her childhood pranks she laughed and shared several of her more heinous crimes. He followed that with an hair-raising incident involving his nephews, aged six and four. Without thinking, she commented, "I don't know why, but somehow I wouldn't have associated you with enjoying children."

"That, Jane, is because you've only seen me as a business man. In fact, I play many parts – brother, uncle and hopefully one day, if I can find someone to have me, husband and father."

At the wistfulness of his expression, she hastened to reassure him, "Oh, there must be dozens of women who'd be delighted to become your wife."

With an amused smile, David leant forward, "Is that so, Jane?"

A blush diffused up her neck and face. She groaned inwardly. If only she thought before she spoke! To her relief, the noisy arrival of a group of people at the next table distracted his attention, and she switched the subject by commenting, "You mentioned your nephews stayed with you. Where do you live?"

"Kensington. I bought the house for its convenient location and as an investment. I lived in a couple of the rooms but then, a year ago, Felicity and my younger, unmarried sister ganged up on me. The pair of them agreed no woman could live in it as it was, so we started to renovate it." A brief shadow crossed his face, swiftly checked by a chuckle. "My beloved sister is still intent on joining me. She's also keeping the poor workmen on their toes because she's determined to be in just after Christmas."

"Do you mind her moving in?"

"Not really, It is a large house. But if she thinks she's going to get away without paying her half of the running expenses...."

"I expect, though, you're glad of her woman's touch? Men don't seem very interested in colour schemes and furnishings."

"Oh, she can decorate her rooms as she wishes but, as to men not being interested, I disagree. Women are natural homemakers, and most husbands just go along with their ideas. But I've found it quite interesting looking at magazines to find out the latest trends. I've discussed ideas with my sisters, my mother and other womenfolk, but the end result will definitely be my decision." He smiled across the table, "Tell me, what kind of décor do you like?"

It was flattering to be asked, but even more so when, after she had talked of her ideas, he seemed to question, ponder and like them. To chat with him so easily made her forget who he was so, when she found herself saying, "I expect Jill would have some good suggestions," she hoped she hadn't been too forward.

It was a relief when he smiled and exclaimed, "Oh, Jill. Yes! She's made some excellent suggestions. In fact, she's been a great help in bringing it all together."

Thrilled that he and Jill were discussing décor – a good sign that things were serious – she smiled and tentatively enquired, "Are you... do you think you and Jill...."

In a brusque voice, David interrupted, "We're just good friends, Jane, that's all." Feeling awkward, she concentrated on sipping her wine while he went on, "I'm very fond of her but, well – I'll say no more. Not just now."

A quick glance showed that he seemed more amused than cross at her prying, but obviously he wanted to change the subject as he added, "Enough of me, tell me about you and Bruce."

David's gentle probing opened the floodgates of her frustrations until she realized how disloyal she sounded. "Oh, I'm sorry. I'm making Bruce sound awful. He's not really. He's a lovely man – but just not for me any more." She smiled regretfully,

"And what kind of man are you looking for?"

"I'm not looking. Not after… you know. I'm leaving it to God. He knows best. It's safer that way."

"I admire your faith, but I like to be in control, to know what I'm doing and where I'm going."

Instantly Jane retorted, "I'd noticed."

David's subsequent roar of laughter made her jump and several pairs of questioning eyes turned upon them..

They left the restaurant still bantering light-heartedly. It seemed only natural as they strolled toward the tube station that she should slip her arm into his. Surprised, he glanced at her, but a quick smile and squeeze of his arm against hers reassured her. The subway steps were now only a few yards away. Happy and carefree, helped by two glasses of wine, Jane pressed against his arm to draw his attention. "I just wanted to say how much I've enjoyed this evening. And mixing business with pleasure wasn't such a bad idea after all."

"Does that mean what I think it means?"

"Um, I rather think it does."

"Good. Then I'll take it from here. Just let my strategy run its course, and within a week I'll be looking forward to welcoming you as Grace's assistant."

In the euphoria of a wonderful evening, she couldn't resist mimicking the popular TV comedian, Dick Emery, by tapping her hand against David and chanting, "Oh! You are awful, but I like you." Bemused ,David shook his head, while she continued mischievously, "It's true. You are awful! What about that time in the canteen – you knew very well I didn't mean to kiss you. Fancy saying , 'if I felt the need to kiss you, could I do so in a more private place'.

120

I was so embarrassed."

David gave a hearty chuckle. "You should have seen your face. There I was, having just received such a public put down, how could I resist such a heaven-sent opportunity to make you squirm."

"That's a pity, because I was just about to ask if this was a private enough place?"

David halted so abruptly that her hand slipped from his arm. Confused, she looked up into the dark unfathomable depths of his eyes. Disturbed by the intensity of his gaze, she could only guess that she'd overstepped the boundary between boss and secretary. His hands gripped her upper arms. Was he about to shake her? His jaw flexed as he searched her face. To compensate she laughed, "David what's the matter — I was joking." Immediately his hands dropped to his side. Now feeling incredibly stupid she spoke to his tie. "Anyway David, thank you for a lovely evening." With a smile and false brightness she said, "See you soon" and headed down the steps into the station.

Halfway down the stairs his voice called her. "Jane! Jane, hold on!" His echoing footsteps caught up with her. "Jane, when I said you'd be home by eleven o'clock it wasn't my intention for you to use the train."

"It's fine, I'll be perfectly safe."

"Maybe, but I'd feel happier to see you to your front door. Come on."

He caught her elbow and drew her back up the steps. Her euphoria had now dissipated and they walked in silence towards the office car park. Aware of the tension that had grown between them, David squeezed her arm. "You are very different from my first impression of you."

Jane frowned. "Am I? But then, I suppose I could say the same thing about you."

"I don't think I dare ask if, on knowing, I get better or worse!"

"I'll reserve judgement."

He gave a good-natured laugh. "I can see having you around, is going to keep me on my toes."

They walked up the drive of the house towards the car park immersed in their private thoughts. David politely held the car door open for her, but before he closed it he bent to comment, "By the way, Jane, if you should feel the need to kiss me I'd   consider outside your house a private enough place!" He didn't wait for her reaction, but closed her door on a bellow of laughter.

The moment David pulled up outside her house he declared, "Well, I must be getting back. No need to invite me in for coffee. I've a busy day tomorrow." Jane hid her relief, but winced when he added, "I doubt your mother would appreciate me coming in anyway at this time of night." Had Jill had passed on her mother's opinion of him?

"Well, thank you again for the lovely meal. It was a good idea to get to know you better and I think I'm going to enjoy working for you, that's if you still want me?"

"Of course... I haven't changed my mind, but I'm glad you have." She moved to get out of the car. "Jane, I think you've forgotten something?" Puzzled she turned back to see David tapping his cheek.

There was no stopping her blush, but she said firmly, "It was a joke, David." His finger tapped on. "Just because you got a 'thank you' kiss last time you brought me home doesn't mean you always get one — I'm not making a habit of it."

David gave a smile and countered, "Yes, but remember, a kiss on the cheek is hardly grand passion is it?"

Jane quickly acquiesced and scampered away.

That was a week ago — it was almost unbelievable that last Monday she'd been walking to the station in gloom and doom. David's strategy had worked like a charm.

Tuesday: Nikki Clarke confirmed to Jane that there

were no vacant secretarial posts.

Wednesday: Nikki received a request from Grace, countersigned by David Reinhardt, for an assistant. As hoped, Nikki mentioned Jane. Grace agreed that she would be very suitable, but pointed out that it could appear that Jane was being promoted over Rosemary. Nikki had countered that, as the job was working for Grace not David Reinhardt, the salary would reflect this and would probably be less than Rosemary's current earnings.

Thursday: Paul unwittingly became part of the plan. He was fed the news by Jill that Grace needed an assistant. Knowing Jane's unhappiness, he 'persuaded' Jane to let him put her name forward. Paul then went to David Reinhardt, where, he confided to him that Jane was looking for a new job and extolled her virtues and abilities.

Friday: David rang Paul to say that Grace had interviewed Jane and was going to offer her the job.

Paul was so pleased that his advice had been taken that he found it almost as hard as Jane not to whoop with delight.

Today, sitting on the train as it rocked along the fast stretch from Acton Town to Hammersmith, Jane gazed at the watery sunshine and hoped it was a herald to a much brighter future. Rosemary was certainly going to be rocked this morning when she found out she'd moved on!

The train drew to a halt. The doors opened to let a few people out. More squeezed in and, to Jane's dismay, one of them was Donna. Of all the people! Of all the days! If she told Donna, her news would spread like wildfire. But not telling Donna now would probably mean her drawing the wrong conclusions later. Jane hid herself in her book and hoped Donna wouldn't spot her.

"Jane. Jane. Hi! I thought it was you!"

She looked up and inwardly groaned. Donna weaved towards her through the crowd. For the next ten minutes, Donna, hanging on to an overhead strap, wobbled over her head and talked loudly and non-stop about men and her love life. Then abruptly she changed the subject to ask, "Why are you up so early today? Don't tell me you've taken up smoking, or having to have a couple of strong black coffees before you can start work?"

Jane screwed up her nose. "Not likely! I'm starting a new job and want to be early."

Donna's face puckered with astonishment. "I didn't even know you'd left, I didn't hear anything about your collection." She gave a derisive laugh, "But then, Rosemary wouldn't, would she?" Before Jane could interrupt, she rushed on with widened eyes, "Oh! Oh, no! You weren't asked to leave, were you? Not another run in with Mr Reinhardt? What about that time in the canteen — oh my, but he couldn't sack you for that, could he!" Donna burst into peals of laughter successfully drawing the attention of those around them.

Obviously Donna enjoyed playing to an audience, for she looked round and smiled. Fortunately the person sitting next to Jane got up, hiding her from view. Donna slid round to take his place. By then most of the eyes had reverted back to reading papers and books or staring blankly out the window into the blackness of the tunnel.

In lowered tones, Jane explained, "I'm not leaving ITP. I'm going to work in Mr Reinhardt's office as Grace Pawson's assistant."

"What!" The exclamation rang out like a pistol shot above the noise of the train. Heads again turned towards them. It wasn't any good pretending Donna wasn't with her, for she was staring at Jane open-mouthed. Incredulous, she questioned, "You! You are going to work for Mr Reinhardt?"

Jane glanced quickly around the carriage. No one was looking their way, but she suspected many were listening. Sheepishly, she murmured, "Well, Paul recommended me to Grace and she thought I'd be ideal."

"Good grief! Did she? I'm surprised Mr Reinhardt allowed it. I'd have thought he'd have preferred someone a bit older and more experienced. Oh! I don't mean that rudely," Donna chortled. "I'd have thought you'd be a bit of a distract...." Jane had had enough. She leapt up and pushed her way through the crowds, glad that they were getting out at the next stop. Undeterred, Donna followed saying loudly, "I don't mean a sexual distraction... but let's hope... he wants his life... and office enlivened... for, my God... oops, sorry Jane, I forgot... with you in it... it could become one hell of a battlefield." When the double doors hissed open, Jane practically catapulted herself out on to the platform and hurried away towards the escalator. Donna caught up with her. "Jane, look I'm sorry, Jane. You took me by surprise. I forgot I was in a public place and that I have such a loud voice."

Jane sighed. "Okay, you're forgiven. But please, if you must tell others, don't tack your observations on the end."

Donna laughed, "Okay. But why you, of all people? Oh! Oh, I don't mean that unkindly." She giggled, squeezing Jane's arm as they stepped together onto the escalator.

"Apparently, Grace has been snowed under for ages and, with the Brussels exhibition coming up, Mr Reinhardt has persuaded her she can't do it all."

"And he chose you?" Donna looked down from the step above, eyeing her suggestively.

"It didn't happen quite like that." Briefly, she explained the set of coincidences which led her to the job, realizing as she did so the value of David's strategy.

Obviously it sounded plausible to Donna, for she said, "So you jumped at the chance. I don't blame you." Her face took on a sultry look, her tone sexy, "Mr Reinhardt is an enigma I'd like to examine more closely!"

"Oh, Donna! Maybe you would! But let's face it, he's years older than me and not exactly in my league. Besides he reminds me of my father." Jane grinned, wondering what David would think of that.

Donna's eyebrows lifted. "So what's wrong with a Sugar Daddy? I say — watch this space. How about, 'ice maiden melts into the arms of notorious, distinguished gent'?"

Marcus Johnson's voice cut into Jane's protest. "So, who's this notorious, distinguished gent then?"

On the step behind Jane, Marcus pulled at the tips of his handlebar moustache as he inclined his ear toward her.

"Honestly!" Jane retorted, although not unkindly. "You members of the Press Department have really vivid imaginations – not to mention ears that flap and noses that stick into other people's business. It seems if ever there is a piece of news, you either worm your way in or sniff it out."

Marcus laughed. "Training, me dear, training. Sniff, poke and pry. You wait and see – one day I'll have my own gossip column in the News of the World." Jane found it impossible not to smile, for Marcus must be at least fifty so he didn't have many years left to fulfil his dream. But he wasn't easily put off. "Well then, Jane Mackenzie, into who's arms might you melt?"

"Nobody's!" Jane stepped off the escalator and pulled Marcus to one side as others streamed by. "Right Marcus, before you put connotations, innuendos, and all the kinds of things you press people do on pieces of information, I am clearly stating now, I am not going out with anyone, I am not interested in anyone, and I'm not even sure that the man called 'notorious' even fits that description."

"Message received, Jane. But...who is he?"

"My new Head of Department."

"Aha! I do smell news! And who might your new Head of Department be?"

"Mr Reinhardt."

Marcus' response was a low whistle and an intrusive stare, before he murmured, "Now that is interesting."

Fortunately Donna, having already been through the score and made her notes, butted in, "Marcus and I are going for a coffee. I'll fill him in, you go on."

Jane gave her a pleading look. Although Donna's apology earlier had seemed genuine, would she make a mountain out of a molehill now? If this was going to be how everyone reacted, Jane hoped David hadn't made a fatal error in his proposals and strategy!

The walk to the office gave her time to ponder on the responses her news had already evoked. Her mother had voiced a dubious, "Do you know what you are doing, dear? He seems a bit high-powered for you."

Bruce had been even more negative, "I wonder what he's up to? You sure he doesn't fancy you? It seems odd to choose you over Rosemary – but then from what you say about her, I suppose I can understand that."

Even Ted's jovial, "Good for you, Jane!" was spoilt when he added, "I expect you'll have to work longer hours, and we'll see less of you," that had brought a peeved look from Bruce.

However, Jill's enthusiasm made up for the others. All week she'd been enjoying the role of go-between as the plot unfolded, and this morning she was waiting at the door to welcome her with a cheery greeting and knowing smile. The laboriously slow, antiquated lift gave Jane time to consider the relationship between Jill and David. A prize piece of gossip, but not one she was going to leak to the Press Department!

Grace was already at her desk and welcomed her brightly. "You're early!" She waved her hand across an empty expanse in the room. "I'm afraid we haven't got you a desk yet, but I am assured it is on its way. David flew to Brussels last night. He won't be in today or tomorrow, so you might as well use his for now, especially as your first task will be to make masses of telephone calls." With a broad smile she went on, "At least I won't have to be rushing round with a white flag just yet."

Jane was aghast, "Oh, no! Not you too." Grace put her head on one side and looked at her inquiringly. "I met Marcus and Donna from the Press Department this morning. I thought they might think it odd if I didn't tell them about my new job. Donna said she thought this office could become … a battlefield. Marcus inferred the same. Oh, Grace, I'm not sure this is such a good idea – perhaps David's made a mistake?"

Grace laughed. "Oh come on Jane – don't look so forlorn! You haven't even started yet. Would I have agreed to this when David rang me last Monday, if I'd thought it would bring more problems than it would solve? Over the years, I've seen many people cut and thrust their way to the top, but not David. And, as for him making a mistake, I would be very surprised. It is rare for him to do anything without a great deal of thought, skill and integrity."

"Whew! High praise, Grace."

"Yes, I suppose it is. Nevertheless, it's true. And for David to find a strategy to keep you at ITP and also be willing for you to work in close proximity to him, means he's recognised that same integrity in you. I've never worked for a kinder, or more generous man, but not everyone sees him in that light. In fact," she smiled, "not many people would believe that under that booming exterior is a quiet, caring and gentle man. Few see behind the business façade, or even trouble to try." Her smile widened, "Some people, though, have the ability to break through that façade without, it seems, trying." At her mortified face, Grace gave an amused grunt, "You're so genuine and natural. He likes that quality and I think he finds you amusing." Grace picked up a file from her desk. "Anyway, enough said. Let's get started on this workload. We've only got a few weeks to get this exhibition in Brussels together and there's a list of telephone calls to work through."

Only a few months ago, Jane had crept into this inner
sanctum to use the telephone. Now she had every right to
be here. Grace found it onerous trying to contact all the
English exhibitors who were going to Brussels, but Jane
thoroughly enjoyed the novelty of swinging in David's
chair and using his telephones! The aspirations of the
Exhibition weren't new to her – she'd typed all the pages of
publicity material. It was now proving useful in answering
exhibitors' questions. This was far better than sitting at a
typewriter all day, although Grace had told her to make
notes of each conversation because later she'd need to
confirm individual requirements by letter.

The morning passed quickly. Even Jane was surprised
at how much she'd accomplished. Grace beamed as she
came across the room just as she finished her last
telephone call before lunch. "Brilliant, Jane! I told you
David knew what he was doing. You've a natural ability —
you make people feel special."

On that praise, Jane practically skipped to the back
stairs on her way to the canteen. On the floor below her,
the door on the stairwell opened and Rosemary's voice
floated up. "Jane! Don't talk to me about her! I thought if I
made her feel uncomfortable enough she'd leave, but it
seemed impossible to get rid of her. I couldn't stand her
loud and pushy ways."

Jane stopped, her hand tightening on the banister.
Richard, who she'd worked with in Accounts, gave a
sarcastic laugh, "Well, you're rid of her now."

Rosemary gave an annoyed grunt. "But, she's still
working here. Of course, she's been sucking up to Mr
Reinhardt for months. You can't tell me that there's nothing
going on there. She's wormed her way into his office —
next stop, I suppose, will be his bed."

Even from a floor up, the coldness in Richard's tone
was clear, "I think, Rosemary, you should be careful in
what you say and who you say it to. That kind of talk isn't

appreciated — especially by Mr Reinhardt."

Rosemary gave a cynical laugh, "Well, in the circumstances that's not surprising, is it?"

"You really don't like Jane, do you?"

"No, I don't, she's too full of herself.This Christian business! What a sham! She's always making eyes at the men, then gets upset when they respond." Although nearly at basement level, Rosemary's voice was still audible, "Did you know she went out with Andrew Carlton? Was it a coincidence Mr Reinhardt sacked him the following Monday? My guess is there was more to that than met the eye. And what about that incident in the canteen that caused talk? In my opinion .... " The stairwell door closed.

Jane held on to the banister, swallowed hard and tried to blink away tears. How could she go to the canteen and face people if that kind of gossip was circulating? Without further thought, she stumbled back to the office to find Grace still there.

"Jane, what's happened? You look as white as a sheet."

"Oh nothing. I think I'll get some fresh air. Buy a sandwich."

Grace stared at her, "I thought you were going to the canteen?"

"I've changed my mind."

The frown on Grace's face deepened. "Has someone upset you? Said something about your new job?"

Nervously Jane bit on her lower lip and nodded. "Then not going to the canteen isn't the answer. You mustn't hide yourself away."

Grace was right, but how could she face people if they were making the same assumptions as Rosemary. On a faint smile, she told herself as well as Grace, "I'll be alright in a minute. Just because one person hates you and says nasty things about you doesn't mean everyone thinks the same."

"Rosemary?"

Jane made a rueful face. "It doesn't matter."

"Did she say these things to you, or someone else?"

"I heard her on the stairs below me talking to Richard Dewey. She said I made eyes at men and had been sucking up to David, but it's…

Grace raised her hand, "Say no more, Jane! I can guess the rest."

Did Grace agree with Rosemary? Anxious to reassure her Jane said vehemently, "It's not true, Grace! As I said to Donna this morning, David is to me like my father, nothing else."

Amusement registered on the older woman's face. "Come on, we're going to the canteen. Everyone is going to hear that I chose my new assistant, and how pleased I am with her. That'll put any insinuations about you and David to rest."

"But you were going shopping."

"Well, I've got something more important to do now, so come on, and do cheer up."

Sam and Ian were already eating and, as expected, beckoned her over. "What's all this I hear?" asked Sam. "You're working for Mr Reinhardt?" She nodded, he looked hurt. "But why didn't you tell us?"

"Sam, I would have done if I'd known. But I was only asked on Friday afternoon. And it's more for Grace than Mr Reinhardt."

Ian chipped in, "But you'll still be working closely with him."

Sam's eyes twinkled in merriment, "Yeah, that'll be interesting. We're a bit far away though to see the sparks fly from the basement. Strikes me one of you needs your head read!"

Ian chuckled, "He'll have his head red, from a handprint on his cheek if he gets out of line."

"Oh, stop it, you two! Here comes Grace."

"I suppose you think I've gone mad?" Grace gave Jane

a fond smile, while Sam and Ian looked uncomfortable. "I have to say, if this morning is anything to go by, Jane's going to be a considerable asset." Nikki, at the next table, turned to agree. "I don't know why we didn't think of asking Jane earlier, seeing she's been involved on the public relations side."

Grace sat down next to Nikki as Donna chirped from another table, "Yes, Jane's good at public relations — kissing Mr Reinhardt was obviously a good move."

Grace laughed. "I didn't take that into account!"

Donna gave her tinkly laugh. "Maybe you should have! For if it isn't kisses at sunset, it could be pistols at dawn!"

By the laughter it was obvious a number of people at the surrounding tables were enjoying their conversation.

Grace responded with mock severity, "Don't worry! At the first sign of confrontation I'll pull out my white hanky and declare a war-free zone."

"And so there goes one very brave lady." Marcus commented loudly, drawing his finger across his throat!

Grace waited for the laughter to die down and smiled at those around. "Thank you Marcus, I'll believe for that to be a compliment. But as Mr Reinhardt is rarely in these days and we've so much work to do. I doubt Jane will have time to raise her head, let alone her voice. But I'll let you know if I need reinforcements! Anyway, if you'll excuse me, I must eat my lunch before it gets cold."

The banter and laughter continued at Jane's expense, but none of it unkind or malicious. Rosemary sitting a few tables away ignored it all, although Richard caught Jane's eye and gave her a wink and a smile. After lunch, thoroughly cheered by everyone's attitude, Jane played table tennis and surprised herself by moving up another place in the league table.

At the end of the day, Grace examined the chart she was working from and commented, "If this is the way you work, I am well pleased. And I'm sure David will be too."

"Oh, thanks. I've loved every minute — the day has flown by. Hopefully, when you and David go to Brussels I'll be able to keep everything ticking over while you're away."

Grace opened her mouth to say something, then seemingly thought better of it.

Jane emerged from the lift as Rosemary came through the adjacent swing door. Not wanting to bear a grudge, Jane gave her a tentative smile. At Rosemary's lift of her nose and toss of her hair, Jane couldn't resist making a face at her back as she stalked past her.

Jill waved enthusiastically from the reception desk and grinned as Jane approached. "Sour grapes and a grand case of jealousy there, I think!"

"It looks like it, but I wish it wasn't." Jane repeated the overheard stairwell conversation but, seeing Jill's horrified expression, hurriedly added, "It's not David she dislikes. She just wants to stir up trouble for me. Don't repeat this to David for heavens sake! Grace stopped any talk at lunch time, and — let's face it — anyone with any sense would realize I'm not one of David's women."

Jill tutted. "I never could understand David's reputation as a womaniser. He's not like that." She smiled at Jane. "But what makes you think people would consider you unsuitable?"

"Oh, Jill. I'm not in his league and he's at least fifteen years older than me."

"He's not, he's only eleven."

"Exactly! I rest my case!" With folded arms, Jane smiled in triumph.

"Now you sound like him! Eleven years age difference isn't too big."

Jane shrugged. "It is to me. He may not be old enough to be my father, but he acts like he is."

"But that can be an attraction."

"Jill, what's the matter with you? David's not interested

in me — he's interested in you. And if anyone should suggest it, tell them I wouldn't get involved beyond friendship with any man who doesn't share my Christian faith."

"David isn't an atheist. I mean, if a man had no objections to you going to church, and might even go with you, wouldn't that be enough?"

"No, there's more to it than that." Seeing Jill's puzzled face, she tried to explain. "You see, I believe that the Bible is the word of God. It says, 'love the Lord your God with all your heart, with all your mind and with all your strength'. That's not so much a command, but more a lifestyle. Six years ago I gave my life — dedicated it — to the Lord. Some people call it being 'born again'. It's a friendship with Jesus. I talk to him each day and He leads and guides me."

"I thought only nuns dedicated their lives to God. And, if you've done that, does it mean that you can't love anyone else?"

"No, of course it doesn't! It just means that God and His will must come first." Had she said 'no' a bit too harshly? She resumed more gently, "It doesn't stop me loving the right man, the one God chooses for me. But, if I marry, then it will be to someone who will share my commitment and faith. In fact, it will enhance our love." Jill fiddled with her hair as she struggled to grasp this concept. "Let me try and explain. Imagine marriage as a two-corded rope. If you include Jesus then the rope becomes three cords, and that makes it stronger." It appeared by her nod that Jill understood, so she went on, "I want a three-corded marriage which will hold together in the difficult times. That's the reason I don't go out on casual dates. I don't want to get involved with anyone unless I feel the Lord is initiating it."

"So what about Bruce?"

"Our friendship developed because we both share the

same faith and interests but, I don't know, I feel something is missing. I've been praying about it, but have nothing clear yet." Perhaps she had said enough. Jill looked worried, so she smiled and joked, "Sorry Jill, sermon over. Don't worry about it. My faith only affects me. If you and David love each other there is no reason why you shouldn't be happy together."

"Hmm."

Concerned, Jane asked, "Is everything all right between you?"

"Oh, yes, fine. Honestly! Best of friends. We're very fond of each other."

"That's what David said."

Jill frowned, then murmured, "He did, did he?"

"How many years older than you is he?" Jane asked, laughingly.

"Nearly eight years."

"Oh, that's okay then. Far better than eleven — that sounds positively ancient!"

Jill's smile was brief and rather distant.

Oh dear. Was Jill worried about the age difference? She hoped not. Not wanting to make things worse, Jane added, "I think you'll be really good together, so don't worry about it. Anyway I must go — I'll see you tomorrow." Jill, deep in thought, barely acknowledged her departure.

CHAPTER 8

The 'fasten your seat belts' sign flickered off as the BEA Trident whined 15,000 ft above the English country-side. Stretched out below, rather like a large patchwork quilt, were fields of different colours and sizes. Jane undid her seat belt, shut her eyes, and let her thoughts drift over the four weeks she'd been working for David.

Her desk had arrived on the second day but the telephones hadn't, so she continued using David's office. She enjoyed twirling in his big, padded leather chair while talking on the telephone. Although to one rather obnoxious exhibitor she'd stopped, facing the window, to concentrate on being polite yet firm by saying, "Yes. I can understand your problem. I see the difficulties, but I don't know what I can do to help." Inside, she could feel she was becoming annoyed and tried to draw the conversation to an end. "Look, I'm sorry you feel that way, do speak to Mr Reinhardt... there is no need to swear...." To cut off further expletives, she stated, "Mr Taylor, ring tomorrow. Mr Reinhardt will be back by then. Goodbye!" Furious with the man, she scowled, whirled round in the chair and slammed the telephone back into its cradle, growling, "And he'll put you in your place!"

"And who is in my place, sitting in my chair?" came that familiar voice, mimicking the bear in the Goldilocks story.

Jane's head shot up. Her stomach did a somersault. A crimson tide flowed over her neck and face as she looked up and saw David sitting on the hard chair opposite her. The surprise had her leaping to her feet in guilt and moving out from his side of the desk. Guilt for sitting in his chair; guilt for telling Mr Taylor she didn't appreciate his language; guilt for losing her temper; guilt for cutting a customer off and guilt that her retaliation had been heard.

Not knowing what to say, she stood by him as he studied the chart on the desk. "You have been making progress – this is excellent. Grace said you'd been doing well – a gift of character and charm."

A pair of black twinkling eyes looked up and met hers. Was he being sarcastic? Hadn't he just heard her conversation with Mr Taylor? In an attempt to be flippant, she replied, "Thank you, and welcome back Mr Reinhardt. We weren't expecting you until tomorrow."

"Obviously!" A wry smile accompanied David's succinct answer as he moved past her to repossess his chair. Amused speculation filled his eyes. "So, Jane, sit down and tell me – are you enjoying your new job?"

David listened attentively throughout her enthusiastic chatter, nodding approvingly until she finally came to Mr Taylor. "Now he's one client I never want to meet."

David's lips twitched with amusement, but his voice was serious as he asked, "Why's that?"

The invitation was all she needed to give full vent to her feelings. "He's like a slimy slug when he wants something, but when he can't get his own way he becomes a nasty bully." She screwed up her face and shivered, "Ugh! His language… he's just a horrible man."

Somewhat bemused by her outburst, David muttered, "Well, well!" causing her to consider if she'd overdone her criticism. Guilt crept in again. She stared down at her hands. "So, Jane… we'll have to hope that when you meet him face to face he'll be more pleasant."

Startled, she gasped, "He's coming here?"

The smile on David's face was close to a smirk as he broke into song to the tune of, 'There's a hole in my bucket, dear Liza, dear Liza'. Instead he sang, "You're going to Brussels, dear Jane, dear Jane, you're going to Brussels, dear Jane, Brussels!" He chuckled at her astonishment.

"I hope you've got a passport?"

"Yes, but...."

"Buts, Jane, are not part of the job! Grace needs someone to help her with hosting the English personnel. There'll be some secretarial work, but mainly you'll be visiting stands, chatting with exhibitors, helping them with their problems, hosting the buffet luncheons each day – oh, and there'll be a couple of evening social occasions."

She could only squeak, "Me? Why me?"

"Why not you? You're Grace's assistant. And by the time you've finished this list of calls, you'll have been in contact with most of the exhibitors." He called over her head, "Grace. It seems sensible to us that Jane should come to Brussels with us?"

Grace entered on cue. "If you're as good at meeting people as you are chatting to them on the telephone – yes, very sensible."

Anxious, Jane jumped to her feet. "But Grace, I've never done anything like this before. What will I say? And what will I wear?"

"Oh, ITP will supply your official clothes – white blouse, navy skirt and navy and red scarf, but I expect...." Grace paused and looked across at David. "Am I right in believing, David, that ITP could help out with the cost of any social garments Jane might need?"

David dismissively waved his hand. "Oh yes, yes! I'm sure that's possible, but you girls can sort that out later. So now, Jane, as to 'what will you say?'" He arose and walked towards her with a taunting smile. "I may have dumbfounded you briefly, but I'm sure it won't last long. And no doubt, should Mr Taylor overstep the mark, you will – in your own inimitable way – put him in his place."

Without thinking, Jane threw him a playful blow in the stomach, along with her favourite punch line! "You are awful, but I like you." But the sight of Grace's stunned face was enough for Jane to clamp her hand over mouth and

138

stare in wide-eyed horror.

David, arms folded, studied her thoughtfully.

Grace spoke first. "Time perhaps to add referee to my job description?"

David's fingers drummed against his upper arm. "That won't be necessary Grace. I think Jane knows that attacking the boss could be rather career limiting. As would dealing with Mr Taylor in a similar fashion. But if the spirit behind it is positive I will enjoy considering a suitable retaliation. It could prove, let's say, interesting!"

Jane didn't dare ask what he had in mind, but she guessed from his expression that he would find some way to amuse himself at her expense!

Surreptitiously, Jane glanced across the aisle of the plane at David, intent on his paperwork. In the past few weeks, David had only been in the office long enough to issue instructions, which she and Grace had worked late most nights trying to accomplish. When she hadn't been too tired to think, she'd fluctuated between excitement at going to Brussels and fear of failure.

Her mother's words echoed in her head: "Working for David Reinhardt is one thing, but foreign travel and hosting exhibitions is another. Whatever next?" Despite Jane's reassurances, her mother still wasn't happy. Neither was Bruce, judging from his rather morose and remote attitude. How fortunate that Grace had been a continual boost to her confidence.

The air hostess, handing out snacks and asking if they wanted tea or coffee, brought both Jane and Grace out of their thoughts. "You're unusually quiet, Jane. Are you afraid of flying?" asked Grace.

Jane frowned. "Not flying, but I am afraid about my role at the exhibition. Do you enjoy this sort of thing?"

Grace smiled. "If you mean being out of the office, yes I enjoy the break from routine. And I love flying. When I see the land mapped out so far below me, it causes me to ask, as David, who wrote the Psalms, 'What is man, that thou art mindful of him?'"

At the mention of his name, David glanced across at them then, realizing Grace wasn't referring to him, returned to his work. Jane, surprised at Grace quoting scripture, was about to speak when she went on, "You know, Jane, in some ways I was like you at your age." Grace gave a wistful smile. "I became a Christian forty years ago at an evangelistic rally held in the Royal Albert Hall. I don't suppose you have ever heard of Aimee Semple McPherson? No, I thought not. She was an American, and not very well received over here. But, as a teenager hearing a woman speak of God's all embracing love, I wanted to experience it. I was so moved that I pushed through the crowds and Aimee prayed with me as I made that commitment to love Him with all my heart, all my soul and all that is within me. And I have never found any human love to match His since."

"I'd say, Grace, you live up to your name. But why haven't you mentioned it before?"

Grace gave a smile. "Thank you Jane. Bless you. I really don't feel that the office is the place to talk on personal issues, I suppose I feel I'm paid to work. I now live quietly with my faith and don't feel the need to talk to everyone about it. It's alright, Jane, don't look so worried. I'm not saying you can't talk about it at work, in fact I find your enthusiasm refreshing. When you're older, you'll realize there's a contentment and peace in knowing that God works through you without having to say anything."

Jane nodded, but reflected that Grace was probably content to go to some staid and boring church, whereas her church was called evangelical because she and others were excited enough to want to share their experiences of Jesus in their lives. "So you're content with your life and being a career woman?"

Across the aisle she heard David said softly, "Jane!" With a quick turn of her head, she saw his frown and realized perhaps her words had been rather blunt. "Oh Grace, I'm sorry. I didn't mean that to come out like it sounded."

"I know." Grace smiled, but her answer was thoughtful. "I've learnt to be content. I believe that has, up to now, been God's plan for me. Certainly I enjoy my job." She shrugged. "But I suppose like most women I hoped I'd have a husband, but... well... it's never too late." There was a hint of sadness as she continued, "God does lead us. He knows what's best for us, even if it sometimes seems difficult or hard."

Jane glanced apprehensively at Grace, and hoped God's best for her life wouldn't be like that. She considered the possibility while eating her club sandwich. When she finished, she found herself voicing what was on her mind. "I wonder if I should be content with my boyfriend, Bruce? He is a good man, but ..." Her face puckered, "... oh, I don't know!"

In a motherly gesture, Grace patted Jane's arm. "You're young – there's plenty of time."

"Yes, I know, but it isn't always easy to know what's right and what's wrong. Look what happened when I went out with Andrew Carlton."

"Just look on every mistake as an opportunity to learn. And I think you probably knew that getting involved with Andrew wasn't right."

Jane was about to say she had only intended enjoying a meal with Andrew, but she held it back. Instead, she sighed with a nod. Grace was right. Even if he'd been all she'd hoped for, she knew it couldn't have gone further.

"Just press into God and he'll guide you." Grace pointed to the 'fasten your seat belts' sign that had just come on. "Now I'll pray the pilot will guide us safely down on to the runway!"

Being a first class passenger certainly had its benefits. Jane had only flown once, to Majorca, and what a difference! They were whisked through, so there were no queues for passport checks or luggage, and a chauffeur-driven limousine delivered them to the hotel. It was even better at the hotel as she found she had a large bedroom with en-suite bathroom all to herself. The bell boy placed her suitcase on a low shelf, David tipped him and moved down the corridor with Grace to the adjacent bedrooms. For a moment she didn't move just taking it all in: the large double bed with the bathroom opposite it, a built-in dressing table and large mirror, and all that wardrobe space just for her.

She opened her suitcase and drew out the gown she'd worn at the Midsummer Ball. When purchased it had been a spur of the moment extravagance in both cost and style. The material shimmered with turquoise and green hues. Holding the thin straps, she held it against herself and twirled in front of the long mirror. Once on, it hugged every inch of her 32-22-34 figure from the built-in bra down to the ankle-length hemline. In June, people had admired the gown, but only Ian had been brave enough to admire her vital statistics! Had it been the dress that incited Andrew's behaviour in David's office? Quickly she consigned it to a hanger, and hoped it wasn't too daring for the Celebratory Ball at the end of the Exhibition.

The suitcase was nearly empty and she was just hanging up her newly acquired white blouses, when a loud and authoritative knock at the door was enough to tell her David was outside!

A wide grin and a chirpy comment were on her lips as she opened it but, before she could utter a word, David thrust several sheets of foolscap paper at her and commanded, "You'll need to study these before tomorrow. Did you bring your swimming things? There's a pool in basement. I'm off to a meeting. I've booked a table for us in the hotel restaurant for eight o'clock. I'll collect you on the way down." With that he was off down the corridor.

At his retreating figure she raised her hand, saluted and said very loudly, "Yes, Sir!"

David whirled, threw her a broad smile, a quick wave and continued his brisk walk to the lift.

With a shake of her head Jane closed the door and finished her unpacking. As she placed the photo of her Mum and Dad on the bedside table she questioned, "Well Dad, what would you have made of me being here?" The telephone shrilling beside her made her jump. It took a moment for her to regain her composure and answer it.

"Jane, it's Grace. I hope you don't mind being on your own for a while, but a friend of mine has just rung so I'm going out. David's booked at table for eight so I'll be back in plenty of time for that."

"That's fine. I've got David's instructions to read, then I'll explore the hotel and have a swim, so see you later."

Down below in the busy street cars were hooting, pedestrians rushing to and fro, but with the sun streaming in the bedroom it seemed a haven of peace. She curled up in the chair by the window and began to study David's sheets of notes and timetable. Tomorrow, the press reception and lunch. After that a tour of the exhibition halls, being introduced to the English exhibitors and ironing out any last minute problems. And, she sighed, no doubt meeting the obnoxious Mr Taylor. Nikki, who had accompanied David and Grace last year, had told her, "The exhibitors are a really friendly bunch. Don't worry – they'll love you." But had Nikki said that because she wanted to stay at home with her new husband?

With David's notes read and hopefully digested, it seemed a good time to venture out of her room. The thought was somewhat daunting, having never been on her own in a hotel or a foreign country before. The long corridor seemed so silent and empty. Opposite her room, glass doors revealed a large room with comfortable chairs facing the TV while on the right, square tables had pretty cloths on. She'd been told that a light breakfast was served between 7 and 10am, and during the day snacks and drinks were available from the pantry. How silly, then, for her to feel like an intruder by walking through the tables to the small kitchen that had a large 'please help yourself' sign. It was well equipped for hot and cold drinks and, having helped herself from the fridge to a glass of orange juice, she sat at one of the tables and nibbled her way through one of the chocolate bars from an overfilled basket. Breakfast wasn't something she usually had time for, so a light pastry with a cup of coffee would be all she'd want each morning. But she suspected Grace and David might go for the full cooked breakfast served in the Starlight Restaurant, or perhaps decide on something from the room service menu..

First, she visited the shops in the hotel lobby on the ground floor, though she expected they'd be expensive. The prices had her eyes nearly popping out of their sockets, and she could only hope Brussels had a shopping centre nearby where she could purchase some less expensive gifts to take home. Next, she located the main bar, the Starlight Restaurant and the Ballroom. Wide stairs wound from ground to first floor, where she found another bar for hotel guests only. The friendly, bored young barman, John, took great delight in chatting to her, and showing her the TV lounge and the leather chaired, newspaper scattered, reading room/quiet lounge. He then directed her to the basement for a swim. But she'd no intention of taking up his offer of a drink at his bar later.

The pool wasn't big, but was divided into four lanes. Several people were taking advantage of the warm water, but it was empty enough for her to swim twenty lengths without interruption and bask in the thought that she was being paid to do this! A few lengths later, she became aware that the swimmers in the lanes on either side of her were shadowing her. Perhaps they wanted a race. She changed from breaststroke to crawl and cut through the water, but after four lengths she realized she was no match for their healthy bodies and slowed in the shallow end where two young men were waiting for her. With a smile, she pulled off her swimming cap, shook out her hair and admitted, "I'm afraid my swimming isn't as good as yours!"

A look passed between them. The taller, and more swarthy, man spoke. "Yes. You don't mind us?"

"Of course not."

"You are staying 'ere?"

"Yes, I'm working at the Exhibition Centre."

"Aha! This fortunate. I, Jacques. Stephan and I, we from France, work at centre too. You'll 'ave drink with us?"

To be polite, Jane introduced herself, but declined their offer, not wanting to seem too friendly.

Jacques nodded. "You 'ave boyfriend, 'usband 'ere?"

"No. Just my boss and his assistant."

"We will see you again?"

"Maybe." She climbed out of the pool and then, remembering her school French, called, "Au Revoir," before disappearing into the changing room.

Afterwards, with nothing much to do until 8 o'clpck, she wished she'd taken up their offer, but this was supposed to be work and David might not have been happy to find her drinking coffee with two young men she'd picked up in the first afternoon!

The restaurant was large, but not very full. Over dinner, David talked of the Exhibition, and the Ball to be held on the last night using both the Starlight restaurant and the ballroom. He indicated the partition which would be opened to make more space, and then discussed with Grace the pros and cons of last year's layout. Jane listened and enjoyed the excellent meal and the warm glow from the wine she consumed. It felt strange having a meal with David and Grace.

Over coffee, David suggested, "Well, we've an early start and busy day tomorrow. I think, Grace, it would be good if we had an early night." Jane allowed a snigger to escape. "Something amusing you, Jane?"

"Err, nothing really." It was difficult to keep a straight face, and she knew how he could be like a dog with a bone.

"Well you obviously thought 'nothing' was funny."

"When I said nothing, I meant nothing you'd want to hear."

David's eyebrows raised, his mouth twisted into a wry smile. "Is that so?" He glanced at Grace. "I'm sure Grace and I will find it equally entertaining."

Grace, with greater discernment, looked doubtful, giving Jane to think she remembered a certain incident in the canteen not so long ago!

"Don't say then I didn't warn you!" Before David could comment further, she continued before laughter at her thoughts burst out. "It struck me, sitting here with you and Grace, it was rather like eating out with my parents." Grace smiled faintly. David stiffened. In glee, she expanded, "So, when you said, 'I think, Grace, we ought to have an early night,' you sounded just like my Dad." Into David's bemused expression she smiled sweetly and rambled, "Of course, my Dad would have said, 'Grace dear' or, because my Mum's name is Joyce, 'Joyce dear', but then, of course he would say 'dear' because they were married, well they would be wouldn't they, being my parents, and then, of course, like you both they are a lot older than me, and probably need an early.... "

Despite being prepared she jumped as David boomed, "Stop! I've heard enough."

Jane grinned, "I was wondering just how much more I could think of to say to get a reaction...." She giggled wickedly.

David gazed at her as though digesting her words. Grace glanced at him and, to break the silence, said, "Well, I think I'll have an early night, and as I am old enough to qualify for the role of your Mum I'll take that as a compliment."

"Well, I'm not!"

With mirth, Jane had to ask, "What, qualified to be my Mum or taking what I said as a compliment?"

David caught up his serviette, tossed it onto the table and stood. "I'm not that old."

Jane made a long face at Grace, who responded with a slow shake of the head.

"So, young lady, my assumption can only be that, as you held you father in high regard, it is to that you make your comparison. That being so, Jane, you'll take my advice on having an early night!" David, now standing behind Grace's chair, indicated she should rise and, as she did, Jane jumped up to chirp happily, "Yes, Dad."

David glowered at her, then strode ahead of them to open the door. As they went through Grace commented, "You know Jane, I thought it was only women who were suppose to get tetchy about their age!"

Jane stole a look at David. His raised eyebrows indicated he was surprised at Grace entering their banter. But Jane was equally surprised to see Grace give David a wry but cheeky smile.

Jane had to admit that David's early night proved it's worth. Yesterday had felt like a holiday, but today had called on every resource she could muster. Before lunch, she walked the entire exhibition with the press corps. During lunch, she'd been followed around by a rotund and spotty youth intent on getting a date with her. After lunch, she handled endless queries from the British exhibitors. Now, most of the exhibitors had packed up for the day and, exhausted, she was looking forward to doing the same.

She recognised his voice even before he accosted her. Mr Taylor was a middle-aged, bespectacled man, who although rather nondescript, used his belligerent manner to make up for his lack of physical presence. His greeting was a tide of verbal abuse and blasphemy. To combat his aggression she gave him her hardest stare and spoke in her coldest voice, which only seemed to fuel his anger.

He eyed her with disdain, raked his thinning hair and, with saliva gathered in the corner of his thick rubbery lips, demanded, his words peppered with expletives, "What the hell is a young slip of a girl like you doing here? And who are you tell me what I can exhibit and where?" As she stepped back to get out of spittle range, she thought how rare it was for her to feel such revulsion for another human being. Her answers seemed to antagonise him further as, finger wagging, he advanced toward her. As her back touched the wall of a stand she tried to sidestep out of his way. Mr Taylor thwarted this move by thrusting his foul-breathed face into hers and, spiced with obscenities, he squealed in his effeminate voice, "My god, you're barely out of nappies. You cheeky little brat. How dare you have the effrontery speak to me like that. You need taking in hand. It's time someone gave you a damn good hiding."

His full-frontal assault upon her senses was beginning to overwhelm her. He was one very nasty man, and she hadn't the wherewithal to know how to deal with him. She prayed for someone to come along, or a strategy to escape him. An idea popped into her head. She drew herself up against the wall and made herself as tall as possible, then stared over his shoulder as if something or someone was there. Mr Taylor stopped mid-sentence and swivelled his head to see what had taken her attention. Jane seized the opportunity, pushed past him, ran to the wooden swing doors that led from the hall and dived into the Ladies' toilet.

Upset and shaking, she leaned against the sink and

looked at herself in the mirror. She shouldn't have come. She should have listened to her mother. She couldn't cope with men like him. Rosemary was tame in comparison. Slowly fear gave way to anger. What a horrid little man, spoiling what had been such a good day. She never wanted to set eyes on him again. She'd avoid him and that area in future. Was he waiting for her outside? A cautious peek revealed not. At least, her comfortable low heeled shoes meant she could slip quickly and quietly down the stairs. Across the lower hall was the Overseas lounge, where they had an office, she'd feel better after a cup of sweet tea. On entering the lower hall she turned a corner and spotted David talking to a group of people. She certainly didn't want to talk to him just now but, as if sensing her presence, he looked across, smiled and, excusing himself, headed towards her.

"Hello, Jane, how's it going?" With his cheery face asking that question, she couldn't stop the tears welling up in her eyes.

David gave a low grunt, caught her elbow and steered her into a quiet spot. "What's happened?"

"I-I can't deal with Mr Taylor."

"Of course you can."

"I can't. He's so awful. He's so rude. I'm just not used to people like him."

"What did he say?"

"I can't repeat it. Please don't make me."

"Jane, nobody is going to make you do anything, but I can't help unless you tell me the problem. Stay here while I find a couple of chairs, then we'll sit down and sort this out." Jane wiped her eyes with the back of her hand as she watched David commandeer two fold-up chairs from a nearby exhibitor and put them around a corner where no one could see them. "Right, Jane," David sat back, held his ankle on his knee, and gave her a brief but encouraging smile. "When you're ready…."

Much as she wanted to tell David everything, she couldn't bring herself to repeat Mr Taylor's foul language but gave an idea of his offensive words. David's smile quickly turned grim, his relaxed manner to sitting up straight, and his face tightened into an intimidating mask. A feeling of triumph soared through her. This would be the end of the horrible Mr Taylor – she warmed to her tale....

David raised his hand. "Right Jane. That will do. So far all I've heard is Mr Taylor's demands and what he called you. Now I want you to start again and tell me, step by step, what he asked and how you answered. Can you manage that?"

Puzzled, she nodded and recaptured the scene. "So he said, 'You're the … idiot who is working for ITP. You're no more than a …. chit of a girl who thinks she knows it all.' Then he went into a tirade about everything, including me, the exhibition, how he exhibits annually and how he should have a stand on the main drag of the exhibition, not some … poxy, dark, poky corner."

David looked thoughtful. "Now give me the exact words of your reply?"

"I think I said – and I was feeling cross at what he'd called me – 'If you would just let me speak Mr Taylor, then I'd answer you. And I can tell you that if you'd booked a stand even two months ago, you could have been on the main aisle. You didn't, so you just have to have what's left.' Well, then he got offensive again, saying how he should get preferential treatment. So I told him that the majority of exhibitors return every year. And it was quite simple – they knew if they filled out their forms and returned them quickly they'd get what they wanted. He didn't like that, and blustered away and then complained that his stand had no electrical points and what was he paying all this … money for if he didn't get the service?"

"Go on – your exact words please?"

"Well, I was finding it even harder now to keep my

temper so it was something like, 'As I said before, Mr Taylor, if you can't be bothered to fill in the forms we send you, then we can't be expected to know your needs'. Then off he went again, saying he'd rung the office to give them. I answered that by saying, 'I told you on the telephone weeks ago that we couldn't complete the forms on your behalf as they have to be signed by you. I also remember telling you then that, if you had a problem with the stand you were allocated, that you'd have to speak to Mr Reinhardt. So, did you do that?' He started off again with more abuse, finishing with he would have thought anyone with any intelligence would have known his stand would need electricity."

"And your reply?"

Jane grimaced. "Err, I think I said I'd have thought anyone with any intelligence would be able to complete, sign and return a simple form. Then he swore again and said it was my job to have reminded him. So I told him we have more than a hundred exhibitors, and if they can all get their forms in on time I didn't see why he couldn't and he had no one else to blame but himself. We aren't mind readers or babysitters."

A faint smile hovered around David's mouth as he asked, "Shall we go on, or would you say we're getting a clearer picture?" Tears filled her eyes as she realized her words and attitude had probably exacerbated Mr Taylor's anger. "However, Jane, that doesn't mean I condone Mr Taylor's behaviour."

That crumb of comfort didn't help. She sat with head bent, the tears trickling down her cheeks into her lap.

David drew his chair nearer, to say quietly, "Look at me, Jane." Instead of the anger or reproach she'd expected, his eyes were filled with warmth and understanding. "There's no need to get so upset. The situation isn't irretrievable." He pulled his handkerchief from his top pocket. "Here, take this and mop up those tears."

"But I've let you down. I didn't mean to. I'm sorry."

"It really isn't that bad. I think between us we can sort this out." He stood and patted her shoulder.

Her voice wavered as looking up at him she asked, "What do you want me to do?"

"I think an apology to Mr Taylor is in order, don't you?"

"Oh no!"

"Oh yes, Jane!"

Not wanting to fail him again, she gave several sniffs and mumbled, "I suppose so, if I have to."

David's response was almost jovial. "That's my girl! Now back to the Ladies', put on a bit of make up, and then I'll come with you."

"Oh no! Couldn't I go on my own? I'll be ever so polite this time."

"I think it would be a lot safer if I accompanied you. I have a few words I'd like to say to Mr Taylor – ones which I think you should hear."

Although she found David's presence during her apology to be intimidating, if he hadn't been there her polite and penitent words would have been even more quickly and belligerently shouted down by Mr Taylor. The tightening of David's fingers at her elbow warned her not to respond.

However, after her apology had been grudgingly accepted, Jane witnessed the awesome Mr Reinhardt in action. With consummate skill he didn't accuse Mr Taylor, but brought him to acknowledge the error of his ways! By the time David had finished, the man was apologising for his bad language, was humbled enough to ask for her forgiveness, had accepted that the location of his stand and his lack of equipment were his responsibility, and mumbled profuse gratitude at David's promise to organise the electricity he needed. No wonder David commanded such respect from and had a reputation for fairness.

The lift rose to the fifth floor. Jane sighed, her back, legs and feet ached. It had been a gruelling day and not one she would want to repeat.

"What's the matter Jane, can't keep up the pace?"

She made a face at David, who was still bright-eyed and obviously still raring to go, as he commanded, "I'll meet you both in Reception in half an hour, then we'll find somewhere to eat. I'm starving."

"Oh, do I have to?"

"Now, Jane, I hope that isn't reluctance to spending time in my company?"

The lift doors opened onto their floor. Wearily, she muttered, "I just want a hot bath and bed."

David headed off down the corridor as if he hadn't heard. Grace followed, while Jane, hobbling painfully behind, stopped, pulled off her shoes and wailed, "It's no good, I can't wear these a moment longer."

Grace had already reached her door, while David was nearly at his. At her wail, he turned and boomed down the corridor, "Oh, by the way, Jane, Mr Taylor asked if we'd like to go to lunch with him tomorrow." He gave his boom of laughter and added in an amused voice, "And, by the way, I'm not a mind reader, but can understand that a mere chit of a girl like you might need an early night and...."

He laughed again, but stopped wide-eyed as a shoe flew through the air past Grace towards him. In a reflex action he lifted his right hand and caught it. Grace stood transfixed with an open mouth, obviously this was not something she expected to experience. So Jane threw the second one – which David caught with equal dexterity in his left hand.

. "Well, well, well, young Jane. Is this the way a lady behaves?" David slowly advanced toward her. "What was it Mr Taylor recommended you needed?"

Now at her door, Jane put the key in the lock. "You wouldn't dare!" But a look at David's face reminded her he enjoyed a challenge! She opened her door, and a glance showed David nearly upon her and Grace shaking her head in disbelief. Without hesitation and on a squeal, she leapt inside and shut the door. The wood barely cushioned the now familiar roar of David's laughter. She berated herself for not standing her ground, for David would never do anything that foolish.

An hour later, having enjoyed a long soak in the bath, the light tapping at her door told her that it certainly wasn't David coming to find out where she was. Cautiously, she peered out. Beside a trolley, a young man smiled and cheerfully announced, "Good evening, Madam. Room 508 has ordered a meal for you."

Jane stepped back to let him in, and noticed that the occupant of 508 had also neatly placed her shoes by the door with a little note. She picked them and it up and read, 'You'll probably sleep better knowing that I declined Mr Taylor's kind invitation to lunch! David'.

A pattern formed for Jane during the next few days. Rise at 8.00am, followed by breakfast with Grace at 8.30 in the lounge opposite. David ate the cooked breakfast in the restaurant, but joined them about 8.45 for coffee so they could discuss the day ahead. Then off to the exhibition hall, where the doors opened at 10.00.

Her first hour or so was spent touring the English exhibitors' stands, supplying information on expected visits or events and answering any queries. In the Exhibitors' Overseas Lounge, she used the facilities to type David's correspondence and reports, and follow up exhibitors' problems and queries. Her short coffee break might be with David or Grace, or an exhibitor using the lounge. If possible, she avoided Mr Taylor, although he was now the epitome of politeness. Jacques, the swimmer, joined her on one occasion. He was a few years older than her, but his courteous attitude made her feel confident and attractive.

She and Grace hosted, and ate at, the buffet lunch for the English exhibitors between 12.30 and 2.30. Conversation became easier as the days went by, as did putting names to faces. By the fifth day, people were making a beeline to talk to her, rather than she sidling up to them. David insisted that after lunch she and Grace take a two-hour break as the exhibition didn't close until 8.00 pm. The latter part of the afternoon and evening were usually quiet, giving her an opportunity to prepare the daily reports and the timetable of special events and visits to be handed to exhibitors the following morning.

Several afternoons, she returned to the hotel and swam. On one occasion, she explored the district with Grace, after which she felt more confident roaming around on her own. The only day she actually tried to rest during the afternoon break was before the English Exhibitors' Dinner, which she knew would mean an extra-late night.

The meal was a very formal affair with after-dinner speeches, the majority extremely boring. Even during David's final address, which was more entertaining, it was difficult to stifle her yawns.

To her embarrassment, David noticed and smiled broadly before unmercifully drawing everyone's attention to her. "I see my secretary is yawning. I'll take that as a sign to say thank you and bid you all goodnight."

In the ensuing applause and laughter, all eyes seemed riveted on her. Fortunately, by now she knew most of those present, so she uninhibitedly grinned, stretched and yawned again before stifling it with the back of her hand and indicating just how bored she'd been. David's eyebrows had risen, but those around her found it amusing.

Next morning, waking with a bit of a headache, she wondered if David would express annoyance at her behaviour. But as they ate their croissants and drank their coffee, he merely talked about the business of the day.

About to move into the day, David stood and pulled out two envelopes from his jacket. "Before we leave, I want you to take these. It's just a little personal thank you from me — a small bonus. A token of my appreciation of your support and hard work."

Jane smiled at his thoughtfulness. Grace spoke for both of them. "David you know you don't have to do this. We are both well paid, especially with the weekend, and extra pay for the late functions, but thank you, it's nice to know we're so appreciated."

"Well give yourselves a treat. I know it isn't long to Christmas, but don't just use it to buy presents for others."

David strode towards the door as Jane echoed her thanks. With a hand acknowledgement, he disappeared down the corridor to his room.

The arrival of a waiter at their table to announce a telephone call for Grace stopped Jane's comment on David's gesture. Back in her room, Jane opened her envelope — the 'small bonus' was enough to buy the whole family and herself a Christmas present.

Elated, she was almost singing as she left her room so, seeing David entering the lift at the end of the hall, she forgot protocol, shouted his name, and ran toward the lift. David's hand snaked out to hold the door. Breathless, she said, "Thanks" and as they were alone, she happily chattered, "And thanks again for that 'small bonus'. It'll buy all my Christmas presents and a leather handbag I saw and liked the other day. What a thoughtful, generous man you are." Without pause or thought, she stretched up and kissed his cheek. "And, about last night — I did overdo the yawning, but it was you who drew attention to me." Her nose crinkled, "You know you are awful — but I love you."

The amused smile froze on his face, his dark eyes seemed to pierce through her. The lift pinged, breaking the moment. As the doors opened to admit others she slipped her hand from his arm. A glance in his direction revealed a fixed stare at the lift doors and, once on the ground floor, he left without a backward glance of farewell. Oh dear. She could only suppose that once again she'd overstepped the boundaries of the secretary and boss relationship.

The tannoy announced, "The Exhibition is closing in five minutes. Will all visitors please make their way to the exits." Time had really sped by since she had returned with Grace from their shopping trip. Probably because she'd been so intent photocopying, and collating the paper as it spilled out of the machine. She hurried her steps to the Overseas Lounge. With her hands full of piled stapled information she backed through the doors and was surprised to find it deserted. Where was Grace? Fifteen minutes later the caretaker arrived, and it was obvious from his gestures, and her smattering of French, that he wanted to lock up. It was strange to feel abandoned, but it wasn't as if she didn't know her way back to the hotel, or have money for a taxi.

The night was dark, the pavements shining and wet with rain. Taxis were few, filled and far between. She began to walk. Light, cold rain started — it was time to call in a favour... "Lord, please find me a taxi." It was as if the request had an instant answer. A taxi came down the road towards her. Seeing her hail, the driver did a swerve turn on the road and swished in beside her. His tyres drew the water on the road into a wave which came up, hit the kerb and drenched her skirt, legs and shoes. Eyes raised heavenwards, she said, "Oh, thanks Lord! Should I have added to my request, because I don't want to get any wetter!"

The taxi driver, probably thinking she was berating him, waved his hands, indicating she should get in. Automatically she gave him the name of the hotel and sat down while he babbled full pelt in French before driving off at speed, throwing her back into the seat and making her wonder if she wouldn't have been safer wet and walking.

Three minutes later, after a bout of unintelligible words, she was at the hotel, his refusal of payment bringing the understanding he'd been apologising for soaking her.

Anxious for a hot bath, she ran up the front steps, smiled at the doorman's gentle smile of sympathy, rushed into the hotel lobby and found herself in the midst of a seething mass of humanity in evening dress. People stood, sat, or milled about as waiters with trays held high delivered drinks, commissionaires matched names to taxis, and people greeted each other as long lost friends. It was as if she'd walked in on a party uninvited and improperly dressed. Embarrassed, and noticing some odd stares at her waif and stray appearance, Jane ducked and dived her way across the foyer and prayed no one she knew would come down in it. But when the doors opened Grace stepped out, looking extremely attractive in a red cocktail dress, her hair freshly set and her face glowing.

"Good grief, Jane, what happened to you?"

"Do you mean I've been missed, because I'm soaked through by the rain, or why aren't I dressed up like you?"

"Oh Jane, I'm sorry! I guess David didn't tell you I'd left early. I've pushed a note under your door to explain. Oh dear, you certainly do look rather bedraggled. I've been invited by a friend to join the dinner dance that the German exhibitors are having in the Starlight Restaurant." Grace's eyes scanned the noisy throng. "It was a bit of a last minute thing, but when I mentioned it to David, he insisted I take time off. I managed to get an appointment in the hotel beauty salon, so I left in a bit of a rush. David's dining with clients, so I'm afraid you'll be on your own tonight."

The evening visits to different restaurants with Grace, and sometimes David, had become a highlight of her day, but she wasn't going to show her disappointment. "Well, I'm looking forward to luxuriating in a hot bath, and I've still got Bruce and Ted's presents to get tomorrow, so I think I'll be happy to have an early night and use room service. By the way Grace, you look absolutely stunning — this friend wouldn't happen to be male, would he?"

Grace blushed and moved past her. "Sorry, Jane, must go." By the time Jane turned, Grace was swallowed up in the crowd.

CHAPTER 9

The following morning, Grace wasn't at all forthcoming about her evening, but she certainly had an after-glow about her. That afternoon, having meandered around the large store's various departments, Jane still hadn't found anything for Bruce and Ted. She was just beginning to despair when she heard someone calling her name.

"Jane! Jane! Ah, 'tis you." Jacques edged his way around the counter, lifted her hand and kissed her fingers. "And why you 'ere in zis Gent's Department?"

"Looking for a present for my boyfriend and his father."

"I 'elp you."

For the next half hour, she and Jacques wrestled with ideas, colours and sizes until eventually she purchased several items that would make nice Christmas presents.

"Now, I think, café?"

Quickly she considered. The fact he wasn't a bronzed Adonis somehow made him seem safer. And she'd seen the range of delicious creamy cakes when she entered the store. How churlish it would sound if she refused!

Jacques was a bit of a clown, and his English was amusing. Also, the man's charm, impeccable manners and dapper clothes had their own attraction.

The coffee and cake were long gone when she remembered she was supposed to be working. Gathering her bags, she thanked Jacques and hurried to the store exit.

Jacques followed. "Jane it has been a pleasant time together, yes? 'Ow about you come out tonight? Stephan and I are going to a nightclub."

Jane hesitated. "Well, I usually go out for a meal with Grace and David. I don't know."

"You speak to them, yes? Stephan 'as Juliette while I

shall be a, 'ow do you say, a raspberry?"

Jane giggled, "No, gooseberry."

"Well, yes – no good berry then for me. You come, please?"

She admitted to herself it would be fun. Jacques knew that Bruce was her steady boyfriend — he'd helped choose his Christmas present — so there was no danger he'd want anything more than her company. With no time to ponder, she promised to meet Jacques in the hotel foyer at nine.

No-one noticed her late return. Grace had left her a note explaining that she and David were at the hotel finalising the details for the following evening's Celebratory Dinner Dance. Oh well, she'd tell them of her plans later. However, on her return to the hotel there was no sign of Grace or David, nor any messages.

Dressed in the black cocktail dress that ITP had generously funded for the English Exhibitors' dinner, Jane paced up and down her room and the corridor, wondering what to do. Well, she couldn't wait all evening — it was already five past nine. Grace had, last night, put a note under her door, she'd do the same. Hastily she scribbled on a sheet of hotel notepaper, 'Met up with Jacques and gone out to a night club with him. Be back late. Love Jane'.

The moment she arrived in the lobby, Jacques was by her side with a flourish of appraisal and the explanation that Stephan and Juliette would meet them at the nightclub. A brief twinge of doubt assailed her as they waited for the commissionaire to call a taxi, but she remembered David's words, 'Not every man of the world is like Andrew'. Was this spreading her wings too far? Jacques was just a friendly exhibitor, and she'd ensured she'd money for a taxi home if there were unforeseen problems.

The nightclub was wonderful — but then she'd never been in one before! From their entry at the top of the circular building, she could see three tiers below her The dance floor was at the bottom of terraces of tables with pink cloths, matching lamps and pretty bowls of flowers. A small part of the circle was taken up with a stage where a six-man band played. Each tier was divided up into different party-sized areas — the top tier into smaller, more intimate, booths. It came as a relief when Jacques pointed to Stephan and Juliette, who were in full view of everyone as they sat among the many smaller tables around the dance floor.

Juliette spoke only French, so Stephan's need to translate everything against the sound of the music became quickly tiresome. Even the conversation between her and Jacques was limited. She was just beginning to wish she hadn't come, when Jacques suggested they dance. The empty dance floor didn't seem to put Jacques off, and the reason became quickly apparent — he was an accomplished dancer.

Ballroom dancing was something Bruce and she did enjoy, and they'd both gained gold medals. The dancing school had a social evening once a month but, outside of that, this was the first opportunity she'd had to show off her skills.

Jacques could almost have been Bruce as they melded together, and she became lost in the steps and the music. It was only when Jacques pulled her close at the end of a cha cha, to tell her Stephan was indicating the food had arrived, that she took breath. A ripple of clapping came from the tiers of tables, causing her to look up with surprise. Jacques laughed. "I zink zese people zink we are part of the floor show." He turned and gave her a low bow. Grinning, she played along and curtsied.

The real cabaret started while they were eating. After that, the floor filled and dancing was cheek to cheek. It was inevitable Jacques would want to hold her tight and, as she was having such a marvellous time, she responded by putting her arms round his neck as they moved slowly around the floor. Later, in need of a drink, they returned to the table. It was then Jane realised it was three o'clock! With widened eyes, she pointed at her watch.

Jacques frowned. "A problem?"

"I hope not." Jane picked up her bag. "We'd better go. I'm supposed to be here to work. I have to be up at eight. I won't be popular if I'm half asleep tomorrow — oh, today!"

Jacques caught the gist and murmured an explanation in French to Stephan as Jane, waving goodbye, was already moving up the stairs to the exit.

The hotel foyer at 3.15 in the morning seemed hushed, with only the night porter and the receptionist going quietly about their business. The eerie stillness of the corridor as they stepped out of the lift caused Jane to giggle nervously.

Jacques took the key from her hand and opened her door. About to whisper 'thank you', she squealed as Jacques, with an actor's flourish, caught her in his arms and kissed her. In essence, his kiss was similar to Bruce's, not heart-stopping but mildly pleasant, so she wound her arms around his neck and returned it. As the depth of his passion increased, Jane broke away and was about to whisper it was time he went home, when Jacques stiffened, his eyes fixed behind her.

Puzzled, she turned to see what he was staring at. There, framed in the TV lounge doorway, was David's large shape. Ignoring his stern face she chirped, "Oh, hello, David. Are you still up? This is Jacques. Jacques, meet David Reinhardt. He's my boss."

Astonished, she saw David very visibly fighting to control his temper.

Jacques moved forward extending his hand, his English stilted in politeness. "'Ow do you do? We see time, late, sorry." Jacques' arm fell by his side as David, eyes blazing at Jane, ignored him. Puzzled, Jane gave him a stricken look.

No one moved. Then, as if a film had started, paused,

and started again, David outstretched his hand toward Jacques who, looking very uncomfortable, took it. David's tone was cold and curt in its politeness. "Thank you, Jacques, for your explanation and apology. We've been very worried as to Jane's whereabouts." Relief was evident on Jacques'. face. Jane realized she'd been holding her breath.

Now understanding his anger, Jane burst out, "But I left a note to say where I was going and I said I'd be back late!"

"Oh yes, Jane! So you did! How thoughtful! A note under Grace's door. Or was it thoughtless? A note so brief. No detail as to where you were. Or who you were with! No thought that we might be worried? And what about the time?" Each short sentence was like a shard of splintered glass piercing her happiness. She hadn't meant to cause any trouble. Tears welled up in her eyes.

Was it despair that made David shake his head at her? She blinked hard to clear her blurred vision. His attention moved to Jacques, his voice tight. "Thank you for seeing Jane to her door. I'm sure we all wish to get some sleep in what is left of the night, so please excuse my abruptness in bidding you goodnight."

Jacques' eyes questioned her. Resentment at David's attitude surged up within her. With a small apologetic smile she said, "Thank you for this evening, Jacques, I really enjoyed myself." David's disapproval was almost tangible, causing her to throw a derogatory look in his direction before adding, "I'm sorry about the evening ending like this. It's probably best you go, I'll be okay. See you tomorrow."

Jacques nodded, gave David a final puzzled glance, and set off down the corridor to the waiting lift.

The doors had barely closed on Jacques before David, with a firm hard grip on her elbow, propelled her into the lounge where he commanded, "Sit down."

Daunted, she found herself obeying and then being

imprisoned as he bent forward grasping the chair arms. Her mouth opened to protest, but she was bluntly told, "Keep quiet! You've caused enough trouble for one evening." Her chin rose in defiance. "Don't you ever learn? Didn't you realize the danger you could have been in? Did you even consider the stupidity of going heaven knows where, with heaven knows who? How were we to know who Jacques was?" Jane attempted to speak, but David cut her off. "Think of it from our point of view. Didn't it occur to you we'd be worried? I ask you — what possessed you to do something so foolish? My God, Jane! It's half past three in the morning." He stopped, ran his hand through his hair, swallowed hard, and asked in a thick voice, "Didn't it dawn on you how I might feel?"

Angrily, she spat out, "How you might feel? What about the embarrassment you've just caused me? Why all this fuss?

"Why? Why?" His eyes flashed like flint. "You ask me – why?" There was a pause. His mouth twisted in fury and then, regaining his composure, he bit out, "Your mother."

Surprised, she echoed questioningly, "My mother?"

"Well, I've no doubt she would hold me accountable if you came to any harm."

"I don't see why!"

"You don't see why?" On a deep breath, he moved his head slowly from side to side as if unable to comprehend her lack of understanding, then closed his eyes as if to preserve his sanity. He re-opened them to say more calmly, "Jane, I can't remember ever feeling so angry with anyone as I am with you tonight." She remembered the report of his row with Andrew, but thought it best not to remind him. "Whether you like it or not, I feel responsible for you."

Granted, given the benefit of hindsight, her note had been brief and they hadn't met Jacques, but even so....

Presuming responsibility for her! What arrogance! She burst out, "Well, I still don't see why!"

The hands that had gripped the chair suddenly caught hold of her upper arms. In shock, she gasped and looked wildly into his eyes, trying to fathom out what was driving him. That seemed to unleash his desire to shake her. One moment he was he wrenching up her toward him, his face so close to hers that for one witless moment she thought he was going to kiss her, and then on an exasperated sigh, she was thrust back on to the chair.

In shock. she gazed mindlessly at him while he ranted, "You just don't see it do you? What shall I say? It's because you are working for me. Because I sanctioned you being here. Because I have your best interests at heart, or believe in a future for you. Is that enough? But what do you do? You act without considering the consequences. Why? You know your judgement of character is somewhat flawed!"

Jane's anger ignited. Oh, trust him to bring that up again!

David gave a heavy sigh, then continued in a more reasonable tone, "You are young, transparent, unprotected, vulnerable and naive. Sometimes you have a maturity beyond your years and, at other times, you act like a foolish child. Was it your intention for Jacques to stay the night? I suspect Jacques thought it was. Mr Taylor may be an obnoxious little man, but tonight I agree with him — you could do with a good old-fashioned spanking."

That did it. That really was the final insult. Without further ado she raised her hand and, with all the strength she could muster, slammed it against his face.

It had two effects. One was to immediately stop his harangue as his face shot sideways under its force, and the other was to bring tears to her eyes as her hand stung painfully. Slowly, David moved his head back. His eyes meeting hers were filled with anger and incredulity.

Strung with pent-up fury, her voice was a quiet, venomous hiss. "You employ me, but you don't own me, or my life!" David flinched. She glimpsed his hurt with perverse delight. "You have no right to speak to me like that. And as it is my life, I will do precisely what I want with it. No one asked you to be responsible for me, or my actions. I didn't expect you to wait up. Nor do you have any right to interfere. Or to be so rude to Jacques. Or thank him on my behalf. And furthermore, you may think you are Mister High and Mighty Reinhardt to whom we should all defer, but beyond being my boss during working hours, you are not my minder! And whether you think I'm a child or not, you aren't my father. In fact you are nothing to me!" His eyes closed against her words. Her anger abated, her voice gentled. "You may not think I can take care of myself, but I did weigh very carefully whether to go tonight. And, believe it or not, I was going to ask your advice."

David let go of the chair. She was no longer his prisoner. Yet, to her surprise, he didn't straighten to his usual stance of authority, but stood as a man crushed. Head bent, his anguished voice was scarcely audible, "It's hard, so hard, not to act like a father, especially when you care so deeply for the child."

Jane frowned. What was he talking about? Did he have a child? Perplexed, she watched him turn and walk away — his self-assuredness gone. Had she unwittingly unearthed some dark secret of his past? It seemed that in the heat of battle her words had, like lethal barbs, found their mark, tearing and lodging in the very fabric of the being that was David Reinhardt. Horrified, she realized how badly she'd wounded the man who had become a special friend. A friend who'd been there to rescue her from Andrew Carlton's clutches. A friend who'd cared for her when she was hurt. A friend who'd given her this wonderful job. A friend who'd listened and advised; and if that wasn't sufficient, a friend who cared enough to stay up and worry about her.

Tears streamed down her face. The old adage, 'Sticks and stones can break my bones, but words can never hurt me', certainly wasn't true. Words could damage and maim a person for life. When would she learn to control her tongue? How could she have been so nasty? In her heart she cried, 'Lord, please forgive me! Let David forgive me.'

In despair, she rushed down the corridor after him, grabbed his arm and placed herself between him and his bedroom door. Whispering hoarsely through tears, she sobbed, "David. Please, listen." Those usually expressive eyes were now dulled and empty of emotion. Dismay filled her but she hurried on, "I am so, so sorry for the things I just said. I was angry. David, believe me, you're the best friend I've ever had — I didn't mean to hurt and upset you. All because of my silly temper. You cared enough to worry, to stay up, to wait for me, and what did I do? Oh, David — please forgive me."

With unseeing eyes, he appeared rooted to the spot. Tears ran down her face, as she pleaded again. Desperate to get his attention, her grasp tightened on his arm, "David, listen to me. I was cruel and unfeeling when you cared so much. Forgive me." Her hand reached up and touch his cheek still red from .her blow, "I'm so sorry." Unconsciously her fingers stroked the spot as she spoke into him a litany of comfort and appreciation.

The movement of his arm gave cause for her to cry, "Please don't push me away."

Instead, his hand covered hers, trapping it against his face. Emotion shuddered through him. Anxiously she watched as he, awaking from his trance, refocused his eyes on her upturned face. With a painful swallow he drew her hand from his face to his chest. In a husky voice he murmured, "Jane," before his arms closed around her and drew her close. Just as she had with her father after their arguments, she turned her face into his warm, strong body. He rocked her gently against his chest while quietly repeating into her hair, "Oh Jane, Oh Jane."

Pushing back against the circle of his arms to look up at him, she asked wistfully, "Am I forgiven?" He nodded and drew her back into him. Pulling away again she asked, "Are we friends again?"

Emotion seemed to shake him — his answer was to nestle her against his chest, his head resting lightly on top of hers. Silently she breathed a prayer of thanksgiving. She was unaware how long they stood in the corridor locked together in mutual comfort but, when she made to move away, his hands gently encased her face and drew her head back, before he bent, lightly brushing her forehead with his lips. "I'll see you in the morning." Then moving her to one side he entered his bedroom and closed the door.

The suddenness of his departure left her momentarily dazed, but as she headed back to her room she was grateful that they seemed to have survived a major confrontation.

"Jane! Jane! Wake up!"

She turned over. That wasn't her mother's voice. It was Grace calling her name. Of course! Brussels; exhibition; work; David! Had the quarrel with him been real? She sat up and caught sight of the bedside clock. Nine thirty!

Grace's voice came through the door again. "Let me in Jane. I've got a cup of tea for you."

Jane jumped out of bed, rushed to the door, opened it and then dizzily sank back on the bed as Grace entered. "Oh, Grace, it's so late. Was David cross when I wasn't there for this morning's meeting?"

"We didn't have a meeting. David went to breakfast with the organising committee for tonight's Ball. Under my door this morning were instructions on what he wants us to do and he's already working on the debriefing report and meeting for tomorrow. No doubt he, and more work, will arrive as the day progresses. You've got about an hour though before he is likely to miss you. What time did you get in?"

Jane nearly choked on her tea. "Miss me? I doubt it!" She rose and moved towards the bathroom while answering Grace's question. "Three thirty."

Grace exclaimed in a horrified echo, "Three thirty!" Sinking on to the end of the bed, Grace spoke to her through the bathroom's half-open door. "I came back at midnight to find David pacing up and down the corridor like a demented lion. When he saw me he began roaring out his frustration. Of course, I found your note under my door — up until then he was imagining all kinds of horrors had befallen you and was on the brink of calling the police!"

Jane's eyes widened. David hadn't got her note until midnight. No wonder he'd been worried!

"It's a rare thing for David to get more than chilly with annoyance. I have seen him in a cold fury, although fortunately not directed at me, but never the hot rage he went into when he read your rather short note. I just stayed silent. It wasn't long before he realized he was directing his anger at the wrong person and was very apologetic. I thought it might be better if I was still around when you got back, so I stayed up until about 1.00am, but in the end he insisted you were his responsibility and urged me to get some sleep. Was he still up when you got back? Had he calmed down?"

Jane emerged from the bathroom to collect her clothes. "Oh yes, he was still up! Look Grace, I'm sorry you had to bear the brunt of all this. As to David calming down — well, er, he did eventually. After I hit him."

Grace's eyes nearly popped out of her head, "You did what?"

"I hit him."

"And you still have a job?"

As she dressed, Jane related the sequence of events and could see that Grace found her tale beyond belief.

"David's note did say you'd probably be very tired this morning, and might need a wake up call. I just don't know what to think. In my experience, those who cross swords with David, whether male or female, rarely come out unscathed." Grace sighed, "Yet it seems you've managed it. There's no mention that we don't carry on as before, so I suggest we get to it." Grace looked at her watch. "And, frankly, if you don't want to find yourself in another skirmish, we'd better get going."

It was a hectic day. The Exhibition closing at 6.00pm with the Ball starting at 8.00pm meant no mid-afternoon break as they had a hundred-and-one things to check or confirm before the dismantling tomorrow. Across the exhibition floor she'd seen David, but was relieved they'd had no chance to speak.

It was already past six o'clock when Grace hurried up to tell her, "David wants us ready by half past seven to help greet the guests."

Jane gave petulant groan. "He hasn't given us much time to get ready, has he?"

"Don't worry if you go now you'll have an hour. You'll be fine. Each country will have two people to greet guests and show people to their tables, so if you are a few minutes late we'll cope."

On her way back to the hotel, she prayed that she'd achieve in the short time that special look which would be mature and worthy of a company representative.

The receptionist handed her the key to her room with a little smile. "This has been left for you, Madam. I hope you'll have a wonderful evening." In a small box was an orchid, which would go so well with her dress. The card attached read, 'This is for you to wear tonight. Thank you for all your hard work. David.'

Jane swallowed hard and blinked back tears, she didn't deserve anything — how thoughtful of him.

To her surprise, she crossed the crowded foyer with three minutes to spare. David, standing by the doors of the Starlight Ballroom, glanced up from talking to Grace. There was no mistaking the admiration in his eyes as he took in the details of her transformation. Grace followed the direction of his eyes. A blush rose to Jane's cheeks, their steady gaze was making her feel uncomfortable.

Grace verbalised her approval. "You look stunning."

"You don't think the eye shadow and mascara are too much?"

"Not at all. I like your hair up in those pretty curls. You look quite perfect, doesn't she, David?"

Before David could reply, Jane observed, "Grace, you look pretty perfect yourself."

Grace smiled, "Thank you Jane. You know, even at my age, I'm still learning never to presume anything. You think you know someone, then suddenly you realize you don't at all."

David gave her a bemused look. Jane, unsure to what Grace was referring, brushed aside the remark by saying flippantly, "Do you know what I think? I think we need two handsome gentlemen to whisk us away."

Grace nodded at David, "Well, we have one here."

A comment from the Midsummer Ball echoed in Jane's head: 'David Reinhardt is vibrant, dashing and handsome'. For the first time, Jane allowed herself to appraise him as others did. The thick black hair brushed back, the warm, questioning black eyes which looked down into hers, the broad smile softening his otherwise harsh, chiselled features. Overall, his athletic body dressed in an evening suit forced her to admit, if only to herself, that tonight he did look the epitome of male virility — which in itself was rather scary.

"So, Jane, will I do?" David's eyes narrowed and,

although voiced with amusement, his words had an edge. "I think I'd prefer it if you didn't allow yourself to be whisked away this evening, Jane."

"No, no. Of course not. I promise I'll be the perfect hostess. I'll stay by your side all evening — oh, oh, well if that's okay, I mean, well, I don't want to spoil your enjoyment, or cramp your style."

The familiar roar of laughter hit the air. His hand slapped his thigh. Heads nearby turned in their direction. Grace raised her eyes in mock horror. Jane grinned inanely.

During the next half an hour, many compliments were made on her sophisticated appearance, bringing her confidence and the assurance she'd got the look just right. Jacques, having been welcome by the French host, glanced in her direction, and she, seeing it, sent him a warm, friendly smile. So she wasn't surprised when, after they'd sat down at their table, Jacques came over and stood hopefully by the vacant chair.

Jane introduced him to Grace, but David's barely courteous smile was enough to know that suggesting Jacques join them would not be a good idea. At her suggestion that he ask her to dance later he gave a nod and, realizing that an invitation wasn't forthcoming, he excused himself and returned to his compatriots.

However, she was a surprised a few minutes later when a tall, distinguished grey-haired gentleman with a German accent greeted them and David immediately invited him to join them. It didn't take her long to figure out why. Wilhelm Schultz was interested in Grace! Wilhelm made polite conversation through the first course but, by the end of the second, both he and Grace seemed to have forgotten Jane and David existed.

David nodded in their direction. "Well, Jane, shall we leave them and go and get our sweet?"

Already feeling full, she looked over the dessert table laid out with enticing and delicious choices, and dithered over what she could manage to eat.

David, his plate already full, added a chocolate mousse and commanded, "Come on Jane, it's time you were fattened up, there's plenty here." He grinned as she pulled a face at him and bent to drawl into her ear, "It looks tonight as if it's going to be just you and me, babe."

Deliberately misinterpreting him, she glanced at his plate. "I certainly couldn't eat it all, but I see you're having a good try." David poured a generous helping of double cream over his chocolate cake and pouted as she murmured, "You'll be sick."

No one saw the pat he gave her rear as he walked away. Astonished, she turned and in response to her wide-eyed look his was innocently quizzical. With a wag of forefinger, and a haughty look she returned to make her selection.

Later, as they watched Grace and Wilhelm dancing, David observed, "I know young people don't go in these days for ballroom dancing, but perhaps we could make an attempt?"

On her lips played the ghost of a smile, her voice prim, as she rose. "Anything you say, Mr Reinhardt."

For a while, he shuffled her around the floor, making her wonder if it was he who couldn't dance. Jacques had obviously been awaiting her return for, the moment they came off the dance floor, he arrived to claim her.

To leave David sitting alone made her feel obliged to ask his permission before accepting Jacques' invitation. But David's curt nod of acquiescence so rankled her that she couldn't help herself whispering in Jacques' ear as they joined the swirling couples, "Come on let's show everyone how well we dance."

On a nod, Jacques twirled her into a foxtrot. A few minutes later, the orchestra changed the mood and played a cha cha. Gleefully, she and Jacques made quite a show. Several couples stopped to watch and the floor cleared to make room for them. Then, when the tempo changed to a waltz, they moved round the floor in a graceful unity that wouldn't have looked out of place on 'Come Dancing'.

With her view constantly blocked by others, she couldn't see David's reaction to her prowess. Finally, when they twirled right past him, he looked right through them. Next time he came into view, she gave a him a quick smile. His response was a faint curve of his mouth, as if rather sad at her duplicity. That touched her. Perhaps she'd overplayed her retaliation. In Jacques' ear she said, "After this I must go back to David. I thought he'd go and mix or dance with someone else, but he hasn't. He's been such a good friend to me."

"That man, 'e have more than friendship on his mind." Jacques gave a contemptuous grunt as he pivoted her round.

Irritated by his assertion, but not wishing to argue, she explained, "He's like a father to me. Sometimes he treats me like a child, but he means well."

Jacques mouth firmed, but he gave no further opinion, seeming intent on whirling her round and round the dance floor as though they were one.

When they eventually rejoined David, Jacques thanked her politely, acknowledged David with a nod, and left. David went back to watching the dancers.

Sorry she'd upset him, she covered his hand with hers to get his attention. "I'm sorry, David. You were so quick to assume I couldn't dance, I couldn't resist showing you I could." To placate him, she smiled softly, her eyes showing her affection. "How about we dance again?"

He gave her a baffled look, but stood, taking her hand. Once on the floor she executed a professional twirl into his body for a quickstep and discovered he was very capable as they crossed the floor in perfect harmony. Several changes of tempo later, Jane had to give him credit. "You know, David, for such a large man you are extremely light on your feet."

His head bent to her ear, "So you can appreciate something about this 'old man'?"

Aghast, she objected, "I've never said you were old."

He chuckled. "No, but you seeing me as a father figure certainly implied it!" Before she could comment he took her through a double twirl which left her quite breathless.

It struck her that the quickstep rhythm was rather like their relationship: slow, slow — pleasant and relaxing, then tempers frayed and they argued — quick, quick — and then back to slow as they relaxed again with each other.

Gradually the floor filled, making it impossible to do anything more than sway to the music. David's hands slipped around her waist. As he drew her closer, her head rested on his chest. Being in the circle of his arms felt comfortable, making her aware of the security he brought her. How strong and tall he was. Even wearing four-inch stiletto heels and with her hair piled in curls at the top of her head she was still tiny beside him.

Memories flooded back of the day he'd carried her along the corridor with her head bleeding. How gentle and thoughtful he'd been, even when she'd been sick over him. Friendship was a wonderful thing. He didn't share her faith, but she could trust him more than some who did.

Jane glanced up to see the cleft in his chin and the outline of his nose. As she pulled backwards to speak he bent his head to listen. "I was just thinking what a wonderful friend you are, thank you."

He drew her closer and said nothing, but in his eyes was the tenderness she associated with her father. The dance tempo changed to rock and roll. The floor emptied as they and others headed back to their tables.

David, his arm still around her waist, guided her off the

floor. "I've never really liked that kind of music, but no doubt you young things could dance up a storm."

In reply, she rolled her eyes and flashed him pert smile. Indeed she could. Bruce had always been a bit conservative as to how far he'd go, but with the dance instructor she'd been game to do the outrageous. David halted, his voice deadly serious. "Jane, I warn you be very careful when, and to whom, you give looks like that. I don't think you realise how provocative they are." Before she could react, he continued abruptly, "Smile. Grace has seen us and I don't want her to think we're arguing."

In obedience, her mouth smiled. But her mind worried as she meditated on his words.

Wilhelm stood to greet them on their return. "David, Jane. This is a wonderful evening and Grace tells me ...."

Was she provocative? Hadn't she overheard Rosemary saying something similar? Did David mean sexually provocative? Oh dear, had she given Andrew Carlton the wrong message? If so, perhaps what happened hadn't been entirely his fault. How awful — but what exactly had she done tonight to warrant David's remark? She must find an opportunity to ask him. In the meanwhile, it was probably best not to dwell on it.

She re-tuned into the discussion. There was nothing she could contribute. This would be a good time to excuse herself, slip away to her room, and get the presents she'd bought for Grace and David.

CHAPTER 10

The lift doors swished shut behind her. Deep in thought, she strolled along the corridor, opened her door, crossed the room and delved through a pile of carrier bags to find the one containing two beautifully blown glass paperweights. In the background she heard the ping of the lift doors and their opening. She pulled out one, and then the other attractive navy blue box. As she turned and put them on her bed, she saw Jacques standing in the doorway. Not wanting to be unwelcoming, she smiled brightly. "Gosh, Jacques, I didn't expect to see you there, you startled me. What are you doing up here? I thought you'd be enjoying yourself downstairs."

"Ma chérie, my enjoyment is with you."

Jane laughed. Fazed by his expression, she chattered on. "I just popped up for these. One for David, and one for Grace. A 'thank you' present. I hope they like them."

Jacques took them from her hands. She watched as he placed them side by side on the dressing table. Puzzled, she'd only a second to gasp, "Jacques," before he swept her into his arms and kissed her.

On a chuckle, she extracted herself. "Oh Jacques, come on!" He took her words literally and pulled her into him, crushing her mouth with his. It wasn't because his kiss was unpleasant that made her push him away, but the realisation of being alone with him in her bedroom. "I must go and give David and Grace their presents."

His reply was husky, "David, 'e killed our 'ope to make beautiful love ...." Jane tried to interrupt, but his fingers rested against her mouth. "Now, 'e is not 'ere, we 'ave time, we do it. Yes? We, 'ow you say, we 'armonise in dance and now in love."

178

His French turn of phrase made her giggle. David's warning echoed in her ears. She stepped back. Had she been giving Jacques provocative looks?

Jacques moved towards her. "Come on, chérie, you do not 'ave to be shy."

"I'm not shy. I just don't — well don't — make love."

"Of course. I make love to you." He laughed gently, "Aha, you English — so, so, shy. 'Tis all part of the game, yes?"

Those words, although uttered pleasantly, brought a swift reply, "No Jacques! No game."

Jacques halted with a frown.

"I think it would be better if you left." To signify her wishes, she walked past him towards the door.

Jacques stepped in front of her and leant nonchalantly against it. "No, no, chérie, that's not, 'ow you say — right?"

"Of course it is. Why should I want to make love with you? I hardly know you!"

His face hardened, he didn't move.

"Go now — please!"

Jacques gave a little smile and allowed his eyes to rove over her body.

Tension coiled in her stomach. Then he closed the gap between them and gently began kissing and nuzzling her neck. His hands roved up and down her bare back. To break his hold, she pushed herself away from him, and stated slowly, "Look Jacques, I like you, but really I — you, must go."

"No. It is not possible. We 'ave such, 'ow do you say, you, me — good together...."

"Compatibility?"

"Aha, yes, compatibility! You English say you don't like, but under it so, so warm and...." Putting his forefinger and thumb together in a circle he kissed them before opening them.

She gathered that he meant 'delectable' and laughed.

179

"Oh Jacques, that may be...."

Her words were cut short as he resumed kissing her. He really was charming, she really couldn't get cross with him, but she needed to explain. The pull at her zip told her now was the time. With a sharp push she uttered distinctly, in one-syllable words, "No! Jacques, No!"

Jacques, his eyes filled with smoky sensuality, looked into hers. His hand slipped into the widening gap, causing the zip to slip down even further. Her hand shot over his to pull it away as she demanded, "Stop! Jacques — stop!"

A low rumble of amusement and pleasure sounded in his throat. It was difficult to keep his hand from pushing the zip down the remaining section. Her voice became insistent, "Stop! Jacques, that's enough. Please!" Stepping backwards, she pushed herself into the wall in the hope she might squash his hand and keep her dress on. Even now, if she moved her arm from across her chest, her dress would fall forward exposing her breasts. Jacques laughed lightly, slipped out his hand out from behind her but, in kissing her again, exerted enough pressure to keep her pinned against the wall.

Icy tendrils of fear doused her response to him. Words weren't going to have any effect. Did he genuinely not understand? If she wriggled against him, would her dress stay up, leaving both her arms free? It worked, and with that freedom she weaved her hands into his fashionably long hair in a parody of passion. Once she'd a good grip she tugged hard, the force drawing his head back, his lips from her mouth. Immediately she twisted away from the wall and pushed passed him. Her dress slipped down, hindering her steps. She hugged it up. Jacques' hand snaked out and caught her hair. She yelped in surprise and pain as it tumbled out of its pretty setting.

"Let go, let go." Desperate to rid herself of the pain, she moved closely to him, her head on one side.

Jacques' scrutinised her face, then obeyed. His sultry

eyes moved from her loosened and tangled shoulder length hair to her bruised and reddened mouth. "Jane, you — so beautiful."

She stared at him and watched as his eyes moved down to gaze hungrily at the exposed white skin of her shoulders and upper chest. Her reaction was to pull her dress higher. Her mouth curled into a snarl, and in the hope of his understanding better, she shouted, "Jacques! I'm not interested! Comprehend?"

He closed in, his body rubbing and pushing itself against her.

"Stop!"

It appeared he couldn't comprehend, for he ignored her, and her squirming to get away from him. Sensuously, Jacques murmured at her mouth, "Aha, ma chérie, you will comprends. I light your fire! Do not be afraid. I show you 'ow it can be." He made a derisive face, "That David, 'e want you, but 'e not 'ave zee passion — you see, I gooder than 'e."

It was rational she supposed, in this day and age, that some secretaries did, when away like this, sleep with their bosses. But the thought that she would do such a thing brought such indignation that she gave Jacques a hard shove. He stumbled backwards. With a swing she landed him a hard slap across his cheek. Her experience, although somewhat limited, told her that this stunned a man enough to realize his attentions weren't wanted.

Jacques hand shot to his cheek.

With a glare she hissed, "Comprehend now — go!"

To make her point clear, she attempted to re-zip her dress while moving toward the door.

"You will not do that again!" Simple words, but the menace in the way he uttered them sent a shiver down her spine. No this couldn't be happening to her again. What did she do wrong?

Inwardly she was quaking, outwardly she stood her

ground and shouted, "Go, Go! Go!" There was no way he could ignore, or mistake the message in that!

An oddly charming smile flashed across his face. He stepped forward. Relief filled her, he was going. But it was not so. He clamped his hands across her ears, his head bent. To avoid another plundering kiss, she clenched her neck muscles. But still it came. Now unpleasant, hard and intrusive, as though to punish her. Was this his 'goodbye' kiss? No it seemed not! His hands moved quickly from her head to her bottom and pushed her against him. He ignored the pathetic kicks of her foot, grabbed one of her flailing hands and trapped it between them.

In repugnance, she stiffened and stood woodenly against him. Tears of frustration welled in her eyes. Why was her 'no' always confused for 'yes'? Life suddenly was full of 'buts' and 'what ifs'. What if she'd not done this, said that, stayed at the dinner.... Jacques mouth felt glued to hers. How long had she been gone? Had David missed her? How awful if he were to arrive and think she was 'entertaining' Jacques. But what could she do? The feel of Jacques' hands slipping inside the back of her dress spurred her on to fight in every manner she could think of.

Unwittingly, she gave a moan of despair. Briefly, Jacques stopped kissing her to nibble her ear and whisper, "There, good, you quiet, now you see you enjoy."

Was that what he really thought? That ploy had worked before. On a more positive sounding moan, she tried to relax. After what seemed an age, Jacques' hold lessened. In pretending to squirm, she managed to slide the skirt of her dress round so the back slit was at the front. This would give her legs the most freedom. Simultaneously with another moan, she swung her body, and jerked her knee up as fast as possible to hit him between the legs.

Jacques doubled over with a loud wail. Now free, she kicked off her high heels, clutched up her dress and pushed past him. She yanked open the door and charged into the corridor. His charm dissipated into what could only be French obscenities. There were only five rooms in this section of the corridor, their occupants at the Ball.

Afraid now she cried out, "Help! Can anyone hear me? Help!"

No door opened in response. At the T-junction she dived through the door into the stairwell. The sound of the door banging above her told her Jacques had decided to follow her, but to her surprise he ran past her. She halted. He turned. And before she could say or do anything, she was slung over his shoulder like a sack of potatoes. Despite her kicking and screaming for help, within seconds she was back in her room. Jacques kicked the door shut and her body was flung unceremoniously on the bed. For a few moments she watched, mesmerised, as Jacques shrugged off his jacket, undid his bow tie and began unbuttoning his shirt.

What did he think he was doing? Self-preservation kicked in. She rolled to the far side of the bed and jumped off. In silence they faced each like animals stalking their prey. Jacques didn't take his eyes off her as he continued to undress. She edged along the bed, gauging the distance between her, him and the bathroom door. Unable to interpret Jacques' words she gave him a poisonous look. Unperturbed, he sat on the bed to take off his shoes. Incensed by his nonchalance she determined to thwart him. Now was a good time! Tucking up her dress, she dashed toward the bathroom door. But, instead of going through it, her face almost hit the door as Jacques pinned her against it with his hard body. A nausea of fear arose in her stomach, her breath came in sharp gasps. Surely this man didn't intend to rape her?

Jacques rubbed himself against her, and nibbled the back of her neck, as though expecting some kind of response. When he got none, his voice rose in agitation. "You say 'yes', then you say, 'no'! 'I don't comprend! You want fight, I fight'. He caught her by the shoulders, twirled her round and pushed her back against the door. With a disgruntled growl he shook her.

Couldn't he see in her face her horror and revulsion for him? Jacques' face contorted with rage. Jane closed her eyes. What a nightmare! Why didn't he just go? A sharp slap against her face shot her eyes open and her head sideways. She howled in pain. The back of his hand hit the other cheek. Her head spun. She reeled against the door. Her hands rose in front of her face to protect her from further blows. Tears flowed down, stinging her burning cheeks. Dazed, with her neck aching from the whiplash effect, she whispered, "You beast, you horrible beast."

An expression of satisfaction appeared on Jacques face as he took in her half-naked appearance. Pleased, he questioned, "You now comprends?"

No, she didn't comprehend anything except that he'd hit her. Her legs gave way under her, and sliding down the door she crumpled at his feet, crying in her heart, 'Oh, please God, help me!'

Jacques, the palm of his hand resting against the door, looked languidly down on her and shrugged. "You 'it me, I 'it you."

Hunched up into herself, she whimpered in shock, her cheeks and mouth stiffening in burning pain. All she could hope was that now, having got his own back on her, he'd walk away and leave her. She huddled tighter into herself.

On an exasperated sigh, Jacques bent and pulled her arm with one hand and her hair with the other. "Up, up."

With no alternative, she wobbled to her feet as his hand slipped into her dress. His moan was one of delight as he roamed unhindered across her naked flesh. Unable to do anything, all energy to resist knocked out of her, her body became like that of a pliable doll which trembled, not with pleasure but fear. Jacques, it seemed, was convinced she was enjoying it. Self-contempt filled her — it was her fault, somehow she must have incited him.

No one had ever touched her like this before. She wanted him to stop, but her brain seemed unable to speak or get her body to act. Dread at the inevitability of his actions caused her to close her eyes, to try and shut out what was happening to her. Her breathing became laboured as, from deep within, sobs began to rise. Jacques' gently stroked her cheek. She opened her eyes. He smiled a knowing and sardonic smile. Paralysed, she watched her dress fall into a turquoise puddle at her feet. Humiliation came fast on despair. Tears rolled down her face.

Perhaps it was better to take the line of least resistance, for there was no one to help her, to rescue her this time. Had God given up on her? The old adage, 'God helps those who help themselves', dropped into her mind. Hadn't she tried explaining? Hadn't she tried to get away? Hadn't she prayed? Her mind focused on the only one who could physically rescue her. What about David, her human friend and self-appointed guardian angel? Where did he think she was all this time? A yearning inside grew into a yawning hole. Where was he? Where was David? Please, please Lord, send David. David? Where was David? David cared. David could rescue her. She needed David. Frightened by Jacques' explorations, her inner cry became a murmur: "David, oh David."

An exasperated volley of words shot forth from Jacques. He caught hold of her, flung her on the bed and began removing his trousers. Horrified, she rolled the bed cover over her and, in so doing, realized at that moment he couldn't run. A sudden spurt of energy burst forth in the name of desperation. She leapt up and charged towards the bathroom. Jacques yelled, the bedsprings squealed, and she was rugby tackled to the floor. The bedspread cushioned her fall. Her head banged against the door frame, stunning her. Tears of anguish and frustration poured down her cheeks. That was it — her last chance of escape. With a sense of fatality she willed herself to endure what was to come. Her tense, stilled body under him seemed to take effect for, worriedly, he spoke her name. When she didn't move, he lifted her in the bedspread and placed her gently back on the bed..

Dazed, she lay there and thanked God. Jacques had finally got the message. There was silence. Had Jacques gone? She waited what seemed like minutes and finally opened her eyes. Jacques was standing by the bed watching her. In horror and dismay her eyes snapped shut.

"So you ready now, no more fight, eh? You mean please now, yes?" His fingers tugged at the bedspread.

She cringed from him and, holding tightly, to it she managed a tearful plea, "Please, no, please don't."

Jacques chuckled as he pronounced, "You 'ave great passion. You will share with me."

Surely no man could mistake a rigid body for one that was receiving pleasure. She willed herself to ignore what he was doing, not to react in any way. It wasn't long before he complained bitterly, "What is ze matter with you? I make love...."

Her muffled, "No", sent Jacques into a tirade of what sounded like French abuse. Believing he was going to hit her again, strength came from somewhere to savagely rake her finger nails into his shoulders. He yelled and grabbed her hands from his shoulders and with a sharp movement wrenched them above her head. Jacques' force jerked through her body.

Her scream of pain covered the sound of a heavy thud. The door burst open with a splintering crash. Through her anguish, she heard Jacques' exclamation, felt a swish of air, her sudden release, a bounce at the far edge of the bed and his crash to the floor.

Instinctively her body shot into a defensive foetal ball, but her eyes rounded to see Jacques on his knees, his eyes level with the bed. He was looking up and beyond her with a face of shock and disbelief. A quick glimpse revealed David towering menacingly over her, his fist raised, his eyes full of crazed fury. But his eyes weren't on her, but on the man crouched by the bed.

Her face stung. Her arms ached. Her body felt a mass of bruises, but she thanked God for David, and listened to the barrage of French being issued at Jacques. David's guise this time was more of a rampager from hell than a guardian angel.

A tidal wave of relief washed over her. Spasms of trembling swept through her. Short, pained animal noises left her throat as she rocked, knowing, it's over, its over. As Jacques gave David an impassioned reply, she felt David's anxious gaze upon her. Something touched her. Defensively she curled tighter. The hotel's thick fluffy towelling robe fluttered over her. She clawed it against her. The only words Jacques used that she understood were English, 'yes' and 'please'. Was Jacques saying she led him on? After David's earlier comments would he believe him? She squeezed into an even tighter ball. She didn't want to see, she didn't want to hear, but nothing could erase what sounded like David accusing and Jacques trying to brazen it out. Jacques gave a sneering laugh which was cut short by the sound of a fist hitting flesh.

David's voice issued a curt command which had Jacques scrabbling by the bed. David bit out harshly further edicts which, by the sounds, had Jacques quickly putting on his clothes. And finally she heard the damaged door scrape shut behind them.

Jane waited for a few moments and then in the silence she slowly and painfully uncurled. Her head and heart thudded. Beaten and battered, she felt abandoned. David wouldn't trust her again. He'd probably sack her. What would she tell her friends, her family? Oh the disgrace! How was she going to bear it? Tears came, she cried bitterly into the pillow — what had she done to cause this?

What sort of world was this? What sort of Christian was she? But God had heard her prayers…. Oh the shame! How was she going to face David again? Or Grace for that matter? It was so awful!

Lord, help me! You, sent David as a very present help in time of trouble, but I need you still — I'm in trouble. So much for 'making love' — what is love? You know about love, Lord. And you were battered and bruised. You forgave. I know I have to forgive, I want to forgive. Help me Lord. I'm sorry if I led Jacques on in any way. How could he have believed I wanted him to… to…? Fear, anger, pain and shame engulfed her.

Deep in misery, Jane's first indication of someone in the room was the feel of hands tucking the robe around her. In the belief it was Jacques touching her she catapulted back into a foetal position.

"It's only me, Jane. Nothing to be afraid of, just cry it out." David had come back!

The bed dipped as he sat behind her. He wasn't angry with her. A consoling hand gently patted her shoulder. That kindness unleashed a deep agony of heartrending grief and sorrow making her cry uncontrollably. Arms slid beneath her and, lifting her like a sick child, he rocked her back and forth. His words, "That's it. That's it. Let it go. Let it go," seemed to stick in his throat, but the reassurance they bought opened up the dam of distress within her. And if she hadn't known better, she would have thought he was crying too.

The anguish slowly diminished in the reality of his comfort. Those words continually repeated, as though on a loop, seemed to go in deeper and deeper as if it were God's message, to 'let it go Jane, let it go'. Then, as though instinctively knowing when, David stopped speaking and nestled her with his strong arms, hugging her into his warm, broad chest. Remorse and shame began to diminish. David's actions were that of a father's love, and it brought the understanding that God, her heavenly Father, was using David to show his love for her. David was his provision for her, his comfort would bring her healing and peace.

What was David thinking? He certainly wasn't angry. Gently drawing away from his chest, she caught his preoccupied eyes and worried frown before he focused questioningly on her upturned face.

"David, Oh! David." A sob arose, but she managed to choke out, "I'm sorry."

His palm felt cool as he touched her burning cheek. He swallowed hard, and muttered, "Oh, what has he done to you?" before drawing her head back against him, and then he asked in a strained voice, "And Jane, what am I to do with you?"

What answer could she give? Instead she pulled back and gazed sadly into his face, her trust and adoration of him mirrored in her eyes.

David groaned, "Oh God," then suddenly tipped her on to the bed and dashed to the bathroom.

Jane stared after him. From behind the door came stomach wrenching sounds. Unsure what to do, she slipped on the dressing gown and sat at the end of the bed. He emerged ashen faced. She stated the obvious, "You've been sick." A weak smile crossed his face. She clicked her tongue, "I told you not to eat so much rich food."

Her comment was met with a long look, followed by an exasperated sigh. "Jane, there is no doubt that tonight, my stomach has sickened with something!" Jane gave a wry smile. David grunted, shook his head and commanded, "Go to bed, Jane." Obediently she slipped under the sheet and was surprised when David sat down beside her. Involuntarily she recoiled as his hand touched her cheek. "It's alright Jane, there's nothing to fear." He stretched out his large hand and stroked back her hair from her face, and sighed heavily. "Jane, I'm not old enough to be your father. I'm a man...." He nodded in the direction of the door, "And like that man, I, too have desires…."

Perplexed, she frowned and bit her bottom lip.

David thrust his fingers though his own hair, frustration evident in his muttered, "Oh God!" Had she done something wrong?

His mention of God, though, reminded her. "David?"

His eyes locked hers in a penetrating gaze. "Jane?"

Stunned for a moment at the unexpected intensity of his stare, she hesitated, then blurted out, "I prayed so hard God would send you — my guardian angel — and he did, didn't he?"

David grunted. She sensed, rather than saw, him grappling with a range of emotions before answering, "Yes Jane, he did." He glanced at his watch. "Oh no, I have to go." He stood and gave a wisp of a smile. "When I last looked at my watch it was because I was beginning to wonder where you were, and how much longer you were going to be. At that moment I had the impression of an urgent whisper, 'Jane needs you upstairs'. I looked round, but no one was near. I leapt up, said to Grace, 'I've got to go,' and raced up here. Your scream…." David's features tightened in pain. "I rammed my shoulder against the door to break the lock." He swallowed hard, "Did I get here before he, he…?"

In embarrassment at what he was asking, she turned her head from him to mumble, "Yes."

It was understandable he should sigh again, "Oh God," but she was at a loss when he muttered, "Oh Jane, Jane, if only you knew." There was no chance to ask what, for he was heading toward the door. Over his shoulder he said, "I have to make the final speech of the evening. I'll send Grace up. You should be safe, but we'd better make sure. Speeches, speeches, the bane of my life!" Taken aback at his hasty exit, she hadn't a chance to say she didn't want to spoil Grace's evening as well as his.

It wasn't long before there was a knock, followed by the door opening slightly and Grace calling hesitantly, "Jane." Grace's head poked around the door and, seeing her in bed, she asked tentatively, "Are — are you all right? David said you needed...." Grace stepped on a piece of splintered wood. Puzzled, she looked at it, and then the door, and saw the chaotic room. "What's happened? You — you and David haven't had a row?"

Jane sat up and winced. Grace's hand flew to her mouth, "Oh, Jane! Your face!"

The rueful grimace hurt. "I got myself into trouble again."

Incredulity crossed Grace's horror-stricken features. "David? David did that? It's inconceivable. David might lose his temper, but hit you?"

"No. Not David."

Grace didn't seem to hear. "It's so out of character. To hit a man in self defence maybe — but a woman? I've always seen him as such a gentleman. It didn't occur to me when David rushed away earlier that it had anything to do with you. I was just worrying if he'd be back in time for his speech. They were just announcing, 'Please welcome Mr David Reinhardt, Co-ordinator of British Exhibitors', when he came in the door. On his way to the stage he grabbed his notes and said, 'Jane's upstairs. She needs you.' Before I could say anything he was gone in a flurry of clapping. I wasn't sure what I find, but I didn't expect to see your scattered clothes on the floor and the room ...." Grace shivered.

"David didn't hit me! He rescued me."

Bewildered, Grace repeated, "David rescued you? Rescued you from what, whom?"

"Jacques!"

"Jacques? The man who took you out last night?"

"Jane nodded, and bit her lip, "One and the same." Tears filled her eyes, "Grace, he — it was so horrible...."

She stopped, as Grace headed for the bathroom.

"Go on Jane, I'm listening, but I must get some cold compresses for your poor face. They'll cool it down and hopefully stop any swelling."

With a cold flannel on each cheek, Jane concluded, "So you see, David was every bit the gentleman. I wish, though, I could have stopped him spoiling your evening, but he just said he'd get you and dashed off."

Throughout, Grace had tried to maintain a composed face, but now it seemed she was more nonplussed than when she'd arrived.

"Grace, please go back to the dance. Enjoy the rest of the evening. At least you'll get the last waltz with Wilhelm — he looks such a nice man."

"David seemed to think I should stay with you. And you've no lock on your door."

"If it's pulled near enough shut, no one will notice. I'm sure Jacques won't return."

"Hmm," Grace nodded. "That's true, if David's dealt with him. David's fair, but this…. That young man will be lucky to have a job tomorrow once David's informed his company of his behaviour."

Jane didn't even want to think about that! "Please Grace. Please go back. Don't let me spoil your evening."

"Well, if you think you'll be okay on your own?" At Jane's nod she added happily, "Wilhelm's a widower and a Christian."

Jane smiled painfully and tried to inject enthusiasm into her voice. "Oh Grace, that's wonderful. I do hope this works out for you. You deserve someone who will treasure you. I'll pray about it as I go to sleep."

Grace bent and kissed her forehead. "Thank you Jane. And you remember what the Bible says: 'In all things, God works for the good of those who love Him, who have been called according to His purpose'. You may have made mistakes, but I'm sure God can bring good out of them. Sleep well, you'll feel better in the morning."

Jane was woken from a restless sleep by Grace's voice outside her door. "....it is important. Can we talk in the lounge?" She was just falling asleep when she heard Grace's voice again. "Just take one step at a time."

David, despite being quieter than usual, was easily overheard. "That's easier said than done. Look at the many obstacles to overcome. Do you really think, in such a short time, you can fall in love and know you want to live with that person for the rest of your life?"

"Well, for Wilhelm and I, being Christians we believe that our meeting was a divine appointment. Even with our age difference, I have no qualms in accepting him."

"And you are considering a March wedding?" He grunted. "It doesn't give me very long. Do you think I can have this sorted out by then?"

There was laughter in Grace's voice, "One way or another, and knowing you, yes! Goodnight David."

"Goodnight Grace, I really appreciate your frankness."

Grace's bedroom door shut, soon followed by David's.

So Wilhelm and Grace were talking about marriage. How wonderful for Grace. Jane snuggled down in the bed. She could see why David was so worried — to replace Grace in three months wouldn't be an easy task.

Waking, Jane looked at the clock — 9.30 am! About to leap out of bed, she noticed Grace's note on the pillow. She groaned with the movement, her body felt so stiff and bruised.

'David will be back around 10.30 to speak to you. Don't worry about work today, I can manage. David's arranged for a light lunch to be sent up to the lounge opposite you. See you about 1.30. We have to leave for the airport by 3.30 for the 5.30 flight'.

Trepidation filled her. Last night, David had been so kind. Was she now going to have to face his anger? Jacques' aftershave wafted through her nose. His smell — ugh! Her first aim would be to get clean. Then all she wanted to do was pack and go home.

The hot bath was so soothing, but she watched the time, it wouldn't do not to be dressed and ready when David arrived. At David's knock, dressed in her twin-set and trousers, her hair washed and dried she ran to open it. Her happy welcome froze on her face as unsmilingly he looked her up and down. "Grace said she could manage without me so I didn't put on my official clothes."

David's attention was drawn by the room service waiter stepping out of the lift with a tray. "That's for me, I think. Room 508. We'll have it in the lounge. Thank you." He turned back to say briskly, "Jane, if you would follow me?" Nervously she did as she was bid. Pulling out a chair, he had her sit and moved to the opposite side of the table. He waited for the waiter to dispense the tray contents on the table, tipped the man, and as he departed asked, "Tea or coffee? Help yourself to a croissant, there's raspberry jam and butter. You're probably hungry, I assumed you'd missed breakfast."

She gave him a tentative smile. "Tea please, and thank you." He may have been thoughtful, but his face was an austere mask. Dread began to bubble in her. Was he going to tell her she was out of a job?

The tea poured and passed, he asked, "How do you feel?"

"I had a nice hot bath. It's helped."

He scrutinised her face. "Good. A little more make up than usual should cover any bruising. Now I think we ought to bring last night's events to a conclusion."

Anxiously she bit her lip and nodded. Tears weren't far away. The knife in her hand shook.

David took in her expression, clenched his jaw and

194

tightened his mouth into a grim line. "First, did you understand anything Jacques and I said last night?" She shook her head. His prompt and unexpectedly positive "Right!" gave her cause to wonder what Jacques had said that he was glad she hadn't understood. After all, she knew Jacques had some wrong ideas about her. David moved on. "Well, the conclusion I drew was that Jacques wasn't entirely to blame."

Silent tears coursed down her cheeks. David ignored them and went on reprovingly, "As I said to you yesterday evening, there are times when you send out what I would term 'mixed messages'".

Her head sank in shame, and without realizing it her body shrank into the chair.

"Jane? Look at me, do you understand what I'm saying?"

Baffled, she lifted her wet face up towards those black eyes and shook her head. David sighed heavily, "Well let me point out the occasions when I've been the subject of those prim, teasing or haughty looks, which are so provocative." Her face burned as he ticked off the incidents on his fingers. ".... then there was the night I persuaded you to work for me. Walking back from our meal you suggested kissing ...."

At that she wailed, "I didn't know. Believe me, I didn't. I just repeated what you'd said. I didn't realize it was provocative. I was just teasing you."

"Exactly! Teasing me!"

How awful! She'd heard the expression, 'she's just a tease', said in a derogatory manner about someone, and now it was being aimed at her. She recalled David's unfathomable look that night and then remembered it on other occasions. "I was, I really was, after, after, what you said, last night, going to ask you what you meant. Honestly!" For a moment she thought she saw a whisper of a smile, but she must have been mistaken for he said severely, "Were you indeed? Shall I go on, or can you see it now for yourself?"

How could she have changed the events of last night? How could Jacques have misunderstood? She was still at a loss to know how she could have done better.

David, watching her face over his coffee cup, must have read her thoughts for he said more kindly, "Drink your tea. The answer, Jane, is to make what you do, and what you say, the same thing. You aroused Jacques until he was, it seems, unable to think straight. He believed your diversionary tactics were just part of a game. And, let's face it, this isn't the first time it's happened!" He gave her a hard, knowing look. Jane was mortified. But there was worse to come. "You state quite categorically you wouldn't get involved with anyone who wasn't a Christian because you don't want to lead them on, yet by flirting, you do just that."

Jane gave a horrified gasp, "I don't!" Rosemary words came back to haunt her, 'she's such a flirt'. And she'd thought Rosemary was just being nasty!

David, his face grim, nodded, "Yes, you do! Can you wonder then why men don't know where they are with you!"

He drained his coffee as she pondered on his words. It was horrible seeing women flirt, and to be told she was doing it, albeit unintentionally.... No wonder David had sighed so heavily last night saying, "Jane, Jane, if only you knew." Now she did know, she was appalled.

"I would suggest you think about what I've said. If you want to talk about it further we can do so another time. Enough said for now, I've work to do." He rose to leave.

"David, I...." He turned. "David, what will happen to Jacques? If what you say is true, that it was my fault, then it wouldn't be fair if he gets punished."

"Look Jane, whatever the rights and wrongs, it's quite unforgivable for a man to hit a woman or, however deluded, to take a woman who says, 'no'. So don't bother about him — he'll get what he deserves."

"But what about the language difference? I've thought about this. I said 'please no' and 'please don't'. Maybe that muddled him?"

Cross, David retorted, "Are you making excuses for him? Why? His conduct was insufferable and his superiors agreed with me."

Jane, remembering Andrew's fate, gasped wide-eyed, "Oh no, what have you done?"

"I have done, Jane, what needed to be done. Let's leave it at that."

"But, don't you see, if it was my fault then it's not fair, he shouldn't have to take all the blame".

"Oh Jane! For goodness sake, stop the histrionics!" David snapped.

Unable to keep eye contact, she mumbled, "But if I'd stuck to my Christian principles, well, I wouldn't have gone off to a nightclub with him in the first place."

David sat back down, leaned across the table and touched her hand. Surprised, she looked up to find him smiling gently. "But Jane, that doesn't excuse his behaviour. I said you gave out mixed messages, not that you were entirely to blame." With furrowed brow he studied her. "You never cease to amaze me. It's rare to find someone who will accept they are at fault and not make excuses or try and shift the blame elsewhere." He shook his head. "And I think it must be even rarer to find someone who's willing to take the blame for someone else to stop them being punished."

Jane frowned and shrugged. "I've never thought about it. Nor had I realized I was a tease or a flirt." Tears filled her eyes again. "I'm so sorry, David, about my behaviour and sorry I've given you such a bad impression about Christianity. Just because I say I'm a Christian doesn't mean I'm better than anyone else. I'm just trying to live by

Christian principles and teaching, but I don't always get it right."

There was scepticism in David's voice. "And as a Christian can you forgive Jacques for hitting you? He nearly raped you."

Jane cringed at his bluntness. Her hand shook. He was right though. A few seconds later.... It really had been that close. "I don't have an option. So I might find it hard now, but I will, especially as I see it wasn't entirely his fault. Unforgiveness brings anger and bitterness — they spoil your life. It grows like a cancer without you knowing it and, before long, it's taken you over. Your outlook on life — your whole personality — becomes negative and embittered."

David glanced at his watch and stood. "Well Jane, I certainly can't see that happening to you. And believe me, you're not the only one who has much to learn! But I should have been at a meeting five minutes ago. You have a rest and we'll see you later for lunch. Enjoy your croissants."

She watched him leave the room and breathed a sigh of relief. At least she still had her wonderful job, but what a mess she'd made! What kind of witness was she? She'd even let the Lord down. Mindlessly she chewed two croissants. Well, there was still the rest of the morning — time to catch up on her Bible reading and ask God some serious questions about friendship, love, and passion.

David and Grace were very late for lunch. Jane had eaten and was ready to go before they arrived to grab a plate of sandwiches, eating them as they packed. Jane felt very subdued. Their rush was probably due to having to do her work.

Once in the airport Grace went shopping, so it wasn't until they were seated on the plane that Jane confessed to overhearing her plans. "Last night I heard you and David talking."

Grace looked taken aback, "Did you?"

Jane smiled. "Yes, about you and Wilhelm. I heard you tell David that will be getting married in March. And I so want to congratulate you — it's such fantastic news."

"Nothing's settled yet." The abruptness of the reply caused Jane to wonder if Grace was cross at her having heard. But a minute later, Grace confided, "We met last year and corresponded a few times, but I wasn't sure he'd be here, or want to meet up again. His first wife died two years ago with leukaemia, and he has four grown children, all of whom are encouraging him to be on the lookout for 'a good woman' to spend the rest of his life with. He may think I fit that bill, but I have yet to be vetted by them — I do feel this is of God."

"I gather David is pleased, but has his doubts because he doesn't want to lose you. He did seem a bit disgruntled at having so short a time to sort it all out."

Grace looked puzzled, and appeared to be rethinking the previous night's conversation before she replied. "I think, Jane, he was more worried about problems that come from feeling you are in love and whether, after the first excitement wears off, there are enough interests in common and a depth of friendship to make the marriage work."

Jane glanced across at David reading a magazine. Was he ignoring their conversation? He certainly didn't ignore his staff's welfare — he'd been really good to her and obviously listened last night to Grace and had given her some sound advice.

"Well, Grace, I know one thing, it would be a lot simpler for me if I just married Bruce. We enjoy similar things and probably have a depth of friendship to make a marriage work." Wistfully she remembered the passion of a few minutes in a blacked out room. Woefully she added, "Both times I've stepped out of my Christian environment, it's been disaster." Jane shuddered, "Last night's incident certainly made me to decide, never again, as David would call it, to 'spread my wings'. I may have to live in this world, but it's best to stick within the confines of the one I know. It's safer! I think it is high time my appointed guardian angel had a well-earned rest." This time David did respond, his expression one of mock severity as he nodded his approval.

Grace, more serious, advised, "Now don't do anything impetuous. Weigh things up before jumping in. And don't go rushing into marriage with Bruce just because you want to escape the world."

Jane smiled. "I caught up with my Bible reading this morning. I do three chapters in the Old Testament, and one in the New, so I get through the Bible in a year. This morning, in Song of Solomon, one verse particularly struck me. It was repeated three times — I think I got the message. It read, "stir not up, nor awaken love until it please."

Grace laughed. "I think we all need to take that on board. It's amazing how God speaks through His word, isn't it? It's spot on for you. And the best way. Wait on God to work it out — that's the wisdom of an old maid who has waited a long time for love to awaken, but now it would seem it pleases God to grant her request!"

Jane smiled, "Wisdom I'm sure, but not so much of the old maid!"

David's broad smile caught her eye. The slow wink in her direction made her glow in pleasure. She was no longer in disgrace!

CHAPTER 11

Two weeks had passed since they returned from Brussels. Now, it all seemed like a dream or a nightmare, depending on which way Jane viewed it. Since their return, David been slightly distant. She'd commented about it to Grace, but her reply had been, "He's got a lot on his mind." That was certainly true. Although they were no longer busy with the Exhibition, David's life still appeared to be filled with endless appointments mostly outside the office.

Last week she'd stayed late with a group from the Social Club, decorating the canteen for today's Christmas staff party, and the conference room for tonight's disco. It had been such fun, but Bruce hadn't been impressed, complaining she spent far too much time at work! Tonight, many were bringing guests to the party but, as usual, Bruce refused to come. People were beginning to think he was a figment of her imagination!

This was the first place she'd worked where they'd had the facilities, money and inclination to provide staff with Christmas festivities, and everyone said it was ITP's highlight of the year. At lunchtime everyone, apparently, got in the Christmas spirit, including the directors, making silly jokes and speeches after what Sam termed a 'slap-up dinner' in the canteen. Under the pretext of Christmas and mistletoe, quite a few men threatened to kiss her and she could only hope David wouldn't think she was encouraging anyone.

The moment the clock struck noon, voices and laughter from people emerging from their offices echoed down the corridor. The stairwell door opening brought strains of 'God Rest Ye, Merry Gentlemen' being sung in the hall two storeys beneath them.

Grace stood and tidied her desk. "I've put notes on

these files for you. It's good of David to let me have so much time off, especially as he has to come in over Christmas. Thank you again, Jane, for filling in for me. I'm sure you'll cope — it should be fairly quiet. You can always...."

She broke off as David's door opened to reveal his tall, well-built figure handsomely dressed in a tuxedo. He beamed at Jane and Grace. "Well, I'm ready. Come on, you two."

The twinkling merriment in his eyes transformed him from the solemn business man he'd been in the last two weeks, back to the light-hearted colleague they'd both enjoyed in Brussels.

Jane muttered to Grace, "Bit overdressed, isn't he?"

"I'll ignore that, young Jane. Just follow me please,"

Jane made a face at Grace, who shook her head reprovingly. Obediently, they clattered down the backstairs behind him to the first floor where, on David's instructions, they tucked their arms into his before making a grand entrance down the main staircase.

While they'd been in Brussels, the Press Department had formed a choir of those who could sing, and they were now under the huge Christmas tree in the hall. As the three of them bowled down the stairs to the chorus of 'Hark, the Herald Angels Sing', Rosemary, in the midst of the singers, saw them and scowled. Grace obviously didn't see it, but David did.

"By the look on Rosemary's face, she should be singing 'Hark, the Glowering Angel Sings'! Methinks she's in need of a little Christmas spirit."

Jane looked up at him. "Methinks it will take more than Christmas spirit to melt Rosemary's icy attitude."

David looked thoughtful, while Jane reflected that only God's Spirit could change Rosemary.

At the bottom of the stairs David picked up two glasses of sherry from the reception desk. "Here, ladies. Cheers, and Happy Christmas."

As Grace accepted, Jane refused. "Not for me thanks – makes me ill. Even a glass of wine can lead me to do things I might afterwards regret."

David gave a broad smile and left them to mingle with the staff emerging into the hall from all directions.

As anticipated, mistletoe had mysteriously appeared. ITP's hundred or so employees were mostly under thirty-five, so budding romances weren't unusual, and the mansion had played host to several ITP weddings over the years. In most instances, kisses landed on Jane's cheek but, she supposed, it was inevitable that David would loom up when one man, already inebriated, decided she should receive more than that.

By taking her elbow, he gently extracted her while giving a low bow, "Now Gordon, you'll have to excuse us as I think it's time we went down to lunch."

On the way across the hall, she grinned. "Thanks, David. I'm relieved to find my guardian angel on duty."

He pushed the swing door and held it open for her to go through. As she passed, he bent to reply quietly, "Since my last call to duty proved I wasn't merely self-appointed, I remain vigilant and alert at all times to ensure that this particular damsel doesn't get herself into any further distress."

A telltale blush spread up her neck and face. Although she was thankful that his 'over and forgiven' attitude had restored a normal working relationship, his words betrayed that it was not forgotten.

The tables in the canteen had been pushed into rows, with more added to get everyone in. It was chaos as people scrambled over each other to find seats. Jill, at the head of a long table by the kitchen door, waved to Jane, who in turn saved places for Sam and Ian. Once the directors, all dressed in tuxedos, their backs to the canteen hatch with their secretaries opposite, were seated, Mr Plaidon banged the table with a spoon and announced, "Please be silent, Mr Reinhardt will say 'grace'.

With a broad smile around the room, David's eyes came to rest on Jane as he proclaimed, with what she could only call devilish delight, "For what we are about to receive, Lord, I ask you that you will bless this bunch, as they drink and munch, throughout their Christmas lunch. Amen."

A cheer went up, the party began. Crackers snapped, hats were donned, whistles and streamers blown, jokes read out and much laughter ensued.

The prawn cocktail was quickly demolished, and once the plates had been gathered up, the directors stood and, in their tuxedos, filed out like penguins into the kitchen, while Grace and the secretaries reached into the hatch and passed out the dishes of vegetables and gravy.

"This is part of the tradition," chuckled Sam.

David was the last to re-enter with the other directors in front of him, each carrying a big silver platter on which lay a huge turkey. David entered into his carving role with much flourishing and gusto, while maintaining non-stop jokes and banter as he sliced his turkey to be passed down the tables. The other directors, ten years and more above David's age, seemed to be taking a more staid approach, but with witty remarks they did encourage their younger colleague to keep his mind on the job. The general noise level grew as the wine flowed.

The directors finally sat to their own dinner, but it wasn't long before those now full of wine began tunelessly singing, "Bring out the figgy pudding." Again the penguin parade moved to the kitchen this time to re-appear with flaming Christmas puddings. From somewhere David found a soda siphon and pretending to put out unwanted fire, sprayed people more than the pudding flames.

Once the coffee was served along with chocolate liqueurs, Mr Plaidon, this time with much spoon banging against the riotous noise, announced it was time for "Directors' Ditties" which he started with a rather boring poem. Jane doubted anyone understood it, or thought it was funny. But by now, with the   majority well inebriated, anything was funny. The other items were better and David, as the youngest director, it seemed was to be the last.

David stood, and bowed at the cheering crowd. His hands holding the lapels of his jacket, he announced majestically, "It is, of course, Christmas. Therefore I felt it would be most fitting to sing a carol." He waited until the cheering and boos abated, and added, "Now, I'm sure most of you will know the tune to 'Joy to the World', if you don't, you'll soon pick it up. Feel free to join in the chorus."

Across the room Jane could see an air of manifest boredom. Several people began talking among themselves. But David wasn't daunted − in fact he looked as if he were sharing a joke with himself! She'd seen that look before!

"To make it more interesting, I've renamed it 'Joy to the Company', and you'll see why." The tittering and chatting ceased as his rich baritone voice rang out.

'Joy to the Company; But then came Jane.
Our lives have been quite changed.
While Grace and I have worked hard each day,
Jane's made us laugh and sing,
Jane's made us laugh and sing,
Jane's made us laugh and sing.'

Jane, the moment her name was mentioned, cringed. She buried her face in her hands and cried, "Oh no!" much to the amusement of those around her. Sam, on a broad grin, said, "It seems you've got yourself noticed again!"

Perhaps this was all part of David's strategy to break down barriers? It seemed that once again he was doing it at her expense. People were laughing, and looking around the room for her. Ian stood and, pointing at her, exclaimed,

"She's over here!" Embarrassed, yet oddly pleased, she didn't know what to do. Blushing profusely, she looked toward David. He nodded and smiled as he continued singing the first verse, which fortunately did involve other people besides her, bringing astonishment to others who, in the spirit of Christmas, had to laugh.

"Jane's made us laugh and sing," he sang across at her, while others began to take up the refrain. Obviously, David had chosen to forget the times when she hadn't made him laugh or sing! It was humbling that others would agree with his sentiments to join him by looking and singing it to her, some banging cutlery in time with the tune.

Each verse David had dedicated to a particular department in ITP, but it always ended with the chorus of 'Jane's made us laugh and sing'. There was no doubt the chorus was the highlight. Amazed, Jane looked around. Grace, Nikki, and the other secretaries at the top table were laughing and singing along, but three of the older directors looked ill at ease, mumbling the words into their beards, or hands.

The moment the song finished, the clapping and cheering started. David bowed theatrically all round, booming, "Thank you! Thank you! And a round of applause please for all those I've embarrassed today, especially the young lady who made this song possible."

As he flourished a hand in her direction, everyone's eyes turned onto her. Not knowing what else to do, she grinned inanely. Sam's shout of "Encore!" was taken up by others.

Now in full swing, David bowed to popular demand and, swaying in traditional music hall style, he sang each verse again, while at each chorus a roomful of raucous voices joined in. In the end he had to bang a spoon on the table to silence the applause, cheers and calls for another encore. "Thank you, but now we really must move on. It is now my pleasure to present the Grand Draw prizes."

After the raffle winners had yelled their delight and scrambled over people, chairs and tables to collect their prizes, David called order again. This time he presented the snooker prize to the new tournament champion who had defeated the holder of the previous ten years. Great cheering went up and he was forced again to bang the table with a spoon for silence. "And now it is my great pleasure to announce the winner of this year's Table Tennis Championship. Known and loved by us all, not least myself, I present this cup to the one and only — Miss Jane Mackenzie!"

It must have been David's song that had hyped them up, for why else would everyone be all cheering so loudly, banging the tables and giving her a standing ovation? Head down, glad her seat wasn't that far from his, she made her way toward him.

David's words reverberated in her mind with her steps. 'Known and loved by us all, not least myself'. What had she done to deserve such words? Did everyone know and love her? Everyone but Rosemary! It would seem like it. And fancy David saying that in front of everyone. She was in front of him now and she lifted her head up, and put out her hands to accept the cup. Her eyes full of her adoration of him, she met his black, amused and twinkling ones. With a gentle smile she mouthed, "Thank you."

David's eyes didn't leave hers. It was expected that David would say a few congratulatory words so she waited for the incredible noise to die down. Just as it ebbed some brave, but drunk, soul at the back of the canteen shouted, "Kiss her!" and from all directions other voices took it up.

Surely she hadn't been gazing up at David in such a way that she was asking to be kissed? Appalled, she looked around. The clapping started again, but this time slow and rhythmic as others took up the chant, until it seemed the whole canteen was echoing in unison, "Kiss her! Kiss her!" The scene associated itself in her mind with a victim in front of a lynch mob and she comforted herself that they weren't shouting as they had at Jesus, "Crucify her!"

David gave a rueful glance at his fellow directors who were smiling inanely at their staff. What should she do? Everyone was looking at her. She moved to walk away, but David's hand caught her elbow, as he boomed over the din, "As it's Christmas, a time of goodwill, it will give me great pleasure to comply with your demand."

The canteen of people it seemed went into uproar. Jane wasn't sure which was more frightening — the sound or seeing David's eyes, filled with mirth, heading downwards towards her. Her eyes widened like saucers, she grasped the cup to her chest as if it would afford her some protection and, in a spontaneous reaction, she turned her cheek in line with his mouth. His lips came within a fraction of her ear, his breath fanned her cheek as he murmured, "I hope Jane you're feeling forgiving today?"

It was then everything seemed to go into slow motion. David with his thumb and forefinger took hold of her chin and gently drew her face around towards him. Hypnotised by his taunting eyes, she watched as his gaze fell to her now uplifted mouth. A quiver of apprehension ran through her as his face drew near. A hair's breadth from her lips, he teased, "Don't look so frightened Jane, you might even enjoy it."

The moment David's lips met hers in a gentle, teasing and to her mind longer than necessary kiss, the canteen of people seemed to erupt into cheering him on. David's hand slipped around her cheek, his thumb gently caressing her neck, his other went round her waist, while she held steadfastly on to the cup between them. The soft exploration of her lips wasn't hot with passion, but was such to make her wonder if this was what a kiss was meant to be — a very tempting entrée to a sensual experience. His mouth nibbled and retreated, nibbled and retreated and until slowly as though loath to stop, his lips slid from hers.

It took her a second to realise he'd finished and, when she did open her eyes, his amused ones scanned her face while blocking her view of the still raucous audience.

Despite her attempt to appear as though nothing untoward had happened, her face felt hot, her body weak, and her mind disorientated! The headiness she put down to drinking too much wine exacerbated by lack of air! Around them, voices cried, "Kiss her again! Go on, Mr Reinhardt. Kiss her again."

David kept her in the crook of his arm and held up his other hand for quiet. With a broad smile, he said wryly, "I think Jane's had enough, and I don't think I'd dare...." He added a wicked wink.

Dazed by events, Jane felt as if the earth was trembling with the noise of stamping feet, cheering and ribald comments. David, with his arm still around her, escorted her back to her table and, as she sat, bent to murmur, "I'm sorry, Jane, that wasn't in a more private place!"

There was no opportunity to respond. Her eyes flashed in indignation at his retreating back. She grit her teeth, longing to retaliate but, for now, sat weak-kneed and shaking. She was thankful that David had called everyone else to sit, and his witty comments whilst announcing details about the evening event had quickly and skilfully diverted people's attention away from her.

Sam, who'd been grinning across the table at her like a Cheshire cat, was the first to speak as the party broke up. "My! Didn't you have an unexpected treat? You looked quite dazed."

"So would you be, if you'd been publicly ravished."

Jill, who was piling crockery on to a tray a few feet away said, "That's a bit strong, isn't it?"

"Well, how would you like him to do something like that to you?"

Jill shrugged. "It was only a bit of fun."

Jane grunted, and stared meaningfully at her. "Well it's

a good job you see it that way!"

Jill momentarily looked awkward as Sam took the subject up. "I never expected 'im to take the request up. Fancy 'im kissing you like that. Thought you'd just get a peck. I 'spect 'e thought 'e was on to a good thing, it being in the spirit of Christmas, because you could 'ardly slap his face."

Jill laughed, "Not even Jane would dare do that!"

Jane responded with a weak smile. So David hadn't told Jill what happened in Brussels! To move on, she asked, "Who was it, who started it off?" She looked at Sam, "I know it wasn't you, but you and your cronies certainly joined in. I have never been so embarrassed in my entire life!"

Ian guffawed, "Oh yes you have!"

"I just couldn't help meself. Best bit of fun I've 'ad in ages. What a turn-up though. One of the toffs doing that!"

Ian sniggered, "It's Jane, Sam. Irresistible! No Jane, don't deny it – he's sung to us, 'you make him laugh and sing'. From behind his back, Ian produced a small piece of mistletoe and held it up. "I was just wondering if, as it is Christmas, could I claim similar privileges seeing as it is Christmas and it was me you beat at table tennis?"

Out of the corner of her eye, Jane saw David looking in her direction. In a desire to show David his kiss was one of many, and forgetting her resolve not to stir up love and desire, she leant forward to plant a kiss on Ian's mouth and found he too turned what was meant to be a peck into a kiss of more passion. The action drew caterwauling from those nearby. Ian proclaimed as he released her, "Mmm! Not bad, but I think as such a good loser I deserve another."

For Jane, she felt she'd gone from a tempting entrée to a meal in a moment, and knew which kiss she preferred. It came as almost a relief to hear David's voice boom, "Jane, there really is no need for you to kiss every member of staff, so if you've quite finished I think we should head back to the office and tidy up."

Jane made a face. Jill got the giggles.

One of Sam's machine mechanics called, "That's the way, mate. Keep her in order."

David grinned nonchalantly. Jane scowled.

Back in the hall, people were standing in groups, smoking and laughing. The place was packed. The carol singers now stood in rows on the steps of the main staircase, their rendering of the more popular carols now assisted by less tuneful voices.

Donna, looking slightly battered, eyes bright, smudged lipstick and swollen mouth, drunkenly lurched toward David waving a huge bunch of mistletoe. "Now then, Mr Reinhardt, you can't refuse a girl a Christmas kiss." She pursed her lips up at him.

Revolted, Jane looked at David expecting him to refuse, but instead he obliged with a peck on her cheek. Donna, however, had other ideas. Her arms wound themselves around his neck to stop him escaping until she'd thoroughly kissed him. Grace, coming through the swing door, stopped, her eyes widening at the sight of David in a clinch. Jane grinned, feeling that Donna was retribution for David's kissing her – and from where she was standing she could see he was doing his best to extricate himself .

Behind Jane, Marcus' voice exclaimed, "Aha! Donna's pounced on him then. And our Mr Reinhardt's certainly full of goodwill today, don't you think, Grace? Is this part of his 'let's rid ourselves of the them and us mentality campaign', or your influence, young Jane?"

Grace seemed to have lost her voice. Marcus bent and kissed Jane's cheek, instructing, "That's it then Jane, you keep making him laugh and sing. This makes life much more entertaining."

There was no doubt of the censure on Grace's face.

With a chortle, Marcus planted a kiss on Grace's cheek and added cheerily, "Happy Christmas, me dear. Don't worry about him. Let him laugh and sing. It's good for us all to see him enjoying himself. It won't do him any harm, especially as most of the staff have drunk enough today not to remember too much tomorrow!"

He moved away as David, now disentangled from Donna, groaned, "Please, you two, save me from any more of that!"

Unsympathetically, Jane chirped, "Now you know the way I felt!"

David gave her a slanted look. "Is that so?"

Embarrassed, she was pleased Grace distracted David by saying, "I need to speak with you."

Jane turned to listen to the choir, but picked up from the conversation that Rosemary had been spreading her personal connotations on David's lunchtime song and kiss.

"Um, let me see. I think that, in the spirit of Christmas, I can find a way to deal with Rosemary. You two wait here for me."

They looked at each other, recognising the rather cheery tone that usually indicated he was up to something. They didn't have long to wait, as David's voice boomed, "Ladies and Gentlemen, may I have your attention. I have just heard that one of these wonderful ladies in this choir has expressed – not directly, mind you, but by her actions – that she's in need of a Christmas kiss."

Grace gasped, "Oh no!"

Jane, hand over mouth, laughed. She spotted Rosemary in the middle of the fourth row, surrounded by other choir members. There would be no way of escape. It was obvious she'd no idea David was talking about her.

His hands on his lapels, his chest stuck out, David viewed his audience and, marching back and forth, drew them into his pantomime. "Now I ask you, should I kiss this lady? Or should I not?"

A good number of people shouted "Yes." Others, bemused or surprised, looked on. Someone called, "Who's the lady?"

David turned round and looked along the rows as though searching for her. The women members of the choir were smiling, or laughing amongst themselves. A few looked nervous, but Rosemary's scowl showed she wasn't finding David's performance at all amusing.

David goaded further. "I think I've found her in the choir. So do I hear a 'Yes' to give her a kiss? What would you have me do?"

Stirred up again, the crowd drew together, obviously trying to work out who the recipient might be. A different voice started the "Kiss her then, kiss her" refrain, and others took it up while female members of the choir looked at each other wondering who which one had been picked out. Rosemary unaware it was she scowled and shook her head as her neighbours spoke to her.

A slow clapping joined the rhythm. David, having now incited his audience, smiled up at the choir, this time with his eyes fixed on his quarry! Rosemary was still oblivious. It took nudges from her neighbours before she realized she was the target. Grace, eyes glued on David, once more shook her head in disbelief. Rosemary's eyes widened as the front three rows of the choir opened up leaving a path before her.

Jill sidled up beside Jane and Grace. "What is he up to? Is someone getting their own back on Rosemary? I can't imagine for one minute she told anyone she wanted David to kiss her."

David waited, hand outstretched toward Rosemary. Jane felt uncomfortable, sure that Rosemary's hardhearted attitude was a cover up for some inner pain. "I know you'll both think I'm being ridiculous, but I feel sorry for her. David may have kissed me, but it was done in the spur of the moment, egged on by others. But this, this is a deliberate act to publicly embarrass her and I don't like it, or think it's funny."

Grace, her eyes watching David, murmured, "There, Jane, we are agreed."

Rosemary had turned looking for escape. But it seemed to Jane that those behind her deliberately closed ranks. Now trapped, Rosemary stood tall, and with almost regal bearing and dignity faced her opponent, her eyes filled with blazing rage. Was it that which made David stop at eye level, one step below Rosemary?

Later, Jill reported from several of the choir members around Rosemary that David said: "Jane won a prize. I didn't single her out, but I have you. I trust you understand why?"

And Rosemary, through clenched teeth, had snarled, "Don't touch me."

At that, David had apparently pointed out, "We have an audience. Unless you wish to become a laughing stock, I suggest you comply."

Amid the general clamour and ribald comments, David picked up her hand and, lifting it high, made to escort her down the stairs. At that point, Rosemary capitulated and they descended like an eighteenth century couple about to enter a quadrille.

Jane, despite her reservations, couldn't stop a giggle as, once in the hall and with great panache, David lifted Rosemary's hand to his mouth and kissed her fingertips, his eyes fixed on hers. It was strange because what had started out as an act of vengeance, David was turning into an act of romance. The kiss moved up to her wrist, but the look of disdain on her face spoilt it. David stepped closer and murmured something against Rosemary's lips before kissing her. The hall fell completely silent as the scene was played out. It could have been a romantic movie, except from where Jane was standing Rosemary's eyes weren't filled with adoration or love, but of a very wary, then frightened, trapped animal.

Grace, obviously disturbed, walked out of the hall. Jane gave Jill a frown and followed after her.

"Are you alright, Grace?"

In a murmur addressed to no-one in particular, Grace said, "I can barely comprehend it. David making a public spectacle...." She stopped speaking.

"I suppose it's Christmas, too much wine, maybe? Anyway if it takes that permanent scowl off Rosemary's face it would be worth it."

"Hardly likely!" Grace entered and closed the cubicle door.

Jane came out of the toilet as Grace was washing her hands. "Not much faith then, Grace, in David's reputation as a hot-blooded male and womaniser?"

"I don't believe in gossip, Jane, and I suggest you don't either. Now, let's get back to the office and tidy up."

As they re-entered the hall, the carol, 'While shepherds watched their flocks by night', had just begun and some of the more inebriated members were singing the alternative words – 'While shepherds washed their socks by night'.

David, it appeared, had been waiting for them. His voice boomed across the hall, "Aha! There you are!" He strode towards them, with a very large piece of mistletoe.

Grace muttered, "How many glasses of wine have you had?"

He laughed, "Not as many as you think! But now it's your turn." His kiss landed on Grace's cheek, she blushed profusely. "Thank you for all your hard work. It's highly appreciated. "

With the mistletoe waving over her head, Jane proffered her cheek and tapped it with her finger. David kissed it muttering, "Spoil sport!" The haughty look she gave him caused him to stare and remembering, his words about her teasing and flirting, she quickly turned her attention to the choir, where half of them were gallantly trying to continue with the official words while others were collapsing into drunken laughter. Rosemary, she noted, was missing.

"So, Mr Reinhardt, may I be so bold as to enquire whether Rosemary melted under your touch?"

David fiddled with his tie and made a play of rubbing his chin, before answering. "Well, Jane, I'm not sure whether the few seconds of our delectably warm moment together has ignited a fire sufficient to melt her but, as you see, she has disappeared."

Grace shot David such a thunderous look that, taken aback, he gaped at her. Grace shook her head, turned and marched across the hall to the back stairs.

Bemused, Jane looked at David, to find him staring after Grace in consternation. "Jane, give me a few minutes with Grace, will you?" In a few strides he caught up with her and together they went through the door to the stairs.

Perhaps now both she and Rosemary had been singled out publicly by David, they'd have something in common. Maybe in sympathising with each other it would help to repair the rift. People were chatting and laughing in groups, but with the choir's efforts finally collapsed, the hall gradually emptied as some made their way home, or back to their offices to sit and chat before getting ready for the evening party.

Not wishing to disturb David and Grace, Jane slipped down the corridor to her old office. The door was open, the room immaculately tidy and empty. Rosemary's coat, which usually hung behind the door, wasn't there. When had she left? Maybe the telephonists had seen her leave? She called in to chat to them, but they had only just returned to the switchboard themselves. Maybe Jill had seen her leave?

Jane strolled back into the entrance hall to see David

and Jill conversing by the Reception Desk. David crossed the hall to meet her.

"Is Grace alright? She seemed very upset."

"She'll be fine. I told her to get her coat and be gone. Her flight to Germany is at 7.30 and I think she is feeling a bit uptight about it — and seeing Wilhelm again, of course. If we go up now you'll just have time to wish her well."

"I couldn't help feeling sorry for poor Rosemary. I thought as we'd both been made a public spectacle of by you today, I'd offer her a crumb of comfort, but I couldn't find her."

David closed the lift gate. "Now Jane, you can't blame me for kissing you — I really didn't have a choice. Rosemary, well, that was different, and...." He paused and considered. "Well... let's just say perhaps not the wisest choice of action. His gaze rested on her. "But surely, Jane, I didn't embarrass you?"

"Let's just say, you may not have had a choice, but you needn't have made such a meal of it!"

The roar of his laughter reverberated around the small area.

"Stop it! It's not funny."

He made a mournful moue, "I'm sorry, Jane, but you really do make me laugh and sing!"

"Not always."

The smile he gave her was reassuring along with the words, "Those times are best forgiven and forgotten."

"Thank you. In that case I'll forgive and forget about today. Just as I hope Rosemary will, because there is something badly wrong with her."

David's face momentarily clouded over before he perked up to say, "It's part of the Christmas festivities to kiss lovely young ladies, and I didn't get the impression you were adverse to my kissing you."

Jane tutted and pursed her lips. "After your comment about wishing it had been in a more private place, I think I need to make it clear that should you wish to kiss me again, on my cheek will be quite sufficient."

David smiled broadly, "Um. Is that so!"

Jane bestowed him a haughty look, "It had better be."

Exasperated, David ran his hand through his hair. "My God, Jane, you're one very provocative, young lady!" The lift jerked to a halt at their floor.

"God doesn't like his name taken in vain."

David, pulling the gate back, stopped. "And you Jane, would do well to remember what I said to you the other week. Provocation can be in a word, a deed, or an expression and another man would probably have taken that look as a come on, not a stay away!"

Anxiously she bit her lip trying to understand exactly what it was she'd done wrong.

David, with a click of impatience, moved back to let her through and said brusquely, "Think about it, Jane. In the meanwhile let's get on, for the quicker we finish today the sooner we get home to prepare for this evening's party."

Jane had accepted Pam's invitation to her flat for tea and as a place to change, but she found Pam's imaginings and questioning about David irritating. It was fortunate she could quell some of Pam's surmising about her by telling her that David was bringing Felicity to the party.

What she didn't tell Pam, and couldn't understand herself, was that David was still not acknowledging Jill as his girlfriend, yet had been willing to tell the whole company that she, Jane, made him laugh and sing! To her surprise Jill wasn't even perturbed, happily commenting, "It's better to keep work and relationships separate. Felicity is a family friend, always happy to oblige — especially if it stops fingers pointing and tongues wagging."

Jane had argued that people would get the wrong impression, but Jill had brushed her off with, "Oh, too bad.

I know they're not together. He and Felicity were never besotted with each other. The family thought David ought to settle down, and Felicity was available. That was okay until David realized his strong attraction...."

Jill had coloured and dried up and Jane, laughing, had finished her sentence, "....to the lovely Jill."

When she saw Jill's weak smile, she wondered whose idea it had been to keep quiet about their relationship.

Jane changed into the outfit she'd bought, which she thought was very Carnaby Street. She'd fallen in love with a lime green dress with concertina thin pleated long sleeves, but it was far too miniskirted for her. Fortunately, in another shop she'd found black trousers with the same pleats so, by putting the two together and adding a chain belt, she had a fun outfit ideal for an informal party and dance.

Pam, it seemed was in no hurry, but continued to try on different clothes so her flatmates could decide which was best. So the party was well underway before they arrived.

The large first-floor conference room was on this occasion turned into a nightclub, one which she'd helped to create a few days before. Ian was helping out at the makeshift bar at one end, and to the side of it, in a gap before the dance floor, were the majority of red-clothed tables with holly-decorated centre pieces with lit candles. Further tables, for those who wanted to talk rather than dance, were in an ante-room connected by double doors. The dance floor area was separated off by wooden partitioning made up by Stan, the handyman. From each of its joists she'd strung a set of coloured fairy lights purchased, along with most of the other items, in Petticoat Lane Market the previous Sunday.

Chris County bowled up to stand beside her as she admired some of her handiwork. "You were right Jane, those angle poise lights covered in different shades of cellophane do make nice coloured spots on the wall — very effective with their different heights. Let's hope everyone collects them back after Christmas. I like, too, those leftover sets of fairy lights on the wall opposite the French windows. Was it your idea to use them to draw a big Christmas tree?"

"No, Nikki's. But it works well. When the dance floor's empty they reflect in the French windows."

"Well this is the best I've ever seen for a Christmas party — well done!" Jane preened with pleasure and was even more delighted when Chris asked her to dance. And after him there were many more wanting to claim her attention. Finally she made it to the bar to get a drink, but Ian only let her take a few gulps before he snatched it from her and, laughing, said, "I've been waiting for an opportunity to dance with you."

Several months earlier they'd discovered they could both dance. Last week, Ian had brought in a tape recorder and they'd not only remembered every step of the ballroom jive they'd ever been taught, but also improvised on others they'd seen at the cinema. Although, as Ian pushed her through his legs and then rolled her over his back, she wondered if maybe they'd gone a bit too far! Still the way everyone stopped to watch, and some to gasp — they were impressed!

Had Bruce been there, he wouldn't have been! Was he a stick in the mud, or was it because she was enjoying the social life at work that accentuated his dullness? Perhaps during Christmas she would pluck up courage and talk to him about their relationship — or lack of it. It would be good if she could start the New Year afresh. The record stopped and so did she, somewhat giddily!

Ian found her a seat and, hot and sweaty, she flopped into it while he went to get her drink. A familiar voice boomed, "Off the dance floor at last, young Jane! Let me introduce you to Felicity."

Jane looked up, wiped her damp hair from her brow and said breathlessly, "Oh, hello!"

Felicity was all Jill wasn't. She looked like a model, or film star. Jill was tall, but she certainly didn't have a devastating figure and face, beautiful long blonde hair and a peaches and cream complexion. But Jill's eyes were always warm and friendly. Felicity's gaze was politely cool, and her words somehow lacked truth as she put out her beautifully manicured hand and said, "Pleased to meet you."

Jane stood to place her sweaty palm in Felicity's cold dry one. It was hard not to feel diminished and by her, which wasn't helped by Felicity's slightly supercilious gaze as it swept over her outfit as she cooed, "David and I have been watching you. Quite a performance!"

Jane detected Felicity's faint disgust as she let go of her hand, and the edge in her voice, but shrugged it off to smile pleasantly, "Oh, thank you. Ian and I have been practising."

"David tells me you had quite a time in Brussels."

Warily, Jane's eyes flicked to David. What had David said? She was sure David wouldn't have told Felicity about her exploits, so she agreed light-heartedly, "Did he? Well, that would cover it!"

Not knowing what else to say, she looked to David for support.

Felicity possessively slipped her arm into his, and looked into his face with a little smile that Jane felt said, 'Come on dear, we've talked to this sweaty little upstart — you've done your duty'. David frowned at her, then declared, "If you'll excuse us, I promised Felicity a dance. See you later."

Relieved that was over, she watched them meld together and execute a perfect waltz manoeuvre.

"So you've been honoured and introduced to the fiancée?" Ian put the drinks on the table and sat down.

Jane grunted. "The answer is 'no' to both. I wouldn't call it honoured, and their engagement ended a few months ago."

"Ruffled your feathers, did she?"

"You could call it that. I felt like a bit of dirt that she had to acknowledge was under her foot!"

Ian laughed, "You do come up with them! But I tell you she's made a mistake there. That bit of dirt is, in fact, a gold nugget – but she's too dim to recognise it."

"Oh, Ian, you really do say the nicest things." She bent forward and gave Ian a kiss on the mouth.

"Umm, I'll have more of that, my little nugget."

Laughing, Jane downed her coke, leapt to her feet and pulled him up. "Come on! Let's show them that when two gold nuggets come together on the floor, they're worth more than just a glance!"

When she and Ian got into the cha cha and began to hog the limelight she noted David's cool smile, and remembered a previous time. Did David think she was overdoing it? Well, what about him? How did he think Jill felt about Felicity? In fact, where was Jill?

Jane looked around and spotted her with a group from the Design Department. Whereas Felicity was devastatingly attractive and the epitome of sophistication, Jill, although tastefully dressed, still looked buxom. Her features were homely and her unruly hair gave her a scatty air! Jane knew who she'd pick – but then she wasn't David. Jill was fun and completely genuine, while Felicity's attitude and smile had been, if anything, condescending. But maybe she'd felt as awkward as Jane had?

It was apparent from Jill's attitude she wasn't finding anything awkward. Indeed, she was now chatting up Chris from the Press Department. Baffled, Jane continued dancing. David, it appeared, didn't seem to notice Jill and was, in fact, smiling and talking to Felicity as if no one else in the world mattered. Jane watched as Felicity put her arms around David's neck, her long body moved seductively against his. He certainly didn't appear averse to her affections. Next time she spotted them, Felicity was laughing and then kissing him. Wasn't this rather overdoing diversionary tactics? Jane looked for Jill and saw her thoughtfully watching them. As soon as the dance ended Jane joined her. "Come on Jill, let's get a drink."

"Is something wrong?"

"Yes! David and Felicity. I don't like it and, from your face, you don't either."

"Does it upset you seeing David being kissed by Felicity?"

"Yes, when he's going out with you."

Jill's expression was pained, but her gaze stayed on the entwined couple. "I think Felicity still wants to be an actress. She enjoys playing a part and does it well, don't you think?"

Jane felt cross. "But Jill, you must mind! I would if I were you! Frankly I can't understand David's behaviour!"

Jill shrugged. "It wasn't David's idea, well not exactly – it was mine. You know me. You know how I feel. I just don't want our relationship to be common knowledge. Not yet anyway." She gave a rueful smile, "I'm not like you. You enjoy being popular. You don't feel ridiculed at having songs sung about you, or being kissed by David in front of everyone." Jane opened her mouth to speak, but Jill rushed on, "I don't mind, honestly, about those two looking like love birds."

"You do love him, don't you?"

"Yes, of course – it would be hard not to."

"Then how can you bear people seeing him with Felicity? Now I know him, I think he's a pretty amazing man, and he'll make a wonderful husband and a good father. If it were me, I'd want everyone to know we belonged together."

"Would you?" Jill paused for thought. "Could you be

interested in him if…?"

"No, you goose, I was talking about you! He is, dear Jill, all you've ever wanted – so don't push him away and hide in the background. In fact I'm surprised he's letting you. I may not have known David long, but I've seen his bulldog tenacity to get what he wants, so I find it hard to understand his casual attitude towards you."

Jill didn't reply. They watched the dancers in silence until Jane was asked to dance.

It was some while later when Jane caught sight of Jill again – this time talking animatedly with David and Felicity. After that, Felicity danced with a few of the directors and department heads while David danced with a number of employees, which included her and Jill. Fortunately for David, the music was too loud to hold a conversation, otherwise Jane might have had a word or two to say on her friend's behalf!

The main lights came on and David stepped forward. "Well everybody, I'm sure you'd agree no Christmas party would be a party without games." There were boos and cheers. "So, can I suggest we get into departmental teams? If you aren't in a department join one of your choice. First game, pass the balloon between the knees, now that's not too difficult."

Jane joined the Print Department team. Ian looked flustered, causing her to ask, "Don't you want me with you?"

"It's not that – it's Mr Reinhardt. Well, I feel he's watching me."

"Oh don't be silly. Of course he's not."

"Well, look round now then."

Jane turned. David was looking thoughtfully in their direction. Seeing her eyes upon him, he smiled and carried on the instructions for the games.

"He's probably working out the numbers in each team. Or keeping a fatherly eye on me. He and Grace seemed like parents to me in Brussels."

Ian shrugged, and seemed about to say something, but changed his mind.

In the games she spent most of the games buckled over with laughter, incapable of passing anything between her knees, her nose or any other part of her body.

When David announced the teams' scores, he ended with, "And, thanks to Jane, the Print Department has no points."

Jane poked her tongue out at him. David gave her an affectionate smile. Ian made a disgruntled sound.

"Now for the finale – my very own version of 'Postman's Knock' which is a cross between that and 'Murder in Dark!'" David grinned around the room as people laughed and groaned. "It's great fun. The only thing is – be careful! If you knock at the wrong door, once the lights go on it could lead to a murder or two!" The dozen or so older people who had bravely taken part in the team games headed toward the other bar. "Don't go! Anyone can play! Just get a partner, any age, any sex," David boomed with amusement, "Although it might be more fun with a member of the opposite one. And if you really want to sit this fun game out, get yourself a drink now from the bar and relax in the other room where there will be a little light!"

Jane, desperate for a drink, slipped out of the dance area to the bar.

Jill found her there. "What are you doing in here?"

"Oh I don't think I am up for one of David's games!"

"Come and sit with me then, I'm to turn the lights on and off. Help me blow out these candles."

"There you are Jane! I've been looking for you. Come and partner me."

"Sorry, Ian, she's sitting this one out!" Jane gave Jill a bemused look. Jill fiddled with her hair, "Oh, go on then."

All the disco style lights were switched off, leaving

only the main chandelier on as she and Ian joined the sixty of so couples remaining in the dance floor area. David, in the middle of the room, was explaining the instructions of his rather bizarre game with a lot of interruptions from those around. "Okay, folks. Now you've got the general gist, you are all in couples and pairs have you now decided on your 'doorbells' sound, then separate to opposite corners of the room."

Jill drew Jane back to the door near the light switch while sending Ian towards the French windows. To her fellow players Jane commented, "This is a silly game, and not difficult, for all we have to do is walk into the middle of the room, make your chosen doorbell sound, attract your partner and together wait until the lights go up."

Marcus still game at 50-something chuckled, "My dear, you've missed the point. Whilst you are finding the right door or bell, every door you bump into you post a kiss on the box!"

Revelation hit Jane. "So Marcus, that's why it's a cross with 'Murder in the Dark'. For, should you bump into the wrong door and kiss the wrong box, you could well find you've been murdered in the dark!"

Men in the vicinity chortled while several women giggled.

"Okay, everyone. Remember you must head out across the room so as not to bump into the partition. And when you have the right door and bell, stay together. Are you ready? Then let's play...." Jill approached David. "Ah, Jill. I thought you were doing the light! Excuse me a minute everyone."

Jane smiled. Perhaps Jill had decided to make sure they had their own secret rendezvous! She then grimaced, it seemed not, as David beckoned a rather bored looking Felicity, said a few words to her, and sent her to where Ian and others were standing. David grinned around the room. "It seems that several of you think I should play my own ridiculous game. I can see that's fair, so I'll turn off the light and Jill will turn them back on again in, say, five minutes!" In ten strides, amid much laughter and cheering, he made it to the light switch. "Okay. Ready everyone? Let's go!"

The room was plunged into blackness. A couple of women screamed, followed by short giggles and rumbles of laughter as people careered into each other trying to cross the room. Jane's eyes just didn't adjust to the darkness. The chosen door bell noises weren't bell-like. Someone was snorting like a pig, someone else was neighing like a horse. The sounds got louder as people got into it.

Arms outstretched, she thought to avoid too many unwanted kisses posted. She and Ian had chosen an owl-like sound, but despite avoiding people by ducking or turning aside if they touched her, and heading straight across the room while making 'twit-to-woo', she couldn't hear or find Ian. Behind her a hand touched her arm. She made her noise and didn't get a responding one. She went to move away, but the hand wouldn't let go and moved to grab her waist, while the other slid to caress ears and neck. Her protest wasn't dissimilar to others in the hall as hands cupped her face and a cool mouth met with hers.

Her first thought was to put up her hands to ward him off. It certainly wasn't tall, skinny Ian. Her second thought, he was a nice kisser. Her third was, 'Well, it is Christmas'. Her fourth thought, that this was very pleasant and, as his tongue flicked seductively along her lips, her fifth came with a mew of pleasure as his kiss, combined with his fingers lightly caressing the back of her neck, sent her body an enticing message. Against his mouth she managed a tremulous whisper, "Who are you?"

His answer was to take her mouth again, his tongue gently and erotically flickering against her lips, willing her to open up to him. There was no sixth thought, and no sixth sense to alert her to the identity of the man – just her mind and body melded to one need. His hands slid to hold her upper arms as her head went back so he could nibble and kiss her Adam's apple, lower jaw and ear. Zones in her body felt they were being switched on, causing currents to eddy through her. Her lips quivered in anticipation as his sought hers again.

Her desire for this man outweighed any thoughts or sense. Her arms entwined themselves around his neck. Her fingers   caressed the short hair at the back of his neck. He shuddered and deepened his kiss. Skilfully and provocatively, his tongue played with hers until she was returning his kiss and delighting in it. Her whirling senses told her this was the stranger from the night of the Ball. It had to be. She caught the sound of his ragged breathing between the various doorbell sounds around them and asked against his mouth, "Is it you, Andrew?"

The answer was a light, yet incredibly erotic, finger circling her ear, as his lips made a similar gesture against hers. His hand slid down and drew her gently against him. This man was aroused, but he was tempting, not demanding, a response from her. He seemed to recognize and match her need – not something she associated with Andrew, but one she recognised from her stranger. His touch, like this, electrified her pulses and brought a reverberating pleasure, which built an ache from the centre of her womanhood. So captivated in a delicious aura of sensation, she barely noticed as he drew her to the wall but, as he left with a final brush of his lips, she leant weak-kneed against it wondering, yet again, who was he?

Abandoned in the blackness, in the ache of desire, she wanted to cry out her frustration. Did this man know the effect of his touch upon her? Did he experience such intensity of feelings? Could Andrew have gate-crashed the party, and seen it as some kind of prank? Yes, Andrew would enjoy doing that, but it was doubtful that to entice her, he would become a kind, considerate and sensitive lover. But if it wasn't Andrew, then who was it?

The angle poise party lights were being switched on one by one. She lifted her head and in the murky light she could see other couples, sitting and standing, some along the wall beside her. Several people were still wandering about in the middle. She slipped from the wall to the nearest chair. David, with Felicity on his arm, appeared in the centre of the room to announce, "Well folks, it's back to disco dancing again, and, if you haven't found your partner or have the wrong one, remember it's Christmas and the time of goodwill to all men, so no murders please." He laughed, and concluded, "Merry Christmas everyone!"

People around Jane laughed, commenting on the appropriate choice of the DJ playing Elvis Presley's song 'Return to Sender' after David's Postman's Knock. And as Elvis sang the words, 'address unknown', she felt an echo in her heart, 'man unknown'. It had to be Andrew – there was no other explanation and, in the general dimness of the rooms, no one would particular notice him. Unless of course it was someone entirely different having some amusement at her expense – married too she didn't doubt.

She felt such sadness because it was obvious, with the right man, her body was capable in seconds of dissolving into aching desire, but it would take a miracle to find a man who could bring her such pleasure and who shared her faith! Could she put up with second best? After two very unpleasant experiences with worldly men, she certainly wasn't trying for a third! God's patience – and David's – had been more than tried.

It seemed thinking about David was enough to bring him to her side. Warily, she looked up at him as he towered over her, booming, "Hello, Jane. What are you doing sitting over here, all alone? Did you enjoy my game?" He sat down beside her, "Good heavens! You look as though you've seen a ghost."

Her voice shook. "In a way...." She trailed off, hugging herself into a ball, and felt a sympathetic tap on her shoulder. Encouraged, she relaxed enough to stammer out, "I — I didn't just see him. I felt him."

"Ho! Ho! Ho!"

The amusement in his voice made Jane scowl and think, rather unkindly, how suited his voice would be to the role of Father Christmas.

Oblivious to her reaction he went on, "This house might be old, Jane, but not that old!"

"I'm not talking about ghosts of Christmas past, but a ghost of Christmas present!"

In a ghost-like voice, David added, "Even perhaps, Jane, the ghost of Christmas future. Oooh...to show you what's to come..." He gave a long low moan. As she didn't laugh, he asked, "Did it touch you? Was it all cold and clammy?"

His facetiousness caused her to snap crossly, "Anything but!"

He peered into her face. "Oh dear. You really are upset."

"More shaken," she muttered with a grimace.

"Tell me what happened." It was more demand than concern.

"Well, I can't believe Andrew Carlton would come here tonight — but I am sure it's the same man as before."

"What man as before? Jane, you're talking in riddles."

"The man who made a pass at me in your office."

David's brow creased. "Which man?" he barked.

Exasperated, Jane wondered how many men he thought had been making passes at her in his office? With a sigh, she declared, "The one on the night of the Ball, of course. I think he's here tonight."

"So?" The smile twitching the corners of his mouth did not escape her notice.

"Don't laugh! It's not at all funny."

His face drew taut in an effort to placate her, "So?"

"Well, in the brief time he was here, he...." She hesitated. It occurred to her that David probably knew more about her than most people, so she blurted out, "He can make me feel the way no other man has ever done."

"How's that?"

"Oh, David!" she exclaimed, "Do stop cross-examining me."

"Sorry." He shrugged, "It's a habit." There was a brief pause, then he rose to his feet. "I thought you might appreciate my showing a fatherly concern and interest."

She leant back in her chair to look up at him before saying irritably, "Well, if you must know, he made me feel as though he'd wired my body to an electric current and switched on the high voltage."

David roared with laughter. Those around looked in their direction. "Oh my! What a description!" He sat down again and while she frowned with annoyance he pulled out his handkerchief and wiped his eyes. "Oh Jane! Sorry – but you do have a way with words!"

Ian arrived to exclaim, "There you are, Jane. Are you okay? What happened?" He gave David a long look and went on, "I couldn't find you in the dark. It felt silly doing those owl noises, and I'd only done a couple and someone grabbed me and kissed me." He laughed somewhat sheepishly and added, "I did try and escape, honestly, but she seemed glued to me and she was some kisser. Wish I knew who she was, but she disappeared as the first light was lit."

Jane grimaced, and put out her hand for Ian to help her to her feet. "Then, Ian, you and me both. I had much the same kind of experience – honestly David – you and your silly games! I suppose we should we grateful that with ghosts about stirring up our lives there wasn't a murder in the dark. Come on Ian, let's go and dance. Let's do one of our best ballroom jives, because I need to do something to let off steam, and I rather think that could do it!"

CHAPTER 12

By the afternoon of Christmas Day, feet up after the Queen's Speech, Jane decided she'd already had enough of entertaining; cooking; washing up; in fact everything and everyone but, most of all, Bruce!

Had the atmosphere at lunch been tense because of her? The incident at the Christmas party had affected her more than she dared admit even to herself. Bruce was morose in his quietness. Ted, Bruce's father, seemed unduly nervous to the point of making himself clumsy, and his over-appreciation of Jane's mother was causing her to be overly bright and extremely animated.

Now, sitting opposite Bruce in the armchair, Jane watched as each of them opened their presents. Within minutes, Bruce was piqued by the expensive gift David had given her. She'd assumed by the weight of the box it would probably contain expensive soap and bath salts. To her astonishment, and the others, David had given her a beautiful leather-bound Bible, with an inscription on the fly leaf:

> *Trust in the Lord, and do good; so you will*
> *   dwell in the land, and enjoy security.*
> *Take delight in the Lord and he will give you*
> *   the desires of your heart.   Psalm 37: 3-4*
>
> *I know you believe God's word is true, so may*
> *   you see the fulfilment of these words in the*
> *   coming year.   David*
> *Christmas 1966*

She supposed it wasn't all that extraordinary for a well-educated man like David to know the scriptures, but what had been extraordinary had been his choice of verse — one that meant so much to her. Had he asked Grace? It didn't matter — his thoughtfulness brought cheer to her heart and spirit, which was good for, on opening Bruce's present, it was a box of inexpensive toiletries that spoke of his boring dullness. She determined the future was definitely going to bring changes.

Jane also realized as the others opened their presents from her that, because she'd purchased her gifts in Brussels with David's money, she'd not thought of how much, but what was special they'd like. But now she realized she had diminished their gifts by her extravagance. Not that they said as much, but in surprise murmured, "Real silk, real leather, 14 carat gold. Oh, you shouldn't have." She had nearly said, 'Well I earn more money now and can afford it', but stopped in time to see just how much more than would have undermined them.

Jane bent down to clear away all the discarded wrappings, assuming as all the presents had gone from under the tree that was it, when Bruce's father announced, "Hold on, Jane, there's still one present to go. Joyce, I hope you didn't think I'd forgotten you, but I hid yours because I wanted it to be the last one." Ted rose and took a small box from the tree that looked like the other decorations.

Jane mused uncharitably that, unlike Bruce, perhaps Ted had put a little more thought into her Mother's present — a pair of pretty earrings, maybe? Was her Mum flushed because she was sitting in the firelight, or from wondering what was in the box that Ted was now giving her? Excited, Joyce ripped off the paper, opened the box, gaped at what was inside and then looked back at Ted who was now on his knees in front of her.

Jane, unable to see the contents, was intrigued. She glanced across at Bruce — his face was devoid of interest. What was Bruce's problem? Sitting forward she tried to see and asked, "What is it, Mum?"

Her mum was about to show her when Ted distracted her.

"Joyce — I feel – you see – being Christmas…it felt right."

Puzzled, Jane could only guess by her mum's rapt expression that she'd seen something expensive in the jeweller's window and Ted had got it for her. Now that was thoughtful and kind.

Tears brimmed in her mum's eyes. Ted put his hand over hers his voice full of emotion, "Oh Joyce, I've hoped – I've prayed you feel the same way. I feel you're God's gift to me. I've loved you from the moment I first met you. I just want to spend the rest of my life with you, so will you…" Ted swallowed hard, his voice a croak as he finished, "…will you marry me?"

Jane blinked the tears from her eyes. Dear Ted — how very romantic of him. He was so genuine, so keen, so obviously in love. He'd never replace her father, but her mum deserved some happiness. She tried to imagine Bruce saying or doing something romantic, but couldn't.

Suddenly, eagerly, like a young girl, her mum cried, "Oh, yes, yes Ted. I love you too. I've felt the same way about you, but was afraid if I said anything I'd never see you again."

"Oh what a silly ninny!" Ted slipped into the seat beside her and, drawing her into his arms, kissed her. They were both so caught up in the moment that Jane and Bruce were forgotten.

Jane stared across the room at Bruce who, in an attitude of resignation, was slumped in the chair staring blankly into the firelight. Perhaps this wasn't such a surprise to him. Maybe it was the reason he'd been so miserable and on edge. Should she too have seen this coming?

Ted and her mother drew apart, but with eyes only for each other. Jane watched as Ted picked up the box from where it had dropped in her mum's lap and pulled out the ring and placed it on her engagement finger.

Happiness beamed from them as they turned to show off the ring.

"Jane, oh Jane! Aren't you going to congratulate us?" Her gaze willed Jane to approve.

Jane jumped up and exclaimed honestly, "Of course I am!" First she hugged her mum and then Ted. "I'm so happy for you both. It's wonderful." Then, kneeling at her Mum's feet, she admired the row of rubies in a Victorian setting. Still Bruce hadn't said anything. Couldn't he have at least tried to be happy for them? How could he be so mean-spirited? Her mum followed her gaze and looked hurt at Bruce's silence.

To compensate, Jane said, "Oh, Ted, what a wonderful proposal. Fancy you falling in love with Mum on sight. Oh, that's what I would like to happen to me." Then, as she realized her words indicated she wasn't intending to marry Bruce, she rushed on, "Have you thought about a date? Is it to be soon?"

Her mum gave Ted an enquiring look. Ted laughed, "Well, I'm hoping sooner rather than later. Would you be in agreement with that Joyce – say the beginning of March?" Her mum, eyes sparkling, nodded happily.

"Bruce, what do you think?"

"Up to you, Dad. You'll do whatever you want anyway."

"Come on, boy, that's hardly fair. I've been father and mother to you for eight years since your mother died, and I'm sure Joyce will agree there will always be a home for you with us. Although, I think it's about time you went out and made a life for yourself."

Anxious to reassure him, Jane's mum chimed in, "Of course there'll be a home for you here. We'd be a proper family then, wouldn't we, Jane? You know the old saying, 'You don't lose a daughter, but gain a son'."

Jane pasted on a smile, but inwardly she groaned, for there were two certainties in her life. One, she didn't want to live with the newly married couple; two, she didn't want to marry Bruce. Somehow, this didn't seem the right time to bring that up, especially as Bruce had just roused himself to thank her mother for her kindness.

Time for a cup of tea. And time was going to bring its own changes. One way or another, she and Bruce would now have to talk about the future.

When David had first asked her to fill in for Grace and work with him for three days between Christmas and New Year, she'd met the idea with half-hearted acceptance. But now she felt relief — an opportunity to escape from home! For two days, she and Bruce had tried to pretend everything was normal for the sake of the happy couple, but their parents' engagement had definitely increased the unease and tension between them.

Jane gathered her coat tightly around her and bent her head against the freezing wind. It was unusual to see so few people about at this time in the morning, and Hyde Park Corner so quiet. Not all the offices opened between Christmas and New Year and some like ITP just allowed for a skeleton staff. She supposed David had volunteered to be 'in charge' as he was the only director without a wife and children. The question though was would she prove an adequate replacement for Grace, who seemed to instinctively know David's mind and decisions before he made them? Who would take Grace's place when she left?

Chris from the Press Department was pacing the hall as she came through the front door. "I don't know what we're going to do! Natalie rang – she's got the flu, and we've no switchboard. All the wrong phones are ringing in all the wrong...."

Interrupting him, she laughed, "Yes, thanks, Chris. I had a pleasant Christmas, how about you?"

He tutted and ignored her remark. "Natalie asked if you were in today and said you'd know what to do. I assume she meant you could find someone to sort it out?"

Fortunately, during her days of sharing an office with Rosemary, Jane used to escape to the switchboard room for a coffee break. She'd always watched with fascination Natalie and Sarah flicking switches, putting in and pulling out plugs across the two switchboards and, if they weren't too busy, they would let her have a go. Before she'd gone to work for David, there had been several occasions when busy and one of them needed to go to the toilet they'd asked her to help out. So, feeling fairly confident she could manage, she exclaimed with bravado, "Okay, okay, Chris. Have no worry, have no fear, for the wondrous Jane is here!"

Chris did have the grace to laugh and enquire about her Christmas.

Jane's confidence diminished once she saw all the night lines plugged into the board. Would she cope now practice was a reality? First she noted where the interconnecting plugs went so she could replace them that evening, and then with a deep breath pulled them all out, freeing up internal and outside lines. Immediately two of the six lines rang, and swiftly she was able to deal with them, before two more rang. Once the initial rush was over, she gave four departments a permanent line to use for their outgoing calls, and kept the first two for incoming. It appeared no-one else in the building could help with the switchboard and she rang Sarah but got no reply. Perhaps warned by Natalie she might be called in! The only thing, Jane concluded, was to combine the switchboard with her other duties. She prevailed upon Chris to bring down the necessary equipment from her office and it proved an excellent solution. There wasn't all that much work to do. There were several reports and letters, none of which were urgent, so she had plenty of time contemplate her present predicament at home, while the occasional interruption of the switchboard stopped her thoughts becoming too maudlin.

The canteen was closed and, with no one else to answer the telephone, it was fortunate she'd made some turkey sandwiches for lunch and wouldn't need to desert her post. She screwed up her empty lunch bag and aimed it at the waste paper basket as the swing door banged. Familiar footsteps came down the corridor. Her door opened, but before she could say 'careful' it was too late. One size 13 shoe bore heavily down on her brown paper bag, crushing a banana skin, an apple core and a couple of pickled onions she'd decided not to eat.

David looked down at the mess under his foot and boomed, "What the hell was that?"

Jane giggled, "Fortunately for you, only the remains of my lunch."

"I'll not ask, Jane. Just find me something to scrape it off will you?"

It was impossible not to laugh at him standing with one foot raised. He didn't look amused. She looked around trying to think of something, "I know Rosemary's got a nice gilt paper knife. I'm sure she wouldn't mind me borrowing it to use to dig at your shoe!" She slipped around him and returned moments later, brandishing it triumphantly.

He shook his head, took the knife from her, and began to remove the mush from the shoe's tread into the waste paper basket. "So this is where you are keeping yourself, young Jane. I've been wondering where you were."

David had taken to calling her 'young Jane' since Brussels and she wasn't sure whether she liked it or not. The switchboard buzzing into life took her attention. Once she'd dealt with the call, she commented, "Funny, isn't it, how everything always happens at once."

Silence.

She swung the chair around. David had gone! She giggled. Of one thing she could be certain – he hadn't been a figment of her imagination, because he'd yet to remove the remains of the bag off the floor. So where had he gone? She didn't have to wonder long for a bunch of flowers, large but not large enough to hide his smiling face, came through the door.

"Aha! The ghost of Christmas Present has reappeared."

David appeared disconcerted as he negotiated the squashed bag. "Pardon?"

"One minute you were here, the next you were gone. Just like the ghost of Christmas Present."

His brow furrowed as though puzzled, then he stated, "Oh! Right! Well, these flowers come as an apology – not for being the ghost, but for drawing everyone's attention to you."

"Oh, you didn't have to do that. I'm getting used to being made a public spectacle; after all it wasn't the first time you've done it, was it?" She took the flowers from his outstretched hand. "But at least you're taking responsibility for it."

With his eyes fixed in the direction of the switchboard, David commented, "I'm surprised that you're taking this so calmly."

"What, the switchboard? Oh, I had a few lessons with Natalie – its not difficult. Grace didn't leave me with that much work, so it's worked out well." She picked up a large empty vase from the windowsill. "I'll just go and get some water. I didn't know you were in, I rang your phone several times. There are some messages on that pad for you."

When she returned, David had taken up residence in the old easy chair in the corner.

"These flowers are lovely, but it was my mystery lover, not you, who upset me." She giggled mischievously at her turn of phrase but, at David's hard stare, she said more sombrely, "His actions made me realize I need to rethink my life. In fact, I've thought of little else since."

Head bent, David rested his mouth against his steepled fingers. He looked thoughtful, and more haunted than she by her 'ghost'.

"As my official guardian angel, you should know who he is. What worries me is, if the 'ghost' tries again, or declares himself, what am I going to do? For it doesn't matter how suited we might be in…err…in anything, it couldn't go further. I'd say the chance of him sharing my faith are zilch." With a stilted laugh she continued, "Darkness and surprise might have enhanced my response, but now I know that kind of compatibility exists, I'm going to pray that when I do fall in love, we have it!" From the blank expression on David's face, she guessed she was boring him and changed the subject. "Oh, by the way, thank you for my amazing Christmas present. It was very extravagant of you, but I am thrilled with it."

With a quick check through the glass partition to see the corridor was empty, she impulsively leant over the chair and gave him a quick kiss on the lips. Instantly he was on his feet, his hands gripping the tops of her arms. Surprised, she gaped up at him. Hard black raven eyes stared down into hers. Bewildered, she stammered, "I'm – I'm sorry. It, it was just my way of saying thank you."

His grip loosened, but his continuing scrutiny unsettled her. Finally he questioned in a quiet, steely voice, "Is this some kind of game you're playing?"

Tears filled her eyes. "No, David! No! Not you too. Please don't be cross! I, I – it was just my way of saying thank you. Like I would to my dad or brother, if I had one." Hoping to appease him, she added, "I checked no one would see…."

His eyes scanned her face, he gave a frustrated sigh. "And that would make it right, would it?"

"Oh! For goodness sake, David, I was only behaving as Felicity would."

His face darkened. "But you aren't Felicity! Nothing like Felicity! Felicity is always willing to back up her actions."

Jane gasped at the inference.

He stepped forward, his face so close to hers that, if the circumstances had been different, she would have thought he was going to kiss her. Instead his hands tightened again round her arms. She half expected him to shake her as he said through clenched teeth, "Heed my words, Jane. Do not play with fire. Fire quickly gets out of control." With a shake of his head, and an exasperated groan he pushed her away. "You know that, so why do I have to keep warning you? Each time you've come out barely singed, but others have borne the consequences of your actions."

He twisted on his heel and, hands behind his back, stalked to the window overlooking the courtyard.

To stop tears brimming over she swallowed hard. She hated it when he was angry and she hadn't meant to hurt anyone. With the back of her hand, she wiped her eyes and looked toward the tall broad figure outlined against the approaching storm-ridden sky.

Bits and pieces of conversation over the past months replayed through her mind. "I'm not your father. Remember I am a man with the same desires as that man." Then, "If only you knew." If she knew what? Had her interpretation of what he meant been wrong? Was he saying he desired her? No, he was in love with Jill. Or was he? He hadn't acknowledged their relationship at the party. But they'd known each other for ages and several times he'd indicated how much he cared for Jill. And Jill cared for him. Jane didn't know what to think. But she did need to make their relationship clear. It was time to pray and ask God for wisdom and words.

In faith she called quietly, "David."

He turned. Even in the semi-darkness she could see he was looking stern.

She forced herself to keep eye contact. "I think I understand what you are getting at." His eyebrows lifted in a quizzical expression. "I really do appreciate your care and concern, though I know there have been times when my actions haven't reflected that." Unable to see him clearly, she couldn't gauge his reaction. She broke off to switch on the light and glimpsed a vulnerability through his unfathomable expression. "I admit at first I did see you as a father figure. I had a wonderful relationship with my father. You and he are similar in the way you bait, banter and keep me in order. But, as you so succinctly said in Brussels, you are not my father. You see, David, you are like the brother I never had – the older brother who keeps his eye out for his sister's welfare; the brother who plays, teases and irritates, and yet you can't help loving; the brother who is so much your friend you would feel bereft if he wasn't around; the most wonderful of brothers – kind, thoughtful, caring, loveable, generous, playful, fun – the nicest brother any girl could ever want."

When she started speaking had she seen a flicker of pain, or disappointment? But her emphasis on the brotherly role had gradually warmed, his eyes mirroring the respect that she had for him.

He took a moment or two before answering. "I think, Jane, you have just paid me the greatest compliment that any man could wish." His eyes glistened with emotion. Hers filled too, in the comfort of knowing a difficult moment had been overcome. In the lull before he spoke again, she thanked God for his help. "Your description of a brother has to be the most wonderful I've ever heard, but I hasten to add it's not one on which my sisters would agree! If you really had a brother I suspect you'd be disillusioned, but – what can I say?" He shrugged with a wry smile, "My endeavour will be to live up to your high expectations!"

Relieved the tension was over, she joked, "So what would your expectations of a sister be?"

"Now there's a good question." His frown contained a degree of glee. He looked to the ceiling for inspiration, and began pacing the floor, his hands clasped behind his back, reminding her of a barrister summing up his case. Why did she suspect that he'd come up with a verdict she wouldn't like?

Jane jumped as the forgotten switchboard buzzed into life. "ITP – good afternoon. Mr Reinhardt? Yes, he's right here, Mr Jordan. Please hold the line, I'll get him for you."

David moved across to take the headset and sat in the operator's chair. Jane slumped tiredly into the armchair. At present, her life seemed fraught with emotions.

It was several minutes before David dropped the headset onto the switchboard, by which time she was curled up half asleep in the armchair. "Well, Jane, I don't wish to disturb you, but you have a job to do and I've pondered enough to give you an interim answer." Blinking, she tried to remember her question. He resumed his stance and paced away from her. He didn't speak until he turned at the partition to face in her direction. "I see the role of a sister to be one which is…" he walked slowly and thoughtfully: "…helpful; pleasant; encouraging; respectful; quiet. You know, Jane – someone who leads a sober life and who doesn't get involved in situations in which I feel obliged to either interrupt or to beat up someone."

He turned to pace the other way as she wailed, "Oh, no that's not fair!"

Unable to resist, he swivelled on his heel to retort with amusement, "Oh yes, young Jane, it's fair!" He clasped his lapels, "And, in the absence of my mother, or a nice little wife, I'd say her duties would include cleaning my house; doing my washing; ironing my shirts; darning my socks; cooking my meals.…"

"That's enough! I've changed my mind. I don't want a brother." In mock despair she buried her face in her hands.

David roared with laughter. Jane got the giggles. "I bet

your real sisters just love you. I bet they'd plot to kill you if you told them your expectations."

"I suspect I have roused that response in them on occasion, yes! Now I'd better go. Neither of us is going to get any work done at this rate."

"There was one thing you are right about."

"Only one – I'd have thought I could do better than that."

"No seriously. I'm going to forget ghosts – and all that other stuff. I told Grace on the plane that I felt God was highlighting to me a verse which said I should 'stir not up love, nor awaken love until it please'. So I'm not going to get involved with anyone until God shows me it's right!

David eyed her sceptically, "Is that so, Jane?"

Ignoring him she continued, "And the other thing I've decided is, Bruce is definitely not for me. Especially after this Christmas."

"Because of your ghost?" She shook her head. A wry smile flickered at his mouth and, bowing slightly, he said magisterially, "And might I be allowed to enquire, as your newly initiated brother, as to what other event or events have occurred to bring about this conclusion? And am I to believe that this is your final decision in the matter?"

"There you go again. Talking more like a barrister than a brother." Jane grinned, stood, and copying all his mannerisms marched up and down as he had. "And on that subject I'll speak as the opposing counsel! In due respect, I wish to submit that although the learned counsel seems happy to take up the role of adopted brother, I do not see that as synonymous to his sisterly expectations. Granted, I am willing to embrace one or two attributes of a sister which would be useful to work in harmony with the learned counsel, but it is not my wish that he should continue as a personal superman, hereinbefore referred to as guardian angel, and therefore it is my intention to bring no just cause before my learned counsel to incite his further action on behalf of the plaintiff."

David began clapping as she stood before him, her expression one of challenge. "Oh, Jane! That's very good – on all counts. And I get the point!" His eyes twinkled with amusement. "Do you know, you really do my heart good. It's certainly difficult for me to remain aloof, pompous, bombastic, or legalistic when you're around!"

It was impossible not to respond with a prim and haughty look. "Is that your description of yourself or how others see you? I'd never have noticed."

He groaned, "Oh, God!"

"There you go again, calling on God – but do you want him to answer? That's the question!"

"I don't know, Jane, I really don't know. But I am seriously considering that the only way to stop the pain you inflict upon me is to acknowledge that God of yours."

Filled with disbelief, she chortled, "That'll be the day."

David leant against the door frame. "Do you have any idea what you have done to my life?" Certainly she'd caused him a few problems, but.... "There I was, a sensible bachelor, enjoying the simplicities of life, keeping everything neatly filed, shelved and in its place, able to access anything when needed. Then you come along and tip my world upside down. You change my ideas, disturb the well-run organisation of my life, and sometimes make me wish I'd never set eyes on you."

True, she'd rearranged his filing system – for the better! What ideas had she changed? She'd question tipping his world upside down.... But there was cause to admit she'd disturbed, at times, the well-run organisation of his life: his last evening in Brussels; the late night she was out with Jacques; the unexpected job offer and dinner; her fall, sickness and visit to the hospital; the police accusing him of theft; spoiling his dinner when he rescued her from Andrew – oh! – and she had probably been the cause of his broken engagement! Mortified by the catalogue of events, she sighed heavily – no wonder there were times he wished he'd never set eyes on her!

To her surprise, David was smiling – he obviously wasn't reading her thought pattern! He continued, "Then, on the other hand, when you aren't disturbing my quiet life, I miss your chirpy voice, cheeky words and innocently flirtatious ways. But enough of that. Tell me about Bruce and this Christmas."

He'd evidently decided to forget work, for he sat again in the big old chair and listened attentively until, with a grimace, she finished, "…so I was glad to come to work to escape."

"Hmm, I see your predicament." His hands steepled, his forefingers tapped his mouth. Then he pointed at her. "By Bruce's reactions, I would guess he's equally disturbed about the future. What I don't understand is why he hasn't discussed it with you?"

Jane shrugged, "Nor do I! Perhaps he's only just beginning to acknowledge to himself that we've been drifting along, and I've been more distant lately. Things may now have to come to a head but, because of Christmas, he's felt – like me – it's not the right time to talk about it. I just wish I knew how to end it. I want us to remain friends. Well, we have to really, for after March we'll be related whether we like it or not. But I'm not sure Bruce will bring the subject up."

"Well, I can see it's been a traumatic Christmas, but nothing is insurmountable. And just think, you've gained two half-brothers in the space of three days!"

"David! This is serious! I certainly don't want to live with Mum and Ted, with or without Bruce. And I assume wherever his Dad goes so will he."

"I doubt it! At twenty-five! I think, when he's had time to adjust, he will see it as an opportunity to make a new life for himself. He may have been happier if it had included you, but I suspect he knows your feelings better than you think."

"Do you think so? I just pray we can talk without it getting too emotional. I certainly see this as my chance to start a new life – perhaps get a nice flat somewhere."

"On your salary you could only afford to buy something small, out of town."

"I was thinking of renting in town. I don't want to tie myself down to the responsibility of a mortgage. And, as far as my salary goes, I thought the Finance Department had made a mistake when I started working for you!" Jane grimaced, "It's brilliant, but I can't rely on that. We may have worked together so far but, once Grace goes, you may decided you don't want or need me any more. It's no good shaking your head, there's every possibility we could have a massive row and you sack me – nothing is assured. That apart, I've now got some savings from my Christmas bonus, the weekend and overtime pay in Brussels, so I could decide to venture out and see a bit more of the world. Whatever right now I've been thinking, it would probably be a good idea to ask around and see if anyone knows of someone with a space in a flat close to town and convenient for work. Although it will be a trek to my church on Sundays and Thursday evenings."

"London's not short of churches."

"True, but there aren't many I'd feel at home in. Still, I suppose a new church would give me an opportunity to spread my wings."

David's eyes narrowed, "Hold on. I thought spreading wings was out these days?"

"I can't go too far wrong in a church, can I? And if I can find a Christian man who is as nice as you, I'd be satisfied."

Frowning, he asked, "You would?"

She jibed back, "Why not? Well, maybe not as old as you – but my mum always says that marriages are strongest when they are first rooted in friendship."

The switchboard buzzing took her attention at what she felt was an opportune moment.

Maybe he felt so too, for he patted her shoulder and bent to whisper in her free ear, "As your newly appointed brother, I feel quite honoured by your last comment. Now I must go. I'll see you tomorrow."

A brief kiss touched her cheek, before he disappeared out the door.

At home, the new-found happiness began to wane. First, her mother sniffed derisively when she realized the large bunch of flowers came from David, "Why flowers, I ask? Wasn't that Bible enough of an extravagant gift to give a secretary?" A few seconds later, in a tone not unlike Rosemary's, she added, "I don't like it Jane. As I see it that man is too high flown for you. Far too bombastic and manipulative, and his influence is having a negative effect on you."

Jane sighed. This wasn't the first time she'd heard similar remarks and knew from experience it was best to ignore them. However, the fact remained that, as her opinion of David appreciated, her mother's depreciated. Was it because her mum had realized he was becoming a rival to her as a source of opinions and advice?

As Jane sat by the fire drinking coffee, she was grateful that neither Bruce nor his father was there. It was a good opportunity for her to talk to her mum about Ted and the wedding. It was time to broach the subject of moving out.

Her mother's reaction was not unexpected. "Jane, this is your home. Just because Ted and I are getting married, there is no reason for you to go. Ted and I love you, so let's be hearing no more about it." She leant across to pat her arm, her eyes focused dreamily, "Jane, you know I appreciate your thoughtfulness, but my feeling is, well, you and Bruce might get together next — has he asked you?"

"No Mum because we're just friends. Anyway, after

March he'll be my step-brother." Tentatively she asked, "As Ted is moving in here, what is Bruce going to do?"

Her mother's brow creased. "That's why Ted's not here tonight, he wanted time with Bruce. You see Ted's decided to sell his house. It'll give us a bit of money to make improvements – central heating and a new kitchen. And although he's offered Bruce a home here, I think Bruce rather hoped he could stay where he was and, with a ready made home, I suspect would have plucked up courage to name the day for you two."

Jane's mouthful of coffee went down the wrong way – she went into a fit of coughing, but waved her hand to say she was all right. Her mum continued, "Still, Bruce moving in here with us will be nice and cosy. It'll be cheaper to run one house instead of two and give you young things time to save up for something of your own."

"Actually, Mum, I've been thinking for a while about flat-sharing in London." A protest was already forming on her mother's lips, so she continued quickly, "I'd save the train fare and travel time, not to mention the frustration."

From that moment the conversation went rapidly downhill. It started with her Mum saying, "You should hear the tales my friends have told me about living in London." It then went on for what seemed ages, to cover treacherous landlords and depraved flatmates, and rounding off with, "To get anything decent, in a reasonable area, would be way beyond your means."

"Not with my new salary."

Her mother gave a grunt of disapproval. "Why would you want to live alone, when you have a home here?"

"Oh, I wasn't considering living alone. I would look for nice people to share with, and nice people don't usually have the nasty sort of landlords you've heard about."

"And do you know any one who fits that bill? Being friends with someone and living with them is entirely different matter. How do you know what they'd be like?

What about your Christian values? It's all too easy to start compromising and find yourself away from the Lord. I'd be worrying all the time about the influence they're having on you."

Annoyed, but trying to be reasonable she tried to reassure her mother. "Look, if I contact some churches in London I may be able to find a group of Christians to share with."

The flurry of negative arguments continued and, rather than have a row, Jane battened down her fraying temper until finally her mother got to the crux of her argument. "I don't know! I think that David is the root of all these ideas. First, executive jobs, more money than you know what to do with, business trips abroad, extravagant presents and now it's flats in London. The next thing you'll be telling me is you're moving in with him!"

For Jane, that was the final straw. "Oh for goodness sake! David has absolutely nothing to do with this. He's my boss, Mum!" The tight-lipped expression on her mother's face infuriated her. "Surely you can understand why I don't want to live here with you and Ted – let alone Bruce!" Her mother gave a knowing smile, which further annoyed her. She lost her temper and shouted, "Mum! Will you get it into your head. I'm not interested in Bruce! I don't want to live under the same roof as Bruce! And I certainly don't want to marry Bruce!" In an attempt at calmness she tried to explain. "Look Mum, I believe that you falling in love and marrying Ted is God's opening for me to do what I've been thinking about for months. Now please, you have to let me live my own life. And while I am on that subject I'll repeat it again, I'm not interested in anyone. David Reinhardt is my boss, a good friend and plays a fatherly role in my life." At the cynical expression on her mother's face, she added, "Well, maybe he's more an elder brother than a father, but I have no more feeling for him than as a brother. Now, is that clear?"

"All right, Jane! All right! You've made your point. What I question is, does David Reinhardt see you in the same light?"

"Yes, of course he does. Anything more would be as ludicrous as your suggestion that I might end up living with him."

"Well Jane, I have to say you are changing, and I'm not sure it's for the better! Bruce is a good man. You'll have to go a long way to find a more decent person. My concern is you're slipping into the ways of the world. And I still say that job of yours has a lot to answer for. Now I don't know what you are doing, where you're going. Even John Myrrh was saying the other day how little he sees of you, and how music practices used to go on for hours and now always seem cut short by your forever rushing off here, there and everywhere – all this travel abroad."

If her life had been that hectic surely she would have noticed! On a sigh she exclaimed, "Mum, I'm merely growing up."

However, Mum's comment, "Well, Jane, it appears you won't listen to anything I say, so you must do as you think best!" had brought some agreement before they both retired early to bed!

Nestled amongst her pillows, Jane considered the day's conversations. Despite her mother's absurd notions that David could be anything more than a friend, Jane acknowledged he was an exceptional man and the more she knew him the more she respected him. Picking up her new Bible, she read again the words ...desires of your heart....

Yes, David would make an excellent role model for her prayer for a husband. Her mind wandered. Was David's sexual prowess all the gossips would have it be? She recalled the feeling of his mouth on hers in the canteen. She compared it with others. Nothing like as exciting and riveting as the stranger's, probably because it hadn't been what she would term a 'sexual' kind of kiss. However, it hadn't been a fatherly or brotherly one either, come to that!

It would be a good idea to write down some of David's attributes as part of her request for the man of her dreams, and plant the card as a bookmark for Psalm 37. The days ahead would bring changes, but the times and places were in God's control and he would stir up love when it pleased him.

CHAPTER 13

Icicles hung against Jane's bedroom window. The freezing weather made it difficult to keep the rooms in the house heated. Even opening the door into the hall brought in a chilly rush of air. Half an hour earlier she'd leapt out of bed to switch on the two bar electric fire, and then dived back into the tunnel of blankets and eiderdown to get warm again. Under her pillow she pulled into the warmth of the bed her underwear. Once that had warmed up she'd put it on in bed! No doubt her Mum had switched on the heater in the bathroom, but it wouldn't be warm enough to have a strip wash. It would be a lick and a promise, as her Mum called it, which meant washed face and hands fully clothed! At least the bathroom was inside the house. She still knew of people who had to go out into their back yard to go to the toilet. Outside it was still dark, but the whiteness of the snow showed that it lay deep and round about, reminding her of the words of the Christmas carol. But she knew the walk to the station would prove it was far from 'deep and crisp and even'. It always looked so pretty when it came down and it would have been better if it had arrived for Christmas, but it rarely did.

Dawn was just beginning to lighten the sky as Jane left the house. Icy blusters of wind strove to penetrate her layers of clothing, while cars driving along the gritted roads threw black slush up onto the snow on the pavement, making that go grey, melt and become slippery. How glad she was of her fur hat and the leather fur-lined gloves she'd treated herself to from Harrods just before Christmas. A coach drove by, churning up the mess in the road and shooting it across the pavement. Her calf-high fleecy lined boots didn't meet the length of her coat and skirt, and icy droplets of spray stung with their coldness through her black knitted stockings.

Once in the relative shelter of the station platform she, along with fellow sufferers, stamped their feet and rubbed their gloved hands together to keep them from going numb. An outbound train proved they were still running, but the groans and grumbles increased as the station tannoy crackled to announce, "Trains to London are delayed due to snow on the line. We apologise for the inconvenience. The next train should arrive in approximately fifteen minutes." People began to move into little groups to mumble their dissent, bringing Jane to think how British people needed a crisis before they talked to each other.

Twenty minutes later, the people on the packed platform had a united moment, cheering as a train slowed into the station. The carriage windows were so misted the passengers inside were rubbing them to see where they were. As the doors opened everyone surged forward to add their frozen bodies to the mass of warm, but damp, humanity already inside. Jane, caught up in the pushing and shoving, found herself propelled into the centre of the carriage as the doors closed.

At each stop, people squeezed up as more people squeezed in. The train's speed seemed to reflect the load it was carrying. Instead of the usual forty minutes, the journey seemed an eternity. Her legs ached from standing in one position and her arm from holding on to the strap, and her body sweated in the heat of so many bodies. The train finally went underground where it raced through the tunnels and, fifteen minutes later, feeling she'd been swallowed, squashed and spat out by an iron monster, she emerged from the bowels of the earth to blink at the snow-covered brightness.

David, bowling down the central staircase heralded her arrival by calling happily, "Good morning, Jane!"

Jane scowled. There was he warm, dry and looking his usual spruce self, while she looked as if she'd been in a steam bath with all her clothes on! She ran her hand through her damp curly locks and growled, "You wouldn't be saying that if you'd spent two hours getting here!"

He looked at her cheerily. "All the more reason then to start that flat-hunting in London."

"My thoughts exactly."

Delighted, he chuckled, "Perhaps, young Jane, God's trying to tell you something?" Eyebrows raised, she pushed back against the swing door. David followed her through. "I can tell you, I'm glad to see you. My telephone, being the first night line, hasn't stopped ringing and I'd no way of transferring them. Without you on the switchboard we are virtually incommunicado! See this pile of messages I have to give out." He fanned them.

Jane threw off her coat and restored the board to daily use. "It seems quiet enough now."

"This is a ridiculous situation. In a company of this size with two permanent telephonists, and several others trained you would have thought someone would have been available. Usually we can use Jill as a back up, but she says she's not coming in. I know it worked yesterday, but I really do need my only secretary!" David gave a forlorn sigh.

"Grace didn't think you'd have that much to do. I'm sure I can manage until she gets back on Wednesday."

"Yes, but for how long? She'll probably want to leave in February."

"Oh dear, I thought it was just me in the doldrums today! I'm sure I can manage – my secretarial skills aren't that bad. Tomorrow Jill will be back – had you forgotten?"

David snorted derisively. "Hardly! Yesterday, when I left home she was plaguing me with instructions as to what I should and shouldn't do in these next two days."

At this unexpected disclosure, Jane said in surprise, "I thought Jill was going home for the Christmas holiday."

For a second he looked nonplussed then, giving a wry

smile, replied, "Ah! Yes! She went there too. Now I'd best go and deliver these messages. In the meanwhile, could you ring round each department? There must be someone in today who could help out here."

It was nearly the end of the morning when she heard David's steps coming down the corridor, As he opened the door, she didn't turn from the switchboard but commented loudly, "This ain't no ghost a-coming!" before pushing in a plug. "ITP. Good morning. Yes, I'll put you through. Hold the line please."

Two pincer-like fingers grasped her ear, then in a traditional pantomime dame voice came the words, "Oh Jane, what big ears you've got!"

Jane pretended to listen, before saying, "Well, yes, Mr Plaidon, I do apologise. Yes, of course I understand that you don't want customers to think we're running a pantomime! Mr Reinhardt? Yes. Yes, of course – he's right here."

A quick twirl of the chair and she caught David's stricken expression as he took the headset from her hand.

"Hello, Joseph, what can I do for you?" Jane began to giggle. Annoyed, he waved his hand to quieten her. "Joseph? Joseph? Are you there?" Dismayed, he groaned, "Oh no! He's gone. You really will be the death of me – this isn't a laughing matter! Plaidon, of all people. He wasn't too pleased at the way the Christmas lunch became a debacle, as he called it. Now he's put the phone down on me because he's put two and two together and realized it was I creating the 'pantomime'. This doesn't bode well."

Jane, trying not to laugh, exhorted, "Well, perhaps in future you'll behave yourself. From what you say, good job Mr Plaidon wasn't there."

"It's not funny Jane, there's nothing to joke about!" He looked so worried she had to tell him..

"David, Mr Plaidon wasn't there, because he never rang up in the first place – it was meant to be a joke! I made it up, I didn't realize you'd take it so seriously."

In disbelief he shook his head, "You made it up.... You, you...." Temporarily, he was at a loss for words.

"One up to me I think?"

David narrowed his eyes at her. Then, similar to the day before, he paced up and down this time, muttering audibly a host of admonitions centred on his foolishness to allow such a cheeky little madam the leeway to act like a wayward sister. Throughout his ramblings she grinned like a Cheshire cat, but when he muttered with glee that he knew just the retribution he had in store for her, she had cause to doubt her wisdom at provoking so astute a foe! The switchboard coming into sudden life took her attention. David waited until she'd dealt with several callers to say, "Very efficient as usual Jane, but I'd prefer someone else here. Have you found anyone willing to learn?"

Jane gave a self-satisfied smile. "Of course! Fran Foster. She may have a cockney accent, but she was the only one available and willing, my Mum says beggars can't be choosers. Here as soon as she's finished her work on the marketing project. And – as I'm your one and only secretary, I'll eat my sandwiches and teach her at the same time. Now with my sacrifice and efficiency, hopefully all planned retribution will cease and my rating in your estimation will rise."

"Umm. Thank you, Jane! I'm sure Fran will be fine. I have no criticism whatever of your choice, arrangements, or sacrifice, and indeed you rate very highly in my estimation." It was his turn to give the self-satisfied smile as he continued, "However, be warned I will return the joke, naturally in the nicest possible way, and be one up on you. In the meanwhile I'll await your return, when hopefully, this afternoon, we can put in a few hours work."

He was out the door and down the corridor before she could issue her retort, but it didn't stop her muttering sarcastically through the glass petition at his retreating figure, "Forewarned is forearmed, Mr Reinhardt! And what do you think I've been doing since I got here, Mr Reinhardt? Sitting here in the armchair with my feet up?"

Fran arrived an hour later, wrote down the various operations and practiced while Jane watched. Once she seemed confident, Jane organised her move back upstairs. Arms full, she staggered into her office. Through David's open door she could see him leaning across his desk reading the newspaper and eating a sandwich. Without even a glance in her direction, he remarked, "Oh, good – normal service is about to be resumed. Once you're settled there's something here you might be interested in."

Curious, she quickly organised her desk and strolled into his office. Intent on reading, David didn't look up. Instead, he commented as he turned over the pages of the lunchtime edition of the *Evening Standard*, "I bought this because I thought you might like to browse through the adverts for flats." The right page found, he laid the paper on the desk to point out, "This one seemed particularly interesting."

Jane moved round beside him to read it. 'Second/third girl wanted – share luxury basement flat off Kensington High Street. Own room, all mod. cons, incl. rent except tel. calls.' Interested, her eyes took in the other details, to which she reflected, "The rent's rather high but, if it is luxurious, it may be worth it. Mind you, what some people call luxurious and what I call it, is another thing. I could afford it, especially if electricity and gas are included."

David murmured abstractedly, "No harm in looking."

Jane frowned. Qualms of doubt and nervousness assailed her as the reality of leaving home was suddenly thrust upon her. "I suppose not, although perhaps it's a bit too soon. I don't want to appear as if I'm rushing from home in some sort of protest."

In thought, she meandered to the other side of the desk

as she considered what to do. It was as though David
sensed her retreat was a reflection of her thoughts, for
he began to draw her attention to the advantages. His
convincing arguments made her aware again of his ability
as a barrister. He was right, though — Kensington High
Street was convenient, and if the flat was suitable it really
didn't matter whether she moved sooner rather than later.

Oddly, after going on about his need of her services, he
stood and instructed, "Ring up now, Jane, before the
opportunity goes," then left her to it.

Had she dialled the wrong number? The voice at the
other end was elderly with a cockney accent. "Yes, dearie,
I know all about the flat. There ain't no one here but me —
I's the cleaning lady. Now, what's yer name?"

"Jane — Jane Mackenzie."

"Right yer are, Miss! Well, master said yer could come
round late this afternoon, 'E'll get 'ome 'bout five."

Jane frowned into the telephone, "Oh! From the advert,
I got the impression it was to share with one or two girls."

"That's right, Miss. They's in the basement flat. Master
lives upstairs on 'is own."

Reassured, she thought out loud, "Well, I'm not sure I
could make it today. You see I'm at work, and this
weather — if the snow starts again it could mean hours
trying to get home."

"Well, if it 'elps, dearie, I could show you round. Then,
if you likes it, I can I'll tell 'em when they comes 'ome."

"It would have been nice to meet the girls I'd be
sharing with. How old are they?"

"There's only one at the moment — 'is younger sister.
I'm sure you'd like her. Them's both lovely people, everso
friendly. She, though, won't be 'ome til 'bout six."

Jane thought rapidly. David was keen to help her.
Would he mind her leaving before time, especially as he
said he was busy? "I'll have to check with my boss if I can

go early. Can I leave it that I'll come if I can, otherwise I'll ring again tomorrow?"

"Course, luv. I'm making a list. Let me give you the address anyway. I expect I'll see you later."

As they said goodbye, Jane reflected the cleaning lady was more sure of her boss' benevolence than she was! In the hope of making his benevolence a reality, she quickly got down to work and had typed several letters before David reappeared.

"Well, young Jane, did you ring up?"

Jane responded with a long face. "I did. I spoke to the cleaner who said the flat had been done out everso nice, but no one's in until five. The snow made travelling this morning awful – if it's going to start again this evening...well, best not to delay getting home." As briefly as possible, she related the phone conversation. "I took the address, but she'd had other calls and was making a list, so the sooner I could see it the better, oh, and I forgot, she said, 'them's both', presumably the brother and sister, were lovely, friendly people'.

Amused, David gave her a wry smile. "That cleaner is a bit a character. She will get lots of calls because decent flats in London are hard to come by, and from what you say this is one not to be missed." He turned on his heel and walked to the window. In between blowing his nose he commented, "The sky's quite blue. That's a good sign. It's probably too cold for more snow tonight. But in case I'm wrong let's do a couple of hours work, then you can go off and see the flat. And if the weather holds, you could stay long enough to meet 'them's both'." David coughed into his handkerchief.

"Good heavens David, it sounds as it you've got a cold coming on."

The coughing fit under control he wiped his eyes, his voice strained as he said, "I'll, I'll be okay. But maybe another good reason to finish early."

"What about all your work?"

"What we don't get done, we don't get done! You finding a suitable flat is more important."

Inwardly she admonished herself for letting the flat's cleaning lady have more faith than she had in David's magnanimity. "Have I told you lately what a good friend you are? Thank you."

David, his voice recovered, said briskly, "Right Jane, let's do as much as we can now. Tomorrow, if necessary, you can make up the time by working through your lunch break." Jane smiled. Perhaps her judgement hadn't been as impaired as she thought!

They attacked the work with such a vengeance that she was surprised by the amount they accomplished in a short time. David gave a satisfied sigh as he surveyed the letters before him. "Leave these now to me. I'll sign, stamp and post them. I think, Jane, we can safely say we work well together. Your idea of typing as I dictated did save time over shorthand or dictaphone. Well done!"

Pleased to be complimented. she nearly skipped out of his office. By the door, she looked back at him to tease, "Well, it just goes to show your only secretary can, it seems, manage the work of two!" In case of retaliatory action she rapidly shut the door.

By 4.15 she was walking down a very pleasant, well-kept street of four-storey, Victorian houses. Even in the dark she could tell it was a very up-market area, compared to some near High Street, Kensington. Number 17 was on the other side of the road, so she could see it was recently refurbished, and different from the others. Usually the basement entrance was down steps in the front garden, but this had been covered over at ground floor level to form a drive to the garage, formerly the front room.

Framed in the doorway, a middle-aged woman wearing an old-fashioned wraparound overall, a scarf bound round her head like a turban, and thick stockings inside lace-up boots was puffing on a rolled cigarette sticking out of the side of her mouth. At Jane's approach, she stubbed it out on the small wall which separated the house from next door and put it in her apron pocket.

"'Ello, dearie. You must be Jane Mackenzie. The Master, 'e don't like me smoking in 'is 'ouse, so I 'as to come out 'ere to do it! Cor! It's cold today. Come on in, luv. I fought you'd be coming 'bout now, so fought I'd look out for yer. The entrance to the basement is through the 'ouse. Me name's Perkins, Mrs Perkins. I does for the Master."

Jane put out her hand, "Nice to meet you, Mrs Perkins."

Mrs Perkins' lined face crinkled as she grinned broadly and placed her hand in Jane's. After a brief, embarrassed shake she offered, "I'll make you a nice cuppa tea, then show you round."

Jane's first impression of the white-walled outer hall was cleanliness. The red quarry tiles shone, as did the row of black dustbins carefully stowed under a shelf, which Mrs Perkins pointed out was just the right height to still lift the lid and put in your rubbish. "'Is idea." She nodded her head in an upward direction, "The master. 'E's a clever gent – good taste too. The master lives on the upper two floors. 'E's letting the basement as a separate flat." They moved through the glass-panelled door into the main hall, where a large lamp shed a warm glow over the cream walls and rich plum carpet.

Mrs Perkins hung Jane's coat on a peg besides hers as she explained, "Them two doors either side of that half-moon table – the first's to the garage, the second to the flat. We'll have our cuppa upstairs, it's warmer up there." As Mrs Perkins ambled upwards, Jane glanced at the individually-lit framed paintings of hunting scenes and wondered if perhaps this was going to be a bit too upmarket for her.

Puffing slightly at the top, Mrs Perkins led her through a rather dark, but elegant, dining room with a large ornate fireplace. As if in keeping with that, a large highly polished mahogany table surrounded by eight elegant chairs filled the centre and a heavy matching sideboard took up nearly one wall. At the far end, through a hatch, she could see a sizeable bright and fairly modern fitted kitchen with dark wood doors and a green Formica work surface which seemed a similar colour to the walls of the dining room.

"I'll just put the kettle on. This'll give you some idea of what downstairs is like. This kitchen was added on to the 'ouse. That arch, the 'atch was part of the original window. Under 'ere is a bedroom, and under that, well, you'll see how the flat's laid out. The master's on his own up 'ere." Mrs Perkins kept up the chattering, which changed rapidly from topic to topic. It stopped Jane from asking questions, but she learnt that Mrs Perkins came in every day, all day, to clean both this flat and the one below and she wondered if her services were included in the price of the rent.

Despite the non-stop talking, Mrs Perkins quickly prepared a tray of tea and home made cake, and was soon ushering her into the large front lounge. The master certainly had a gem in Mrs Perkins, and if this room was anything to go by, the flat downstairs was going to be just the kind of place Jane would love to live in. She eyed the baby grand piano – if she could persuade the master to let her play that, it would offset any lack in her flatmates!

Mrs Perkins heartfelt sigh drew back Jane's wandering thoughts. "...easier now, but it's been as much as I could do to keep these floors clean with all the building work. The master bought this 'ouse nearly derelict on the lower floors. Far too big for 'im alone. Used to live in two rooms upstairs. But by the time I come a few years back, he'd finished this. No central 'eating then. I used to fink what a waste of an 'ouse! Place was only alive when 'is family came. In the end it was 'em who suggested 'e make it into two 'alves. I 'ave to say 'e weren't too bothered, but 'is sister persuaded 'im." The grin on Mrs Perkins face indicated his sister knew how to twist her brother round her finger. "She's been responsible for the main ideas, though 'e does 'ave a mind of 'is own. I 'eard 'im say," Mrs Perkins mimicked a refined accent, 'This is my part of the house and I will decorate it as I wish.'"

To Jane, his decoration and taste seemed much like her own. The walls were a warm shade of peach, the paintwork cream and the carpet patterned with pale shades of peach, cream and green, making the room restful, yet bright and airy.

She tried imagine what the master was like as she listened to Mrs Perkins. "Real bachelor, though, 'e is. Quite content with 'is own company, but 'e goes away a lot. A proper businessman. Not stuck up though – friendly. 'E always has a word to say. Generous too! I often find a little bit extra in me pay packet. Funny really, I always feel a bit sorry for 'im. I fink 'e's an attractive man and 'e's 'ad ladies, well, you know, in 'is life." Mrs Perkins gave a derogatory grunt, then frowned. "Can't understand 'im not 'aving a nice wife. The last one I fought would get 'im to the altar – been in and out of his life for years, but it came to nuffink. Between you and me I was glad. Too flighty!"

Jane found it hard not to giggle as Mrs Perkins looked her up and down as though she might be a prospective candidate for the master.

"Anyways, when I'm 'ere I usually do a bit of cooking, then, if 'e comes 'ome alone, there's something in the fridge for 'is tea. Well, luv, if you've finished your cuppa we'll 'ave a tour round. Might as well show you the bedrooms upstairs while you're 'ere."

"Are you sure Mr...?" she paused, waiting for Mrs Perkins to fill in the name.

"No, ducks. The master, 'e'll not mind." Mrs Perkins

was heading towards the door. "Come on, luv."

"Does he, the…master play the piano?"

"Don't fink so. Never 'eard him. Belonged to some relative I fink who wanted it stored so, being as the master had so much room, it came 'ere."

In her mind, Jane was beginning to form a portrait of the master. A refined, somewhat reclusive professional gentleman, perhaps a headmaster, for he'd be one to know his own mind, and would give a reason for Mrs Perkins' title for him. To own and refurbish a house in this area he would either have money or earn a good salary, so a guess would be late forties or fifties. Apparently he wasn't unattractive to women, but not anxious for a permanent relationship. Mrs Perkins might not feel the master would mind her seeing the whole house, but the impression was he wouldn't be the type of man who'd appreciate intrusions into his privacy when he was home.

Half-listening to the nineteen-to-a-dozen chatter, Jane kept smiling politely as she took in the luxury of the upper rooms. The two main bedrooms, one double-bedded, one twin-bedded were rather bare of fripperies, but the bathroom was quite luxurious, with the latest shower device. The other door was to a smaller room overlooking the front of the house. Mrs Perkins switched on the light which revealed a study with a large old-fashioned desk in front of the window with several neat piles of books and papers. Jane barely glanced in, but noted the walls were lined with bookshelves filled with large, heavy volumes.

"The master was so 'elpful, when me 'Arold passed away – 'e did all the paper work. Couldn't have managed on me own. I only flick the duster round 'ere, unless we need to use the studio couch to put up his family. Don't like to disturb 'is work."

Curiosity made Jane interrupt the flow. "Does the master entertain much?" The size and luxury of the kitchen might mean he loved to cook, but the general size of the accommodation wasn't in keeping with the lonely, balding, bespectacled, bachelor she'd pictured.

"Oh, 'e likes things nice. 'E sometimes has a lady stay." Mrs Perkins blushed and added quickly, "They don't always share his bedroom. And, of course 'is family comes if they want to go to the theatre or shopping in town. 'Is sister is organising a New Year's Eve Housewarming Party!" Mrs Perkins turned, eyebrows raised. "Now she enjoys a bit of entertaining! Not the cooking kind, mind! Her mum's been trying to teach 'er that – hopeless." Jane looked at her watch – it was nearly five o'clock. Mrs Perkins smiled. "Yer time's getting on. Better show you downstairs, the master said 'e'd be 'ome about now." As if on cue, the front door closed with a bang. Mrs Perkins smiled, "Aha! Now that'll be 'im."

As Mrs Perkins led the way down the stairs to the first floor she said, "I hope he won't mind me being up here. I feel an intruder."

"No, luv, 'e won't mind. 'E said to show you round."

CHAPTER 14

A voice called from below, "Hello, Mrs Perkins! Is the young lady still here?"

Jane stopped, rooted to the spot, two stairs up from the middle floor. Her hand gripped the stair rail as the master came into view to join Mrs Perkins on the landing. Amused eyes flicked over her as Mrs Perkins prattled on. A variety of thoughts and emotions washed over Jane. The moment Mrs Perkins stopped, the master bowed slightly and said with a wide smile, "So, Miss Mackenzie, how good to see you."

Not wanting him to know how flustered she felt, she pinned her eyes on his, shook his hand, and played along. "And good evening to you too, Mr Reinhardt. This is an unexpected... surprise!"

"That's what surprises are Jane – unexpected! But a pleasant one, I hope?"

Her lip curled, "I'm not sure. You, I gather, aren't here to be viewed as a potential flatmate."

David's mouth twitched wickedly. "That, Jane, would depend upon the flatmate with whom I might be sharing." Jane blushed. David roared with laughter and an enthralled Mrs Perkins glanced between them. "Oh, Jane, you should see your face!" Mrs Perkins frowned and shook her head. "With that advert coming out today, it was just too good an opportunity to miss — especially after your little ruse this morning!"

Before she could berate him for his duplicity, Mrs Perkins interrupted. "I'll get me bag, sir, then I'll be off." Having drawn David's attention, she gave him a knowing look before scurrying into the dining room. Politely they watched and waited as she gathered up her things. "I'll be going then, sir."

"Yes. Yes, thank you, Mrs Perkins." Jane saw his wink, and the responding quirk of Mrs Perkins' mouth.

"Goodnight then, sir. Goodnight, Miss."

Jane gave a weak smile and then, remembering her manners, called, "Oh, Mrs Perkins – thank you for the tea and delicious cake and for showing me round."

With a broad smile, David gestured towards the lounge, "Come in – sit down." As she complied, he pretended to lick his finger and draw a mark in the air, "That's definitely one up to me. That makes us even."

There was no doubt that his retaliation had been swift. She threw him a sardonic smile and tentatively perched on the edge of the nearest armchair. He walked across the room to close the curtains and switch on a lamp by the hi-fi. He gave her a boyish smile, "Do relax Jane, make yourself comfortable. You know, I couldn't believe it this morning when you said you'd decided to look for a flat in London. What a coincidence! It was such fun baiting you, and difficult to hide my laughing, especially as you thought I had flu coming on. Am I forgiven?" David slumped happily into the chair opposite her, took in her churlish expression and, fingers steepled against his mouth, waited for her to speak.

Still perched on the edge of the seat, she countered, "And to think I was so sympathetic toward you! I suppose this would be termed a brotherly prank? But it strikes me, even before I played that joke on you this morning you must have had this planned. But too, I'll admit it was good, and I fell for it, and given similar circumstances I'd have probably been tempted to do much the same. But, don't look quite so gleeful because your sister might not be as forgiving as I for your interfering in her selection of flat mate. That's assuming I am a candidate and get the chance to view the flat downstairs." Before he could say anything she gave him the prim and haughty look she now knew to be provocative, and teased, "Or was this just a ploy to get me into your den? Though the way I hear it, you're a shy, lonely, retiring bachelor."

Amused, David retaliated, but his tone had an underlying edge. "Look at me again like that, Jane Mackenzie, and you might find I am not shy or retiring!" At his hard, open-eyed look, she found a sudden interest in the carpet. David grunted and continued, "I presume that's Mrs Perkins' description?"

Glad of the diversion, she looked up answering quickly, "That, and a few other things, which I just couldn't repeat." At the tightening of David's jaw, she rushed on, "I'm only joking – she didn't say anything you wouldn't like." Feeling awkward, and to divert his attention, she glanced towards the piano and asked, "Do you play?"

His gruff, "No!" made her shudder. Oh dear. She hoped that nice Mrs Perkins wasn't going to get into trouble. With a cynical look he asked, "So, Jane. Do you? Another of your secret talents?"

Cross, she bit back, "You're a fine one to talk about secrets! And, yes, I do play. But it's no secret. I play at church every Sunday, and on other occasions. But not the kind of music you're probably used to." She nodded at the shelves under the hi-fi, which contained records and tapes.

"You might be surprised. Go on – take a look through my records and tapes."

It felt like he was issuing a challenge rather than an invitation. Her discomfort was made worse as he arose, waved his hand in their direction and, leaning nonchalantly against the mantelpiece, said with a wry smile, "Now don't be shy, Jane. Be my guest."

There was no alternative now, but to get up and flick through them. Reluctantly she acknowledged, "It would appear we have the same taste in classical music." David moved from the fireplace to the settee as she continued, "although I'm not keen on jazz!" The third and final shelf was shared between Elvis Presley and the Beatles, the latter, more of a surprise. And as she rambled through an explanation of modern church music being of similar music style to the early Beatles', she weighed up what to do next. She couldn't sit in the nearest chair because that was slightly behind the settee facing the now curtained window. So the only other choices would be to sit next to him on the settee or return to the chair on the far side of the room, which meant either climbing over his outstretched legs, or walking around the block of furniture.

The decision was made for her as he demanded, "Then Jane, as you play, treat me to a selection of your kind of music."

Was he being rude, irritating, or did he genuinely want to hear her play? Was he as relaxed as he appeared? Suddenly she felt completely out of her depth. He may have become her 'big brother' and enjoyed playing a prank on her, but this wasn't work. What was she doing in his living room? It just didn't feel right. But his request would be a simple solution to her unease, so she acquiesced with a nod. Piano playing, like typing, was something she could do without concentrating. Her mind wandered, her fingers ran over the keys, her emotions often played out and reflected through music.

In the working environment she knew her place – although perhaps she didn't always keep it! In that relationship he was boss, she was his assistant, and they were friends. But tonight, she had to agree with her mother, she didn't belong in his world. What had she got in common with him: an interest in music, a sense of fun and humour?

A working relationship was uncomplicated. You knew what was expected and could enjoy another's company without fear of emotional entanglements that might become hurtful. Admittedly, theirs had been a little more unusual! Jane squeezed her eyes tight in humiliation. In order to face him these past weeks, she'd deliberately pushed out of her mind his view of that scene in Brussels. But being here now, in his house, was personal. There were no working boundaries and no specific role to play.

His sister might need a flatmate, but who was to say they'd have anything in common – they might dislike each other on sight. Had he even told his sister about her? Had he thought about work? That could be awkward if people found out she were living in his house. Worried and unsure, she began playing one of the songs her friend Lou had written. This music normally brought her peace, but tonight when the last note faded away, her misgivings hadn't.

She glanced at David but he didn't stir, giving the appearance of being asleep. So much for wanting to hear her play! What should she do now? He broke the odd silence by opening his eyes and turning to ask, in a quiet, rather choked voice, "Has that last piece of music got any words?" It was clear to see something had touched him. Dumbfounded, she nodded. He smiled faintly, "I suppose you can sing too? Bewildered she bit her lip and nodded again. "Then, Jane, could you…" he hesitated as though afraid to ask, "…could you, would you sing them for me?"

The realization that the music, which often reached into the depths of her being, had affected him made her qualms vanish. The lyrics were even more powerful than the tune. She didn't doubt this was a God-given opportunity to introduce David to the person to whom she'd given her heart. Without further thought her fingers slid over the keys in the classical introduction. The power of the music swept over her, wiping out every thought, as not only the notes but also the words became an extension of her, and all that was within her. Every word filled with deep meaning and relevance. Finally she sang the last two lines:

My heart is like a wayward child prone to go astray,
And it's knowing that I need you keeps me by your
side.

Tears filled her eyes. A deep peace filled the room. Loath to disturb even the air, she remained with head bent over the keys in worship of her creator.

The clock struck six. Sounds from the street merged into the silence. The house's general creaking echoed in the stillness. There was the gentle rustle of clothing; she glanced up to meet David's gaze. His were eyes full of deep, dark warmth, his voice unusually quiet and slow, as if contemplating as he spoke. "That's one of the most beautiful pieces of music I've ever heard. You played it with such feeling. The words really mean something to you don't they?" Before she could answer, he continued, "It's God that keeps you by his side, isn't it? You made it sound like a love song."

"In a way, it is." She moved from the piano to the chair by the side of him, and admitted, "I didn't write the music or words, but they express how I feel."

David's eyes glazed over, and she relaxed for the first time since he'd arrived. Without further thought she curled up comfortably in the chair and prayed for the wisdom to know what to say next. A few moments later he refocused on her. She responded with a gentle smile, then sensing she should say more she went on, "When I sing those words, it's my worship – my response to Jesus' love for me. I often have a sense of God's presence when I play or sing that song."

David's attention returned inward. Peace enveloped them.

Later, Jane wasn't sure how long they'd sat like that, but the atmosphere was broken by the sound of a car drawing up, its door and then boot being opened and shut. David stretched lazily, as if he had been sleeping. When they heard the front door open, David turned and smiled. "Ah, that will be my beloved sister returning, and I haven't shown you the flat yet."

The flat! Good heavens! Uncurling from the chair, she'd a sense of returning from a far-off place and the need to jerk herself back into reality. The twinkling laughter in his eyes was enough to make her jump up and retort, "Oh, I am here then to view the flat?" In Brussels she'd glimpsed facets of his relaxed manner, homely attitude and lazy smile, but in the last hour their relationship seemed to have moved into a new dimension – although she couldn't discern how, when or why.

With a yawn, David arose from the settee drawing his body up to its full height then, with an impudent smile, he held out his hand. "Come. Meet my sister and see what you think."

She could ignore his outstretched hand, but not his high-handedness. "You may have organised this, but I'd say it's more what she thinks, not what I think. Does your sister even know she has a potential flatmate to interview?"

"Oh, yes!" He grinned, "She knows."

Jane remembered Mrs Perkins saying that his sister liked to interfere in his life – she guessed he was now enjoying interfering in hers.

"I rang her to tell her you were interested. She's really looking forward to seeing you. I expect she went straight to the flat because she thought we were already there." He gestured toward the door, his mouth twitching with irritating amusement, "So, if you're ready, let's go."

With a grimace she swept past him. He was really enjoying this – she only hoped his sister would be equally entertained. As she descended the stairs, she remarked over her shoulder, "Do you know, I don't think Mrs Perkins told me your sister's name." David didn't answer, so on reaching the bottom she stepped back to ask, "So, what is her name?"

He passed in front of her to lead the way. He pointed to the first door on the left. "The garage. Door straight ahead

273

is the washing, boiler and drying room." He ushered her through the second door on the left into a corridor behind the garage. "On your right is my sister's bedroom with its own bathroom. Beyond, you will see on the right the stairs down into the flat."

"You still haven't told me your sister's name."

David started down the first flight with her following. "This is an extension. The back wall of the original house was blown out by a bomb in 1944 and it's now nearly all window-partitioned into sections. Fortunately, being a terraced house, although the inside was badly damaged from the blast, the rest of the walls remained intact. He turned on the landing, "You can't see the garden in the dark but, it's accessible from the flat and mostly paved." The stairs turned and went down alongside the window, but on her right she could now see into a fair-sized room with white walls and plain green carpet. Teak units filled the space between the door in the opposite wall toward the fireplace, and in front of them two rust coloured settees were placed at right-angles in front of the fire. David, from the bottom, looked up to ask, "So what do you think so far?"

From the final stairs, the door opposite was open enough for her to glimpse a bright, white modern kitchen. It was fantastic, the sort of thing she might expect in an American movie. Not wanting to seem too enthusiastic, she said casually, "So far so good."

David moved into the centre of the room. "Don't just stand there. Come on down and look around."

Although the room wasn't very wide it felt spacious, due to the reflection in the large glass windows. Under the first flight of stairs down was tucked a round table and four chairs. David pointed to the two doors behind her. "Those are the bedrooms. I'm sure my sister will let you choose which one you'd like."

Jane was about to ask what had happened to his sister,

when the sound of a flushing toilet made David grin. "No need to point out that the bathroom is next to the kitchen!"

A door opened and Jill emerged.

Perplexed, Jane gasped, "Jill? What are you doing here? Have you come to view the flat too?"

Jill's features tightened as she looked across at David. Then it dawned on her – Jill was working tomorrow so had obviously come back early and taken the opportunity to be with David. She was probably in on his prank to get her here and had popped down here to talk to his sister.

David's mouth twitched with amusement. "Hello Jill, have you had a good day?" Then oddly, not waiting for a reply he turned, walked towards the stairs and said, "Here, Jane, is the back door into the garden."

Jill glared at his back, drew in a sharp breath and said in an exasperated voice, "He hasn't told you, has he?" Jane turned from glancing at the back door, to Jill, then at David's back before he turned to face her. A glance at his expression told her he was up to something. Jill's frustration was confirmed by the abrupt away she blurted out, "I live here!"

Puzzled, Jane looked at her and frowned. Why, when he knew she and Jill were good friends, hadn't David told her that Jill had already taken one of the vacancies? Wide eyed, she enquired, "So, David, another of your little surprises?" His response was to merely nod his head, for by now he was blowing his nose, which she now knew to be a cover up for his laughter. Irritated by his obvious glee at once more surprising her, Jane turned to Jill. "I suppose you and he have been in cahoots about this too?" Before Jill could speak, she turned back to David, "And where is your sister? Is she to get any choice of flat mate? What will she think of this?"

David's frame shook. What was the matter with the man? What was so funny? Jill sent her a tight smile and glowered at David before declaring harshly, "Jane, I have no hesitation in telling you exactly what David's sister thinks of him. She has every reason to consider him to be a scheming, conniving, conceited brother who is insensitive, inconsiderate, thoughtless, aggravating, irritating and his little jokes not funny, but the bitter end for those he entraps." Jill pursed her lips and stared at him.

David mopping his eyes, managed to say, "Steady on Jill, that's a bit harsh, isn't it?" before sinking on to the fourth step of the stairs to guffaw into his handkerchief and mutter, "This is the best, the very best...."

What was going on? It was obvious Jill knew David's sister well enough to know that she wouldn't appreciate his interference in her life, or her choice of flat mate. What a pity – she would have really enjoyed sharing this beautiful flat with Jill, but obviously it wasn't to be. She adjusted her shoulder bag and gave Jill a sympathetic smile. "Look, Jill, I'm sorry. I don't want to make this any worse – I'll go before David's sister gets here."

David pulled himself up to his full height and blocked her exit, while spluttering, "Oh Jane. Oh Jane," before he sink into further hysteria.

If she hadn't known better she would have thought he was drunk.

As she was about to push past him, he drew himself up by the stair rail, and clenched his jaw in an effort to bring about a semblance of self-control. "Wait Jane! Please! Let me introduce you to my...." He obviously caught her fierce look, for he rushed on and nodded toward Jill, "You see, Jill over there...well, she is my sister." David pulled in his mouth to stop his laughter, but mirth filled his eyes as he watched her digest his words.

Jill was David's sister. The words repeated themselves several times in her head. She couldn't take it in. Slowly, as if in a dream, Jane turned towards Jill, who gave her a nervous smile and moved toward her. Bewildered, Jane allowed Jill to steer her to a dining room chair.

"Are you all right?" Worry etched Jill's features, her hand fiddled with her hair. "I asked him to tell you before I came home, but it seems he thought it would be far more amusing to spring it on you. I'll make a cup of tea. He can explain himself."

As he sat beside her, it seemed David was blissfully unaware of how upset she was. Her thoughts were in turmoil. Explain *him*self – Jill needed to explain *her*self! How they must have laughed about her assumptions of romance between them.

Between his chuckles David observed, "You have to admit… I've pulled a cracker this time… you just didn't get it… didn't get it at all. Definitely more than even, one up to me I'd say!"

It may seem funny to him, but to her it felt like a cruel joke. If she didn't believe they really were her friends…. Her eyes filled with unshed tears. She wanted to hurl abuse at David, but the only words she could spit out were, "You're a mean, mean toad!" That only seemed to delight him further.

Different things she'd told Jill came to mind. Had she repeated them to David? Jane remembered that there had been times when Jill had looked anxious – probably feeling guilty at their deception.

When Jill returned with the tea, Jane could see the similarities — the black hair and eyes, the chiselled features and tall and broad figures, David muscular and Jill generously curved.

Jill put out the cups. "I told him you'd be upset. I don't mean just today, but because we hadn't told you before. When the job at ITP came up it was just what I wanted. I didn't tell David, just applied and got an interview. When I got the job, I explained who I was. No one seemed to think it a problem, but David felt it would be better not to make our relationship public. Of course payroll had to know — my payslip name and address with the company is under

Hart — but in all other things I'm a Reinhardt." Jill smiled. "Like my driving licence and – if we'd gone on holiday together – my passport! I thought you'd guess, but then suddenly you had the idea we were a couple...." Jill jerked her head toward David, "He thought it very diverting!"

David, now calm, was listening with a sickly grin on his face. Jane sighed wearily, "Well, he's amused himself twice today at my expense."

With a snort, David was laughing again. Jane grunted, and went on to tell Jill the dastardly tale of David pointing out the advert, generously letting her go early, and the meeting with Mrs Perkins. By now quite enjoying herself, she concluded, "So, here I am just picturing this shy and retiring bachelor of at least fifty, when Mrs Perkins' master arrives home." Screwing up her nose, she went on, "So you can imagine the shock when I hear the master's voice!" Rudely, she pointed at the unrepentant gentleman, who, having thoroughly savoured her saga of the day's events, was dabbing his eyes with a now sodden handkerchief. "Him! So I'm really pleased I got the better of him this morning."

"You did? Oh tell me!" Jill rubbed her hands in glee.

Jane, now over that first shock, enjoyed relating her switchboard joke on David.

"Brilliant! Well that served him right! David thinks the things he gets up to are so, so funny, so it's good for him to get a taste of his own medicine!" Jill threw him a poisonous look. "There have been times when I could have gladly throttled him – remember when he butted into our conversation in the canteen!" They groaned together.

A mirth-ridden voice piped up, "Jane gave me such a lovely kiss."

"I didn't kiss you! You stuck your head between us — I was going to speak to Jill."

Jill shook her head. "Jane, just ignore him. I find it's the best way. And, if my dearest brother hasn't completely put you off the idea of being anywhere near him, I'll show you around the flat. I'll tell you one thing this has taught me, I need to get a lock put on the flat door, otherwise we'll get no end of bullying."

"Oh, come on! Jane's comeuppance today wasn't entirely undeserved."

Jill banged down her cup, "Come on, Jane, let's leave the moron to his own company."

Still cross at David's double duplicity, Jane gave him a contemptuous look and followed Jill.

The kitchen was a dream. Modern, shiny, fitted cupboards top and bottom, masses of work surface, a huge cooker, large larder fridge and a dish washer! Jill opened cupboards to revealed an array of modern electrical equipment, and all Jane could do was repeat over and over, "It's wonderful, amazing."

"What do you think of my garden, then?" Jill flicked a switch and pointed through the window. This original entrance to the basement had been blocked off because of the garage above, but the gap, no wider than two stone staircases, was covered by heavy metal gratings which would allow enough air and light into the area for the original stone steps to act as shelves for potted plants and herbs, and would in summer make an attractive display. Jill had even squashed in a small wrought-iron table and chair under the top steps.

"It's all fantastic, Jill. I didn't know you liked cooking and gardening and."

Jill laughed. "Oh, I don't mind gardening, but I hate cooking. Mum designed this kitchen. Domesticity is just not my thing! But I think Mum's hoping a lovely kitchen will inspire me. Anyway, let's move on. The bathroom is under the front entrance. That small window in my garden gives a bit of light, but you can't see out, so I've put a couple of plants in the bathroom to cheer it up. Not sure they'll like it though."

They left the kitchen to look into the bathroom, and ignored David relaxing in the easy chair by the window. A quick peek at the bathroom showed its luxury features: heated towel rail; shower head on the bath; constant hot water and fully carpeted. Oh so different from home! With the central heating there were no drafts from doors, and everywhere was so warm. How her Mum would love that and, when Ted sold his house, she knew it was their first priority.

The two bedrooms on this floor were a good size, one oblong L-shaped and the other L-shaped. Although the L-shaped room was perhaps narrower and shorter, she liked its character.

Jill explained, "This was the only bit of the back wall that remained. It makes the room a bit shorter, but those original French doors mean you can open them and have your own private patio. The sun shines this way of an evening.

"Dad thought David was barmy when he bought the house, as it had lain derelict for ten years after a bomb had blown out the majority of back wall, killing the family who owned it. After the war, it took years for lawyers to trace relatives who had gone to America. Then it became part of a legal wrangle which took more years, until those involved agreed to sell the property in its appalling state and get what they could for it. David was in the right place at the right time. At 21, he'd just come into Grandfather's inheritance, and he was working at the law firm handling this house in his summer holidays from University, so put in a ridiculous offer and was astonished when it was snapped up.

"The first thing David had to do was make the house secure and weather proof. I remember coming here — it was sad seeing it all broken, full of damp and mould. An architect friend suggested that rather than rebuild the broken walls and badly damaged interior at the back of the house, it would be more cost effective to dig out new foundations, extend the property and convert it into two flats."

They left the first bedroom and inspected the second. David was nowhere to be seen. "We got two bedrooms out of the same area by making one L-shaped. This square one has the advantage of floor-to-ceiling windows, but the built-in wardrobes take up bedroom space. As you saw in the L-shaped room, we used the corridor into the bedroom for that, making a similar sized bed space." Jill preened. "The one large room made into two was my bright idea."

Jane smiled. Jill obviously had enjoyed being part of the refurbishment. "But why has it all taken twelve years to come together?"

"I'll show you my room. It's above this lounge. Unfortunately the original work cost so much that David hadn't enough to finish the inside. He even thought once of selling, but Dad by then had seen the value of David's purchase and persuaded him to live on the second floor which, except for a bit of decorating, didn't need anything major done. Little by little, floors and plastering were done on the first floor and a proper kitchen installed about four years ago. But two years ago, when he and Felicity decided to get married, David was keen to do more than have three empty basement rooms accessible only by a ladder from what you now see as the flat door. He thought of borrowing from the bank, and it occurred to me why didn't I invest my part of Grandfather's inheritance into it?"

Jill opened her door. "This room, the hall and staircase has only just been finished, built across the two huge joists that support the new back wall on the ground floor and first floor. You can't see now, but in the summer it will be a lovely room with a view of the garden below. So bright with all the windows, it was expensive to curtain!" She opened a door on her left. "This is the bathroom – it is internal but has a duct out, so when you switch the light on it starts drawing away any steam or smells!"

"You must find it amazing, having seen it in all its awfulness, to see it now. Do you have photos?"

"Oh yes, you know what David is for documenting things. Just like all the legal stuff he went into when accepting my money to do this work. I don't own anything, but my money is invested into the building as a whole. So the percentage I put in against the value of the building now, I will be able to take out against the value of the building in years to come. Dad says property, especially in London, will rocket in price. It already has, because David would today get at least six times back his initial outlay and all the money he's spent since. So with my 10% investment, one day I might be a rich lady! But he's not letting me have anything for free. If I live here, I have to pay the rent like anyone else and my share of the expenses. I suppose that's fair, because he's had to buy furniture, equipment, etc. — all of which will wear out and need replacing. And of course, one day, he will either have to sell the house or buy me out when I need the money. Mind, it's tied up for ten years, but with the proviso that if I needed it he would pay the interest if I had to borrow, or take a mortgage himself to release the capital at that day's value. He does have his moments of real sense! Anyway, I thought about the cost if I was to live here, and how much I pay out now to live in a grotty bed-sit, and decided — with three bedrooms, why not let out two by finding others to share? And so here we are. Well, Jane, what do you think? Will the luxury of the flat, and sharing with me, offset the troublesome landlord?" Jill played with her hair, "Please, please say 'yes'."

"I'd like to, but…"

"It's not the rent is it? It sounds a lot, but it includes Mrs Perkins' services. David worked out the running costs and – her eyes rose heavenwards – the only way I can afford to live here is by charging you and someone else that sort of rent. You could help choose our other flatmate. I really hoped you'd ...."

"Stop, stop, Jill. It's okay, I'd love to move in. Hold on — don't get too excited. My reticence was because I'm not sure that living in the same house as my boss is a good idea."

"He's not that bad really! Although I was jolly cross with him tonight. Mind you, it would be better not tell anyone at work that he's our landlord, for heaven knows what they'd make of it. Probably accuse him of having an inbuilt harem."

Jane grunted. "Not a rumour to be desired! However, if I know anything about David, he would have considered that before he invited me here."

"Well, he did say I'd have to be rather circumspect in who I invited from the office," giggled Jill, "but as long as he doesn't turn up when they're here, who's going to know? His address is hardly common knowledge."

"Right then, let's go and find that brother of yours and tell him you have your first tenant." Jane rubbed her hands together and grinned. "Although he may regret that in the days to come."

To Jane's surprise, when they returned to the basement, David had cleared up the tray of tea cups, everything in the kitchen was neat and tidy and he was seated in the chair awaiting their return.

When Jane commented about it, Jill grunted. "David's not just fastidious in the office. Remember how you quoted him, 'Everything, Jane, has a place and everything, Jane, should be in it'. I'm the opposite, but if you can live with that, we'll get along just fine."

David gave Jane a quizzical look. Jane blushed and mumbled, "It looks nice and tidy now."

"That Jane is because Jill's not moved in yet. Just wait

and see." He gave her a wry smile. "I assume then, you've agreed to join us."

"Yes, she has, but no thanks to you, brother dear."

"Well, I'm sure you'll be very happy here, Jane."

To keep onside with Jill, she jibed, "Just as long as you understand that I won't be that sister you desired. You know, the one who does your cleaning, washing, ironing shirts, darning socks, and cooking meals."

David grinned as Jill, astonished, gasped, "He never said that?"

"Oh, yes he did – only yesterday!" David gave her a wide-eyed look, that irritating twitch of a smile hovering round his mouth. "Oh, and another thing, while I'm thinking about it, boss in the office is one thing, but don't go getting any ideas like that here. For instance, if I ring in sick one day I shan't expect you to bowl down the stairs to check up on me – or bring a typewriter home in case I might feel better later."

With a humble bow and pretending to doff a cap, David said, "Yes, me lady, just as you say, me lady."

"I mean it!"

"Of course, me lady! Now, perhaps, me lady this might be a good time to offer you a lift home in the Rolls?"

David sounded so like Parker from the TV programme *Thunderbirds,* that she imitated Lady Penelope, "Oh, no Parker, that won't be necessary. I'll get the tube."

Jill burst out laughing. "Good job. It'll be a long time before he can afford a Rolls."

Jane wagged her finger toward David, "And remember I'm fleeing the family nest, not building another."

"Oh, don't you worry, young Jane. I don't intend to be your watchdog, but it won't stop my concern for your welfare. It's dark, cold and probably very slippery out there, and despite it only being a five minute walk to the station in a fairly respectable neighbourhood, things do happen."

On a heavy sigh, she had to agree 'things' did happen to her.

At her expression, David suggested, "It's alright, don't look so worried. How about a compromise? I'll walk with you to the station."

Having accepted David's company, she graciously allowed him to tuck her arm into his as they strolled down the road. "Jill's very lucky to have a brother like you." Hastily, she qualified the remark. "Except, of course, when you play your practical jokes!"

He squeezed her arm and smiled down at her. "I told you only yesterday that my sisters wouldn't agree with your flattering description of a brother. Jill would say an older brother was far too domineering, and Paula would groan and ask when I was going to grow up!"

The street was quite dark and, having slithered on a frozen puddle, she admitted she was glad to be with this tall, broad man. To walk beside him made her feel very small, but very secure.

"By the way, Jane, it might be wise not to mention your new address too freely. You will need to inform Personnel, but I'd prefer it if you didn't tell anyone at work I was your landlord!"

Primly she chirped back, "Yes, it would be awful to be discovered to have a secret spy in Reception, and your secretary living with you."

He frowned, "Put like that, I think you can see my point."

Jane giggled. "Actually it's quite funny, because last night my mother said she thought you'd influenced me and that my behaviour and attitudes had changed. To make her point, Mum went on about you organising my work and expanding my mind by travel abroad." David gave her a brief wintry smile. As they crossed the road, Jane went on, "Then guess what Mum said?" She didn't wait for a reply. "I quote, 'the next thing you'll be telling me is that you're going to live with the man!' At the time I was furious with her for even suggesting such a thing, but I was not to know that twenty-four hours later I could be seen to be doing just that!"

David's response to her laughing was to ask gruffly, "Have you got a season ticket?"

With a nod, she slipped her arm from his, fished in her bag and produced it just as a train could be heard arriving at the platform below.

"Good. Right then, I'll see you tomorrow."

Before she could hoist her bag back on her shoulder, he was several paces away. He lifted his hand in a brief wave, called, "Goodnight, Jane," and was gone.

For a moment she stared after him then, turning, she ran down the steps to catch her train. Had she offended him by repeating her mother's comments? She shrugged. Well, he'd just have to get over it. Life was too short to waste time worrying, and life for her was definitely changing for the better.

CHAPTER 15

When she arrived home, she discovered Bruce's dad installed for the evening, bringing a foretaste of the future at home. The sense of Ted's permanence was already making her feel like an outsider. From the kitchen her mum's voice called, "Why so late home tonight, Jane? I heard the trains were delayed this morning. I suppose David made you make up the time?"

So David was again the scapegoat of her mother's thinking! It might be best to confine her news to just sharing a flat with Jill. "Actually, I've got something amazing to tell you both."

"Let me get your dinner out of the oven. It's a bit dried out, but some tomato ketchup will improve it." In between mouthfuls she told of Jill needing a flatmate.

Ted listened and nodded, then he poured himself another cup of tea, picked up the newspaper and headed for the door. "I'll leave you two to talk."

Had Ted left because he felt an argument might ensue? Quiet and sensitive, Ted hated any discord.

"Anyway, Mum, I couldn't believe it! It was really fabulous and really safe because it's a house with two maisonettes and you have to go in the main door first." Jane was amazed that, as she delighted in describing every detail, her Mother's reaction was to smile and nod. "Jill said I could move in any time, I'd really like to do it sooner, than later." She waited, expecting a negative response at her enthusiasm to leave home.

Instead, with a warm motherly smile, her Mum reached out her hand and covered hers. "I think, Jane, I'd better tell you that when Ted came in this lunch time I told him about our conversation yesterday, and he convinced me that you are quite old enough now to have a life of your own."

With a rueful expression she went on, "I know I can't keep you at home for ever, as much as I'd like to! It's incredible you've found something so quickly, and with someone you know and trust. Today's events have to be more than coincidence – one of those 'God-incidences', especially as Ted and I talked and prayed about it earlier."

Inwardly, Jane raised thanks to Ted and sighed with relief. Fighting not to grin stupidly, she gave a hum of agreement. Tomorrow would be time enough to tell her Mother that although sharing with only one, there were actually two people under the same roof whom she'd grown to know and trust.

Next morning as Jane walked by the Reception desk, Jill's first words were, "I hope you haven't changed your mind?" Despite Jane's assurances and asking when she could move in, Jill seemed anxious to point out that her wayward brother and his antics would be kept out by lock and key.

"Jill I'm sure it will work out. My worry is having to behave one way in work and another at home, but I'm not going to let that…." She stopped speaking, seeing David strolling towards them.

"Are you two ganging up on me already?"

Jill glanced round the hall, then scoffed in a low voice, "So what if we are, brother dear? We're not going to put up with any of your mischief, are we Jane?"

Jane bit her lip nervously suddenly realising if this went wrong she could be out of a job and home at the same time. David glanced at her and laughed. "Oh, I think Jane knows her boundaries. But, should she overstep them, I'll inform her in the nicest possible way! By the way, have you asked her yet?"

"Asked me what?"

Before addressing Jane, Jill made a playful moue at David. "David and I – well mainly I – have arranged a New Year's housewarming party tomorrow night, and we – I – would like to invite you as my new flatmate. Actually, it's a bit more than that. You see, I wondered... wanted to ask... and, well it's a bit awkward really.... You remember yesterday you told David that you didn't intend to do his cleaning, washing, cooking and such like?"

Jane took in the mock innocence of David's smile and Jill's hair fiddling and wondered what was coming next, so she answered with conviction, "I do indeed!"

Jill gave David a dispirited look, but having pushed back her straying hair, asked, "So, I suppose you would think it an awful cheek if I asked you, as my friend and new flatmate, to help me cook for the party?"

Jane looked at David, but he held up his palms in defence. "It's nothing to do with me, Jane!"

"It was my idea. I've organised the party, but it would be so much better if we could have some proper food, not just crisps and things, and it occurred to me how much you love cooking, and know all about catering, and you liked the kitchen, and please Jane you see I'm so hopeless at anything like that."

It wasn't the cooking that was the problem, but where Jane's loyalties lay. For the past few years on New Year's Eve their church had held a party. The kids brought sleeping bags for when they got tired, they played games and everyone contributed to a meal. Half an hour before midnight, they worshipped and praised God and half an hour after they prayed for each other.

As though sensing Jane's hesitation, Jill went on, "We're not just asking you to the party because we want a cook – we want you to come and meet our family and friends. Stay overnight and test out your new bed! Please, please, Jane!"

"Jill – stop, stop! You needn't plead, beg any more, I'll happily help you with the cooking."

Jill gave David a smile that said, 'I told you so' and then went into raptures, "Oh, Jane that's great! Oh, thank you, thank you, Jane. It's going to be such a great party."

"Yes I'm sure it will, but I can't stay for that."

After being so excited, Jill looked crestfallen. "Don't you want to come?"

"It's not that. It's just – well there's a party at church. I usually go to that."

David turned as Mr Plaidon called his name. "I must go. I think it's really good of Jane to help out, so leave her be. Let her decide where she wants to be and what she wants to do." Jill frowned at him. David winked at Jane, and added, "However, we'd both love you to be there."

When Jane arrived home, her mother was alone. On the train home, she'd tried to work out a simple way of telling her that David was Jill's brother and her new landlord. Somehow she didn't think her mum would appreciate hearing about David's pranks. In the kitchen, her mum was finishing the final preparations for dinner, and so it was easy to help out, chatter away, and hope her mum might be too distracted to ask any awkward questions.

"I told Jill you were happy about the flat. Jill was worried and said perhaps you wouldn't be if you knew she was David's sister and it was his house we were living in. I said I'd tell you tonight, but couldn't see a problem as ours is the basement flat with it's own door, and David lives on the first and second floors, but anyway you are invited round to see if for yourselves. And guess what? They've invited me to their New Year's Eve Party. I said I'd go for the day, and thought if I leave there by six, I should be back and ready to go to the Church party by 7.30."

"Jane, if you want to stay on, we won't mind – you don't have to come to the Church party. We'll miss you. Everyone at church will miss you. But they'll understand that next year you'll be living in London and won't want to return twice, or three times a week to be part of the church here. And it won't do to just come to church here on a

Sunday for we both know that's not what it is about. You need commitment to a church and friends to support, and who will support you. It is so easy otherwise without opportunity to meet, talk, study and discuss God's word, for your life to drift away from His principles. You will look for a new church and become part of it, won't you?"

At her mother's worried expression, she reassured her. "Of course! I might be leaving home, but I'm not leaving my faith."

"Glad to hear it. Obviously, I worry about the influence others have over you, but I have to believe you will be strong enough to stand against the pressures of the world. I can't remember you telling me Jill was David's sister, but although Jill and David might not see themselves as Christians or go to church, from what I've heard from you they sound decent enough. I doubt they'll lead you astray and, who knows, it might be of God for you to lead them to a church."

Jane laughed. "David and Jill in church – now that would be a miracle." Her thoughts went to the miracles of the past two days. God certainly was working on her behalf. She had no idea what David did in his spare time, it was none of her business. But if he had integrity at work, he'd be much the same at home. She did know of Jill's search for Mr Right, which often led her into the arms of the wrong men, but that was something her Mum didn't need to know, and something she certainly wasn't going to embrace after her experiences!

"There is one thing Jane, what about Bruce? What does he think about your plans?"

"He doesn't know about them. I've wanted to talk to him about us for ages, but I couldn't find a way. I'm just hoping that with you and Ted getting married and me leaving home, he'll understand I want to be completely free."

"Yes, I must admit I'd wondered if you might feel that

way. I thought you might get over this restless period, but I suppose it was inevitable your relationship with Bruce would change. Still, let's look on the bright side – Bruce will one day meet someone else, and so will you. Then we'll have two families instead of one to take an interest in our old age!" Jane smiled. It was something of a miracle the way her Mum had so calmly taken her 'living' with David. It seemed Ted, love and marriage were having a positive effect. She could only pray that the Lord had prepared the way with Bruce and he might also be so accommodating.

When Bruce and Ted arrived an hour later, her mother took Ted into the kitchen, leaving Jane and Bruce to sit by the fire. She felt awkward, and by the way Bruce kept his eyes from hers he probably felt the same. For a few minutes neither of them spoke, then both started together. Bruce invited her to go first, so she explained she didn't want to live with her mum and Ted, and what seemed God's amazing provision for her to live in London.

He didn't seem unduly surprised. Perhaps Ted had told him her plans. But he couldn't have known that Jill was David's sister and he was her landlord, so she was amazed when he responded so positively. "The flat sounds great. Can I come round and see it? I'd say you've found good friends in Jill and David."

Glad that he was no longer dispelling gloom and doom, she felt more at ease to ask him his thoughts on the forthcoming marriage.

His answer was somewhat grudging. "Well, I suppose they're entitled to their happiness, as long as I'm not expected to tag along."

"So what will you do?"

Bruce sighed heavily and sat back in the chair. "Something different. I've seen you breaking out like a butterfly from a chrysalis these past months, and I suppose,

292

deep down, when I saw you stretching your wings, I knew it wouldn't be long before you wanted to fly away – away from me." He laughed derisively, "But I don't suppose it would matter quite so much if I didn't feel a boring ugly duckling, and unable to swan off like you."

The hurt in his voice brought tears to Jane's eyes. "Oh, Bruce, of course you could swan off like me. Don't even say such things about yourself. I've been growing up, my needs are changing, my vision stretching. We both need opportunities to experience, to learn, to build, so we can become rounded human beings. I was attracted by your kindness, patience, trustworthy nature, your ability to make music speak, your love of the Lord...."

Miserably he interrupted, "But it wasn't enough?" .

"Bruce, that's silly. I value you as a person and the fact you've been there for me these past years. But, I have realized lately you represent a brother rather than a lover." Bruce winced at her turn of phrase, making her hurry on. "You're a good man and have the potential to go far. Without me around you'll be free to find the right person. Even if we drift apart, we're going to have a common bond. We're going to be brother and sister, and in years to come we'll be able to enjoy each other's families."

To her relief Bruce's face had begun to brighten.

"You're right. You've always been the one with vision, while I'm just happy to potter along. Maybe that's all we've ever been – friends. I've never considered, well what you said, the lover thing, I thought time enough for that when we got married." Jane gave him a shy smile. Neither had she until she'd met the stranger, ghost, or whoever he was. "Seeing you pushing ahead, I think I was jealous of your success, but it has sparked me to think of my career. I've seen adverts for librarians in universities, which would be more interesting than the local library, but I didn't do anything about it because it would have meant moving away, and I felt if I did that, then I really would lose you." He looked sad, then perked up, "But everything's changed, and for the better because, as you say, you'll soon be my sister and we will always be friends."

Now their feelings and futures were uncovered, the restraint of the past few weeks vanished, leaving them both lighter in spirit and able to discuss and advise each other as friends do. As Bruce continued talking she thanked God. He'd heard her prayers and had been working in the lives of those around her in a way she couldn't have envisaged, in such a simple yet wonderful solution. It was hard to believe after the months of struggling that she was now free! Free from living at home; free from parental control; free from Bruce as a potential husband; free from guilt at wanting to break up the happy foursome, and free to go where she liked, when she liked and with whom she liked.

It felt odd to be travelling on a Saturday into London. There was only one other person on the platform and three sharing her carriage, making her wonder why offices didn't stagger their weeks to include Saturdays. Brunswick Gardens in daylight was even better than at night. The short walk from the High Street meant everything was very convenient, including buses to travel to work or, if it was a nice day and she got up early, she could walk to work through Kensington Gardens and Hyde Park.

A warm welcome awaited her. The front door opened immediately she'd rung the bell. David bounced down the stairs in grey slacks, open shirt and v-necked jumper. He looked so different from the man she worked for that a sister-like affection arose for him. Jill, seeing her suitcase, immediately asked, "Have you come to stay?"

Jane smiled. "I'm so excited about coming to live here I thought I'd make a start by bringing a few things with me."

The time flew by as she cooked, baked and instructed Jill, but it wasn't long before she realized why Jill had been anxious for her help – she really didn't have a clue!

David, though, didn't need any clues when it came to timing his arrival in the kitchen. The moment she took something out of the oven he always seemed to appear, to carry out what he called 'quality controls'.

Jim and Paula, David's older sister, arrived early in the afternoon with their two boys to add to the happy chaos. Straight away Paula, who was decidedly fat, fun and forty drew Jane into the continual family bantering, making her realise she felt happier today than she had for ages. The two little boys, Richard and Philip, though were mischievous terrors! Paula was constantly divided between helping to prepare the food and admonishing them for eating it. When Philip was found climbing on David's dining room table, with his fingers and face dripping with chocolate sauce after having demolished the carefully constructed tower of profiteroles, Jane shuddered and decided if she ever had any children they'd be properly disciplined.

There was heartfelt relief when David intervened. With a boy under each arm, he entered the kitchen to announce, "These two have come to say sorry to Auntie Jane for messing about with the food."

There was much wriggling and screaming at this, but David grinned nonchalantly. Lowering them, he put a hand on each boy's shoulder and, to Jane's surprise, they both apologised. Paula gave a benign smile, told them Mummy would clear up their mess and now, try to be good. David swirling them up again under his arms and marched away saying, "Of course you'll be good me hearties, a nice bath awaits ye." Both Jane and Jill clapped their hands over their ears as the boys wailing outdid David's booming voice, but the din faded as they headed upwards to David's bathroom.

Half an hour later Jane went upstairs to find all was peaceful and in order. Paula had done such a good repair on the profiteroles that even she wouldn't have known they'd been rolling over the dining room table earlier. On her return to the kitchen, Jane commented to Jill, who was just finishing the washing up, "I can't believe how quiet it is up there. What happened to those tearaways?

"Oh, that's Uncle David for you. He can get those boys to do anything. They absolutely adore him and the stories he tells them. I'll go and tell David, when he's ready we're finished here, and he can carry up the plates, etc. from the kitchen."

Jane pulled off her apron as Paula walked in. "I'm sorry I haven't been much help. The kids proved to be more of a hindrance than expected. Still, it looks as if you've done it all. You've worked so hard and done brilliantly with the food. Go and relax in a leisurely bath – I doubt many people will arrive much before 8.30. David and I can sort out the other things."

"Oh, I enjoy cooking, and thanks. But I must go – I'm not staying for the party."

"Not staying? Of course you are! After all that hard work you've put in – what is Jill thinking of?"

Jane was explaining about her other engagement as Jill came running down the stairs to announce, "The parents have arrived."

Paula frowned at Jill. "Jane says she's got to go. Surely you're not going to allow that, after all her hard work?"

"Oh, I've been instructed to leave Jane to make her own decision." Jill smiled across at Jane. "And I've also been instructed that the cook must be presented to the parents. They will be most disappointed if they don't at least get the chance to say hello to you. They've just seen the food. Mum knew it wasn't my cooking!"

A glance in the mirror in the hall had Jane pulling at her now greasy hair, and smelling under her armpits. "I can't meet your parents looking like this, I've been sweating over a hot stove all day, I'm disgusting."

Jill giggled, "You look wonderful. Rosy cheeked,

ruffled and homely. Anyway, they'll understand. And by the sounds of it, you've no choice − they're coming this way."

Two little boys in plaid pyjamas shrieking 'This way, this way," heralded their arrival, with Richard sticking his head through the banisters to remark, "Lay down here. Look, look Philip, you can see Auntie Jill. Auntie Jill − I can see you."

"Yes, hello Richard. I can see you too. You see, Jane, that's the problem with little boys, they have ways of spying you out."

David laughed as, having by-passed the children, he was now bounding down the stairs toward them closely followed by his parents.

"Mum said she just had to meet you, she is so impressed with the food. So, Jane, this is my Mum, otherwise known as Margaret."

Margaret was petite, her white hair beautifully coiffeured, and her small body encased in an attractive peach suit. David's father, introduced as Franz, was a big-built man. His loud guttural voice welcomed her, his hand stretched out to shake hers. His air of authority made her feel if she addressed him it should be as Mr Reinhardt. Margaret's friendly conversation made up for her husband, whose hard stare was making her feel uncomfortable. After a few minutes Jane said apologetically, "I'm very sorry, I'm afraid I have to go, but it's been nice to meet you both."

"Oh, that can't be right! Jill, surely you've invited Jane to the party?"

With a boom similar to his son's, Franz demanded, "Going! Oh no! We can't have that! David, make her stay!"

David's warm, twinkling eyes caught Jane's before he addressed his father. "And how am I supposed to do that?"

"Good heavens, son. Haven't I taught you anything?"

David chuckled, "Ah, but Dad, you've never had to deal with Jane."

Franz's penetrating black eyes fixed on Jane as though she were some strange anomaly; Margaret assured her she was welcome; Paula asked couldn't she possibly stay; and Jill added she'd feel awful when their guests arrived if she couldn't introduce her friend, the fabulous cook.

Torn, Jane looked around and didn't know what to do. David intervened with broad smile, gesturing to the others. "Well, Jane, after that you'll gather I'm not the bully in this family – the women are!"

As the three female members of the family cried out at his unfairness, Jane smiled and was pleased she'd taken her mum's advice to pack a small suitcase of things she could leave in the flat with a view to moving in, and things she'd need if she took up the option to stay to the Reinhardts' party.

With hands held up in surrender, David begged the women, "Stop! Stop! As I said before, it's Jane's decision. Jane, if you really must go, then the least I can do is to run you home in the car. But I think you can tell, we would all love you to stay."

It was heart warming to look around the faces of the Reinhardt women and hear their pleas. She grinned at them, then addressed David in a lofty manner, "It's very kind of you to offer to drive me home, Parker, but as I think I said the other day, your services will not required – in this case, not because I wish to be independent, but because I'd love to stay to the party."

The Reinhardt women cheered.

Franz patted David's back. "Good boy! Knew you could pull it off."

To that, the Reinhardt women made a host of scornful comments. Franz caught Jane's eye and, unsmiling, gave what she could only hope was a nod of approval.

Paula queried why Jane had referred to David as **Parker**

and, once informed, laughed. "Oh yes. You boys, you love the Thunderbirds on TV, don't you? I thought, Jane, it was because you'd discovered that he's a nosey parker."

David retorted, unabashed, "I'm not nosey, I've just got an enquiring mind! Which is why I ask now, has our Cinderella got anything with her to wear to the party? It's a bit late to go to the shops!"

All eyes focussed on Jane. "It's okay. In the stuff I brought this morning I included a dress and change of clothes, just in case I decided to stay. I'm looking forward to trying out my new bed.... Oh no! I forgot to bring any sheets...."

Margaret was quick to offer, "David will lend you some, won't you, dear?"

He looked sheepish. "Sorry, Mum, they're all on the beds."

Promptly, Jill piped up, "That's okay – I've got a new unopened set of double ones. Jane, you could probably fold one of those in half for your single bed."

Paula pretended to wipe sweat from her forehead. "Phew! That's a relief! I thought after all that Parker's services would be required later tonight."

Jill gave David a sarcastic smile. "I'm sure, to save that, our dear brother would have let her have his bed."

"Only if I could have shared it with her!"

Jane blushed to the roots of her hair. Margaret, Paula and Jill chorused, "David!" while he grinned like a naughty boy.

The bedroom still looked empty even when she'd unpacked her suitcase. The built-in wardrobe was huge, far bigger than she would need. It was good though to have central heating and, even more luxurious, a sink in her room. Armed with her soap and Jill's bath foam, she padded across to the deliciously warm bathroom to relax in a hot bath. This really was wonderful. Not just the flat, but friends who were including her in their lives. She soaked for ages and wished she'd brought her watch with her, but it was probably time she got out — her fingers were getting wrinkly. She reached out for her towel and groaned — she'd left it hanging in the bedroom. The only towel in the bathroom was the hand one! To stop dripping all over the floor, she used it while wondering what to do next.

She was damp and didn't want to put back on her dirty clothes. Her own towel was big enough to be quite decent to walk from bathroom to bedroom, but this one was decidedly skimpy. In the mirror she held it against her, it covered her front, but left her rear quite bare. She assessed the possibility of anyone coming down the stairs in what couldn't be more than six strides to her bedroom. Even if they did she was decent from the front. And she couldn't stay in the bathroom all evening. Carefully positioning the towel and holding her clothes on her arm, she opened the bathroom door and peered out. No sound of anyone approaching and the stairs were clear. Good — she made a quick dash to her bedroom and opened the door. From behind her a voice boomed, "Well, well, there's a sight to behold."

The surprise made her jump, rush forward into her room and shut the door, but not before she had a quick glimpse of the ever-present David Reinhardt standing in the kitchen doorway, a stack of plates and serviettes in his hands. Oh why was it that man always caught her in embarrassing situations?

By the time she joined the party, three ITP directors and their wives had arrived, along with several other guests she didn't recognise. David, dressed in his tuxedo, excused himself from a group and joined her, observing in an amused tone, "Well, well, well, Jane. You're looking even more beautiful than when I last saw you." He tucked his hand under her elbow as he drew her across the room.

With pursed her lips, she took a deep breath and commented grittily, "If I'm going to live here, I would appreciate it if you didn't come downstairs without announcing, loudly, your presence. And, in your case, that shouldn't be too difficult!"

"Ah, Daphne, this is Jane." instantly changing her expression, Jane smiled sweetly at Mrs Plaidon as David went on, "Jane, as you know, has been working for me. She and Jill have become great friends and now she's moving in to share the downstairs flat with Jill."

This was the first of many introductions. To Jane's surprise, all the directors appeared unperturbed that David was about to be her landlord, their friendliness showing in their continued conversation.

Janet Truman, the wife of a retired director, praised her on the food, then waved her stick to beckon David over. "Wonderful spread, wonderful. Let me tell you, young man, this girl's a valuable asset." David smiled. "I gather, though, you've already noticed that. Eh? I believe she works in your office. Now I hear she's going to be sharing your home. All this living together malarkey! Whatever happened to good old-fashioned marriage, that's what I want to know?" Jane looked at David, expecting him to clarify the situation but Mrs Truman, warming to her theme, said with asperity, "You should make a decent woman of her, you hear me!" David stared hard at Mr Truman, who'd been attempting to stem the flow by drawing on his wife's arm. "When I was young this sort of...."

Mr Truman intervened, "Now, now, my dear, come along. Jessica's dying to have a chat with you." But as he led her away she was still talking. "We didn't do that sort of thing. Living in sin, that's what it is!"

Jane, incensed by her words, attacked David with hers. "Why didn't you say something? You need to put her right. We certainly don't want people jumping to that sort of conclusion! Go and talk to her, explain...."

"Jane, there's no need! And there's no need to look at me like that. It's nothing to worry about. Everyone here knows Mrs Truman. She is old, gets confused, and often says inappropriate things. There is no point in trying to correct her, she will only get upset. And Henry will counteract anything she says with the truth."

Jane grimaced, "I sincerely hope so – otherwise I'll be moving out, before I've barely moved in."

David grunted, glanced briefly at his watch, said, "Excuse me," and walked across the room to join two of his friends.

Jane stared after him. Had he'd been more disconcerted at Janet Truman's assumptions than he made out? People kept arriving and after about half an hour David, having overcome his odd mood, was once again bouncing between conversations and introducing her to people. David's legal and accounting friends tended to be older and rather staid. They greeted her pleasantly, but conversation was difficult for they hadn't much in common. Jill's friends, on the other hand, were younger and full of fun and laughter.

Being used to church functions, Jane found it easy to flit between the different groups in David's lounge, usually offering food, but stopping to talk or laugh when there was an opening. At one group she was just offering a tray of canapés when, behind her, came a man's mocking laugh, followed by another commenting, "Like you, she's not what I expected, but she is bringing him out of himself. I've always thought he was far too staid for his years – too much study, his mind always set to achieve. I felt it was good when he changed direction from law to business. He lacked social skills, but these past three years have opened up things for him, he's allowing himself time to enjoy life. Let's hope she..." Jane offered the tray to the group. The man speaking stopped, looked slightly taken aback and then selected a canapé. "These are simply marvellous Jane.

David's lucky to have such a good cook for a friend." The other men seemed rather amused, as they helped themselves and murmured their agreement of their friend's sentiments.

David, she noticed was chatting animatedly with Felicity. Obviously it was their friendship to which those men had been alluding. Jill had said they were no longer involved since the broken engagement, but perhaps the break and being together at Christmas had helped them to see their relationship afresh.

She wondered had David seen her observing him, for he looked across, smiled at her then continued talking to Felicity. Later as she went to the dining room for fresh supplies, she and Felicity met head on.

Felicity waved her hand In the general direction of the table. "Oh, Jane, I hear all this is your doing. I, like Jill, am positively hopeless at anything quite so domesticated. You, my dear, obviously have a flair as a cook, but you really don't have to act as a hired servant – the art is to just mingle." The remark was followed by a tinkly laugh before she sashayed back into the other room.

Did Felicity just have an unfortunate way with words, or had she been implying that Jane didn't fit in? If that were the case, she'd prove her wrong! In offering food, she'd show Felicity that to serve wasn't degrading, but an important part of putting different people at ease. She plastered on her 'hostess with the mostest' smile, collected a fresh selection of vol-au-vents and sausage rolls from the oven, and moved in amongst the nearest arrivals, a group of David's friends. As they pondered over the selection, she chatted, calling on her excellent memory for names, bringing comments from the men, and laughter from the women.

Throughout the groups she repeated this, then began to draw people from the different groups together introducing and helping to start up conversations between them. At her instigation, a mixed group of David's and Jill's friends were now heavily into a debate on justice.

A hand touched her shoulder. "I hope you're enjoying yourself, young Jane?" David smiled down on her and chuckled at her fervent, "Oh, yes, thank you."

"I'm glad, because you are doing an excellent job of helping others to enjoy themselves." He moved away as his father came into view. Thrilled that David thought she was doing an excellent job, she sent Franz a beaming smile. His response was to half smile, so perhaps under that harsh exterior Franz was just a shy man.

Her attention was drawn by Jill's friend, Peter. "Jane, who is that beautiful tall, willowy blonde in the corner."

"Oh, Felicity. Would you like to meet her?"

Peter looked sceptical, "I wouldn't think she'd be interested in me."

"Oh come on...." She drew Peter across the room and introduced him. He was at least three inches shorter and five years younger than Felicity. The look on her face was hardly welcoming, but Jane was not to be put off. "I assured Peter you loved to mingle and would be interested in talking to him. He works for a magazine where, I believe, they like to feature the beautiful people. You never know, Felicity, when you might get a break. Now please excuse me – things to do, people to see."

Ten minutes later, a scowling Felicity caught her in the kitchen and hissed, "That spotty little scumbag wasn't much more than the post boy. What do you think you're doing?"

"I was doing as you suggested, just mingling – you know, bringing people together!" As she burrowed in the fridge, she continued, "And to prove I'm not the hired help, I'm making everyone feel welcome. Are you?" Without looking, she knew Felicity had left.

Sherry trifle in hand, she returned to the dining room where Felicity was admonishing David. David glanced over at Jane. Jane replied with a rueful smile and was rewarded with a wink. Seconds later, Felicity marched out of the room while David, with contorted face, waved his hands in mock defeat.

Midnight struck. Immediately, people began shaking hands, hugging and kissing each other. David drew her aside. "Happy New Year, Jane. You've been quite a hit at this party – I'm very glad you stayed." His eyes fell to her mouth. Before she could proffer him her cheek, his breath whispered across her lips, "This year could be very special."

His kiss was like that at the Christmas lunch, except there was no cheering or bantering from a canteen full of people and no excuse of dizziness from wine or heat. And there was only a moment to savour the pleasant sensation which ran through her, before a general clamour of good wishes assailed them. She turned in one direction and David the other and she found herself face to face with Felicity, with an expression not dissimilar to one of Rosemary's scowls. Quickly, Felicity moved forward to kiss David. Jane felt saddened by her dislike, but as she was pulled in to link arms with others ready to sing, 'Auld Lang Syne' she was amused at the length and intensity of their kiss. At the words, 'We'll take a cup of kindness yet', she smiled at Felicity, but her gesture of friendliness was ignored.

Around one o'clock the guests began to leave. And as David and Jill said their 'goodbyes' she began tidying up – just as she would have at home. In turn, Paula, Margaret and Jill told her to go to bed and not worry about it. David, having just seen the last guest out overheard Jill's exhortation and that they'd clear up in the morning, intervened. "Come on Jane, you heard Jill." That wry and irritating smile twitched at his mouth. "And if you don't get down those stairs to bed, I will personally despatch you there."

Hands on hips, Jane responded. "Oh, will you indeed! And you obviously need reminding that you have no authority to despatch anybody or anything, anywhere. In this house you are my landlord, not my boss and, as I'll be paying you rent, what I do and where I go will be in my time, not yours."

Margaret's expression was one of fascination as she glanced between them. Jane guessed it was a rare thing for her tall, authoritative son to be challenged. During the evening she'd overheard Franz say to Margaret, "...Jane's no more than a mere slip of a girl", so she was about to prove that she could stand up to his bossy son, even though Franz had already gone to bed and wasn't there to see it. Jill, knowing their confrontations, fiddled with her hair, while Paula cheered her on, "Go on, Jane, you tell him – about time someone did."

The support egged Jane on, so she continued, "So, David, if you will move out of my way, I'll just pop that cutlery in some hot ...."

She squealed as she was swept off her feet and cradled against David's chest. "There's one thing you forgot Jane, I'm bigger than you and, in the law of the jungle, I win!"

Still fighting, Jane retorted, "Oh, so the name's Tarzan now is it? Put me down you big ape!"

"That seems fitting with me Tarzan, and you Jane!"

The women laughed and watched as he carried her down the stairs, while she struggled to be set free.

On the ground floor, he questioned, "Will you go the rest of the way, or shall I take you?"

Crossly she muttered, "I'll go on my own, thank you!" He put her back on her feet but, once out of his reach, she shouted "Bully!" before fleeing through the open flat door.

His voice boomed after her, "Sleep in. We don't want to see you until lunch time."

CHAPTER 16

It was Jill tapping at her door that finally woke Jane from a deep exhausted sleep. She looked at her watch – eleven-thirty! Jill opened the door slightly and called, "Jane! Oh sorry! Were you still asleep? I've been sent down to make sure you that you knew you were welcome to join the family upstairs. That brother of mine really is awful, isn't he, but you have to admit it was funny last night. Don't let him put you off being here. Come up when you're ready, lunch won't be until about 1.00 anyway – Mum and Paula are cooking it."

Jane washed and put on her royal blue, pencil-slim skirt, a cream twin set and a long string of royal blue beads. David and Franz stood as she entered the lounge. Margaret patted the settee beside her, "Come and sit here. David, dear, pour Jane a glass of sherry."

Before Jane had the chance to refuse, David said, "Sorry, Mum. Apparently Jane and sherry don't mix but I expect, Jane, we can find something else you'd like." Was Franz' grunt at her request for a cup of tea approval or disapproval? There was no doubt of Margaret's approval as she chatted to her. She seemed interested in everything Jane had to say, her friendliness taking off the edge of what felt like an interview.

Paula delivered a tray with a pot of tea, milk, sugar and a china cup and commented, "I thought you might need more than one cup, the way Mum's keeping you talking." With a wry smile, not unlike her brother's, she added, "Be warned, Mum's been asking all sorts of questions about you that Jill and David can't answer."

Aghast Margaret blushed vividly.

Jane laughed. "You just fire away Mrs Reinhardt, sorry —Margaret. I've nothing to hide." And to put her at ease Jane poured herself a cup of tea and told her, in a way to make her laugh, the tale of David's advert, Mrs P and finding out her friend Jill was his sister.

"Oh Jane, you've a good sense of humour! And it seems you are well able to cope with that son of mine. So what do you think of him?

Jane glanced over at him and Jill playing a game of chess. He would obviously hear her reply, although it seemed they were in deep concentration over the board. "Well, Jill summed him up during that incident and although I may agree with some of her adjectives about his brotherliness," she grinned and looked across at them but they didn't appear to be listening. "I think his heart is in the right place. He's been kind, generous and thoughtful towards me."

"Well, I'm glad to hear it. David tells me you are a Christian. I suppose we'd all like to think we were that, but he says it is different for you."

Faced with such a statement she felt she should explain, but a sense of inadequacy filled her, causing her to pray she wouldn't come over as being a religious freak. "I suppose it all started when Mum and Dad, who would have called themselves Christians, went to a Billy Graham evangelistic rally in Harringay Arena in 1954. It's a bit hard to explain in a nutshell. Basically, they realized that to really know God they needed to have a relationship with Him, and that was more than believing in Jesus' death and resurrection and going to church on Sunday. Once they had acknowledged they were sinners in the sight of God, they asked Jesus for His forgiveness, and asked Him to come into their lives in the form of the Holy Spirit so they could learn from Him – in other words become disciples.

"At ten, I didn't really understand all that but I enjoyed Sunday School, the stories, activities and fun centred around Jesus and, because He was so much part of our lives every day, I suppose I fell in love with him. A few years later I made the same commitment my parents had. You asked about my Dad and I told you he died a few years ago. We miss him but, because of our faith in Jesus, we know to those who believe in Him He gives eternal life. So Dad shed his earthly body, but that spirit which is within him lives on, and that too makes such a difference."

"Really! How can you be so sure? There's no evidence to believe that." The sharpness of Margaret's tone made her wonder if she'd lost someone dear to her. "Oh Jane, I'm sorry, that sounded rude."

"It's okay, Mrs Reinhardt, don't worry about it. But I can assure you there is evidence, in the Bible and in recent years. I have heard about people who have died and come back, but there was real evidence for me. My dad's death was sudden, he said 'goodbye' to us in the morning, went to work and," her voice choked but she finished, "never returned."

"Oh no, my dear. Oh, please don't upset yourself."

At Margaret's consternation, David and Jill both turned to look at them. Franz continued reading his paper, but she'd felt all along it was just a cover for his listening to their conversation.

With her hand she waved away the tears that had filled her eyes and addressed the three of them. "It's okay. Honestly! Because you see I took my tears then, and I still do, to my best friend, Jesus. I cried and cried and asked him why he would take my daddy. He didn't give me an answer, but several nights later I dreamt of my dad in this beautiful place where colour and light and music melded. I saw the back of a man in a white robe come and put his arm around my dad as if sharing some special secret and, as they laughed together, they sort of went like translucent gold oil, and then my dad and Jesus turned as if they knew I was behind them, and their faces were full of joy and radiance and I felt it flow from them over me and fill me. When I awoke the dream seemed so real, and within me I knew it had been. I'd had a taste of heaven, because that joy unspeakable and full of glory that the Bible talks about had filled me, and when I spend time with the Lord it always returns and brings an incredible peace and a sense that God is in control."

While speaking she'd relived the dream. Now she saw that Margaret had tears in her eyes and was trying to find her handkerchief up her sleeve. Franz had put down his paper and was staring into the fireplace and David and Jill were deep in thought, but not over the chess board. Not knowing quite what to do, she leaned forward to the low table in front of her and poured herself another cup of tea. No one said anything, so she was grateful when the front door opened, two loud but small voices could be heard and, as it banged shut, those in the room slowly stirred back into life.

Richard and Philip's shouts came up the stairs, "Mum, Mum, where are you?" Their boots removed, but coats still on, they rushed in and then out of the room again, as Paula's voice came from the dining room. "We made a huge, huge snowman in the park and Dad said...."

Margaret stood. "I'd better go and help Paula. Thank you, Jane. Perhaps we can talk again later."

Jill offered, "I'll lay the table," and followed her out.

David boomed after her, "I'll get the wine opened."

Franz picked up his newspaper, so didn't see David stop and briefly rest his hand on her shoulder as he walked behind the settee. But he must have heard David say quietly, "I experienced that presence the other night. When you sang that ...."

Whatever else he might have said was interrupted by Jim. "I must sit down. Those boys wear me out, but it was such a good idea to take them to the park. That will quieten them down and hopefully they'll sleep well tonight."

Seconds later, Jane wished they were still outside. They hadn't quietened down as, to her discomfort, the boys began whooping around her as though she were the latest sacrifice, while Jim talked to Franz.

To her relief, David returned and called them to order. But immediately he sat down next to her and asked if she'd been to the latest Billy Graham rally, the two boys seemed determined to interrupt, dive bombing them with either their cardboard planes or their small bodies. But she managed to say that she and her mum had attend on the night when Cliff Richard had declared to the world that he'd become a Christian. And, in between David play fighting with one or other of the boys at their feet, they managed to discuss whether Cliff would give up his singing career, or even if declaring his faith might ruin it. "He'll probably find God blesses him. What's the betting he doesn't become another Frank Sinatra and still be popular in forty years time."

David grinned, "It's a good job you don't bet, because that's one you certainly wouldn't win. He's not that talented."

She opened her mouth to protest on Cliff's behalf but squealed instead, because Philip in play had just rolled over the side of the settee into her. She definitely wasn't talented when it came to boisterous kids and wondered how obvious it was that she didn't know how to interact with them. Paula tutted as she came to announce lunch, "Please David don't wind them up." To her mind they already seemed pretty wound up.

Because of the boys, it was impossible to have a conversation with anyone without Jim or Paula telling them to sit up, be quiet, or eat the food on their plates and not get down from the table. They were just in the middle of the main course when Philip, grabbing his orangeade, knocked it over. In unison, Paula and Jim cried out and leapt up.

Seated at one end of the table, Jane watched the drama unfold. Rivulets of liquid speedily coursed their way across the table towards Margaret who dropped her napkin in their path and pushed back from the table. Paula dashed forward to add her napkin to stem the flow. In the process, her sleeve caught Margaret's wine glass. Wine then went swimming in the other direction, bringing David to jump into the fray and lift the table cloth in the hope of keeping it from dripping over the side. In the midst, Jim, red faced, was dragging Philip out the door. The boy was crying, "It was an accident, I didn't mean it, I'm sorry."

Jill, remaining calm, moved to the sideboard drawer and took out several tea towels while Jim admonished Philip, "Yes, and if you'd been behaving yourself before, I'd have let it go. But you weren't. Go upstairs and sit on your bed, and don't touch anything in Uncle David's study."

Franz seemed determined not to get involved as he picked up the gravy jug to deliver gravy to his dinner. David boomed, "Jill give me one of those, quick. I don't want wine on the carpet." Jill shot forward to deliver a cloth into his outstretched hand, and Jane gasped in horror. All eyes turned first to her and then followed the direction of her gaze. Franz's hand with the gravy took the hit. The jug swayed alarmingly, the gravy waving and slopping over. It added brown blobs into what was becoming a colourful design on a once white, starched table cloth.

"Oh God, Dad, I'm sorry."

Franz shook his head, put the hot dripping jug carefully back on its saucer and demanded, "Give me one of those towels."

This, she presumed, was family life – which as an only child she hadn't experienced, and rather wished she hadn't now. Had her thoughts been mirrored on her face? Suddenly Franz barked across at her, "Not what you expected then, Jane, this family?"

He was right there. This scenario wasn't something she, or anyone at work, would link with the fastidious David Reinhardt. She shrugged, "I'm an only child, not used to large family meals with children."

"Umph. As you can see, this one's bedlam when it gets together. It'll take a bit of getting used to."

Jane gave a weak smile. She didn't know how to answer. Franz seemed to mean it as encouragement. But she had no intention of getting used to it. Not for her, unruly kids, and she didn't intend to make a habit of eating with the Reinhardt family. Franz said nothing more, but continued eating his meal and she did the same.

There was a rather subdued atmosphere as members of the family reshuffled around the table to eat where the cloth wasn't wet and daubed with red, yellow and brown.

It cheered up when left-over puddings from the night before were brought in, and every member of the Reinhardt clan had praise for her food, including the two wayward boys. Perhaps they weren't so bad, after all.

Jill, having just eaten chocolate cake and following it with lemon meringue pie, chirped up, "Jane's going to make someone a good wife."

Franz stated bluntly, "Being a wife leads to being a mother – I don't think Jane's ready for that." He looked pointedly at the table which resembled the aftermath of a bloody battle and added, "Now how about some coffee?"

Franz was right. Motherhood wasn't something she aspired to, especially if this was an example of family life. She gave him a small smile and noticed everyone else looked embarrassed. Fortunately or unfortunately, Philip, having been allowed to return, tipped up his trifle to see if he could make the jelly wobble, and Margaret used the diversion to point to the kitchen. "Franz, dear. David won't mind if you make the coffee. While you are there, get a damp cloth and see if you can get those gravy spots off the front of your sweater. Now, does anyone else want coffee?

Your father's making it."

To Jane's surprise he got up to put the kettle on. David threw Jane a reassuring smile and a grimace at his dad's back, followed by a look that gave the impression that Dad might think he wore the trousers, but Mum knew how to handle him!

The family adjourned to the lounge for the promised coffee. In automatic mode, Jane stayed behind to pack up dirty dishes and take them to the kitchen, but Paula hustled her out, "Jane, you are our guest." She followed her into the hall, and said more quietly, "Oh, and don't mind Dad. He can be a bit gruff, but he's got a good heart. David, make sure Jane doesn't get out of that chair. She's trying to clear up again."

Jane protested, "I was only doing my bit now because I must go soon."

"Go?" cried Jill and Margaret in unison.

Paula frowned. "I hope you're not going because of… well all that… it's not always like that, I'm really sorry, it was awful, wasn't it?"

Jane shrugged and hurried to reassure her. "These things happen. I have enjoyed myself and it's been great to meet you all. In living downstairs, I'll probably see you again, but if I'm going to make tonight's meeting I shall have to leave soon to catch the train."

At the puzzled faces in front of her, she explained, "It's Sunday – I usually go to church in the morning and evening."

David, as if by way of explanation, stated, "Jane plays the piano."

Jill gave an apologetic smile, "You'll have to forgive our family for our lack of religion."

Margaret was quick to disagree. "I'd like to think we have Christian beliefs, we just don't go to church."

Much to Jane's relief Franz brought in the coffee and its distribution distracted the discussion.

Her coffee finished, Jane stood and returned her cup to the tray, catching Margaret giving David a speculative look and she noted his puzzled frown. A moment later, Margaret asked, "David, why don't you take Jane by car? That's the least you can do, considering how hard she's worked."

Obediently he rose to his feet.

"No, no, please. I don't want to drag you out, and away from your family. The train will be fine. But thank you for the offer." She addressed the rest of the family seated around the room. "And thank you for having me, and the party and everything. I must go and get my things together so I'm afraid you'll have to excuse me."

Under their gaze she suddenly felt awkward and backed towards the door. David stepped forward as if about to speak, but before he could, she was amazed to hear Margaret say decisively, "Let's all go to church. That way, Jane won't have to rush off – and I'm sure it would do us all good."

The astonishment on the faces of the Reinhardt family was such that Jane rushed to put them at ease. "Oh, please don't do that on my account. And it isn't like you probably think of church. Our evening service has a music group. It's modern, not traditional. We meet in the hall – don't sit in pews. It's, err… it's not quiet – often noisy, it's not one man at the front – we all join in." The more she said, the more confused their faces became. "Honestly – you really don't have to come. The train will be fine." Thoroughly embarrassed at her inadequacy, and at being the centre of their puzzled attention, she hurried away leaving them in dumbfounded silence.

Oh dear, her words hadn't exactly encouraged them. However, she guessed the Reinhardts would be more turned off than turned on by the informal way the services were conducted.

Jane looked at her watch. The trains today were only

twice an hour from High Street Kensington, and she'd have to change to get to Osterley. She hadn't intended to leave quite so early, but it would be about half an hour before she needed to get the next train. She stripped her bed so Jill could have her sheets back. There were only a few things to put away and, having done that, she sat looking at the snow through the narrow French doors.

Hadn't she said to her mum that the Reinhardts coming to church would be a miracle? And, when the miracle could have occurred, she'd been negative and stopped it. Oh Lord, I'm sorry, I've messed up again. Non-Christians were frequently invited to join with them – but the Reinhardts! Well, Margaret wanting to come. Perhaps what Jane had told her earlier had roused her curiosity.

If her mum and Ted were still sceptical of what Christians were beginning to call a new move of the Holy Spirit, what would the Reinhardt family make of the new freedom it was bringing? For so long the church had been associated with religion, but now young people were being drawn in and, across the country in concerts and rallies under the banner of 'Youth for Christ', new modern songs were being written and sung, bringing changes to the face of Christianity. Well, who wanted to sit and be bored every Sunday morning? A tapping at her door cut through her thoughts. She called, "Come in."

Jill's head popped round the door. She gave Jane an apologetic smile and fiddled with her hair. "Hi. I've been sent down to tell you everyone is interested and wants to come to your church tonight. Don't look so astounded. I think we were just a bit surprised when Mum suggested it. Jim's going to stay here with the boys, and David said the service was probably at 6.30 – if he's right, we won't have to leave for a couple of hours, so time for tea and cake before we go – so please come upstairs again."

The others were playing hide and seek with the boys. Jill disappeared to tidy up, while Franz snoozed in the armchair and Margaret quizzed her about her faith, her music, the church and her family until finally, to bring the conversation to an end, Jane shrugged and said, "You see, I'm really very ordinary."

Margaret smiled at Jane and patted her hand, "No one is ordinary. Everyone has something, and I know David thinks very highly of you."

Jane frowned. "Oh I don't know about that!" Not quite knowing what to say next, she jabbered on, "You really don't have to come to church tonight. It's not, of course, that I don't want you to come, but, well, it'll break up your family party."

"Don't worry, dear, I'm sure we'll find it fascinating. It'll also give us a better understanding of what makes you tick."

Jane gave her a questioning look, fearing sarcasm, but there was none. Another warm, friendly smile and pat on her arm reassured her. She was amazed. David had told his mother that he felt highly of her. What had she done to deserve such praise?

Even with Jim left behind with the boys, they still needed to take two cars. Paula and Margaret went in the Jaguar with Franz, while she and Jill went in David's Rover. David led the way and they arrived at the church hall as it was beginning to fill, with the hum of chatter and laughter making a warm, friendly and welcoming atmosphere. Jane was pleased when Bruce came straight over to shake David's hand. "Hello. It's good to see you again. Welcome to our church. Is this your family?"

David did the introductions while Jane smiled, feeling really proud at how Bruce was handling the unexpected. She'd had just time to introduce the Reinhardt family to her mother and Ted, before she and Bruce took up their places on the platform. She could see her mother and Margaret in conversation while the others seemed bemused at the noise and lack of holiness.

From her elevated position, she waited for John to welcome everyone, and began playing the introduction as he announced the first hymn. Phil, a retired trumpet player from a local jazz band, let rip during the chorus and, around the Reinhardts, people raised their hands above their heads in worship. It was difficult not to let a stupid grin appear on her face at the astonishing scene.

Over the last few months, she'd prayed she might get Jill along to a meeting, but never dreamt the Lord would answer by sending her whole family! The Reinhardts, with her mum and Ted, spanned a whole row and even though David was four rows from the front and across the aisle from her, his baritone could still be heard. She felt she ought to pinch herself awake.

Heaven only knew what the Reinhardt clan were making of what could only be termed, by them, unusual behaviour. Once or twice she saw them discreetly glancing round when someone in the congregation prayed, rather than those at the front.

When they got into singing one of the favourite Billy Graham hymns, Paula joined in with David and others clapping along with the words,

Oh happy day, O happy day, when Jesus washed my
  sins away
He taught me how, to watch and pray, and live
  rejoicing every day.

Jill, although looking uncomfortable, followed their example. However, Margaret and Franz were, like Jane's mum and Ted, more inhibited and just mouthed the words.

As the music finished, Keith stood. He smiled and then announced, "For those of you who have your Bibles, I'm reading from the RSV – Matthew, chapter 18, verse 12."

Jane propped up her open Bible on the piano's music rack as he read, 'What do you think? If a man has a hundred sheep, and one of them has gone astray, does he not leave the ninety-nine on the hills and go in search of the one that went astray?'

Keith looked over the congregation and continued, "Tonight, I want to talk about Jesus as our shepherd, and how he cares for each one...."

A loud, discordant sound broke across his words. Everyone looked toward the piano. Jane, having tried, but failed to catch her Bible as it toppled off the music rack on to the piano keys, was now retrieving it from the floor.

Keith smiled and quipped, "Let's hope my notes are better than Jane's!" There was laughter from the younger members of the congregation, and mild amusement from others.

Unabashed, Jane ran her fingers over the keys, playing a few bars of Tchaikovsky's *1812 Overture*. David was one of those who quickly caught on to the joke and clapped.

Keith grinned across at her. "Thanks Jane! So from Tchaikovsky's 1812 we'll return to Matthew 18:12!" He looked down and began to read. "What do you think? If a church has a hundred sheep, and one of them goes away, will not they, the ninety-nine who are remain miss the one who has gone to search for new pasture?"

Those who had their Bibles open, tittered and looked up. Jane could see the Reinhardts glancing around, sensing something was wrong. Some of the young people giggled, and Ted and Joyce looked at each other and back at Keith.

Keith, looked out across his audience and smiled. "Sorry folks – couldn't resist it. I wasn't going to say anything tonight, but I feel the Lord and Jane have pre-empted it. Some of you know Jane will soon be leaving us. And at some point, Jane, we'll give you a good send off. But my point tonight is – we'll miss you! You will leave a big gap in our worship group and in our lives. You help to make God real here, and I want you to know that."

Several members of the youth group had expressed audibly their shock at Keith's announcement, but now began clapping. Embarrassed, she looked across the hall as others took up the clapping and in groups began to stand. Within second the whole congregation rose to follow suit. The Reinhardts looked bemused, but joined in. David, smiling broadly, was clapping enthusiastically. He may not know exactly why he was clapping, but he obviously wanted to show her he appreciated her too. Bruce moved forward to speak to Keith who nodded in agreement. "Bruce has just suggested that it would be good if Jane could play one of the Lou Hayles songs we all enjoy, and then maybe, just maybe, I'll come back to my sermon!"

People laughed and everyone settled back in their seats as Jane, having conferred with Bruce, began the first chords. This wasn't to entertain the congregation, but to give glory to God, so she forgot the people and sang as though alone with Jesus, in a clear voice of worship.

> *I guess it's no surprise... I see it in your eyes*
> *I always knew you'd do it*
> *And I want to learn to trust... I know that I*
> *   really must*
> *I wish I always could*
> *But you're teaching me to come to you, to open*
> *   up myself to you*
> *When I tell you honestly, 'I need you Lord', you*
> *   come to me, come to me:*
> *Suddenly there's movement on a bare and empty*
> *   stage*
> *Suddenly there's writing on a black and empty*
> *   page,*
> *Suddenly the shadows are exploding into light*
> *Doubt and fear disappear, stampeding out of*
> *   sight.*
> *'Joy springs up when you least expect the light'.*

Jane's audience were spellbound as the group joined in and harmonised each time that last line was sung, and joined in the remainder of the song with their varied instruments. When, after several verses, that same line finally faded into silence there was a very real sense of the Lord's presence.

For several moments no one moved, then Keith, taking up his position once more at the front of the hall spoke. "Thank you Jane. That's precisely what I mean when I say Jane makes God very real to us. And I was wrong – Jane's notes were better than mine! Life is like that song...."

Jane barely heard the rest of the sermon for suddenly, for her, it wasn't joy that had sprung up, but a realization of how difficult it was going to be to leave these people who had shown so much love to her. Almost in a dream, she played the final hymn, and was then surrounded by people wanting to know where she was going and what she was doing.

From her vantage point, she was gratified to find that people were talking to the Reinhardt family. Her mother and Margaret seemed to be getting on well, and David and his father were about to be descended on by one of the church elders. A few minutes later, David's booming laugh echoed across the hall. She shuddered. Was her mother thinking how loud he was? But, to her surprise, when she joined the group she found the Reinhardt family had been invited back to the house for coffee.

Once home, the two mothers chatted non-stop. David's father looked on before being drawn into conversation by Ted, while Bruce and Jill swapped thoughts about a novel they'd both read. Meanwhile, Jane, Paula and David discussed the meeting, which led on to their thoughts on God. David was more knowledgeable than she'd imagined but, when he and Paula began to argue, she took the chance to slip away under the guise of collecting dirty cups.

Engrossed in mulling over the events of the day, she

jumped when a hand lightly rested on her shoulder. The familiar voice taunted, "Well, young Jane, this has proved a successful exercise. Do you think your mother will now approve of us living together?"

He knew that a facetious remark like that would bring retaliation, and he was already retreating – but not quickly enough to avoid the soaking wet dishcloth she hurled across the kitchen. He ducked. It hit the top of his head, making his hair wet and water to drip down his face. The cloth, now a wet lump, lay at his feet. David looked at it, then at Jane. He bent and picked it up. There was something ominous in his expression, that made Jane back against the sink and hiss, "Don't you dare! Do that, and then what will my mother think?"

He closed the short distance between them, his eyes staring at her mouth. "If you scream, I know an excellent way to stop you."

There was no doubt of his meaning. She blushed profusely, but managed to draw herself up to answer pertly, "Are you threatening me, Mr Reinhardt?"

"Me, Jane? No, Jane. And, it's not Mr anything – I'm a loving brother playing with his dear sister." David's voice took on a seductive note, "Although, if you so wish I'm open to changing that!"

Unsure how to answer or react she turned back to the sink.

His response was to drop the cloth in the water with a large splash dousing the front of her jumper. "Dear me, Jane, what a mess you've got yourself into. You really must be more careful when washing up. What will your mother think?" With a chuckle, he beat a hasty retreat.

A few minutes later, when she returned to the sitting room, David was talking to Ted. He ignored her, but her mum exclaimed, "Ah! There you are Jane. I was just saying to Margaret... Oh, my goodness, what have you done to yourself?"

"The cloth dropped into the water and splashed me."

"Perhaps you'd better go and change your jumper."

"It's okay, it'll dry out." Her Mum turned back to Margaret who, having given David a thoughtful look, caught the exchange of David's wink for Jane's scowl. Quickly, Jane changed her expression to smile at Margaret and raise her eyes in mock despair, which Margaret returned with a knowing nod.

When the Reinhardt family took their leave with best wishes for the New Year, David shook her mum's hand and, thanking her, invited, "And, Joyce, if you want to visit at any time, you know you'll be most welcome."

Jane stopped handing out the coats. "Hold on a minute. Don't go getting any ideas about inviting Mum to your house unless you want to entertain her yourself. When I want Mum round, I'll ask her. We may be under the same roof, but you run your life, and I'll thank you to let me run mine!"

Out the corner of her eye, Jane saw Paula nudge Margaret, their attention now fixed on her.

David, for a moment, looked nonplussed and then bowed. "You're quite right, Jane. It's not my place to invite your mother – I'm sorry." He gave a wry smile and addressed Jane's mother. "However, Joyce, if you visit Jane, please feel free to call on me too."

It was then her mother's turn to look nonplussed. Margaret stepped in. "Yes, do come up and visit next time I'm in London. We can share some of those recipes you were telling me about."

Later, snuggling in bed, Jane hugged her knees. This new year had certainly started with a few surprises! She grinned. God had risen to the challenge to prove He was a miracle worker – fancy the Reinhardt's coming to church! And her Mum had invited them back and they all seemed to get on so well together. David was very different at home than at work. His sisters might say he was a bully, but she had to admit – an amusing one. But he was naughty to threaten to kiss her, for he wouldn't do that to Jill or Paula. She would have to make it clear again that, as a sister, only kisses on the cheek were allowed. Hopefully, David would keep to that in the future and not make living in the flat difficult – but only time would tell.

CHAPTER 17

It was Wednesday morning and Grace was due back. When Jane arrived, Grace was already sitting at her desk, her face aglow. "I don't have to ask, I can see you had a wonderful time." Grace held out her left hand, displaying a square cut emerald surrounded by diamonds. "Oh, Grace, it's beautiful! You've decided then. When's the wedding?"

"Brussels, the last Saturday in March, and you're invited."

Jane frowned. "Mum and Ted are thinking of a March wedding – let's hope they don't choose the same day.

"So, by the sound of it, I'm not the only one who's had an eventful Christmas. When did you find out about your Mum and Ted? Are you pleased?"

"I suppose I shouldn't have been surprised, but I was. Ted asked her on Christmas Day. And I am pleased. Mum's like you, positively radiant. Anyway, that's just one of many surprises since you left." She glanced round, fearful that the ever-present Mr Reinhardt might appear, "Probably best to tell you the rest later."

With raised eyebrows, Grace breathed, "I dread to think! All well with the work I hope?"

"Yes, we got masses done. David would sit with his feet up on your desk, dictating as I typed, which saved time. I was in alone yesterday doing filing and bits and pieces, so you shouldn't be too busy today."

Grace, reverting to the previous conversation, asked, "Do you think if your mum and Ted haven't fixed a date, they would mind choosing another Saturday? You see, I'd like you to be my bridesmaid."

"A bridesmaid! Oh, Grace, I'd love to! Good heavens, I'll be walking down the aisle twice in one month!"

Grace laughed. "Well, maybe the third time you'll be the blushing bride."

"Hardly. I don't know anyone who'd have me!"

David's voice boomed behind her, "Oh, I don't think you'll need to look too far to find the right man. So, Grace, am I to understand that congratulations are in order?"

Grace, having given David a hard stare, then blushed like a young girl, held out her hand to show off her engagement ring and announced, "Wilhelm couldn't put off his trip to Australia in April so he wants me to go with him. The wedding is set now set for the end of March, I'm sorry I couldn't give you more notice."

"Grace, I think that Wilhelm is a very wise and lucky man, the ring is beautiful, and at least you've got two months to find your replacement. Better get on to it right away – you will be a hard act to follow. I doubt anyone else will have that intuitive way of being one step ahead of my demands. Still, if it comes to the worst, Jane and I can muddle along. We managed to over Christmas."

Hands on hips, Jane retorted, "Oh thanks very much. We muddled along did we? I thought we'd worked really well together, but if we only muddled along perhaps you'd better look for a replacement for me too."

David hit the palm of his hand against his forehead. "Oh grief! What is a man to do? Let's not start off on the wrong footing – you are wonderful Jane. Your work is excellent, your typing is fast and accurate, and yes, we did work well together which was delightful, encouraging and efficient. Will that do? However, I need that extra input of experience to think of the things I don't, is that acceptable? Now I suggest that you and Grace have half an hour to catch up with each other, then let's concentrate on getting this year off to a good start."

Not having been able to get a word in, Jane jumped to

attention and saluted. "Yes, Sir!"

David gave her a long look, shook his head, walked into his office and closed the door behind him.

Grace raised her eyes to the ceiling, "I see you are still being very trying to our Mr Reinhardt!"

"Not half as trying as he's been to me, I can tell you." Jane launched into an account of events and found that Grace already knew that Jill was David's sister. However, she didn't seem to share Jane's enthusiasm about the move into David's basement flat. She was, though, suitably flabbergasted on hearing of the Reinhardt family going to church and their subsequent visit to Jane's home for coffee.

The tale took rather longer than the half an hour and David, obviously guessing he'd been the subject of the majority of their conversation, finally put his head out of the door. "Grace, this is a five minute warning. Could you get your notebook. Nikki's away, so I want you to take the minutes of the directors' meeting. Jane, here's a list of telephone calls that need to be made. I also need this letter to go to the Exhibition Centres I'll be visiting on my next trip – it would be good if you could get these out tonight."

Jane didn't notice the time and only realized she'd missed the first sitting at lunch when Grace returned. David had obviously gone off somewhere else, and Grace seemed a bit preoccupied. But once down in the canteen, Jane made sure everyone knew of Grace's engagement and soon Grace was smiling happily, immersed in telling of her romance and wedding plans.

At lunch on Monday and Tuesday it had been hard for Jane not to tell Sam of her plans to move to London. But she had told them about her Mum and Ted, and breaking off with Bruce. There was no doubt about the gleam in Ian's eyes at that news, so she was quick to point out that if she did meet someone else he'd have to share her faith. Last night she'd slept at the flat and could hardly wait to move in, but time enough to tell them when she felt more accustomed to the idea herself.

She and Grace had been back from lunch half an hour when David passed through the office to command, "Right Grace, give me a couple of minutes. You might as well bring in your shorthand pad, I've some letters to dictate."

David's door closed. Jane sighed, "Oh dear it sounds as if someone, or something, hasn't agreed with him!"

Grace didn't answer. Lifting a document out of her tray, she asked, "Jane, I need this photocopied. Could you do it for me now?"

Jane frowned, took the document from her and was about to ask if this was more important than the letters David had asked her to type by the end of the day, when his office door opened.

"I suggest Jane does that photocopying."

"I thought the same thing. Jane's just going."

She sensed a tension in the air. To ease it she chuckled, "I've gone!" With that, she was out the door, down the corridor and into the waiting lift. It wasn't until she reached the ground floor that it dawned on her that Grace hadn't specified how many   copies were needed − it would only take a minute to pop back up.

About to enter the outer office, she stopped on hearing Grace saying, "David, I merely said I thought it unwise. If I've overstepped my role, I'm sorry, but I am concerned."

"Look, Grace, I appreciate your concern – I even understand it − but, believe me, it will work out."

"How can you be so sure?"

David gave a brief, cynical laugh, "I have a trump card, which I have yet to play."

"This isn't a game, David. This is someone's life."

Jane wondered, should she interrupt or wait?

"I'm treading carefully, softly, softly – but I am making inroads." David's voice became amused, "Every now and then I test the ground!"

Grace obviously didn't find it funny. "Well, whatever this trump card is, I hope it's more sensible than those you've been playing recently. At Christmas, you shocked me into speaking my mind. And here I am doing it again. I can only assume you've resolved the other major issue in this?

"Well, not entirely. But the more I delve into it, the more understanding and interesting it becomes."

"That may be so, but it's a commitment. And the decision you make won't be valid unless you do it for the right reasons. I think you have gone too far too soon. It's the most important...."

"Grace! I know! I know! But the way it came together was incredible. And in answer to whether it's wise or not – the more involved I get, the more I'll find out, and the more I'll see a clearer picture of whether it could work out."

"But you are getting embroiled. Just think of the consequences if it doesn't work out. These past few weeks have given me cause to question your integrity...."

Not wanting to stand outside any longer Jane rushed through the door as though she'd just arrived to ask, "Grace, I...." she broke off. Grace, as well as startled, was obviously upset. David's expression was one of annoyance, which he proved by pivoting on his heel and slamming his office door behind him. "Oh dear, I'm sorry. I – I didn't mean to interrupt. I just came back because I wanted to know how many copies of this you wanted."

In an attempt to recover, Grace gave a poor imitation of a smile. "That's alright Jane. My fault – I'm sorry I didn't say, but one will do."

"What's the matter with him? Jill would say, don't let him bully you – he always wants to get his way because thinks he's right."

Grace picked up her notebook and files. "Just a difference of opinion! David wasn't bullying me, and, I

329

have to say, in most instances he does have an uncanny knack of being right." With her hand on David's door, she said dismissively, "Enough said. Do me two copies, I expect we'll need them."

On her return Grace looked up, thanked her and gave her a happy smile as David's voice boomed through his open office door, "Ah, Jane, the very person! Can I have one of those?"

If she hadn't overheard their argument, she wouldn't have believed it had happened.

He dangled two keys on a ring at her. "I'll swap you a document for these. Jill tells me you have arranged for your mum and Ted to go round the house tonight. I gather Jill's just got herself a hot date, and I've arranged to take Grace out for a meal to celebrate her engagement. Feel free to show your mum and Ted the whole house, just so they are clear about the setup."

A sense of relief filled her as she took the keys. It would have felt awkward him being in the house. She wouldn't have known whether to ignore his presence upstairs, or take her mum and Ted up to meet him. On the other hand, he may well have come bounding downstairs to welcome them, which would have given them reason to wonder just how separate their lives were going to be. Now, with him out, and his permission to view the whole house, they'd see for themselves he had his own flat, and lived his own life.

Her mum walked around the flat, taking notes and gleaning ideas. "Ted, can you imagine a kitchen where you don't have to pull out the cupboards to clean underneath and around them? And we'd get so much more in ours if we also had a sink unit instead of that huge, deep sink and draining board. Once your house is sold we'll have money to spend. And I'd like one of those showers over the bath, too."

330

Ted gave her a loving smile and put his arm going around her, before ruefully saying, "I'm not sure we could afford a fitted kitchen quite like this, dear. They don't come cheap. I thought central heating was the priority?"

By the time they reached David's lounge, Ted stated with amusement, "Now, Joyce, please don't get any ideas about us having a baby grand – we've neither money nor space." To Jane he commented, "I bet you hope to have use of this?"

"David said I can come up here any time I like. Oh, poor Mum, you look quite envious. Come on, you play for us. David wouldn't mind even if he were here, especially as you play better than I do." She pulled out the stool to encourage her mum, who didn't need to be asked twice to play such a beautiful instrument. Her fingers flowed over the keys, filling the lounge with glorious music, but it was an odd feeling to be sitting beside Ted on David's settee listening to her.

After a variety of music had given the piano a good testing of its tone and dynamics, her Mum rose to declare, "I can't imagine why anyone would dump as beautiful an instrument as this on David just to store it. But at least with you here it will get some use. I'd say, Jane, you've certainly fallen on your feet here. I can understand why you want to move in next weekend."

Jane agreed. Yesterday, she'd come back with Jill to stay the night, and found a huge bouquet of flowers on her bed and a welcome card attached. Thrilled, she took them into the kitchen where Jill was making a cup of tea. "These flowers are beautiful – you didn't have to do this." She opened the card, it read: 'Thank you for all your hard work at New Year, and welcome to your new home. So pleased you're my new flatmate. Love Jill'. On the other side David had scrawled at the bottom, 'You're too good to be true. Please marry me? Love David'.

Jane burst into laughter, "Have you seen this?"

Jill looked over her shoulder, "What's your answer?"

Jane chuckled as she unwrapped the flowers. "I doubt he wants one. You know your brother – it's just his amusing way of saying he appreciates me." Jill gave a small smile as Jane took a vase from the cupboard.

An hour later David, changed from his business suit, bowled down the stairs, booming, "I'm on my way! I'm coming down the stairs! I've arrived!"

Jane emerged from her bedroom at the same time as Jill from the kitchen.

"Okay, okay, brother dear. There's no need for you to announce your presence as though you were an incoming train!"

Jane chuckled at Jill's analogy. David, undaunted, gave Jane a knowing look, which she ignored by saying, "Oh, David, thank you for the lovely flowers. There really was no need." David's face lit up and he smiled over her shoulder at Jill. "Anyway, I think it should be me thanking you for inviting me to the party, and for providing me with such a lovely home." Puzzled that his eyes didn't return to her, and his smile seemed less enthusiastic, she went on, "All I need now is to find a church with lots of young people in it and I'll feel I've started a whole new life."

Inexplicably, David seemed somewhat deflated. There was an awkward silence until Jill said over-brightly, "I had to borrow a couple of vases from your kitchen. Some of the flowers are in Jane's room and the rest are in here. You certainly chose a magnificent bouquet."

David's rather gruff, "Good. Yes." reminded Jane of his father.

Well, whatever his problem, her mum always said there was nothing like a cup of tea and once it was made David recovered enough to enquire, "So, Jane, did I announced my presence loudly enough?"

Jane noticed Jill's quizzical glance at first her, then David. She felt herself reddening, as she answered, "Err, yes, thank you!" Then, wagging her finger at David, she said primly, "And when I'm around just make sure you keep it up."

At David's sensual expression she frowned, but realized how he'd taken her simple sentence when he responded, "That won't be difficult." The blush deepened, but she stared at the carpet, not wanting to acknowledge his remark. A second later he started a conversation with Jill and glad of an excuse Jane took refuge in her bedroom.

Ten minutes later she ventured out to find they'd gone. But she'd barely sat down to read the TV magazine, before Jill came running down the stairs. "You'll never guess what that brother of mine has done now! He's kept quiet about it since New Year's Eve. Apparently you weren't the only one who saw that advert in the paper. David said that, between him and Mrs Perkins, they took sixteen names and addresses and said they'd get back to them. So, do you know what he's done? He's had them all sent application forms! I ask you! Have you ever heard of applications for flat sharing? It's supposed to be us choosing – not him. He really is the limit!"

Several days later, they were eating breakfast when David announced his incoming presence and steamed in brandishing some printed papers as though they were trophies of war. "Application forms girls, thought you might be interested in seeing them."

Jill shot up from her chair to snatch them out of his hand as he passed her on the stairs. "Ours, I think. And you can stop protesting. It's our flat, our choice, our flat mate and our private business, and thank you, but no thank you to your help. Jane and I will expect you to give us any other forms that arrive, preferably without reading them first." Hands on hips, she gave him a hard look and pointed back up the stairs to proclaim, "That, brother dear, is the way out. We'll see you later at work."

Much to Jane's amusement, he did as he was bid, although not without some muttering about how little his efforts were appreciated. The moment he was out of earshot, Jill commented, "Round one to us, Jane. Start as we mean to go on – he does so like to interfere, but not this time."

Only six girls returned the forms. As Jill said, probably put off by the formality and all the questions. In the end they decided to invite only three, as the other three ticked that they smoked. Despite sniffing scornfully when David scoffed, "See what a good idea those forms were?" Jill had the grace to admit, that although unusual, the forms had saved time in interviewing unsuitable candidates.

Jane also conceded that, but had to ask, "I know Grace didn't make up the forms, so what poor soul did you inveigle to type and send it out?"

David stuck his hands on the sides of his V-necked jumper. "Oh, I do have people who are willing to do me a favour just for the chance to bask in my appreciation."

"Now let me guess – you've cast your spell over Rosemary?"

David's mouth curled in scepticism. "Rosemary is not likely to do me any favours!"

"What? After you kissed her so passionately?"

"My dear Jane, I am coming to believe that in that area I am sadly deficient." David gave a downcast stare at the carpet.

Jane chuckled, "Oh, I'm sure that's not true," and added sarcastically, "Brother, dear."

Jill gave a derisive snort, then piped up, "I can guess – it was Beryl, for she loves to mother him."

"Umph. Pity she doesn't smother him!"

David drew himself up to his full height. "Now, young Jane, that's a very unchristian remark, especially after saying you held my brotherly role in such high esteem."

There was no answer to that, so she addressed Jill. "I

think, when these three girls come to view the flat, we must neither mention nor allow them to meet, David. We don't want them put off in the first instant!"

"You're right! He's definitely not an asset!"

Raising his hands in defeat, David plodded up the stairs, muttering, "You do your best for them, and what do you get? I don't know how I put up with it, why I allowed it in the first place." His muttering fell to a mumble as he turned the corner on the second flight of stairs.

Jane and Jill smiled gleefully at each other. They'd won that round too!

More by accident than design, David had gone to Birmingham the night the three girls were scheduled to come and, in fact, the evening turned into something of a hen party. The first girl didn't leave before the second arrived, and the second was still chattering to the first when the third arrived. It had been hard to choose as they were all pleasant, with similar ideas and interests, and two of them earned a higher salary that Jane.

Jackie was older than both Jane and Jill, obviously very independent, and had seemed slightly fazed when they told her the landlord was Jill's brother, the form had been his idea, and he had a habit of popping down to join in whatever was going on.

Liz was the same age as Jill. She was obviously husband hunting, and seemed more interested in David than them, making Jane comment perhaps she'd be better sharing with him, not them.

Helen, it appeared, was a year older than Jane, and did all kinds of crazy things in advertising, which she said 'gave her loads of fun and pots of money'. With brothers of her own, she was probably the best qualified to deal with an errant brother who couldn't keep out of their space! It was only after Helen moved in that they found out her brothers were younger, smaller and quieter!

Three Sundays later, while Jane was rummaging in the drawers in the lounge for a pen, a familiar boom announced his arrival. She and Helen looked at each other and Jane groaned, "We really must get a lock on that door. Ignore him. What is it with pens – wretched things! I'm sure they walk."

David offered, "Pen? Oh here, borrow mine, but keep an eye on it – I want it back. Have you seen Jill?"

"Thank you. Yes, I'll look after it. And no, she's either fast asleep, if your voice hasn't now awoken her, or stayed over from the party she went to last night."

David frowned at the latter part of the answer, then asked, "So which of you two is cooking lunch today?"

Helen had walked into the kitchen the moment David had arrived, so Jane answered, "Helen is."

David, his voice loud enough for Helen to hear, said with a hint in the air, "Right! I expect Helen, with a large family, is a good cook."

Jane grinned. For the past two weekends when first she, then Jill with her assistance, had cooked the roast dinner, David had appeared around breakfast time in the hope of an invite. They'd succumbed, but she guessed Helen wouldn't.

"Helen's cooking roast lamb, mint sauce and all the trimmings with sherry trifle for pudding. Jill and I are looking forward to it." When there wasn't a response from the kitchen, David's face dropped. Amused, she coaxed him away. "Let me get my coat, for it's time I went to church. You can walk me to the front door."

To her surprise, he offered, "I'll do more than that. How about I come with you?"

With a grab at her coat, she exclaimed, "You want to come with me? Well you can if you like, but I warn you I haven't been to this church before, I've no idea what it's like. It's great Mum being a substitute pianist to release me from my church, but I'm not sure I'm going to find release in a substitute church. The ones I visited on the last two Sundays were the pits!"

"How can a church be the pits?"

Companionably, she thrust her arm through his and led him up the stairs. "There are churches and churches. The first week, the building was large, cold and damp. The thirty people were miserable, they sang miserably to miserable hymns with miserable music, followed by a miserable sermon on a miserable message!"

David laughed, "Am I to understand that you'll not be going there again?"

"Definitely not. The second week, I went by train to a church I'd heard about. It was very up market, everyone was dressed smartly, everything was in place, the music was perfect, the sermon academic, and it was a place to be seen rather than a place to worship a living, loving God. This week, I looked in the local paper – hopefully, if a church goes to the trouble to advertise, they'll have a bit more life in them. This one's a short bus ride away."

"Come on then, what are we waiting for?"

The Church of England service was less traditional than some, but the service was led by a vicar who didn't expect the congregation to do more than respond to the prayers in the prayer book and sing the hymns. At least the hymnbook was the same as Jane's church used, but it was strange to enjoy the music without feeling responsible for it. It was also strange sitting next to David, and shaking his hand when the vicar asked them to turn and say, "The peace of the Lord be with you." The sermon did have a few funny stories within it, and afterwards the people around welcomed them and were friendly. However, she was quick to point out when someone referred to her as David's wife that he was only her landlord!

David was conversing with a couple who had several little children running around their feet, so she left him to go with Magda, who introduced her to members of the youth group, whose ages ranged from fifteen to thirty. While she was enjoying coffee and biscuits Jane noticed two women, probably late twenties, eyeing David up and down, and when he came over to speak to her she guessed they were probably discussing their relationship.

"Jane, you know the couple I was talking to? They've invited me to lunch. I said you were already booked, is that alright?"

"Yes, fine." A giggle bubbled up inside of her. How did he manage it? He'd come to church and scrounged a lunch! She grinned as the two women seen earlier sidled over to them. "Hello, I'm Pat, this is Frances. It's nice to see new faces. Did you enjoy the service?"

David put out his hand and introduced himself, and added, "And this is Jane. She lives in the flat below mine."

Pat and Frances briefly acknowledged her, but it was obvious in whom they were interested as they asked, "So David, do you live around here?" Jane moved away to look at the church bookstall, but from her viewpoint she could see several other young women noticing the tall, broad, raven-haired man.

The people's genuine friendliness was enough to make her decide to attend the evening service, which she'd been told was livelier. It was better than the morning, with choruses instead of hymns. There were about twenty people of her age and another twenty either older or younger. David had obviously caused a stir that morning as several women asked questions about their relationship and, if he was single! There was no sign of David when Magda dropped her back at the flat around ten o'clock, but his coat was there and she made sure she placed his pen in the inside top pocket.

When, the next day, Jane told Grace about David's sudden urge to go to church, his invite out to lunch, and the interest he stirred in the single women, she didn't seem particularly surprised. But when David appeared just after their conversation, Grace couldn't resist saying, "Good morning, David. I hear you had an interesting weekend. Did you enjoy your lunch?"

David groaned. "Is nothing about my private life sacred? I suppose, that's what I get for having her living under my roof!!" Grace smiled sweetly, Jane grinned. "Actually, the answer is yes it was interesting, and yes the lunch was excellent. And so, Jane, how was Helen's?"

Jane rubbed her hands in glee. "Lovely. You really missed a treat. Well, that's if you like your meat done to a crisp, potatoes half cooked and soggy cabbage."

"And the sherry trifle?"

"Lumps of sponge in half-set jelly and not a taste of sherry to be found. Poor Helen was full of apologies, but we told her it wasn't her fault, but yours!"

"Mine! How do you work that out?"

"For such a punctilious gentleman, I'm afraid you were very remiss. It was that questionnaire of yours. You forgot to ask, 'Can you cook?'. Now I've got two flatmates who can't – so next week it's your turn! And no suggesting you come to church with me so you can scrounge lunch out of another unsuspecting Christian."

"Ouch, Jane – that's unfair!"

"Maybe, maybe not – let's see how you do next week. Your place, or ours?"

David shook his head, walked into his office and shut the door, leaving Jane with no clue as to whether her challenge had been taken up. Grace eyed her quizzically. Jane opened her hands and shrugged!

Each day, Jane had a lift into work with Jill, who drove David's faithful 1951 Morris Minor which he'd had since he was sixteen. Jane laughed with Jill on hearing David didn't want to part with it because he felt one day it would be a historical treasure! Finally, Jill had persuaded him there was no point in keeping a historical treasure if it turned into a piece of rusty, dusty junk in the garage. Its value would be far greater if it were in good running order!

Typically, the very day she was in a hurry to get home, the car David hailed for its wonderful reliability wouldn't start. As he was at a meeting the other side of London, the choice was a walk home in the rain through the park, or take the bus. By the time they'd waited for the bus, then found the traffic totally snarled up from Knightsbridge to High Street Kensington, Jane wondered if walking would have been the better, even if wetter option!

At the bottom of their road, she could see her mum and Ted standing under their umbrella outside the house waiting for them. Jill opened the front door and led the way to the flat as her mother scoffed, "So much for your argument that living in town would mean you got home earlier each evening!"

"It's not always like this. We're usually back in twenty minutes, but the car wouldn't start. Probably something to do with all the rain we've been having. David wasn't there to help then the...."

Her explanation halted as Jill had stopped on the stairs into the flat, her mouth open in astonishment.

Jane, wondering if they'd been burgled, leapt forward, but also stopped, stunned at the sight in the living room. Ted and her mum jostled together on the stairs behind them, bending to see what they could see. Ted was the first to utter, "What on earth...?" while, surprisingly, her mother giggled.

Strung around table and chair legs, stretched criss-cross from wall to wall, forming a intricately woven barrier between them and the rest of the flat, were dozens of ballpoint pens. Each one was individually tied to the string, which was pulled taut so that the tips just touched the carpet, giving the appearance of walking!

Jane breathed, "David!"

Jill clicked her tongue. "Oh! Trust him! And how are we supposed to get through this?"

Puzzled, Ted asked, "Why would David want to do this?"

Jane sighed. "Oh, I can guess why! On Sunday, I said pens seem to walk – obviously this is one of his little jokes!"

Jill groaned. "When he was young he played some pretty awful tricks on me, but I thought he'd got out of it. Mind, he's always been a bit of a challenge."

Ted produced a penknife. "This isn't exactly the kind of tool to use through the jungle, but I'm sure I can hack a way through to something more suitable from the kitchen."

He stepped forward, and put one foot in a rectangle and the other in a diamond shape, then bent to cut. But it wasn't easy and with a wobble he managed another step, overbalanced, and brought down a dining room chair and a few lines of pens! Jane's mum sank onto the stairs with the giggles.

Jill was still dithering on the brink. Jane stepped forward. "Look, I've got the smallest feet, I am sure I can step through the gaps to the kitchen and get some scissors."

Carefully she began picking her way across, but half way she got the giggles, caught her foot in the next step, and collapsed across a row which broke her fall, although the majority of pens remained upright and only a small dent had been made in the web of netting across the carpet. It was at this point Helen arrived home and viewed the scene.

Ted, dishevelled, was sitting on the carpet covered in string and biros, and appeared to be attacking himself with a penknife. Jane, sprawled headlong on the carpet, was twisting round trying to untangle her feet, while her mother sitting on the stairs was creased up with laughter, and at the same time, bemoaning her need of the toilet.

Jill, looking like a swimmer popping her big toe in the water to test the temperature, confessed, "I'm afraid, Helen, this is one of David's little jokes!" Helen didn't look overly amused. Jill grinned wickedly. "You know what we should do? Clear all this up and then not mention it to David when he comes in. I did that once before. He got so frustrated wanting to know what happened, that he finally owned up so he could enjoy our reaction. Stay where you are. I'll get scissors from his kitchen – Joyce, come and use my loo. We'll be through this in no time."

Jane, having freed herself, surveyed the scene and decided to take Jill's advice and stay where she was. How had David, in the midst of his busy schedule, found the time and opportunity to play such a prank?

Disgruntled, Helen plonked herself down on the bottom stair to comment sadly, "I didn't like to say anything in front of Jill, but that brother of hers is a bit strange! And what about the way he comes down the stairs always hollering his arrival – if that's not peculiar...." The shudder in Helen's tone sent Jane into a fit of giggles.

Jill arrived back with two pairs of scissors and, as soon as a path had been cut to her door, Helen disappeared into her room probably thinking they were all quite mad. It wasn't long before they'd gained entrance to the kitchen and, while Jane and her mum prepared tea, Ted and Jill hacked and untied all the pens from the furniture. It took the four of them, after tea, a further hour to untie each pen. The final tally was 150 black and 150 blue, which they shared between them.

The escapade hadn't made her mum and Ted think David was strange. Amazingly, it had warmed them to him. Jane noticed how friendly and pleased to see him they were when he came in the front door as they were leaving. However, in accordance with their pact, no mention was made of the prank. Ted and her mum played their part wonderfully, but she guessed once outside they'd been creased up in laughter.

It was a miracle the way she and Jill kept straight-faced. David, having hung up his coat, headed without invitation to the basement – off, no doubt, to see the scene of the crime! They looked at each other, and while Jane struggled not to laugh, Jill went into silent hysterics and dived into her bedroom. Jane took a deep breath and headed down the stairs. David had seated himself on their settee and was reading their TV magazine. He thought he'd come down for chat did he?

Straightening herself, determined not to blow the plot, she said briskly, "Well, I'm off to bed. Helen went earlier. Turn out the lights when you leave, David. Thanks. Good night!"

The moment she was through her door, she slapped a hand over her mouth and rushed to grab a towel so she could muffle her laughter. Within a minute, she saw from the light under her door going out David had gone. She gave it a few minutes then slipped out and tapped on Jill's door, for what she called a good belly laugh and an extremely silly debate as to how to get back at David.

For days, David had an air of expectancy, but he confessed to nothing. He even came down one evening to ask Jane if she had a biro but, before she could answer, Jill rummaged in her handbag, saying, "I had a stack of the things, but I'd swear they find a way of vanishing. Ah! Here you are, let me have it back when you've finished with it."

Jane, no longer needing to respond, continued watching the TV and pretended not to see David's hard stare in her direction before he returned up the stairs.

A couple of weeks later, Jane, flicking through a file for some information, came across a letter from the Passport Office. An idea stirred for revenge on David. She shared it with Jill who loved it, and they giggled, plotted and hatched a plan. Having prepared carefully, they waited until the right Friday to ensure maximum effect.

Due to their excitement at what the post was going to

bring on Saturday morning, Jane awoke early and found Jill already in the kitchen. They tried not to look at each other, or make silly comments because it started them giggling and they needed to get a grip on being serious.

They'd set the breakfast table in advance, so all they had to do was await the doorbell ringing. There was a mild panic when it did ring, but they quickly took up their positions to look as though they were innocently eating their breakfast. To make it look realistic, they each took a mouthful of cornflakes as the anticipated thundering tornado came rushing down their stairs.

Neither of them dared look at the other when David charged into the flat waving a letter and raving, "This is ridiculous. You're never going to believe it. The Passport Office has sent me this, this...I'd go as far as to say 'offensive' letter."

They gave him their full attention while chewing on their cereal.

He grunted derisively and smacked the letter. "They think I've been involved in extremist activity! It's absurd! Why – who would have reported that to them?"

Jane swallowed, then commented, "So you have been involved in extremist activity."

"No! Of course not!"

"But you just said...."

"I know what I said, and I know what I mean, and I know what I'm not!" He slammed the letter on the table, as though so doing would punish the originator.

Jane, with the straightest of faces, shrugged, "Well, they must have some grounds for suspicion."

Jill patted his arm comfortingly. "Never mind, brother dear. Have some breakfast?"

David growled loudly and sat heavily. "Breakfast – I couldn't eat a thing. If this is to be believed, it could hinder my whole trip. They want a report of the business I'll be conducting, and the names and addresses of all my contacts in each country I'm visiting. Hell! I'm going to the five major continents, several cities and numerous meetings. I'm not sure it's even feasible. "

Jill in a strained voice asked, "Are you sure you've never done anything anyone could consider subversive?"

"Rest assured Jill, I've done nothing underhand in my entire life so it has to be a mistake, but its a damned inconvenient one."

Unable to speak because she'd stuffed her mouth full to stop laughing, Jane proffered the cornflakes.

David waved them away and re-studied the letter.

For a few seconds there was silence except for Jane and Jill's rhythmical, and very controlled munching!

Then David, exasperated, boomed again. "What am I going to do if they invalidate my passport? I'm due to leave next Saturday, and I've a heavy schedule to keep. Oh really, it's too bad! The timing of this letter is pretty awful too – now I've got to wait the whole weekend to do something about it."

Incapable of saying anything they made sympathetic noises through their cornflake crunching.

"Just wait until I speak to this – what's his name? – Unwin R. Courtout." Menacingly his finger prodded the signature.

Jane put another spoonful of cornflakes in her mouth, she tried to chew, it was impossible. Desperate to abort the chortle of stifled hysteria, she began to cough, then choke. David leapt up, and thumped her back. The shock made her mouth open and a tide of cornflakes and milky spittle shot over the table.

Jill used the opportunity to release her suppressed laughter.

David kept thumping Jane's back as she continued to choke, while he insisted, "Cough it up now. Come on, cough it up." Glancing at Jill he berated, "I don't know what you're laughing at! It's not funny."

Tears were now pouring down Jane's face, both from choking and disguised laughter. She fought to control herself and insist, "It's alright. David, it's alright!"

David looked bewildered and grunted, "Well I can't see what's funny about nearly choking. Any more than I can understand this, this offensive letter." He stabbed the letter with his forefinger.

Her eyes followed his finger. The letter, spotted with chewed cornflakes and milk, was now very offensive! Helpless mirth encompassed her. Jill was blowing her nose. David muttered something inaudible. From his pocket he pulled a handkerchief and proceeded to flatten, smooth and clean off his letter. "This whole thing is a...."

"What the hell is going on here?" All three of them stared open mouthed as Helen, bursting from her bedroom red faced with fury, continued shouting, "It's Saturday – it's only 8.00 am. I was asleep." Her eyes rested on David. Her lips pursed – her expression revealing her thoughts.

David, taking that as a cue to leave, picked up his be-spattered letter and waved it at Helen. "Sorry! My fault. Bit of a crisis. Just going." He took the stairs two at a time and declared at the top, "You have no idea how serious this is. It could take weeks to iron out. I tell you, if my trip is delayed, someone is going to answer for this. John Forsyth, deals in extradition and Home Office affairs – I think I'll have a word with him."

With that he was gone, leaving them holding their breath until they guessed he was out of hearing. "Oh God, Jane, did you see his face? I can't believe it! He was so taken in." Jill mimicked, "You've no idea how serious this is. In fact, I'd go so far as to say this letter is offensive."

Jane nodding went into fresh giggles, "It certainly was after I'd spat milk and cornflakes all over it. Did you – did you – see how he tried to clean it off?" Helen gave them a sad look and returned to her bedroom. Jane wondered how long it would be before she handed in her notice.

Jill spoke with punctuated laughter. "And, oh my! Oh my! He's – he's going to consult one of his friends! In the Home office no less. He's going to be so mad when he finds out! We – we've certainly got him this time!"

Later, they explained to Helen how they'd photo-copied the Passport Office heading, having blanked out the original letter so they could write their own and send it to David. However, it seemed Helen was more interested as to when and how long David was going to be away, than enjoying their prank!

A Sunday routine had developed after the first couple of weeks. Jill now prepared the vegetables and put the meat in the oven. When Jane returned from church, she put on the vegetables, checked the meat and, if beef, cooked the Yorkshire puddings. Helen provided the sweet course of her choice.

Much to Helen's irritation, David joined them each week because Jane and Jill had told him if he wasn't taking his share in the cooking, then he could at least pay towards it. Generous as ever, David insisted he pay for all of it, every week, which meant Helen couldn't refuse to have him join them. But she barely acknowledged his presence, despite every effort by him to engage her in conversation.

Jane noted David's car wasn't in the drive as she left for church, but he'd arrived back by one o'clock and seemed full of his usual jovial chatter over lunch, and made no mention of the offensive letter. Finally, itching to know what was happening, Jane couldn't wait any longer so, as Helen served the sweet course, she asked in a tone of pure innocence, "Oh, by the way David, did you speak to your friend, about your letter? Did you say he was in the Home Office? It struck me having a friend there could be helpful. Perhaps he could give you a character reference?"

David answered in a grim voice. "Yes. I spoke to John.

There was nothing he or I could do until Monday, but he assures me that, if I can't sort it out with the person who wrote the letter, he will contact the Passport Office and speak to Mr U. R. Courtout."

At David's slow pronunciation of the name, Jane only just managed to hold a serious expression, so merely nodded sagely.

Jill pulled out her handkerchief and blew her nose.

David gazed speculatively at her. Jill fiddling with her hair could be such a giveaway when she was nervous, but to her credit she put her handkerchief away and began eating her bread and butter pudding. It was obvious David had got the inference from the name and suspected them, but she wasn't going to give in yet. She knew David was now considering her, so she looked up and faced his scrutiny, smiled, and with wide, guileless eyes murmured, "I'm sure you'll work it out."

Jill snorted noisily and pulled her handkerchief from her sleeve.

Helen diverted David's attention by leaping up. "David, would you like some more pudding? There's still some left. I'll take your plate. Jane? Jill? Have you finished?"

David passed his plate, but his eyes were now resting suspiciously on Helen's smiling face. To put him off track, Jane leant towards him as Helen disappeared into the kitchen. "I think Helen felt a bit bad at shouting at you yesterday and, as her sweet has turned out rather well, I think she's pleased that you wanted seconds."

David hummed although, when Helen returned from the kitchen, he gave her a broad smile. "I must say, Helen, this is most enjoyable. Now I'll just eat this and then I have something I want to say to you all."

Helen gave him a barbed smile. Jane and Jill looked at each other and wondered what was coming.

It didn't take David long to finish and, putting his

spoon down, he launched straight in. "I wanted to speak to you with regard to the letter I had from the Passport Office. I shall, if all is not resolved, be contacting Mr Courtout tomorrow. However, I felt you may not be aware that the unauthorised use of headed company paper is considered as fraud. The seriousness of this offence would depend on where the letter is purported to have originated – in this case, The Passport Office. As this is a government agency, misuse of their notepaper would be deemed a crime, and would bring a conviction and the possibility of a prison sentence."

"Really?" Jane questioned, her face full of innocent surprise. "Do you think your letter is a forgery? I mean – who would want to do that?"

David gave Jane a long look, rested his eyes briefly on Helen, who was smiling at him, and then at Jill who was blowing her nose. "Considering the man's initials and name, I am led to believe I have no further to look than this room."

Jill gave several pig-like snorts.

Feeling the hoax was rumbled, Helen sniggered.

Jane, determined to hang this out as long as possible, managed to maintain an air of detachment and looked at them both as though puzzled, then added slowly, "The man's name... oh yes, I see. How extraordinary – U.R. Courtout!"

Both Jill and Helen now laughed openly, while she smiled happily.

David stood. He gave each of them a hard stare before proclaiming, "Yes! I believe U R all Courtout! And Jane – you can stop trying to act the innocent." He stood, strode into the kitchen and returned dangling the car keys. "I think a week of walking to work will help cool your amusement at my expense, and the exercise will tire your over-active brains." With that he tossed the keys up and snatched them from the air, before taking the stairs two at a time and vanishing from sight.

Jill, unperturbed, grinned. "Oh well, girls, I think we can say we're definitely rumbled."

Now worrying that perhaps that she'd overdone it, Jane asked, "Do you think he's really cross?"

Helen shrugged with a grin, "Who cares! I bet he was furious when he realized the U R Courtout name!"

"Helen's right! He'd hate to admit to anyone that he could be so gullible. And caught out by us! He would be especially cross if it was John who pointed it out. If he did, and had a good chuckle at David's expense, David would be so embarrassed. Serves him right, though, after some of the embarrassing things he's put me through! I tell you what Jane, I'm thrilled we got one over on him, but that's not all...." Grinning broadly, Jill fished in her handbag and produced a set of keys. "I borrowed these several weeks ago from his desk, when I couldn't find the others. He may think we're walking, but we won't be!"

CHAPTER 18

Winter had turned to spring. Jane looked out on the walled garden. It wasn't large, but it had an old-world charm with crazy paving, small flowerbeds and a little pond containing a fountain in the form of a small statue. Inside, she sipped her coffee and relished the warmth. Outside, it was bitterly cold, the sky a miserable grey. It was amazing to think that the Saturday before it had been sunny and relatively warm for the second week of March. She looked at the two fruit trees, and guessed that in summer they would bring privacy and protection to the garden from the sun – it wouldn't be long before they started to blossom.

She thought how her mum had blossomed over the past three months. Outside the church last week she'd looked so young and pretty, her arm hooked into her new husband, who too seemed to have grown in stature and confidence. Their obvious togetherness made that lump rise again in her throat and she had reminded herself she hadn't lost a mother, but gained a father and a brother! But it did feel strange, as though she didn't belong in their lives any more, but of course life would never be the same again, they'd gone their different ways.

The radio was playing a track from *The Sound of Music*, 'I must have done something good'. It was such a romantic yet true story, she'd already seen the film twice. Her mum called it her special song, having been so blessed with Ted that she must have done something good! Jane smiled, Grace probably felt much the same in Germany, preparing for her wedding next weekend.

Suddenly she felt very alone. The house was empty. Jill

was staying the weekend with her parents. Helen was away, visiting friends, and David was travelling between exhibition centres in a variety of countries. And she had a whole day and evening ahead of her with no plans.

Dear Sam, he was always jesting about the 'high life' she and Jill must lead living in the heart of London. He, like her mum, had been a bit reticent when she'd said she was going to move to London, but when two days later she told him Jill had offered her a room in her flat, he'd been really pleased for her saying, "You'll be safe with Jill. She don't smoke, don't overdrink and don't strike me she'd do drugs." So Sam's version of the 'high life' didn't involve those! Maybe it was the two parties she'd gone to with Jill, a few cinema visits, the Sunday and Thursday church meetings and two invites out to Sunday tea, one with Donald and Tricia who'd entertained David to lunch – but it didn't feel a high life! Nor did the occasions when she'd tagged along with Jill to a pub, club or dancing at the Hammersmith Palais or Lyceum Ballroom in the Strand. She'd felt then as if she were on show – like an animal in a cattle market waiting to be picked up! But then she hadn't been bored either, in fact, she loved the proximity to the shops, the park and work. Central London was a good place to live and to be.

Once David had gone on his month's tour, she and Jill had invited round several people from work. Pam was eager to move in if Helen left. Jill had smiled and said the landlord vetted everyone with a long questionnaire. She'd invited Sam and Ian. Sam said his missus wouldn't like it, so she invited her too, but after several excuses she didn't push it. Ian and Phil from the Printing Department came together and seemed rather awestruck and uncomfortable in what Ian called a 'posh pad'. Grace came but, although invited, she was very reluctant to view David's half of the house, saying she felt like an intruder.

Jane agreed that it did feel strange, and she had to force

herself to go into his flat to play the piano although, in other ways, she felt she was living with David, for she saw him more at home than work as he often spent days away from the office. When at home he seemed to find plenty of excuses to appear in their flat – especially if something was cooking! There had been times at work when she'd received a quelling look because she'd been too familiar, and times in their flat she told him he was being too bossy, but they usually got along.

Her coffee finished, she put the mug on the table and curled up in the chair by the window. She had to admit, if only to herself, that she was missing David. Was he missing her? She gave a grin, she doubted it – not with his busy schedule!

For three weeks before her mum's wedding, she'd been so heavily involved in arrangements she hadn't had time to think of him except to wonder which country and time zone he was in. However, each day he found time to post a card to either the office or flat. Each one was dated. Sometimes two or three arrived in one day, often from different countries. He was an amazing man!

Generous too, for having established she could drive, he insisted she take him to London Airport in his large Rover. Once there, he'd leapt out, gathered his luggage from the boot, tapped on the car window and proclaimed, "Your name is on the insurance – feel free to drive it any time. Oh, and anyone over 25 is insured. As it's white, it might come in useful as a wedding car." All she could do was gape as he'd leant in and pecked her cheek. Before she could thank him or say goodbye, he'd entered the terminal.

It was odd, she'd felt quite thrilled he'd trusted her to drive and use his car, and remembered now how bereft and sad she'd felt that she wouldn't see him for a few weeks. But once she'd called in on her old home and told Mum and Ted of David's offer, she'd forgotten about it, until now. Probably because she was feeling so alone today, she considered telephoning Bruce. Perhaps he'd like to come round. She smiled. He had been quick to volunteer himself as chauffeur for the wedding, and had found plenty of excuses to have the car at his disposal beforehand. In fact, perhaps they could go out somewhere in it this afternoon. And then she realised it was his first weekend living in Southampton. No doubt he was probably settling in and finding his way around.

A sense of despondency began to set in, so she pushed it away, recalling how good Bruce looked as he doubled as best man and chauffeur, while she as bridesmaid had doubled up her roles and given her mother away! They hadn't wanted a big affair, but it seemed everyone at church wanted to come, and everyone wanted to help. With little expenditure, Mum and Ted had had a wonderful day to remember.

Grace's wedding next weekend would be entirely different. Grace had been told to indulge herself. And if Jane's expensive and exclusive bridesmaid dress was anything to go by, it was going to be a very posh affair.

How wonderful God was. He'd not only fulfilled the desires of Grace's heart for a husband, but Wilhelm was a rich man. Grace would never again have to struggle to keep herself and her elderly mother. Despite this, Grace worked up until the last possible moment, because she didn't want to let David down. Once David had left, Grace stayed for one week to hand over to Jane, on the understanding that she could manage until matters had been resolved. These matters, she assumed, would be David finding someone who he felt could replace Grace. No candidate had yet proved successful. She just hoped when David did it, he would ensure it would be someone she could work with.

Jane shrugged. She had offered — she didn't think she was too young to take on such a responsible position permanently, but David and the other directors did. David was due home tomorrow evening. He'd probably start organising the interviews on Monday.

Having washed and tidied up her lunch things, she gave the kitchen a final check and turned off the lights. It was certainly easier to be tidy when Jill wasn't around! Two o'clock – this time next week, she and David would be at Grace and Wilhelm's marriage ceremony.

She walked into her bedroom and ran her hand along the built-in wardrobe, and wondered for the tenth time what she ought to take to wear! It would be odd being away alone with David – rather like a weekend date as they were going Friday afternoon and returning Sunday night!

She sat heavily on her bed, causing the wooden surround of shelves containing books and ornaments to rattle. The bed was cleverly designed to slip under the bookshelf surround. It had large box cushions matching the bedspread, and when they were stood up in place it became a comfortable settee. She leant back now, curled her arms around her knees and glanced appreciatively around. In the time she'd been here, she'd come to love her L-shaped room with its bright matching bedcover, cushions and curtains – they gave a sunny feel on the dullest of days.

Through the narrow French doors, she could see her own private bit of patio, and beyond into the garden where daffodils were bringing colour to the winter barrenness. She grinned, David certainly had brought colour into her life. It was nine months since their first meeting over that bouquet of flowers. How her opinion of him had altered! How her life had altered from the night of the Ball and the stranger. None of it her doing, but like a divine hand guiding her into a new job, new flat, new church, new Dad, new brother, new adopted brother.

But what about that recurring nightmare of searching for something or someone – her fear that even if she found the answer she wouldn't recognise it? The panic it caused made her wake suddenly, her body aching for that which was lost. Last night it had been particularly vivid and she'd woken, calling out, "No, no, don't go!" to a dark shadow. Perhaps until she found a man who could substitute for the stranger, or the identity of the ghost, the dark shadow would always be there to haunt her and disappear?

There were a few available men at church, but they seemed so wishy-washy, and she knew it was because she was comparing them to David, which was hardly fair considering he was older and more mature in his outlook. Mum was always quick to point out there was no future in their relationship beyond a brother and sister friendship. She was right, for even if Jane forgot the social argument and age difference, David didn't share, or seem interested in, her faith.

This was ridiculous. Why sit here contemplating these things when she had a whole house to enjoy and no one to disturb? She needed to exercise her fingers on the piano keys and practice some songs for, having played some of Lou's songs at her farewell supper, they'd insisted she come back as a guest and lead the worship, which was now only two weeks away.

It did feel odd bounding up David's stairs and him not being there. In fact, even when he was there she only went up if invited – it was, after all, his home. It felt private. She grinned, not that David felt the same way about their flat! This house, though, was great when it was full of laughter and voices, and with the chaos of David's family visiting it felt like one big house, one happy family. She shivered – it wasn't quite so warm up here as in the flat below, but it would be a while before she got too cold to play. Her thoughts, as she exercised her fingers up and down in scales, once more drifted to David and the value he seemed to put on her small contribution to his life, and to his world.

On the Sunday evening, after their treacherous letter had been rumbled, David had found her in the kitchen making a hot drink before bed. His expression was rueful, and she thought he'd come to bring the car keys back. Instead he asked, "Jane, I've got a favour to ask. You can say no, because I've not invited anyone yet! I'll bring you back a special present from my travels."

Jill, overhearing, leapt to the kitchen doorway in her defence. "David, you're making it impossible for her to refuse. This is the only place that she gets to be away from you, but you continually pop up and down. She's not here to be at your beck and call." Wide wistful black eyes focused on Jane while Jill continued to point out, "Jane clearly stated when she moved in the things she wasn't going to do, and cooking for you was one of them, yet here you are every Sunday for lunch – not to mention other times. Crumbs, she's only got to put the oven on and you're down here to see what you can scavenge!"

David's gaze hadn't wavered from Jane's face even as he answered Jill. "But Jane's cooking is so delicious, I just can't resist inviting myself."

"The trouble with you is you're such an accomplished bully, Jane hasn't even noticed your tactics."

It had been so fascinating to hear Jill going on at David that Jane hadn't spoken, but at that she'd acknowledged, "No, I hadn't noticed. How did he manage to get us to give him Sunday lunch every week?"

With hands on hips, Jill curled her lip, "As David would say, he made a good investment! Isn't that right, brother dear? He pays for all the ingredients, we buy them, prepare them, cook them, he gets a good meal without leaving home and it costs less than going to a restaurant!"

David gave a quizzical frown at Jill, "That's a bit harsh isn't it?" Then returning his attention to Jane he gave a charming smile, "I'm quite sure Jane doesn't see it that way."

Jane folded her arms. "I'm thinking about it. "

David's eyes slanted seductively. As he moved towards her, Jane's gaze hardened. In front of her, he looked down and stroked her nose with his finger as though she were a favourite cat, and murmured, "Yes, do that."

Jill muttered something about her need to get to bed and left the kitchen.

Disconcerted, Jane moved from under his finger, but her heart had quickened seeing the tenderness in his eyes. She broke eye contact, only to be drawn back as his hands encompassed her arms and his eyes scanned her face, as though taking a mental picture.

"Oh, Jane, I'm going to miss you."

"Don't be silly – more like 'out of sight, out of mind'."

"Never that Jane. Never that."

Unsure of how to respond to the intimate inflection of his voice and words she moved away, picked up a cookery book and bantered in a cockney accent, "Well Sir, as your 'umble cook living in yer basement, Sir, perhaps Sir, you would like to choose a menu, Sir. And for 'ow many would it be for, Sir?"

David boomed with laughter as she bobbed a curtsey and tapped her forehead before flicking through a book of recipes. His reply had a seductive edge, making it one of those occasions she wished she'd not started something. "Well Jane, in my view you are far from a humble cook, but I'll agree you live in my basement. In the past in these big houses, 'Sirs' had reputations for enjoying more than the cook's food. Is there anything special I might indulge in on your menu?"

Embarrassed, she'd kept her eyes on the recipe on the page and tried to make her answer sound nonchalant. "I expect I could come up with something everyone would like. Who are you inviting?"

"Paula, Jim, Mum, Dad, Jill, you, and myself. The boys can eat early and be in bed."

Without raising her head, she'd answered, "That's fine. I'm happy to cook, and you don't have to buy me a present." She gave a little laugh and wished he'd go.

For a few moments there was silence as he stood behind her, then he said, "Thank you, Jane. You know, I really appreciate you."

She knew he was waiting for her to turn round, but for some unknown reason she didn't want to, and had continued reading a recipe until she knew he'd gone.

That same disquiet she'd felt then, now seemed to reflect in her music — it wasn't flowing as naturally as usual. Frustrated, she got up and wandered into the dining room. The furniture was large and dark, a bit old fashioned for her taste — but it was a family room and, when the family were gathered around the table with the candles lit, it seemed warm and welcoming. Today, though, it felt cold, dark and empty, exacerbating her loneliness. This was the first time since she began living here that she'd had time alone in the house. What were all her friends doing? Where would David be now? Los Angeles or New York. The time difference was complicated.

She returned to the piano and recalled the last time the dining room had been filled. She smiled. David had first said she could have Friday afternoon off to do the cooking for his family, and then added it would be time in lieu of her using Saturday morning to take him to the airport! Paula's boys had apparently been so upset when they were told they wouldn't be joining in the family meal, and eating Auntie Jane's food, that it had spurred her to suggest that if they chose something they liked she would cook it just for them. Toad-in-the-hole and chocolate mousse was the choice, and she'd chuckled, "Hopefully not together," while David had laughed, "Why not? It all goes down the same way."

David, probably provoked by her silly act as cook, had acted as butler to the boys eating early in the dining room, and their meal had become quite a pantomime. The boys loved it. So much more fun, Richard said, than having dinner with boring old adults! In the end, she wasn't sure who'd enjoyed it most, or who had made the most mess. Sausage dipped in chocolate mousse wasn't a delicacy she'd recommend.

The more conventional meal she'd cooked for David's family had been equally appreciated, especially the tomato roses and the other vegetables Jane had used to decorate the dishes. The final course had brought a gasp when she brought in the huge oval platter with profiterole swans resting in blue and green swirled sauce! An idea adapted from the disastrous evening with Andrew Carlton.

Between courses, she'd left the table to visit the toilet and discovered the 'terrible pair' playing a spying game on the stairs. Their surprise at being discovered rooted them wide-eyed to the spot, so she suggested in a whisper that they had better get back to bed before Uncle David found them – which she knew was a stronger threat than either Paula or Jim. Relieved she wasn't about to 'dob them in' as Richard put it, they scurried off up the stairs, but not before Philip slipped back to whisper, "Auntie Jane, are you going to marry Uncle David?"

Momentarily stunned, she recovered enough to pat his backside, point him upstairs and answer, "No, Philip, I'm not," to which he muttered to his brother, "She's not. That's a pity." Shaking her head, Jane wondered where the little mites got their ideas from.

On her return to the dining room, David's mother was saying across the table, "Your father and I haven't any reservations. We can't understand why you're...."

Margaret had broken off talking to David to smile at her, and he picked up from where she'd left off. "I don't think you're interfering. However, the time isn't right, but I do have high hopes of bringing about a very satisfactory conclusion."

Jane, having been made to feel so much part of the family, felt she could comment. "Oh dear, I recognise that tone of voice. It's the one David uses in the office when he's faced with a   challenge and determined to solve it. What poor soul is going to be persuaded to do something they don't want to do?"

There was an awkward silence before Margaret laughed, "It hasn't taken you long, Jane, to understand the way that boy of mine works. And talking of boys, perhaps you should go and check on Richard and Philip, David. As David obediently rose, Paula began asking questions about how to make profiterole swans, and her question hadn't been answered.

Maybe that broken conversation was something to do with the unresolved matters Grace had mentioned. Surely David wasn't thinking of leaving ITP? The place wouldn't be the same without him. Her fingers raced over the keys, bringing the music to a crescendo and, as the final chords faded away, she heard the front door opening and closing. Puzzled, she left the piano and peered down the stairs.

"Hello, luv. It's only me!" called a familiar voice.

"Mrs Perkins! What are you doing here on a Saturday?"

"Oh, me, oh my! I did a silly fing yesterday – took me purse out to the shops in me shopping bag, then came back 'ere, grabbed up me bits and pieces and left leaving me 'andbag behind. Fortunately, me 'ouse keys are on the same ring as 'ere, so I could get in 'ome, but I feels sort of lost wivout me 'andbag."

Jane smiled, "Well, now you're here, how about a nice cup of tea?" Mrs Perkins hesitated. "I've hardly seen you since that day I came to view the flat." From Mrs Perkins' face, it was obvious she wasn't used to having cups of tea made for her. To put her at ease, Jane added, "Everyone's away, so I'm a bit lonely and could do with both a cuppa and a bit of a chat. What do you say?"

After several cuppas, and mentions that she must be

going, Mrs P, as Jill called her, chattered on. There was a brief pause, during which Mrs P seemed to be plucking up courage, before she ventured, "So how do yer like living 'ere, ducks?"

"Oh, I love it, especially when the house is full. But it seems so quiet today."

Mrs Perkins pondered, then piped up, "Likes you, don't 'e, the master." She gave a wicked smile and wink.

Jane chuckled. "Oh, we have our moments. He's like a big brother who's always teasing and trying to gain the upper hand!"

"Ah! Is he now!" Mrs Perkins nodded knowingly. "That's what it's all about, innit?" Jane stifled a laugh – getting Mrs P's meaning but thinking how wrong could she be. "Changed 'e 'as, yer know."

"Has he?" Amuse him she may, but her presence certainly wouldn't qualify to be a life changing experience!

"Oooh, yes! Since you've been 'ere. Mind, even a few months before yer came 'e seemed brighter, like as if 'e suddenly found something amusing which gave 'im a new interest in life. Yeh, 'e's always bin a quiet and retiring man, 'cept when 'e's with that sister of his. They spark each other off. Still I fought 'e'd never find the right one." She whispered conspiratorially across the table, "In my opinion he usually chooses 'em flighty types." Jane forced herself not to smile as Mrs P went on, "Yer know, 'em's who throws themselves at any good looking man. Never lasted long – well, 'cept that Felicity woman."

Mrs P raised her eyes towards the ceiling and Jane tried to look serious. Mrs P gave her the once over, then continued with her observations. "Now you – you'd keep 'im 'appy. 'E'd never know a dull moment with you. I fought the minute I set eyes on yer – now this one, she'll do the master. I could tell 'e were interested in yer and not just 'cause he reckoned you'd make a flatmate for 'is sister. No! The minute 'e came in that night, 'e looked lit up, and when you replied so 'aughty, I fair knew there were something afoot. My though, I was a bit surprised when 'e rang and tells me what 'e what 'e was up to. Not like 'im, I fought, but I was pleased to oblige. 'E's a good man, pays me good wages – better than me friends get."

Jane found it impossible to keep the amusement from her voice. "I think I should tell you, Mrs Perkins, David – I mean, Mr Reinhardt – and I are merely friends. We do enjoy playing tricks on each other, but I can assure you that's all there is in it."

Mrs Perkins was not to be put off. "Don't yer believe it, luv. I saw the way 'e looked at yer. 'E thinks the world of yer."

This was becoming farcical. "I think the world of him too, Mrs Perkins. I agree he's a wonderful man, but I am no more than just a sister to him, and he a brother to me."

"Hmm. There's a pity then, me dear. I was 'oping it was more than that. Yer should see the hours 'e spends studying up there." She nodded her head to the upper floor. "'E told me a few months back, when I asked if 'e 'ad gone all religious, 'cause of all 'em Bibles and fings that I ain't seen before that a young lady at work 'ad made 'im take an interest in religious fings. I s'pose I put two and two together. I mean you've a Bible and fings, ain't yer? I've seen 'em by your bed." Unable to fully comprehend what Mrs Perkins was saying, Jane stared at her. Mrs Perkins, looking uncomfortable, shrugged, "So I fought see – with 'im fixing for you to live here, well it must be you."

Jane considered as she answered. "I think, Mrs Perkins, I might have started David's interest in religion, maybe even Christianity, but my coming to the flat was sheer coincidence, and honestly there is nothing more...." she trailed off in thought.

Mrs Perkins rose and picked up her bag. "Well ducks, I'd best be off. I 'ope I ain't spoke out of turn? I do get things wrong." Her face creased into a worried frown.

Jane reassured her and followed her to the front door, her mind racing with questions. Was David taking an interest in Christianity? If so, why hadn't he talked to her about it? Surely, knowing Grace was a Christian, he would have talked with her, so why hadn't Grace mentioned it? Perhaps David had taken seriously her comment, 'If I ever find a Christian man who is as wonderful as you, I'll be satisfied'? Did he have romantic notions about her? Did he think if he became a Christian she would seriously consider him?

Having wished Mrs P a safe journey home, Jane ran up the stairs to find out for herself what David was reading in his study. Part way up the second staircase to the top floor she halted, feeling guilty. David had told her to treat the whole house as her own, but somehow his bedroom and study felt off-limits. Peeking round the open study door, she created enough gap to see inside! It was just as Mrs Perkins had described it. Slowly, she sidled in to get a better look. Piled together on his large desk by the window were two Bible commentaries, a huge concordance, a Bible dictionary and two different Bible translations, one of which was similar to her Christmas present.

Torn between David's privacy and her curiosity, she finally overcame her scruples and pulled at the ribboned bookmarks in the uppermost Bible to see what he was reading. The first bookmark was at Psalm 37 – the same verse he'd written in her Bible at Christmas. The second, in Romans, referred to Christian marriage, and the third was in Corinthians at the place where Paul explains why a Christian should only marry another Christian.

An interest in Christianity was one thing – but marking passages about heart's desires and Christian marriage? Was Mrs Perkins right? David had never given her any reason to suppose he wanted more than friendship. She frowned. Or had he?

She pulled out the chair and sat at the desk, drawing

the commentaries towards her. They also had marked references on the topic of marriage. On the other side of the desk in a pile of study books was one on marriage. Because he wasn't a Christian, she'd never allowed herself to consider him more than a friend or a brother. But what if he became one – would that put a different complexion on their relationship?

Perplexed, she pondered on words he'd spoken. Perhaps they hadn't been as flippant as she had assumed. Since Christmas and New Year, he had done as she had asked and acted toward her in the same way he would Jill – an affectionate arm around, a quick hug, a kiss on the cheek. Inevitably, she arrived back to the kiss in the canteen at Christmas. His public approval had been both unexpected and embarrassing. He hadn't instigated the kiss, yet he'd taken great delight in administering it and, if she was truthful, she wouldn't have minded him kissing her again. The New Year kiss had also been pleasant and enjoyable.

But what did she consider falling 'in love' was about? After all, she had thought she loved Bruce until the 'stranger' and the 'ghost' showed her how a spark could ignite between two people. Friendship was always a good basis for a loving relationship, so they had that. In front of her, without thinking, she flopped open the pages of the Bible. Her eyes were arrested by the words, "Haven't you read that the one who created them from the beginning made them male and female and said, 'For this cause shall a man leave his father and mother, and shall cleave to his wife; and the twain shall become one flesh'? So they are no longer two separate people, but one. No man therefore must separate what God has joined together."

She shut the Bible. Had God been answering her question? When she opened the Bible again, it fell open to the same verses. This was no way to get guidance from God, but she couldn't resist trying it again. This time it didn't open up anywhere near the same place and the verses weren't relevant, so had God been speaking? If so, what would she think about marriage to David?

It was ridiculous to even consider he'd be interested in her. She liked him – perhaps even loved him – but in a romantic way and marriage? It was too much to take in, or even think about. She bent her head to pray, "Lord, I'm so confused. I can't think any more. You know the plan you have for my life. Please help me not to try and work it all out, but just trust in you, for I know you'll show the way when the time is right."

Springing up, as if getting away from the books would make it all go away, she ran down the stairs. Music was what she needed, but she was too tense to play. Perhaps David had some music she could enjoy. She found a tape recorded six months earlier in her church. It was a good mix of hymns and new songs. She put it on, determined to worship God and not dwell on what she had seen.

Halfway through the second song, a startling thought hit her. What was Christian music doing in David's collection, and from her church? Urgently, she fingered her way through the tapes and found others. Would she have found these if she'd have gone further than just flicking through his records that day she came to see the flat? Or had he collected them since? At least, when he came home she could ask him about the tapes, whereas to admit to rummaging around in his study could be taken as an assault on his privacy. She lay back and let the words of the hymn sink in.

When peace like a river attendeth my way,
When sorrows like sea billows roll;
Whatever my lot, Thou has taught me to know,
It is well with my soul
It is well, it is well with my soul.

Curled up on the settee, she cuddled into the cushions believing those words to be true. The music flowed over her and by the time the last words of the hymn, 'Blessed hope! Blessed rest of my soul,' were sung, Jane was asleep.

CHAPTER 19

Daylight had faded into darkness before Jane stirred. She stretched languidly and clicked on the lamp by the settee. Her eyes blinked in the light, she looked around the sitting room. It was incredible to think that, less than a year ago, David Reinhardt had been someone whom Rosemary had inferred wouldn't mix with the likes of her. What would Rosemary say if she knew that she now not only worked for the imposing Mr Reinhardt, but lived in his house, had use of his flat, sat on his settee and was treated as part of his family! She gave a quiet chuckle. These days the opportunity to mix with Rosemary rarely happened!

In those days though she'd thought of David Reinhardt probably much the same as others and, despite their run-ins, had been slightly in awe of him. He was distinguished, prominent, sometimes outrageous and with a desire for justice. He was almost feared in the business circles in which he moved, yet he'd become a brother she delighted in. A sense of privilege stirred within her at being close to such a man.

How long had she been asleep? She shivered, and slid her feet to the floor. Hugging her arms across her chest she jumped up and down, but that and her thin jumper didn't bring her warmth. In her mind, she tossed up whether to go back down to the warmth of her flat or slip upstairs and take another look at David's books. Maybe she could borrow one, it would give her something to read.

The house was in darkness, so she put on the landing light. She ran up the stairs, across the short landing and into the study. Once in the room she had to fumble about a bit to find the reading lamp on the desk then, having put it on, she brought the books under its light and sat down in the comfy chair.

In the silence the house creaked, but a slightly louder creak caused her to look up and listen. On a notepad were a series of reference to verses in the book of Romans which started with 'the wages of sin is death' and ended with 'if you confess with your mouth that Jesus Christ is Lord you will be saved'. No doubt then that David knew that Jesus died on the cross for his sins and the need to acknowledge that.

Jane looked up. There was that noise again. Then silence. It was probably the faint rustling of the wind in the tree below the window. It had sounded more inside, but then houses often creaked for no reason. Oh dear, perhaps there were mice in the roof, or even scampering around the house! Not that she'd ever seen or had evidence of that. Cautiously she looked over the floor, then told herself she was bigger than any mouse. He would be more frightened of her, than she of him. Then she shivered again at the prospect of meeting one! It was time to go back to the nice snug warmth of the basement.

In the pile of books, she glanced through and picked out *The Normal Christian Life* by Watchman Nee. She'd heard of it, but not read it. Her thumb flicked through the pages. Arrested by the words, 'God's desire is for sons...' and 'joint-heirs with Christ...', she sat to read on. If David was questioning faith and Christianity, this did seem a good book to read.

A dull, but definite creak with an accompanying squeak made her tense. It was rather like the sound of a bed when someone turned over in it! It certainly wasn't David. He'd spoken to Jill yesterday morning from Los Angeles, and still had a meeting in New York before arriving into Heathrow tomorrow afternoon. Jill was picking him up from the airport on her way back from their family home in Berkshire, so it couldn't be her either. Fear tightened her throat. Was it a burglar? Had she shut the front door properly? She had been rather distracted. How ridiculous! Of course she'd shut it – she remembered leaning against it. Still tense, she waited for another sound, but the house remained silent. Her imagination was running riot in more ways than one! A slight noise became a burglar.

Bibles, commentaries and books signalled that David was interested in becoming a Christian. Highlighted verses in a Bible and a book on marriage indicated David's desire to marry. And Mrs P's observations were enough to make her wonder if it was his intention to make her his blushing bride. The only evidence here was of a man who, when he got his teeth into something, was like a dog with a bone.

It was time to tidy up and leave. A dull thud came from David's bedroom. She stiffened. It came again, slightly louder. There was someone in the house, but who? Her stomach churned. If it was a burglar, she need something to defend herself. Quickly glancing around the room, she saw a pair of scissors sitting in the pen pot. Good as a deterrent, but she'd never have the courage to stab someone. Another louder thud made her draw breath. On the other hand....

Jane prayed and tried to keep calm. If someone was in David's room, and it sounded as if they were now opening his wardrobe door, what should she do? The telephone was down one flight in the hall. The squeaking sound of the bedroom door knob being turned was enough for her to back up against the desk. At the sound of the bedroom door being opened, she spun round, lurched across the wide desk and grabbed the scissors. Almost instantly, a hand fell on her outstretched arm and a body pinned her to the desk. In shock, her eyes closed. Her body froze. Warmth against the back of her legs from her assailant's body reminded her....

Her eyes flashed open. The desk light was enough for her to see her face mirrored in the uncurtained window.

And behind her a large, distorted reflection. Immediately, she looked at the hand covering hers. The heavy gold signet ring on his little finger confirmed his identity. Annoyed, she didn't bother to speak but made to escape with the same action as she had the night of the Summer Ball. Instantly, and instinctively seeming to know her mind, his body leant into hers, stopping the turn and gently removing the scissors from her hand.

Upright, she could see him more clearly, and the memories of the 'stranger' flooded back. Dazed, she looked numbly at the mirrored image but, as his hands stirred into a slow but provocative dance over her, her body responded. And seeing the movements seemed to magnify the sensual pleasure. He said nothing. She felt mesmerised by that feathery touch that made tiny electrical charges build into minute shocks, causing her to draw breath. But she determined not to show her response.

The voice she knew so well challenged, "So… Jane?"

"You? Was it you?"

A seductive whisper purred in her ear as finger tips ran over and around her neck. "What do you think?"

In their wake came darts of electric pulses sending messages to her brain, that brought a cry of pleasure from her throat and weakness to her knees. She felt she was drowning in a warm sea. It was a struggle to rise above the delectable waves of pleasure to grasp the concept that this man had been her stranger. She whimpered in pleasure. His murmuring, "You like this. How about this?" fuelled her desire. So effective was his assault on her senses, her whole body seemed to throb and ache in a delirium that needed sating. But he wouldn't let her turn toward him, despite her writhing against him.

There was no doubt now of her stranger's identity and, as then, all caution, all propriety, all reason flew from her mind, although the desire for the pleasure he was stirring was intensified because it was David. She was safe with

David. The thought exalted itself above the tide of passion engulfing her, enough to speak in a barely audible voice, "It was you?"

The pressure of his body lightened. His fingers gently pulled away the soft, knitted neck of her jumper and his lips sought out new areas to torment her. Huskily, he murmured near her ear, "Don't ask me Jane – tell me."

With difficulty, she controlled her lolling head to straighten and put up a hand to touch the side of his face. He was real – this wasn't just an erotic dream. Secure in the knowledge of her tormentor, her body ached to respond – to touch, feel, kiss and to bring him pleasure in return. Subconsciously, she registered the rough drag of his breath. His hand splayed out against her stomach, drawing her tighter against him and showing that his passion was as great as hers. This wasn't one his jokes, or a game. It was as real to him as to her. Dizzy with revelation and weak from the bombardment of his caresses, her head drooped again. In a breathless whisper, he asked, "Who do you think I am, Jane?"

Incapable of answering, now understanding that the stranger wasn't a stranger at all, she snuggled against him. To provoke a response, his dancing fingers wove up and down her body while, with the tip of his tongue, he caressed the nape of her neck, her hairline and ears asking, "Does this – and this – and this – bring back memories?"

Night after night she'd relived his touch, but this was far beyond that original kindling. Disjointedly, she whispered, "Yes, oh yes! David – it was you!"

Her answer was rewarded with a very familiar, but muted boom. "At last, Jane, you recognise our déja vu!" He drew back, teasing, "So what took you so long?"

Suddenly she felt vulnerable, afraid – was he going to disappear again? Alarmed, she turned. His hands caught her and held her upper arms. Embarrassed to see such naked desire in his eyes, her gaze diverted to his mouth.

But, seeing the seductive twitch of his lips, her eyes lowered to where his tie usually rested.

"Come here." Hugging her against his chest, he murmured, "Don't be afraid, or shy. It's me, David, known also as Tarzan, and you Jane!"

Even though held against him, she trembled and responded with a watery smile. What did he think of her? The passion she'd displayed in his office, and now in his study. Would he think her wanton, deserving all she got from Andrew and Jacques? A finger tucked itself under her chin to gently tip it upwards. When her eyes met his, she saw more than desire; she saw sincerity, she questioned, love?

"Oh Jane! Ever since the Midsummer Ball, I've longed to rekindle the fire which I so inadvertently started that night. And the more I got to know you, the more I realized how precious that had been." Jane stared him. His rugged features were softened by the desk lamp, and a warm, almost rueful, smile danced on his lips. He bent to observe her more closely, his eyes dark, seductive pools. "For a while there, I wondered if I'd lost my touch. However, it wouldn't appear so."

A blush began to arise at the intensity of his stare. She tried to turn away, but his finger kept her chin raised. Mesmerised, she watched his mouth descending towards hers. As his lips brushed hers, his hands moved to cup her face, his fingers sending quivering pulses along her neck and ears, before sliding into her hair. Lost in time and space, she trembled as the kiss became that of the ghost – one of such slow precision, it brought a spiralling of need over which she had no control.

Her arms found their place around his neck. Her body yielded into his strength. A desire to give as well as receive matched him, caress for caress, with both her hands and her lips. Then it was David who groaned and murmured her name over and over. And with a heaving sigh and impassioned voice, be murmured, "Oh Jane, Jane, how I've dreamt and longed for this." Then, as if he couldn't stop himself, he picked her up, rained kisses over her face and neck, twirled her round and round, and finally tumbled her on to the studio couch with the words, "Enough, enough. I don't think I can take any more!"

The sight of him heading out the study door was enough for her to cry out, "David. No! Don't leave me."

With a smile, David reassured her. "Don't worry, I'm not going far. I'll be back in a minute. Believe me – the 'stranger' and the 'ghost' didn't want to go either, but had no choice."

True to his word, he returned in a few minutes and, as he entered, switched on the main light. She was hugging her knees and trying to come to terms with what had just happened. David Reinhardt was the 'stranger', the 'ghost' and the friend she adored. It was as if, in denial, she'd squashed the love she had for this man. Now, as it inflated she felt she would burst with happiness.

"I need to see you to talk to you." Unable to take her eyes off him, she watched as he pulled the curtains. Then, as he lowered himself beside her, their eyes met and locked. It was like a dream, and as if David needed to believe that it was true as well. In almost a trance, his finger moved forward to gently trace back and forth along her lips, bringing a sensation both hypnotic and erotic.

Just when she felt she could bear it no more, he murmured, "I think, my love, that we need to get more comfortable, with me so tall and you so small. Here, cuddle up under my arm." Overwhelmed that he should call her 'my love', she could only look at him wide-eyed. "Don't look so worried. I'm not going to take advantage of all that unleashed passion I seem to create in you. And I'll have you know, that comes as much as a surprise to me as discovering I'm your stranger, and the ghost from the Christmas party, was to you. I thought you'd guessed we were one and the same person, but your despondency that night had me worried."

She snuggled against his warmth, "I didn't, I didn't know it was you."

"I know. But, for a brief time in the switchboard room, I thought you were playing with me to pay me back." He sighed heavily. "However I was slightly more heartened when you began on the brother tack – at least, then I knew you felt something for me." His dark eyes roved over her face. "Oh Jane, you have no idea what you do to me."

Her lips parted in a soft invitation. He bent and kissed her again with such gentle provocation that her body responded instinctively. It arched up towards him, her arms entwined round his neck, pulling him closer to writhe against him. Now she'd allowed herself to acknowledge she loved him, the need to offer herself wholly to him overcame all her preconceived ideas and resolutions. Her responses became wilder and more reckless.

"Whoa, Jane! Whoa! What have I unleashed?" David broke free from her and groaned playfully. Despite his light-heartedness, those black eyes above her were heavy with desire! Wistfully he sighed, sat her back and, tracing her neck and ear with his finger, chuckled, "Now Jane, as much as we may long to continue this and take it to its final conclusion, I want you to know it is my intention to savour that privilege and that precious gift for our marriage bed." He became serious, "That is, if you'll have me?"

Had she heard him – David Reinhardt – say he wanted to marry her? What would her mother say? What would her mother say if she had seen her moments ago? A deep blush began to rise up her neck as, mortified, she realized how frenzied and unrestrained she'd been. What must David think of her? How could she have behaved so? Anxious to redeem the situation, she drew apart from him and asked the first thing that came into her head, "So – so, what are you doing here?"

His roar of laughter made her jump, and rocked the poor settee. "Oh Jane, what am I to do with you?" He shook his head, "This, my dearest Jane..." he said with a flourish of his hand, "...this is where I live." He gave her a hard stare and wagged his finger. "And this is my study – which it seems is about as private as my office to the likes of you, young lady!"

Was he cross? Nervous, she bit her lip. He'd been very cross on Midsummer night! Her flushed face became even redder for, until then, her attack on him and his response had been conveniently wiped from her memory. With a sudden urge to put space between them, she curled up away from him, drawing herself into the corner against the settee arm. In a childlike gesture, her thumb found its way to her mouth.

"Jane? Look at me!" The command was of a man who expected to be obeyed. Instinctively, she curled tighter and shook her head. She had to think this out. No one who knew him would say he was a harsh man, but he had standards he expected to be kept, and when roused, his anger could be awesome. Jill might be right in saying he was a bully, but he wasn't cruel. He liked to be in control, but was more kind and persuasive!

"Jane?" The faint tremor in his questioning tone was enough to draw her attention. His facial tension eased. Compassionate eyes gazed across at her. "Oh, Jane. Please don't be upset. And I will understand if the thought of being married to me is too awful to contemplate!"

Her thumb moved nervously back and forth across her lips as she sought the words to express her feelings. Astute eyes seemed to penetrate her innermost thoughts, for he stated, "Maybe there are one or two points that need clarifying."

To give her space, he moved to the opposite corner of the settee and settled himself where he could comfortably see her. "For one reason or another I have been annoyed, even furious, with you on occasions since the night of our first encounter." He paused long enough for her to raise her head. Giving her a rueful smile, he continued, "But, hopefully, you've noticed that I have exercised incredible self-control when my patience has been tried to the limit. Despite my threats, I have not repeated my rather unorthodox behaviour of that particular evening, and I assure you, it is not my intention to do so ever again!"

The soft tenderness in his eyes confirmed his sincerity. Her stomach quickened, confirming in her heart just how much he meant to her. Tears filled her eyes.

"Now will you come and sit next to me while I explain my actions that night?" Passively, she nodded and moved next to him. He tucked her back under his arm as he went on, "I'd been caught in traffic. Arriving late, I asked my fellow directors to speak while I fetched my speech. When I saw the light in my office, I wasn't in the mood to appreciate your audacity – first in being in my office, and second for using my telephone for something so trivial as a chat with your boyfriend." He ruffled her hair, "Since, I've come to appreciate your intrusion into my life – which, I might add, my family and friends say has changed me for the better!"

That made her head twist to look up into his face. "Your family and friends?"

David chuckled, "Oh, yes, Jane. Oh, yes!"

Her brow creased as she eyed him questioningly.

A wry smile flickered across his mouth, "It seems, Jane, the only person who failed to receive the message that I'd fallen head over heels in love with you – was you!"

The words 'head over heels in love with you' echoed around in her head. It made her feel distinctly naïve. She buried her face into his chest.

He cuddled her. "To most people in the company, my office is considered sacrosanct. So, I asked myself, who was the slip of a girl with the dainty, upturned bottom leaning over my desk?" Again, she looked up at him, her finger touching her lips. "As I looked at that swaying little bottom, it struck me how entertaining it would be to find out if you appreciated my audacity as much as I did yours!" There was no concealment in the slanted, seductive look with which he held her gaze. Jane lowered her head to vividly relive the scene. "I don't quite know what I expected to happen, but I certainly didn't anticipate being so unexpectedly and viciously attacked."

With a quick glance at him, she murmured, "Sorry." Then she pulled back. "It could have been worse, you know." And she threw him one of her haughty looks.

He groaned, "And you have no idea what those provocative looks of yours do to me." His eyes narrowed, "And to other men...." He shook his head. "You have no idea how many times I've had to restrain the urge to pull you into my arms and thoroughly kiss you."

She frowned. He'd certainly hidden that response well!

David viewed her down his nose, and she felt as if she was a minion in the Courtroom who'd the impertinence to interrupt his case for the defence. Then he stated, "You have caused me to digress." An unstoppable giggle bubbled out from her. "Jane! Let me finish. I still want to tell you about Midsummer night. I was convinced that you were enjoying my tantalizing, so I decided to turn you round, then kiss and run, when to my surprise you turned on me. Whew! When I next sat at my desk and saw the paper knife on the blotter, I realized how close my manhood had come to being punctured." He paused, and she slid her face up his chest to look at him. He gave a wry smile, and teased, "You will, I'm sure, be glad to know that no lasting damage was inflicted." The contortion of her face in embarrassment made him chuckle, as she snuggled back against him. "Anyway, I was as much stunned as hurt. To think that some slip of a girl had not only the temerity to enter my office, and use my telephone, but had also tried to inflict grievous bodily harm upon my person – with my own ruler – astounded me! I certainly wasn't going to let you get away with that.

"At first I'd no idea how to deal with you, but the way you fought, kicked and screamed, hurling such polite abuse at me, so reminded me of Philip and Richard that I retaliated by treating you like a naughty child." The hug he gave her now made her wonder if he was afraid she would run away. "I expected your reaction would be similar to the boys – although I don't make a habit of chastising them in that way – but almost instantly you went quiet.

"I thought this was another ploy so, in anticipation of another attack, I beat you more soundly than I had intended. Can you imagine how horrified I was when it seemed I'd beaten you senseless? I didn't know what to do. I wanted to say 'sorry' but didn't dare reveal who I was. All I could do was hug you and hope, like the boys, you'd understand. I didn't want to leave you with the impression of a sadistic, unfeeling man, so I kissed you in a way I knew to be provocative, but was taken aback when you responded so passionately – making me want more and to find out more about you."

In telling his story, he'd relaxed and sunk back into the cushions so, as she sat up, she could now look down on him to question, "But how did you know who I was when you couldn't see me?"

David chuckled. "I could say I'd recognise that pert little bottom anywhere but, actually, I did have an unfair advantage. I saw your profile before I turned out the light. And, by a stroke of luck, I was talking to Jill one day when you were walking up the drive, and she told me the story of you giving Ian a slap for kissing you. So here, now, was a worry! Had you guessed my identity? If you had, it was quite possible you'd appear at the Ball somewhat bedraggled, and accuse me of molesting you. I had to think quickly. Fortunately, I can run fast so I hared down to the taxi rank. Whatever happened, I then had it covered. Either you'd take a nice, quiet, comfortable taxi home or, if you caused a stir, I had a taxi ready to bundle you into."

Lips pursed, Jane's eyes flashed in outrage, "Oh! So you had it all worked out. How convenient! Did you ever think about me and the effect that had on my life? I suppose Jill was in on that too, and knew who the stranger was right from the beginning."

"Jill's never known. She may have had her suspicions, but I've never admitted it to her. I was afraid she'd let it slip to you."

"And the flowers?"

"It was the way you eyed me so suspiciously across the canteen. I thought it would be a good way to say 'sorry' and find out your reaction. I knew that dear sister wouldn't miss out on a bit of excitement, and that she'd tell me all about it. Imagine, then, my amusement when I discovered you in the hall with her, and could ask you myself!"

"I don't have to imagine it, I was there. Remember?"

"Ah, but despite our altercation, I did learn that I was forgiven!"

He took her hand, kissed her finger tips and looked into her face. "Jane, I've agonised over you finding out the identity of your stranger. My behaviour was totally alien – even to me! My actions brought you discontentment, pain, trouble, and," he smiled gently, "changed the course of both our lives. I nearly confessed that evening when you lay in my office after your altercation with the washbasin, but Grace interrupted. Then I'm afraid I lost courage. I just hope when you know everything, you'll be able to forgive me."

What else was there to know? The trepidation in his voice seemed strange coming from a man who was usually so self-assured. And what else was there to forgive? This was the first time she'd seen David Reinhardt totally vulnerable – the man behind the facade. It didn't make her reject him. It made her love him all the more. A lump lodged in her throat as she gazed up into those eyes, so tender, so loving, so for her.

"You see, I've worked hard to carve myself a career, I just couldn't risk losing it by confessing to a foolish impulsive act. But I found you'd carved yourself into my heart and, for the first time in my life, I haven't found a way of being in control – either of you or my feelings." He looked rueful, "Not that I didn't try."

"I didn't know," she murmured.

"That's just it. It's your innocence and trusting nature, coupled with your spirit and unexpected maturity, that makes you special. It makes me want to hold you, cherish you, protect you, yet give you space to be yourself and reach the goals you desire. It's a new dimension for me. It's not something that comes from study and research." On a heavy sigh, he sat up. "This brings me to the stranger-ghost. I don't want to disillusion you, but actually we don't have some unique wonderful chemistry between us. It's like everything else – just something I've studied and researched." David's face contorted ruefully, "I won't deny I've had a fair bit of practice over the years but, in learning to stimulate a woman's responses, I confess it's always been to further my own pleasure."

Thinking of Bruce, she had to ask, "Are you saying that if people took the trouble to learn, they could all be as expert as you?"

"Oh, Jane, I feel gratified that you think I'm an expert, but expertise doesn't necessarily come from books and experiments. I haven't a clue about love. I've never been in love before. I only know you can't control it. I suspect it's that extra, vital ingredient which can take you beyond an act, or an art, into an all encompassing, rich experience which doesn't begin and end with the physical side of a relationship.

"My life has been in separate pockets. You entered one, then broke into the next, and the next. Suddenly, it seemed each part of my life – which up until then had been reasonably fulfilling – now became merely the border of a much bigger space which I want to fill with you. You make me feel young, alive. It seems everything before was colourless, empty, meaningless...."

"That's funny! Earlier today, I was thinking life without you was pretty colourless! I've missed you, but I hardly dared to think about it."

His eyes twinkled in amusement, but his voice was solemn, "Is that so? And that was before you discovered my expertise in love making?"

"'Fraid so! You've spent all those years perfecting an art which, in the end, made no difference to my loving you."

David peered into her face, his lips twitched. "Hmm, really, Jane? There's no point in me doing this then?" His lips touched and tantalised hers. She moved toward him and he pulled back, laughing. "Um, no interest there then. What about this?" His hands cupped her face. His fingers in her hair brought shivering waves of pleasure down her neck and spine, "Does that do anything for you?"

With a pert look, she determined not to respond..

"Aha! You asked for this." His mouth took hers, as his hands played havoc with her body's erogenous zones. In seconds, she was a whimpering wreck, craving for more of him.

Her eyes flashed open as he held her from him. His mouth curved into a knowing smile. "So, Jane, I think I've proved my point."

"No you haven't!" Chin up, she retorted, "I said it didn't make any difference to me loving you, not that I didn't appreciate your expertise."

"Is that so! Well, I've proved a point to myself! Whatever expertise I may think I have, I fear I may lack the self-control needed to ensure I don't sacrifice my intention to marry you before bedding you."

How could she ever have thought of him as being unattractive? That dear, wonderful, rugged face – the square jaw, the long nose, those dark expressive eyes and the way his skin crinkled around them as he smiled. To just look at him now made her stomach curl in desire. She'd never tire of this man, life wouldn't be boring with him, but she sensed it wouldn't be easy, with his strong character and somewhat pedantic ways. He made her react, whether in laughter or tears, in anger or delight. There was no doubt he was the man of her dreams, the man who would fulfil her heart's desires, the man God....

There was a catch in her heartbeat. She stiffened and stopped breathing. Her eyes widened in anguish. Her mouth fell open as the tears overflowed down her cheeks.

David gave her a gentle shake, eyes full of concern, "Jane, what is it?"

Blankly she stared at him. She swallowed, try to get a grip and think. But it was if the whole world was caving in on her. God! How could she have forgotten God?

Exasperation and desperation gave a hard edge to David's voice. "For goodness sake, what's the matter?"

To think she'd been so taken up with the moment, she'd allowed herself to be drawn into dreams of love and marriage with this man! But without God – without Jesus – it just couldn't be. Thoughts swirled through her brain like wisps of mist. Unable to grasp them, she finally choked out, "David, I...." She broke from him, and sobbed, "It's no good! No good!" before she flew out the door heading for the sanctuary of her bedroom.

As she ran down the flights of stairs, she was torn between the Bible command, 'be ye not unequally yoked', and her love for the man who literally was of her dreams. Maybe David was interested in God, but it wasn't a commitment. To be equally yoked, he had to believe as she did. Sobs caught in her throat as she stumbled down the last few steps into the flat. Deep grief rose from the pit of her stomach. Doubled over, she struggled forward, trying to hold down the pain with her hand. Her heart felt it was being rent in two. Which was it to be? Love for Jesus and faith to believe the Lord knew best, or love for a man who clearly loved her and was all she could desire for a husband? She wanted both, but had to give one up. Wildly, she looked around the flat. She couldn't stay here – she had to get away. Mum and Ted were away another week, she had the keys to the house.

Blindly, she pulled her overnight case from the wardrobe and began filling it at random. God's word said he wouldn't tempt her beyond her strength, and she would need all of that to walk away. This probably would be the hardest thing she would ever have to do. But God had never failed her and she mustn't fail him. She determined not to question the Lord, but trust in him.

With grim determination, she pulled her clothes from the wardrobe, her wash things from the cabinet. There'd be enough time to cry out the bitter tears, the agony of heart, in the days and weeks ahead.

David was calling out her name. She closed her case, clipped down the lock, put on her coat, slung her handbag over her shoulder, grabbed the case and opened her door.

David's eyes mirrored her misery. "Oh Jane, I'm sorry, I should have told you. I meant to but...."

Jane pushed past him, but he moved to block her.

"Let me pass."

"Jane stop! Put that case down. This is ridiculous. Hear me out at least. I know why you rushed off. Jane, I've become a Christian. That's why you rushed off, isn't it?"

"I can't stay. I've got to go." Tears threatened. The pain of seeing him, of loving him.... She tried to push past him.

In frustration, his hand swept back through his hair.

"Jane, didn't you hear me? I just said I've become a Christian."

Determined to remain firm, her hand clenched her case even tighter as she said, "Yes, I did. But if you have, then it was for the wrong reasons." She saw his body flinch as though she'd dealt him a blow. "Please, David, don't make this any harder for me, just let me pass."

"Not until you've given me a fair hearing. I deserve that surely?" Jane knew that grim look. Nothing would move him so, wearily, she put down the case, deliberately hardened her heart and stared at him.

David sat heavily on the fourth stair, so their eyes were level. It was impossible not to see his desperation. Or hear the raw emotion in his voice. "I'm only declaring my love to you now, Jane, because I've found God for myself. My plan was to get a little sleep then take you out for a meal. However, the moment I saw you in my study, bending over my desk, just as you had that Midsummer night, I lost all sense of reason and saw it as an opportunity to reveal myself as your stranger."

Jane blinked back the tears. She was not going to weaken.

"You are right to question, but I assure you I have not made a commitment to follow the Lord because of you. Yes, I sought after God because of you, and your faith. And Jill told me you wouldn't be interested in anyone unless they shared your faith. But as I then spent hours studying, I began to see you just didn't become a Christian and that was that. It was, as I heard you once say, a life time and daily commitment. I knew I had everything to gain and nothing to lose, but Grace said it had to be something you did with your heart, not with your head, and so I did it with my head and asked God to make it real in my heart."

David faltered, swallowed hard, and then continued, "Whether you loved me or not, whether you could accept my love or not, became the lesser issue because gradually my heart took over from my head, and I slowly began to understand God's love for me. I knew that he'd sent his son Jesus to die for my sins that I might be forgiven and could have eternal life, but it became more than that. I feel as if a whole new realm of the meaning of life has opened up to me."

It was true, it really was true. He'd never be able to say those things if it wasn't. Her heart leapt, but she remained silent and said nothing. She wanted to hear him out.

"These past weeks, I sense the Holy Spirit helping me see people and situations differently. I'm learning to trust him with my life. And I know now, even if I had to live without you, he still has a plan for me and my life. I will always find fulfilment in him." David studied her bleakly, then said with conviction, "So, Jane, believe me when I say I love you, but I also know I have to let you go."

David stood. Why – if he'd become a Christian – was he now saying he had to let her go? His face was now set – steely and resolute. In disbelief she frowned at him.

"I realize it will be impossible for you to continue to live here, and obviously it would be far too painful for us to work together. But, naturally, I'll give you a glowing reference." A shudder of pain coursed through her body. She opened her mouth to speak, but he silenced her by saying, "Please don't say anything. But don't rush away – you need to pray, to sleep on it. And I'm certainly not turning you out without home or job. Give yourself time to find somewhere else and, rest assured, I will not set foot down here again unless it is you who invites me."

Head bent, David turned. With a hand on the banister, he climbed the stairs. He didn't look back and when the flat door closed she knew he'd meant it – he'd walked out of her life forever.

Stunned, she sank to her knees and cried out in agony to the only one who could understand. If she'd any doubts of her love for David, they were banished forever. The thought of never seeing him again was too much to bear. David's body language showed he was hurting but, for once, he'd not tried persuasion, just given the facts and been willing to let her go. Didn't that say something? Didn't that count for anything? If God had been testing them, David had certainly passed with flying colours! Would she have been strong enough to walk away? She sighed. Only the Lord knew that, but she did know that if God hadn't taken them along this path, she would have always wondered if David had become a Christian for the wrong reasons. Only the Lord knew what life would throw at them, but if David could trust God now to take him through this, then he'd proved his faith. Actions spoke louder than words.

Throwing off her coat she ran up the stairs.

The main hall was in darkness. The upstairs flat was dark and empty. Where was he? Should she go to his bedroom? It didn't seem right, but then she couldn't leave him to suffer. On the top floor landing, Jane was relieved to see the light under his study door. The door wasn't shut. The sound of deep groans indicated a man wrestling in prayer.

The overwhelming need to hold and comfort him swept over her. Not bothering to knock, she burst in upon him. David was sitting on the chair by his desk, his head in his hands, bent over his knees. At her entrance, he looked up with eyes glazed in pain.

Jane's heart felt it would burst. She ran to him, drew his head against her, and stroked and cuddled him, not unlike the way he'd done to her in Brussels. "David! Oh, David! I do believe you love the Lord, I love you and know you love me. I don't want to leave, be apart from you, so don't push me away. I don't think that's God's will for our lives."

Silently, their emotions mingled in their tears. His arms wound around her waist, drawing her against him. This was the real David Reinhardt, their relationship now on level ground. Jane's heart filled with joy, which was quickly dampened as David stated in a flat voice, "It's not as simple as that – I've much to confess. Come and sit on the settee. I can't tell you how much I want to believe we can work this out, but there are still things you don't know, that will hurt and upset you. I promised God I would tell you those things before I revealed to you I was the stranger. If I had," he took a deep breath and said sadly, "maybe we could still be friends. As it is, Jane, stay in the flat. I'll put on that lock. And, if you want it, I can get an opening for you in another company, similar to the job you've...."

Her body flinched in misery – why was he still pushing her away?

Staring ahead, he continued, "I should have listened to Grace. You see, she put two and two together after the incident with Jacques. She gave me good advice – back off, and go and seek God. But I didn't. After Christmas, when she found you were about to live here, she was furious – said I was playing games, manipulating your life." His voice was full of self-contempt, "She was right, but she didn't know the half of it."

"David, stop it. Just stop it! There's no need for this. You didn't force me to live here. And I did say, if I could find a Christian like you I'd be happy. So you were only fulfilling my wishes." Jane shrugged. "What's wrong with that? Especially as I was always telling Jill that I thought you were good husband material."

David gave a derisive grunt, "But my manipulation started before that. I organised everything. I thought if you came to work for me, it would lessen my desire for you. Instead it grew, along with the need to know your God."

"Excuse me! I chose to work for you. And as for your

desire – well, through it you found God! That can't be bad."

"But that's exactly what manipulation is all about. You thought you'd chosen but, if my memory serves me correctly, you told me quite clearly it wouldn't work. You even came up with some good arguments. So I then manipulated you at the same time as manipulating others to make it work."

There was no answer to that.

Flexing his shoulders, David took a deep breath and exhaled it. "After that came the coincidences. First, in Brussels, the 'still small voice' – I read about that later in the Bible; then you mentioning the need of a flat the day before the advert came out; my mother organising for us to come to Church with you, then getting on so well with yours. Did you know they chat on the telephone?" He clicked his tongue, "I suspect about us."

"You're joking!" But even as his eyebrows arched, she realised how her mother and Ted's attitude had changed toward David, and she'd thought it was because of him lending his car for the wedding.

"Remember the night you came to see the flat...."

"Could I ever forget?"

"And your song? Two weeks previously, I'd asked Jesus to come into my life and take it over, but until that night, nothing seemed to have changed or happened. But that music and the words filled me with such a desire and a love for God, I really felt his presence in the room and wanted to know him so much more."

"Why didn't you say something?"

"Because, Jane, several hours later you casually mentioned your mother's observations of my interfering and changing you. If I'd told you then about my new relationship with God, you'd have either thought it odd, not believed me, or wondered if I was saying that because I had designs on you. All of which would be understandable, since I'd been manipulating your life ever since the Midsummer Ball. It was just too early to say anything. I needed to be more sure of my relationship with the Lord and with you."

"Honestly David! You're making it sound as though you were the big spider trying to trap the pathetic little fly. I didn't have to fly into your web – I came willingly!" Taking in his tired and weary face, she longed to comfort him, to kiss him, but she could accept that he needed to unburden himself. However, she attempted to reassure him. "I see those things as God's hand bringing us together – not you manipulating everything."

David grunted, "Don't you believe it. There's more to come. After the Midsummer Ball and the row in the hall, I was curious about you. That night you'd been putty in my hands, yet later had firmly put me, and previously Ian, in our places. So, weeks later, when Andrew Carlton's secretary had been kicked and beaten with the successful intention of aborting the four-month unborn baby in...."

Jane gasped, "Oh, my goodness! The poor girl!"

"Keep that to yourself. If ever they find Andrew, it'll all come out. At the time we had our suspicions but, as Evangeline was too frightened to reveal the man's name, we couldn't do anything. It wasn't the first time we'd suspected he'd a dark side, but without evidence we could do nothing, and he needed a replacement secretary. So, when the temp agency couldn't come up with an older woman, and the choice came down to you or Rosemary, I was sure you wouldn't stand any of his nonsense. So, you can imagine how worried I was when Jill told me you were working late and going out to dinner with Andrew. The least I could do was try and keep an eye on you. Felicity wasn't with me that evening, but she was annoyed that I preferred to chase around after you instead of being with her and announced, if I decided to act as your bodyguard, our engagement would be over. Somehow, that didn't seem important, when put against your safety."

"Oh, David, I'm sorry."

"Don't be. It was a blessing in disguise. It jolted me into realizing I'd drifted into a relationship because my family had a campaign to marry me off! But after Andrew nearly...." He closed his eyes and winced. "Well, you'd have thought after that I'd have learnt not to dabble in your life. But no – two days later I had you taken into my office to recover when you fell and hurt your head."

"You can't call that manipulative. You did it because you were grateful I'd stuck up for you with the police."

"Oh, Jane, you are very good at finding excuses for me, but that argument didn't convince Jill. After that, it didn't take her long to put two and two together and see I'd been taking more than a passing interest in you."

"Jill knew? Why didn't she say?"

"Jill knows better than to break a confidence. In fact she aided and abetted me! Although she was very reluctant about letting you continue to believe we were going out together.

"Then, of course there was Brussels – just think what nearly happened there! I've got a lot to answer for. I hoped, once you were living here and seeing you day and night, so as to speak, my crush, as I called it, would fizzle out. The rest you know." With a sad little smile he invited, "Feel free to ask questions."

Did she have any? All she could do was think how much she loved him, and how drained he looked as he wearily continued, "My appointment in New York was cancelled, so I came home on the first available flight. The thought of seeing you again and thinking of how I was going to tell everything, means I've haven't slept properly for 36 hours! It's true what they say, that confession is good for the soul. I do feel a weight has been lifted off me, but I'm exhausted."

Love for this man flowed through her. She knelt beside

him. "David, I don't feel hurt or upset by any of your so called 'manipulations'. We all make mistakes, do things wrong, and if you want my forgiveness you have it. I love you. You are the fulfilment of my heart's desire. You can believe it or not, but it's true – after the stranger, I asked God for a man who'd turn me on." Jane grinned as David's eyebrows rose. "Later, I based my prayer for a husband on you. Seems to me, God has answered in the form of you, my dear Mr Reinhardt!"

Slowly she moved forward and let her lips touch his mouth, then gently nuzzle, then nibble and using similar techniques that he so skilfully exercised on her, it wasn't long before he warmed enough to take over and kiss her more thoroughly, and the fire that sparked between them quickly fanned into flame.

It was David who broke away. She opened her eyes to see his serious face above her. Immediately, she wondered what was wrong, then she caught the twinkle in his eye. "I hope, Jane Mackenzie, you're going to accept my marriage proposal, for it would seem I've made a wanton woman of you."

She drew herself up and gave him a haughty wide-eyed stare, "Actually, Mr Reinhardt, I don't remember being asked. However, if you should beg me to marry you...."

"Is that so, Jane? Well, if I wasn't quite so I tired, I don't think I'd have to resort to begging you. But as it is, I'll do it the conventional way. However, I promise you, when I'm licensed to have my way with you, rest assured, there will be times when you'll be begging for me!" David's mouth curved into a long, knowing smile.

Jane immediately rose to the bait, "Umph! We'll see about that!" But, even as she pooh-poohed it, she felt the frisson of excitement his words created within her. He slipped to his knees before her. A gentle finger lifted her chin. "Jane Mackenzie, you may have led me a merry – and not so merry dance – but I can't resist you. You torment my dreams, excite my days, and I have fallen madly, passionately, in love with you and your God. So, as I can't imagine another day without you, will you please, please, say you'll marry me?"

Her manner appeared to be one of quiet deliberation, but on the inside she was so full of joy. God had worked a miracle, it and he were amazing. Patiently, David waited before her. She guessed her eyes were reflecting her thoughts, for he just looked at her with such love. This was such a special moment. "David, I believe it is God who has brought us together and, however long we have together, I give you my love. I've no doubt we will laugh and cry, have our rows and disagreements, but that will never alter my belief that you are God's gift to me. So, yes, I will marry you. It will be my privilege to become your wife."

"Whew, Jane, that's a relief, although I'm not sure about the privilege bit. When you described my brotherly role, I said you'd probably be disillusioned. I've not been a husband before. I've read up on marriage. I'll not be a saint to live with, although, on occasion, I have been a guardian angel!"

Jane laughed, "No need for preening! In Brussels, I'd say you were more a rampager from hell, but you served your purpose. But this is a new era, and we'll both have things to learn, but we'll work it out together."

David laughed and ruffled her hair. "I know I'm a mite older than you, but what's this about 'however long we have together' – do you think by marrying you I might end up in an early grave?"

"Could be – you've already seen me as a wanton woman. That'll keep you busy. You've said many times I'm very trying, so I will probably knock years off what was your well ordered life. But I will try as your wife to become more...what's your word? Yes – 'circumspect' in the future."

Delighted, he kissed and nibbled the tips of her fingers.

"Umm, yes, young lady. You can be very trying, and I suspect you'll keep me on my toes, but I love the challenge you bring, and I love you. Anyway, in the hope you would marry me, I bought these on my way through Amsterdam." He pulled a small suede bag out of his pocket and dropped it in her lap.

Puzzled, she pulled at the draw string and tipped the contents of three small boxes into her lap. "Oh, David! Oh, my goodness – diamonds!" Seven unset petal-shaped diamonds sparkled in the light. The next box contained a dozen rounded stones like small seeds, and the final one held a single round diamond reflecting rainbow colours from its many facets. Tears filled her eyes and, with a lump in her throat, she choked out, "All these?"

"I bought a choice. You can use as many, or as few, as you like to design your own engagement ring – they'll buy back any not needed."

"Oh, David! How did you know I've always thought I'd like to design my own ring?"

"Jill. That romantic sister of mine was more than willing to draw you to a jeweller's window and ask you which ring you'd choose."

"Good heavens. You've been planning this for a while. I remember that. I laughed and said designing my own ring was as much a dream as finding the right man, and one rich enough to buy the diamonds. David, you may not be poor, but I do have an idea of the cost of these – it must have been a fortune. When I told Jill – well, it was just a whim!"

"My dear Jane, nothing is too much for you. I delight to fulfil your whims because you have given me so much. Not just fun and laughter, companionship and love, but, best of all, you showed me the way to God who has already taught me new things about love and life. And I know he has so much more for us." David stood, yawned and stretching his weary, travel-worn body, said, "Oh, and by the way, if you want different diamonds, or other stones, that can be arranged. Don't take the diamonds out of the boxes, they easily bounce and get lost, but do make a start on your design. Oh, and you're taking Monday as a day's leave."

"I am? What was that you said about manipulation?"

"Umm! Yes! Sorry! But I'd really like you to have your ring made by Friday. I'm sure you would want Grace to see the evidence that, despite my not heeding her advice, God still won the day, and you've honoured me by consenting to become my wife."

"Honoured you, indeed?"

David gave her a taunting smile. "Indeed! And, whilst you're still honouring me, perhaps you could name the day and, as it seems you are unable to resist me, it had better be soon!"

The seductive expression with which he was looking at her forced her to agree. "I know just how you feel. How about the nearest Saturday to Midsummer Night? It would seem to be appropriate, providing you can be circumspect for that long?"

"I'll do my best, Jane, but I've yet to seal the deal."

That strong, handsome face came toward her, his eyes filled with love – love for her. Should she pinch herself to see if it were a dream? But the lingering kiss was a reality and, as David left her, she knew he'd return.

Dear Reader,

Thank you for reading this book. I hope you have enjoyed it and will be interested in reading the other books in this series as they are published.

The characters and story line of this book are fictitious, but underlying it there are real and available spiritual truths to all who would seek to know more.

In 1971 I shared an office with a girl called Jane. It was her unreligious way of talking about Jesus, her mistakes, and yet her love and trust in Him, that made me curious. Next came a series of unexplainable and supernatural happenings. On the 29th July 1972, Jane invited me to Pip 'n' Jay, a lively church in Bristol. That night the minister, Malcolm Widdecombe, knew things about me that he couldn't have known, and I realized it was the Lord speaking to me through him. In a very matter of fact way I gave my life to the Lord and told Jesus He had a month to prove Himself to me.

That month, and to this day, my experiences of a supernatural God, who so desires to have a relationship with those He has created, make for tales far more extraordinary and stranger than any fiction I could write. It is a path of discipleship, not always easy, but when His love for you meets with that for Him, there is a joy unspeakable and a peace that is beyond understanding.

I hope and pray that something of that truth and reality in this story has touched your heart and you will read the next few pages. And, as I did, give the Lord the opportunity to take you on a journey which is the greatest adventure through this lifetime into the next.

RUTH JOHNSON

3 GOOD REASONS TO TRUST IN JESUS

1. Because you have a past
You can't go back, but He can. The Bible says, 'Jesus Christ the same yesterday, and today, and for ever.' (Hebrews 13:8) He can walk into those places of sin and failure, wipe the slate clean and give you a new beginning.

2. Because you need a friend
Jesus knows the worst about you, yet He believes the best. Why? Because he sees you not as you are, but as you will be when He gets through with you. What a friend!

3. Because He holds the future
Who else are you going to trust? In His hands you are safe and secure – today, tomorrow, and for eternity. His Word says, "For I know the plans I have for you…plans for good and not for evil, to give you a future and a hope. In those days when you pray I will listen' (Jeremiah 29:11-13)

Jesus loves you! He desires to have a relationship with you, and to give you a life full of peace and purpose.

Try it. Begin a personal relationship with Jesus today by praying the prayer below. And once you have done it, ask Him to become real to you.

Lord Jesus Christ,
I am sorry for the things I have done wrong in my life. I ask your forgiveness and now turn from everything which I know is wrong. Thank you for dying on the cross for me to set me free from my sins. Please come into my life and fill me with your Holy Spirit and be with me forever. Thank you Lord.

FOR MORE INFORMATION:

Access the website run by United Christian Broadcasters at www.lookingforgod.com

Need prayer: UCB prayer line is manned from 9.00am – 10.30pm Monday to Friday on 0845 456 7729

UCB *Word for the Day* – daily stories of ordinary folk touched by an extraordinary God. It has Bible references for each day and when followed means you get to read the whole Bible in a year. Telephone: 0845 60 40 401 to get your copy.

IF YOU HAVE PRAYED THE PRAYER:

Give the Lord a chance to prove Himself to you

1. Get yourself a Bible - New International Version

2. Ring UCB for *Word for the Day* to be sent to you.

3. Ask the Lord to become real to you and even if you don't understand what you read follow the plan for each day asking God's Holy Spirit to open it up to you. It took 3 weeks at about 15 minutes a day before it began to make sense to me.

4. Try out the churches in your area. Find one that you feel comfortable in, then join it and get to know the people in it.

5. Please email me: Ruth.Johnson@blueyonder.co.uk so I can rejoice and help you in those first few weeks.

If you would like to make contact with a local Christian, or would like further help from someone living locally to you please write giving your full name, address, telephone number and email — include your age group, to:
3 reasons, FREEPOST, WC2947, South Croydon, CR2 8UZ

Copies of Lou Lewis' CD, 'Healing Stream', available from Zimrah Music — address at the front of this book: £10.00 each. Cheques should be made payable to Lou Lewis.

ACCESS www.emanuel-publishing.com
FOR SIGNINGS, MEETINGS & PUBLISHING DATES
Or be kept personally informed by email:
Ruth.Johnson@ emanuel-publishing.com

JILL (1968)

Jill, despite failed relationships, is looking for Mr Right. A chance encounter sets off a chain of events which threatens her, her friends and family. In this, Jill discovers there are many faces of love, but there is only one who will bring her the fulfillment of her heart's desires....

DAVID (1970)

David likens his marriage to riding a rollercoaster blindfold, their shared love the track that holds, keeps and guides them. In going from the greatest exhilaration to the darkest despair he draws on love's strength and finds it casts out fear, brings restoration and expands his vision to re-evaluate his heart's desires....

ROSEMARY (1972)

Rosemary has found love and contentment, but anguish squeezes her heart as history seems to be repeating itself. Hurts and fears taunt her as she struggles to decide if a marriage of convenience is too high a price to pay for the joy of motherhood. The tenacity of love draws her to confront her heart's desires....

JANICE (1974)

Janice, battered and homeless finds an unexpected refuge. Her arrival causes shock and dismay, her attitudes and behaviour lock those involved into a battle to hold onto love. Even as she holds them to ransom, she experiences an unforeseen love growing within her, making her rethink her heart's desires....

MATT (1976)

Matt's past haunts him across continents, in spite of unexpected friendship, love, provision and fulfillment in his chosen career. His caring heart brings a chance encounter and brings rewards he hadn't envisaged, unveiling that love that has no bounds as he is set free to know his heart's desires....